INHERIT—OR DIE!

The sailor turned to Sterren and explained, "She says she was sent by her king, Phenvel the Third, to find the heir of your grandmother's brother, the Eighth Warlord, who died four months ago. She consulted a magician — I'm not clear on what sort — and that led her to you. She is to bring you back to Semma to receive your title and inheritance and to fulfill your hereditary duties as the new warlord — you're *Enne Karnai*, the Ninth Warlord."

"That's silly," Sterren replied. He relaxed somewhat. If the story were true, then his worries about vengeance were groundless, and he saw no reason for the woman to bother lying.

"That's what she said," the sailor replied with a shrug.

"What if I won't go?" he asked. While it might be nice to have an inheritance waiting for him, that bit about "hereditary duties" didn't sound good, and he wanted nothing to do with wars or warlords. Wars were dangerous. Besides, who would want to live among barbarians? Particularly among barbarians who apparently didn't speak Ethsharitic.

The idea was ludicrous.

The interpreter relayed his question, and Lady Kalira's face fell. She spoke an authoritative [...] the sailor hesitantly translated it as "S[...] to perform one's duty to [...] treason is punishab[...] tion."

"Execution?" The [...] much more attractive.

The Unwilling Warlord

Lawrence Watt-Evans

COSMOS BOOKS

Original Dedication:

*Dedicated to Julian Samuel Goodwin Evans,
who won't appreciate it for years yet.*

Note for the revised edition:

Now he appreciates it!

THE UNWILLING WARLORD

Published by
Dorchester Publishing Co., Inc.
200 Madison Ave.
New York, NY 10016
in collaboration with Wildside Press LLC

ISBN-10: 0-8439-5943-6
ISBN-13: 978-0-8439-5943-7

"We are plain quiet folk and have no use for adventures. Nasty disturbing uncomfortable things! Make you late for dinner!"
— *The Hobbit*
J.R.R. Tolkien

Part One

Warlord

One

The dice rolled, smacked against the baseboard, then bounced back and skittered to a stop. One showed five pips, and the other two each showed six, clearly visible even in the flickering light of the tavern alcove.

The paunchy farmer in the greasy gray tunic stared at the dice for a moment, then snapped his head up and glared suspiciously at his opponent. He demanded, "Are you sure you're not cheating?" His breath carried the warm, thick aroma of stale wine.

The thin young man, who wore a patched but clean tunic of worn blue velvet, looked up from raking in the stakes with a carefully-contrived expression of hurt on his face. His dark brown eyes were wide with innocent dismay.

"Me?" he said. "Me, cheating? Abran, old friend, how can you suggest such a thing?"

He pushed the coins to one side, then smiled and said, "Still my throw?"

Abran nodded. "Make your throw, and I'll decide my wager."

The youth hesitated, but the rules did allow a losing bettor to see the next roll before wagering again. If Abran did decide to bet, though, it would be at two-to-one instead of even money.

That probably meant the game was over.

He shrugged, picked up the bits of bone again and rolled them, watching with satisfaction as the first stopped with six black specks showing, the second seemed to balance on one corner before dropping to show another six, and the last bounced, rebounded from the wall, spun in mid-air, and came down with five spots on the top face.

Abran stared, then turned his head and spat on the grimy floor in disgust. "Seventeen *again?*" he growled, turning back. "Sterren, if that's really your name," he said, in a more natural tone, "I don't know what you're doing — maybe you're just honestly lucky, or maybe you're a magician, but however you do it, you've won enough of my money. I give up. I'm leaving, and I hope I never see you again."

He stood, joints creaking.

An hour earlier the purse on his belt had been bulging with the proceeds of a good harvest; now it clinked dismally, only a few coins remaining, as he walked stiffly away.

Sterren watched him go without comment and dropped the coins of the final wager into the purse on his own belt, which had acquired much of the bulge now missing from Abran's.

When the farmer was out of sight he allowed himself to smile broadly. It had been an exceptionally successful evening. The poor old fool had stuck it out longer than any opponent in years.

And of course, where two could be seen having a game, others would sit in for a round or two. A dozen besides poor Abran had contributed to Sterren's winnings.

For perhaps the thousandth time in his career as a tavern gambler, Sterren wondered whether he *had* been cheating. He honestly did not know. He knew he certainly was not guilty of anything so common as using weighted dice or muttering spells under his breath, but there were magicks that needed no incantations, and he *had* been apprenticed to a warlock once — even if it had only been for three days before the warlock threw him out, calling him a hopeless incompetent. His master had *tried* to give him the ability to tap into the source of warlockry's power, and it hadn't seemed to work — but maybe it had, just a little bit, without either his master or himself realizing it.

Warlockry was the art of moving things by magically-enhanced willpower, moving them without touching them, and it was quite obvious that a warlock would have no trouble at all cheating at dice. It wouldn't take much warlockry to affect something as small as dice, and it was said only warlockry could detect warlockry, so the wizards and sorcerers Sterren had encountered would never have known it was there.

Might it be that he controlled the dice without knowing it, using an uncontrolled trace of warlockry, simply by wishing?

It might be, he decided, but it might also be that he was just lucky. After all, he didn't win *all* the time. Perhaps one of the gods happened to favor him, or it might be that he had been born under a fortunate star — though except for his luck with dice, he wasn't particularly blessed.

He stood, tucked the dice in his pouch, and brushed off the knees of his worn velvet breeches. The night was still young, or at worst middle-aged; perhaps, he thought, he might find another sucker.

He looked around the dimly-lit tavern's main room, but saw no promising prospects. Most of the room's handful of rather sodden inhabitants were regulars who knew better than to play against him. The really easy marks, the back-country farmers, would all be asleep or outside the city walls by this hour of the night; he had no real chance of finding one roaming the streets.

Other serious gamers would be settled in somewhere, most likely on Games Street, in Camptown on the far side of the city, where Sterren never ventured — there were far too many guardsmen that close to the camp. Guardsmen were bad business — suspicious, and able to act on their suspicions.

A few potential opponents might be over in nearby Westgate or down in the New Merchants' Quarter, which were familiar territory, or in the waterfront districts of Shiphaven and Spicetown, which he generally avoided, but to find anyone he would have to start the dreary trek from tavern to tavern once again.

Or of course, he could just sit and wait in the hope that some latecomer would walk in the door.

He was not enthusiastic about either option. Maybe, he thought, he could just take the rest of the night off; it depended upon how much he had taken in so far. He decided to count his money and see how he stood. If he had cleared enough to pay the innkeeper's fee for not interfering, the past month's rent for his room, and his long-overdue bar tab, he could afford to rest.

He drew the heavy gray curtain across the front of his little alcove for privacy, then poured the contents of his purse on the blackened planks of the floor.

Ten minutes later he was studying a copper bit, trying to decide whether it had been clipped or not, when he heard a disturbance of some sort in the front of the tavern. It was probably nothing to do with him, he told himself, but just in case he swept his money back into the purse. The clipped coin — if it was clipped — didn't really matter; even without it he had done better than he had realized, and had enough to pay his bills with a little left over.

Only a *very* little bit left over, unfortunately — not quite enough for a decent meal. He would be starting with a clean slate, though.

The disturbance was continuing; loud voices were audible, and not all of them were speaking Ethsharitic. He decided that the situation deserved investigation, and he peered cautiously around the end of the curtain.

A very odd group was arguing with the innkeeper. There were four of them, none of whom Sterren recalled having seen before. Two were huge, hulking men clad in heavy steel-studded leather tunics and blood-red kilts of barbarous cut, with unadorned steel helmets on their black-haired heads and swords hanging from broad leather belts — obviously foreigners, to be dressed so tackily, and probably soldiers of some kind, but certainly not in the city guard. The kilts might possibly have been city issue — though if so, some clothier had swindled the over-lord's officers — but the helmets and tunics and belts were all wrong. Both of the men were tanned a dark brown, which implied that they were from some more southerly clime — somewhere in the Small Kingdoms, no doubt.

A third man was short and stocky, brown-haired and lightly tanned, clad in the simple bleached cotton tunic and blue woolen kilt of a sailor, with nothing to mark him as either foreign or local; it was he who was doing most of the shouting. One of his hands was clamped onto the front of the innkeeper's tunic. The other was raised in a gesture that was apparently magical, since a thin trail of pink sparks dripped from his raised forefinger.

The group's final member was a woman, tall and aristo-cratic, clad in a gown of fine green velvet embroidered in gold. Her black hair was trimmed and curled in a style that had gone out of favor years ago, and that, added to the shoddy workmanship of the embroidery and her dusky complexion, marked her as as much of a foreign barbarian as the two soldiers.

"Where *is* he?" The sailor's final bellow reached Ster-ren's ears quite plainly. The innkeeper's reply did not, but the finger pointing toward the curtained alcove — toward Sterren — was unmistakable.

That was a shock. It was obvious that the foursome meant no good for whoever they sought, and it appeared they sought him. He did not recognize any of them, but it was possible that he had won money from one or all of them in the past, or perhaps they were relatives of some poor fool he had fleeced, come to avenge the family honor.

He tried to remember if he had won anything from any barbarians lately; usually he avoided them, since they were reputed to have violent tempers, and the world was full of gullible farmers. He did not recall playing against any barbarians since Festival, and surely, nobody would begrudge *anything* short of violence that had happened during Festival!

Perhaps they were hired, then. In any case, Sterren did not care to meet them.

He ducked back behind the curtain and looked about, considering possibilities.

There weren't very many.

The alcove was absolutely simple, comprised of three gray stone walls and the curtain, the plank floor with betting lines chalked on it, and a beamed wooden ceiling, black with years of smoke, that undoubtedly served as a floor for an upstairs room. There were no doors, no windows, and no way he could slip out. No hiding places were possible, since three wooden chairs were the only furniture. Smoky oil lamps perched on high shelves at either end provided what light there was, as well as the fishy aroma that combined with stale ale in the tavern's distinctive stench.

No help was to be had in here, that was plain, nor could he hope to rally the tavern's other patrons to his aid; he was not popular there. Gamblers who usually win are rarely well-liked — especially when they play for stakes so low that they can't afford to be lavish with their winnings.

Sterren realized he would have to rely on his wits — and those wits were good enough that he knew he would rather not have to rely on them.

They were, however, all he had, and he had no time to waste. He flung back one end of the curtain and pointed at the door to the street, shouting, "There he goes! There he goes! You can still catch him if you hurry!"

Only two of the foursome paid any heed at all, and even those two treated it only as a minor distraction, giving the door only quick glances. The two immense soldiers did not appear to have heard him. Instead, upon seeing him, they turned and marched heavily toward him, moving with a slow relentless tread that reminded Sterren of the tide coming in at the docks.

The other two, the sailor and the foreign noblewoman, followed the soldiers; the sailor flicked his forefinger, and the trail of sparks vanished.

Sterren did not bother ducking back behind the curtain; he stood and waited.

It had been a feeble ruse, but the best he could manage on such short notice. As often as not, similar tricks had been effective in the past; it had certainly been worth trying.

Since it had failed, he supposed he would have to face whatever these people wanted to do with him. He hoped it wasn't anything too unpleasant. If they had sent by one of his creditors he could even pay — if they gave him a chance before breaking his arm, or maybe his head. Even if someone demanded interest, there was no one person he owed more than he now had.

The quartet stopped a few feet away; one of the soldiers stepped forward and pulled aside the curtain, revealing the empty alcove.

The sailor looked at the bare walls, then at Sterren. "That was a stupid stunt," he said in a conversational tone. His Ethsharitic had a trace of a Shiphaven twang, but was clear enough. "Are you Sterren, son of Kelder?""

Cautiously, Sterren replied, "I might know a fellow by that name." He noticed the tavern's few remaining patrons watching and, one by one, slipping out the door.

The spokesman exchanged a few words with the velvet-clad woman in some foreign language, which Sterren thought might be the Trader's Tongue heard on the docks; the woman then spoke a brief phrase to the soldiers, and Sterren found his arms clamped in the grasp of the two large barbarians, one on either side. He could smell their sweat very clearly.

It was not a pleasant smell.

"Are you Sterren, son of Kelder, son of Kelder, or are you not?" the sailor demanded once again.

"Why?" Sterren's voice was unsteady, but he looked the sailor in the eye without blinking.

The sailor paused, almost smiling, to admire the courage it took to ask that question. Then he again demanded, "Are you?"

Sterren glanced sideways at the unmoving mass of soldier gripping his right arm, obviously not in the mood for civilized discourse or casual banter, and admitted, "My name is Sterren of Ethshar, and my father was called Kelder the Younger."

"Good," the sailor said. He turned and spoke two words to the woman.

She replied with a long speech. The sailor listened carefully, then turned back to Sterren and said, "You're probably the one they want, but Lady Kalira would like me to ask you some questions and make sure."

Sterren shrugged as best he could with his arms immobilized, his nerve returning somewhat. "Ask away. I have nothing to hide," he said.

It must be a family affair, he decided, or his identity wouldn't be a matter for such concern. He might talk his way out yet, he thought.

"Are you the eldest son of your father?"

That was not a question he had expected. Could these people have some arcane scruples about killing a man's first heir? Or, on the other hand, did they consider the eldest of a family to be responsible for the actions of his kin? The latter possibility didn't matter much, since Sterren *had* no living kin — at least, not in any reasonable degree of consanguinity.

Hesitantly, he replied, "Yes."

"You have a different name from your father."

"So what? Plenty of eldest sons do — repeating names is a stupid custom. My father let his mother name me, said there were too damn many Kelders around already."

"Your father was the eldest son of his mother?"

This made no sense to Sterren at all. "Yes," he said, puzzled.

"Your father is dead?"

"Dead these sixteen years. He ran afoul of . . ."

"Never mind that; it's enough we have your word that he's dead."

"My word? I was a boy of three, scarcely a good witness even had I been there, which I was not. But I was told he was dead, and I never saw him again." This line of questioning was beginning to bother him. Were these people come to avenge some wrong his *father* had committed? He knew nothing about the old man save that he had been a merchant — and of course, the lurid story of his death at the hands of a crazed enchanter had been told time and time again.

It would be grossly unfair, in Sterren's opinion, for his own death to result from some ancestral misdemeanor, rather than one of his own offenses or failings; he hoped he could convince these people of that.

It occurred to him that perhaps this sailor with his pink sparks was that very same crazed enchanter, but that idea made no sense, and he discarded it. It was far more likely that the pink sparks were part of some shop-bought spell.

In fact, they might well be all there was to the spell, a little something to impress the ladies, or anybody else, for that matter.

"His mother, your grandmother — who was she?" the sailor asked.

His grandmother? Sterren was even more baffled than before. He had been seven when she died, and he remembered her mostly as a friendly, wrinkled face and a warm voice telling impossible tales. His grandfather, who had raised him after all the others were dead, had missed her terribly and had spoken of her often, explaining how he had brought her back from a tiny little kingdom on the very edge of the world, talking about how she got along so well with everyone so long as she got her way.

"Her name was Tanissa the Stubborn, I think; she came from the Small Kingdoms somewhere." As did these four, he realized, or at least three of them. The questions suddenly began to make sense. She must have stolen something, or committed some heinous offense, and they had finally tracked her down.

It had certainly taken them long enough. Surely they wouldn't carry their revenge to the third generation! "She's dead," he added helpfully.

"Was she ever called Tanissa of Semma?"

"I don't know; I never heard her called that."

There was another exchange in the familiar but incomprehensible language, including his grandmother's name as well as his own. By the end of it the woman seemed excited, and was smiling.

The smile didn't *look* vindictive, but that was very little comfort; whatever crime his grandmother had committed must have been half a century ago, and this woman could scarcely have been born then. She wasn't exactly young, but she didn't look *that* old — and she didn't look young enough to be using a youth spell. She must have been sent on the hunt by someone else; perhaps her father or mother was the wronged party. In that case she'd be glad to have the job done, but would have no reason for personal dislike.

A glance to either side showed the two soldiers as impassive as ever, and he wondered whether they understood what was going on any better than he did.

The interpreter, as the sailor apparently was, turned back to Sterren and asked, "Do you have any family?"

"No." He didn't think it was worth trying to lie.

"No wife?"

Sterren shook his head.

"What about your mother?"

"She died bearing me." Perhaps, he thought, they would take pity on him because he was an orphan.

"Since you're the eldest, there could scarcely be brothers or sisters if she died bearing you. What about old Kelder, your grandfather?"

It occurred to Sterren, a bit belatedly, that he was removing the possibility of spreading the blame or getting off on grounds of family support, but it was too late already, and he continued to tell the truth. "He died three years ago. He was an old man."

"Uncles? Aunts? Cousins?"

"None."

"Your other grandparents?"

"Dead before I was born, from drinking bad water."

"Good!" the sailor said with a smile. "Then you should be able to leave immediately!"

"What?" Sterren exclaimed. "Leave where? I'm not going anywhere!" He made no attempt to hide his surprise and indignation.

"Why not?" the sailor demanded. "You're not still an apprentice, are you?"

"What if I am? Where are you taking me? Who are you?" His remaining assurance faded a little more; they wouldn't dare kill him here in the tavern, probably not anywhere in Ethshar, but if they managed to remove him from the city they could do anything they pleased. There was no law outside the walls — or at least Sterren knew of none.

"I'm just an interpreter . . ." the sailor began.

"What were those sparks?" Sterren interrupted.

The sailor waved the question away. "Nothing; I bought them on Wizard Street to help find you. Really, I'm just an interpreter. I'm not the one looking for you."

"Then who are these others, and what do they want with me?"

"The Lady Kalira is taking you to Semma," the sailor replied.

"The hell she is!" Sterren said. "I'm not leaving the city!" He was close to panic; visions of death by slow torture flickered through his mind.

The sailor sighed. "I'm afraid you are, whether you like it or not."

"Why?" Sterren asked, letting a trace of panic into his voice in hopes of inducing pity. "What do these people want with me?"

The man shrugged. "Don't ask me. They hired me in Akalla to get them to Ethshar and find you, so I got them to

Ethshar and found you. It's none of my business what they want you for."

"It's my business, though!" Sterren pointed out. He tried to struggle; the soldiers gave no sign they had even noticed. He subsided, and demanded, "You can ask, at least, can't you?"

"I can ask Lady Kalira," the sailor admitted. "Those two don't speak Trader's Tongue, and for all I know they're the ones who want you." He seemed appallingly disinterested.

"Ask her!" Sterren shrieked.

The sailor turned and said something.

The tall woman did not answer him, but stepped forward and spoke directly to Sterren, saying very slowly and distinctly, "*O'ri Sterren, Enne Karnai t'Semma.*"

"What the hell does that mean?" Sterren asked. He was about to say something further when he realized that the two barbarians had released his arms. He looked up at them, and saw that their huge flat faces were broken into broad grins. One stuck out an immense paw and shook Sterren's hand vigorously, clasping it hard enough to sting. Utterly confused, Sterren asked the sailor, "What did she say?"

"Don't ask me; that was Semmat, not Trader's Tongue. I don't speak Semmat."

Lady Kalira saw Sterren's continued incomprehension and said, "*Od'na ya Semmat?*" When he still looked blank, she said, "Et'sharitic is bad." Her pronunciation was horrendous.

Sterren stared for a moment, then turned to the sailor and demanded, "Is she telling me my native tongue isn't fit for her to speak? Is this some sort of barbarian ritual thing?" He was even more thoroughly confused than before.

"No, no, no," the sailor said. "She's just saying she can't speak it very well. I don't think she knows more than a dozen words, to be honest, and I taught her half of those on the way here."

The Semman aristocrat apparently gave up on direct communication with her captive, and gave the interpreter a long message to relay. He interrupted her twice, requesting clarifications — at least that was what Sterren judged to be happening, since each interruption was followed by a careful repetition of an earlier phrase.

Finally, the sailor turned to Sterren and explained, "She says she was sent by her king, Phenvel the Third, to find the heir of your grandmother's brother, the Eighth Warlord, who died four months ago. She consulted a magician — I'm not clear on what sort — and that led her to you. She is to bring you back to Semma to receive your title and inheritance and to fulfill your hereditary duties as the new warlord — you're *Enne Karnai*, the Ninth Warlord."

"That's silly," Sterren replied. He relaxed somewhat. If the story were true, then his worries about vengeance were groundless, and he saw no reason for the woman to bother lying.

"That's what she said," the sailor replied with a shrug.

"What if I won't go?" he asked. While it might be nice to have an inheritance waiting for him, that bit about "hereditary duties" didn't sound good, and he wanted nothing to do with wars or warlords. Wars were dangerous. Besides, who would want to live among barbarians? Particularly among barbarians who apparently didn't speak Ethsharitic.

The idea was ludicrous.

The interpreter relayed his question, and Lady Kalira's face fell. She spoke an authoritative sentence; the sailor hesitantly translated it as, "She says that failure to perform one's duty to one's country is treason, and treason is punishable by immediate summary execution."

"Execution?" The inheritance suddenly sounded much more attractive.

Lady Kalira said something in Semmat; the smiles vanished from the faces of the soldiers, and each dropped a hand to his sword-hilt.

"But it's not my country!" Sterren protested. "I was born and raised here in Ethshar, of Ethsharitic parents!" He looked from the sailor to Lady Kalira and back.

The sailor shrugged, a gesture that was getting on Sterren's nerves. Lady Kalira said, in halting Ethsharitic, "You, the heir."

Sterren looked despairingly at the two soldiers; he could see no chance at all that he could outrun or outfight either of them, let alone both. The one on the left slid a few inches of his blade from its scabbard, in warning.

"*Hai!* No bloodshed in here! Take him outside first!" The innkeeper's voice was worried.

No one paid any attention to his outburst — save that Sterran hoped he would call the city guard.

Hoping for the city guard was a new experience for him.

Even if they were summoned, though, they could not possibly arrive in time to do him any good. He had no way out. Struggling to smile, Sterren managed a ghastly parody of a grin as he said, "I guess I'll be going to Semma, then."

Lady Kalira smiled smugly.

Two

Sterren stared at the decaying, sun-bleached town of Akalla of the Diamond in dismay. It lived up to his worst imaginings of what the barbaric Small Kingdoms would be like.

He had had very little warning of what to expect. His captors had spirited him out of the tavern, paused at his room on Bargain Street only long enough to gather up his few belongings, and then taken him, protesting vigorously, onto their chartered ship.

He had looked desperately for an opportunity to escape, but none had presented itself. At the last minute he had dived off the dock, only to be fished ignominiously out of the mud and dragged aboard.

After that, he had given up any thoughts of escape for a time. Where could he escape to from a ship? He wasn't that strong a swimmer. Instead, he had cooperated as best he could, biding his time.

His captors had separated him from the interpreter, and made it plain that they expected him to learn their barbaric tongue — Semmat, they called it. He had swallowed his revulsion at the thought of speaking anything but proper Ethsharitic, and had done his best to oblige. After all, if he couldn't understand what was being said around him, he would have little chance of learning anything useful.

His language lessons had not covered very much when the ship docked in Akalla of the Diamond, just ten days after leaving Ethshar of the Spices. The weather had been hot and clear — and fairly calm, which is why it took ten days just to cross the Gulf of the East and sail the South Coast. One of the two immense Semman soldiers, the one who called himself Alder d'Yoon, told Sterren in a mixture of baby Semmat and sign language that the voyage in the other direction had taken only four days because the ship had been driven before a storm much of the way — a very expensive storm, conjured up for that very purpose, if Sterren understood him correctly.

Alder guessed the total distance between the two ports at less than a hundred leagues, a figure that surprised Sterren considerably. He had always thought of the Small Kingdoms as being a very long way off, on the far side of the ocean, and a hundred leagues across a mere gulf didn't seem that far.

Of course, Sterren was not absolutely certain that he had understood Alder correctly. He knew he had the numbers straight, because he had learned them from counting fingers, but he wasn't completely sure of the Semmat terms for "day" and "league." He wished that he could check with the interpreter, but Lady Kalira — or rather, *Aia* Kalira, in Semmat — had expressly forbidden the man to talk to him in *any* language, and she was paying enough that the sailor would not take any chance of losing his job.

Several members of the crew spoke Ethsharitic, but Lady Kalira had paid each of them to not speak it to Sterren except in emergencies. He was to communicate in Semmat or not at all.

Too often, it was not at all, leaving him unsure of much of his limited vocabulary.

Whatever the exact distances, there could be no doubt that on the afternoon of the tenth day their ship put into port at Akalla, in the shadow of the grim pile of guano-whitened stone the Semmans called Akalla *Karnak*. Sterren thought that *karnak* probably meant castle, but again, he was not quite sure. He had never seen a castle before, and the forbidding fortification at Akalla did not encourage him to seek out others.

He had gathered that Semma lay somewhere inland, and that Akalla of the Diamond was the nearest seaport to it. He was not yet clear on whether Akalla was a separate country, a conquered province, or a district within the kingdom of Semma. The truth was that he didn't much care, since it did not seem relevant to any plans to escape back to Ethshar.

And Akalla looked like a place that very few people cared about. It consisted of three or four streets lined with small shops and houses, all huddled onto a narrow stretch of beach in the castle's shadow, between two jagged stretches of broken cliffs.

The buildings of the town were built of some sort of yellowish blocks that looked more like brick than stone, but were far larger than any bricks Sterren was familiar with. The joints all seemed to be covered with faded greenery — brown mosses or gray lichen or half-dead ivy climbing the walls. The roofs were of turf, with thin, scorched brown grass on top. He saw very few windows. Flies buzzed in clouds above the streets, and the few people who were visible on those streets seemed to be curled up asleep, completely covered by dirty white robes. The whole place smelled of dry rot.

Sterren was not at all impressed by the town.

The castle was far more impressive, but it, too, was streaked with dying plant life and seemed lifeless, almost abandoned.

As Sterren watched the sailors tying up to the dock, he asked the soldier beside him — not Alder, but the other one, Alder's comrade Dogal d'Gra — how far it was to Semma.

Rather, he tried to ask that, but his limited knowledge of Semmat forced him to say instead, "How many leagues is Semma?" That assumed that he was using the correct word for leagues and hadn't screwed up the grammar somewhere.

What he had thought was a simple question plunged his guard into deep concentration; the Semman muttered to himself, saying in Semmat, "Akalla, maybe one; Skaia, four or five; Ophkar — hmm."

Finally, after considerable calculation, he arrived at an answer. "Twelve, thirteen, maybe fourteen leagues."

Sterren knew the numbers up to twenty beyond any question, and a good many beyond with reasonable confidence, but to be sure he held up his ten fingers and said, "And two, three more?"

Dogal nodded. "Yeah."

Horrified, Sterren stared back out at the port. Thirteen leagues? The entire city of Ethshar was little more than a league from corner to corner, yet he had never managed to explore it all. It took a good hour just to walk from Westgate to the Arena — more, if traffic was heavy. They would have to walk all night to reach Semma!

In the event, as he later learned, they would not walk at all, and certainly not at night. Instead, when the ship was secured at bow and stern, and the gangplank in place, he found himself escorted not out onto the highway to Semma, but to a small inn near the docks — small by Sterren's standards, that is, since it was, except for the castle, the largest structure in town.

The interpreter, to Sterren's consternation, stayed behind on the ship; he had fulfilled his contract and would not be accompanying them further.

Upon learning this Sterren suddenly wished he had tried even harder during his language lessons. Now if an emergency arose he would have to rely on his limited command of Semmat, rather than finding an interpreter.

He felt more cut off than ever.

Once inside the inn, out of the hot sun and into the cool shade, Sterren looked around, and his opinion of Akalla went up a notch. The inn was laid out well enough, with several cozy alcoves holding tables, and one wall lined with barrels. A stairway at either side led up to a balcony, and the rooms for travelers opened off that. A good many customers were present, eating and drinking and filling the place with a pleasant hum of conversation, while harried but smiling barmaids hurried hither and yon.

Most of the customers wore the thin white robes Sterren had seen on the street, but here they were thrown back to reveal gaily-colored tunics and kilts beneath.

Lady Kalira ignored the bustle and headed directly for the innkeeper, who stood leaning against one of the barrels. She took two rooms for her party — one for herself, and one for Sterren, Alder, and Dogal.

Sterren glanced around, and decided that even though it was a pleasant enough inn, he did not really want to be there, not with Alder and Dogal watching him constantly, and with, he presumed, nobody around who spoke Eth-sharitic.

Since he had no choice, however, he resolved to make the best of it. While Dogal took the party's baggage up to their rooms and Lady Kalira settled with the innkeeper on the exact amount of the party's advance payment, Sterren attempted to strike up a conversation with a winsome barmaid, using his very best Semmat.

She stared at him for a few seconds, then smiled, said something in a language he had never heard before, and hurried away.

He stared after her in shock.

"What was . . ." he began in Ethsharitic, and then caught himself and switched to Semmat. "What was *that*?" he asked Alder.

"What?" the soldier asked in reply.

"What the . . . the . . . what she said."

Alder shrugged. "I don't know," he said. "She was speaking Akallan."

"*Akallan*? *Another* language?"

"Sure," Alder said, unperturbed.

Sterren stared about wildly, listening to first one conversation, then another. Lady Kalira and the innkeeper were speaking Trader's Tongue, he realized. A couple at a nearby table was whispering in some strange and sibilant speech that didn't sound like Trader's Tongue, Akallan, *or* Semmat, and which certainly wasn't Ethsharitic. Other voices were speaking any number of dialects.

"Gods," Sterren said, "how does anybody ever talk to anyone here?"

Alder asked, "What?"

Sterren realized he'd spoken Ethsharitic again; he wasn't sure whether he wanted to weep or scream. He did know he wanted a drink. He sat down heavily in the nearest chair, and resorted to a language understood everywhere; he waved a finger in the air in the general direction of the barmaid, and threw a coin on the table.

That worked, and the barmaid smiled at him as she placed a full tankard before him. He began to feel more cheerful.

After all, he reminded himself, he was in a port. Naturally, there would be a variety of travelers, speaking a variety of tongues. "In Semma," he said to Alder, "all speak one language?" He knew, as he said it, that his phrasing was awkward, but it was the best he could do.

"Sure," Alder said, settling down at Sterren's table. "Everyone in Semma speaks Semmat. Just about, anyway; I guess there might be some foreigners now and then who don't."

Sterren struggled to follow his guard's speech. He had been resigned to learning Semmat, but now he was becoming really eager to learn. Whatever the ignominy of being forced to use a barbarian tongue, it was nothing compared to the isolation and inconvenience of not being able to speak with those about him.

And it looked as if he was, indeed, going to be stuck in Semma for the foreseeable future, if he didn't get away very, very soon. Thirteen leagues inland! There was simply no way he would be able to slip away and cover that distance without being caught and dragged back — not if the Semmans had any sort of magic available, as they surely did.

If he was going to escape, he would have to do so tonight, here in Akalla, and stow away aboard a ship bound for Ethshar.

And how could he do that when he couldn't find three people in Akalla who spoke the same language as each other, let alone anything that he, himself, understood? How could he learn which ship was bound whither, and when?

Even if he once got aboard a ship, how could he earn his way home, when he couldn't even understand orders, or argue about the rules of a friendly game?

No, it was hopeless. He was doomed to go to Semma, a country that his grandmother had been only too glad to flee, even at the loss of her noble status.

Being thus doomed, all he could do was make the best of it. He would have to find some way to fit in.

He might even have to actually be a proper warlord.

First, though, he needed to know the language.

"Alder," he said, "I want to learn Semmat better. Fast."

Alder gulped beer, then nodded. "Sure," he said. "What do you want to know?"

Three

At first, the discovery that he would not be required to walk thirteen leagues came as a relief. By the end of his first hour on horseback, however, Sterren was having second thoughts, and wishing he had found an opportunity to slip away during the night. Riding had always looked so easy! All you had to do was to get up there — which was simple enough when one had two burly guards willing to hoist you into place — and then sit there.

He hadn't realized how hard it was to just sit there, with the saddle bobbing up and down underneath, on and on and on unendingly, as the four horses Lady Kalira had bought carried them up out of Akalla of the Diamond onto the high flat plain to the east. His backside already felt very scraped and raw.

He was surprised to see, between bounces, that they were not following either of the main inland roads, which led north. In fact, the road they did follow faded quickly away, leaving them on featureless sun-washed grassland that seemed to extend clear to the horizon in every landward direction. To the south and southwest, at least at first, the plain was chopped off short by the cliffs and the sea below.

The only structure in sight anywhere was the castle, gradually diminishing behind them. Sterren had no idea how his companions were finding their way once the road had vanished, but they seemed confident of the route, so he did not question it.

For one thing, he was far too busy trying to minimize the bruising of his backside to worry about where he was going, or why. He put aside all worries about wars and warlords and life among the barbarians, concentrating solely on matters closer to hand — and closer still to his seat.

By the time the party stopped by a tiny stream for a midday rest and refreshment, out of sight of even Akalla *Karnak*'s highest tower, Sterren's throat ached from dryness, his hands ached from clutching the reins, his feet ached from being jammed into the stirrups, his back ached from trying to keep him upright, and worst of all, his rump ached from the constant abrasive collisions with his saddle. He did not descend gracefully, but simply fell off his mount onto a tuft of prairie grass.

Alder and Dogal politely pretended not to notice, but Lady Kalira was less kind.

"You haven't ridden before, have you?" she demanded without preamble.

Sterren took a moment to mentally translate this into Ethsharitic. "No," he admitted. He was too thirsty, weary and battered to think of any sarcastic comment to add, let alone to translate it into Semmat. Her blithe assumption that an Ethsharitic street gambler would know how to ride seemed to call for a cutting remark, but Sterren could not rise to the occasion.

"You should have told me back at the inn," she said. "I could have gotten a wagon. Or we could have walked. Or at the very least we could have given you a few lessons."

Sterren tried to shrug, but his back was too stiff for any such gesture. "I . . . It was . . . It did not . . . damn!" He could not think of any word for "appeared" or "looked" or "seemed." Before any of the Semmans could volunteer a suggestion, he managed, "I saw it was not bad, but I saw wrong."

"It looked easy, you mean."

Sterren nodded. "I guess that's what I mean."

"A warlord really should know how to ride," Lady Kalira pointed out.

"I'm no warlord," Sterren said bitterly.

"You are Sterren, Ninth Warlord of Semma!" Lady Kalira reminded him sternly.

"I'm Sterren of Ethshar. I play dice in taverns," Sterren retorted.

Lady Kalira backed away slightly. "You know, you mustn't tell anyone that when we get to Semma," she said.

"Why not?" Sterren demanded.

"Because you're the warlord!" Lady Kalira replied, shocked. "You hold a position of great power and respect. We can't let it be common gossip that you made your living cheating at gambling."

Sterren did not follow all of this speech, but he guessed one vital word from context. "I didn't cheat!" he shouted; the effort sent a twinge through his back and legs, and more than a twinge through his buttocks.

"Then how did you win regularly enough to live?"

"I was lucky," he muttered unconvincingly. He had learned the word aboard ship.

"Ha!" she said. "Wizard's luck, if you ask me."

"Wizard?" Sterren asked. He knew the word meant one variety of magician, but wasn't sure which. "Warlock," he said in Ethsharitic.

Lady Kalira did not recognize the word; instead she changed the subject.

"You must relax," she said, demonstrating my letting her arms fall limply, "when you ride. Move with the horse, not against it."

Sterren nodded, not really believing that he would ever learn the skill.

"And we can pad the saddle — that velvet tunic in your pack will help. And you can walk sometimes."

Sterren nodded again, with a bit more enthusiasm.

By mid-afternoon, thanks to additional cushioning, a slower pace, and walking when the blisters on his rump became unbearable, he had improved enough that, although he still ached in every joint and in several unjointed places as well, he was able to think about his future and to carry on some limited conversation with his companions as he rode.

He began by pointing in each direction and asking what lay there. All they could see was sand and sun and grass, which made it obvious that he was asking what lay beyond.

Ahead, of course, was Semma; behind was Akalla of the Diamond. To the left, the north, Dogal told him, "Skaia." The name meant nothing to him.

The reply when he pointed to the right was more interesting.

"Nothing," Dogal told him.

"Nothing?"

"Well, almost. A couple of leagues of sand, and then the edge of the World. If you stand up in the stirrups and stare, you may be able to see it."

"See it?"

"Yes."

That, Sterren thought, was a very interesting concept, seeing the edge of the World. Standing up in the stirrups, however, was a *terrifying* concept, so he decided to forgo the view.

How, he wondered, could one see the edge of the World? What did it look like? What lay beyond it? The southern horizon, he noticed, did look slightly different from the others; there seemed to be a yellowish tinge to both ground and sky in that direction. He stared, but could make out nothing.

The very idea fascinated him, all the same. To be so close to the actual edge!

He had thought that Ethshar of the Spices was in the center of the World, but if he had come so close to the edge so quickly, then that could not be so; he knew the World was bigger than that. He had heard travelers speak of Ethshar as being in the southeast, but had, until now, put it down to a distorted worldview.

Obviously, it was his own view that had been in error.

That was quite a realization, that he had been wrong. He wondered if he had ever been wrong about anything important.

Dogal distracted him from that line of thought. "Might be Ophkar to the north of us now," he remarked. "Skaia's not that big. Bigger than Semma or Akalla, smaller than Ophkar."

"Semma is next, beyond Ophkar?" Sterren asked.

Dogal nodded. "That's right. Your accent is improving greatly, Lord Sterren; congratulations."

Sterren said nothing in return, but felt a touch of pride. He had tried very hard to get the accent right on the barbaric names of the surrounding kingdoms, and it was good to know he had succeeded.

He had come to realize that Akalla, Skaia, and Ophkar were all indeed separate kingdoms, squeezed into the thirteen leagues between Semma and the coast, and he marvelled that the Small Kingdoms were *that* small.

He also wondered all the more just what he was getting into. If the kingdoms were crowded together that closely, they must surely rub each other the wrong way every so often. No wonder they needed warlords.

"What is Semma . . . What . . . Tell me about Semma," he said unable to come up with the words to ask, "What is Semma like?" or "What sort of a place is Semma?"

Dogal shrugged. "Not much to tell."

"There must be something you can tell me; are there many cities?"

"No cities."

Sterren could not think of a word for "town." Instead, he asked, "Are there many castles?" The word for castle was indeed *karnak*; he had checked on that back at the inn.

"Just one, Semma Castle. That's where we're going."

Dogal was not exactly a torrent of information, Sterren decided; he nudged his mount over toward Alder, on his right.

"Hello," he said.

Alder nodded politely. "Hail, Lord Sterren."

Sterren sighed; he supposed he would have to get used to that pompous greeting. "Tell me about Semma," he said.

Alder glanced at him curiously. "What do you want to know?"

"What it . . . what I . . . how it is there."

"What it's like, you mean?"

Gratefully, Sterren latched onto the phrase he had been missing. "Yes, what it's like."

"Well, Lord Sterren, it's hard for me to say, because it's the only place I've ever been, except for this trip to Et'shar to fetch you. I was born there, never lived anywhere else."

"Ethshar, not Et'shar," Sterren said idly, pleased to be the one correcting for once, rather than the one corrected.

"Et'th'shar," Alder said, spitting messily as he struggled with the unfamiliar combination of aspirants.

"Are there many people?"

Alder shrugged. "I don't know, really," he said. "The castle is certainly crowded enough."

"I didn't just mean the castle."

"Well, that's where everyone lives except the peasants."

That startled Sterren, and caused him to wonder if

he was still misunderstanding the word *karnak* after all. "Everyone?"

"Just about."

"Peasants?" The word was new to him.

"The common people, the farmers," Alder explained.

Sterren nodded — he knew about the easy marks from outside the walls. "Are there many peasants?" he asked.

Alder shrugged again. "I guess so."

"Are you a peasant?"

"I'm a soldier, Lord Sterren." The reproof was obvious in Alder's tone.

"You weren't born a soldier," Sterren pointed out, proud he had remembered the word "born" from Alder's earlier comments.

Alder reluctantly admitted, "True. I was born a peasant."

"Nothing wrong with that," Sterren said, seeing he had hurt the big guard's feelings. "I was born a peasant, too."

This was a lie, of course; he had been born into the merchant class. He meant, however, that he had been born a commoner.

Startled, Alder corrected him. "No, Lord Sterren, you were born a nobleman."

"Well, I didn't know it," Sterren retorted.

Alder considered that, then smiled. "True," he said.

Sterren rode on in silence for a long moment, marshaling his thoughts.

At least, he thought, he would be living in the castle, which would presumably be at least an imitation of real civilization. He had feared that he might find himself in some muddy little village somewhere. A castle was not a city, but it was, he hoped, better than nothing.

In the remainder of the afternoon, and around the campfire that night, Sterren pieced together a rough idea of what Semma was like from a constant questioning of his two guards. This also served to improve his Semmat considerably, adding to his vocabulary and giving him practice in pronunciation and sentence construction.

Semma was a quiet little kingdom, almost all of it occupied by peasants on small family farms, scraping a living out of the sandy soil by growing oranges, lemons, dates, figs, olives, and corn, or by raising sheep or goats or cattle. At one time some peasants had grown spices for export, but Semma had lost its spice trade long ago, when Ophkar had temporarily cut off all the routes to the sea and the markets had found other, more reliable sources. The soldiers knew of no mines, or towns, or any sort of manufacture or trade.

In the center of the kingdom stood Semma Castle, with a large village clustered around it — the closest thing to a town or city that the kingdom could boast. The castle itself was home to something over a hundred nobles — Sterren had balked initially at believing that, but both Dogal and Alder had insisted it was the truth. Sterren could imagine a hundred people willingly jammed into a single building readily enough, since he had seen the crowded tenements of his native city, but he could not imagine a hundred people living like that who called themselves *nobles*.

Back home in Ethshar, Azrad VII surely had a hundred or more people living in his palace, but only a few could call themselves nobles; most were servants and courtiers and bureaucrats.

Alder had noticed his disbelief, and had explained, "Well, that's counting the kids, and besides, a lot of them are lesser nobility, and it's a big castle. You'll see."

Sterren considered that, and Lady Kalira took this opportunity to present him with a salve for his developing saddlesores.

"It's always a good idea to bring a healing salve when travelling," she said, "though this wasn't exactly the use I had in mind."

Sterren accepted it gratefully, and crawled away from the campfire somewhat in pursuit of privacy. Lady Kalira discreetly turned away, and the Ethsharite slid down his breeches and applied the ointment liberally.

That done, he rejoined the others. He had just begun to inquire about the army he was supposed to command when Lady Kalira announced it was time to shut up and sleep.

Sterren obliged, leaving military matters for the morning.

Four

They spotted the castle's central tower by mid-morning of the third day, scarcely an hour after they had buried the ashes of their breakfast fire and set out again. Sterren had to admit that it looked like a *big* castle, as Alder had said.

At that point they had just begun to pass farms, rather than open plain — compact yellow houses surrounded by small stands of fruit trees, patches of tall corn, and miscellaneous livestock grazing the native grass down to stubble. The various inhabitants of these establishments, intent on their own concerns of herding or cultivation or hauling water, invariably ignored the travelers.

The plain was no longer quite so smooth and flat as it had been for most of the journey; the ground they traversed had acquired something of a roll, though it was still far from hilly.

Sterren had never gotten around to asking much about the army, but he had learned that Semma was roughly triangular, bounded on the southeast by the desert that stretched to the edge of the World, on the north by the relatively large and powerful kingdom of Ksinallion, and on the west by Ophkar. Semma had fought several wars against each of her neighbors over the last two or three centuries — particularly Ksinallion — but under the Seventh and Eighth Warlords had stayed at peace for an amazingly long time. Alder and Dogal did not remember any of the wars themselves, but Alder's maternal grandfather had fought against Ksinallion in the Sixth Ksinallionese War, about fifty years ago. Sterren was still patiently listening to tales of ancestral bravery when the castle came into view.

Not long after that a cloud of dust appeared ahead of

them, and grew until a dozen horsemen emerged from it. Sterren was worried, but the three Semmans seemed very pleased by this welcoming committee.

The horsemen were all large dark-skinned men dressed much like Alder and Dogal, riding horses in red and gold trappings, and Lady Kalira announced that this was an honor guard, sent to escort the newfound warlord to the castle.

Sterren was relieved to discover, when the party came to a halt a few paces away, that this was correct. The government had not been overthrown since Lady Kalira's departure.

The conversation between his original escort and the new arrivals was too fast for him to follow, so Sterren simply sat astride his horse until it was over.

The newcomers wheeled about and formed up into a column around Sterren, Lady Kalira, and the two soldiers, and waited.

Sterren looked about, puzzled, and saw Lady Kalira gesturing with her head. It dawned on him that *he* was in command; this guard was in *his* honor, and they were waiting for him to start.

Reluctantly, he urged his mount forward, and the entire party rode on toward the castle.

Sterren found his inquiries about Semma's army inhibited by the presence of a dozen uniformed strangers. He shrugged and accepted the situation. After all, he would be able to see for himself, soon enough, just how matters stood. He rode on in dignified silence, up the dusty road and into the village that surrounded the castle.

The travelers were greeted at the castle gate by a ragged fanfare of trumpets — at least one trumpeter was always a fraction behind the others, and an occasional sour note could be heard, but in general it was an impressive and gratifying experience for Sterren. He had heard far better, far more stirring music played in the Arena, or in the overlord's occasional parades, or even by impromptu street bands, back in Ethshar, but never before had he heard more than a brief cheer in his own honor. He counted a dozen trumpeters spaced along the ramparts; impressed, he tried to sit up a little straighter on his horse, to live up to his role.

Certainly, being a warlord had its positive aspects; as long as he could avoid any actual wars, he thought it might be enjoyable. Unfortunately, he doubted he would be able to avoid wars; the Small Kingdoms were notorious for constantly going to war over stupid little disputes.

On the other hand, Alder and Dogal had said that Semma had been at peace for more than forty years. Maybe that peace would last.

Or maybe a war was overdue. He simply didn't know anything about the situation.

It was time, however, to start learning as much as he could, as quickly as he could. With that in mind, even as he tried to ride with dignity and pride, and to *look* the part of a warlord despite his shabby, travel-worn clothes, he was studying everything in sight.

The castle stood upon a slight rise, the closest thing to a hill that Sterren had seen since leaving Akalla; Sterren could not tell if the little plateau, standing eight or ten feet above the plain, was natural or man-made, but it was certainly not new, in either case. Surrounding the castle and its raised base were scattered two or three dozen houses and shops, all the same dull yellow as the outlying farmhouses, all built of some substance Sterren had never seen before and could not identify, all with thick walls and only a few heavily-shuttered windows. Gaily-colored awnings shielded most of the doorways and served as open-air shops; there was no single market square, just a small plaza at the castle gate, and the streets were rather haphazard. All the ground in the castle's vicinity was dry, hard-packed bare dirt, trampled smooth and even, and the houses and shops were not arranged in clear, sharp streets, but just ragged lines that wiggled every which way.

Outside the village in any direction Sterren could see scattered farmhouses, built in the same way as the village's structures, strewn unevenly across the plain.

The castle itself was a stark contrast to these humble dwellings; it was an immense and forbidding structure built of dark red stone. An outer wall topped with iron-braced battlements stood more than fifteen feet high, with no opening anywhere in it save the gate by which Sterren's little party entered.

As they passed through this portal, Sterren saw that the wall was roughly twenty feet thick, and the gateway equipped with three sets of heavy doors as well as a spiked portcullis, and openings overhead through which assaults might be made on anyone trying to enter uninvited.

It was not, perhaps, as overwhelming a piece of engineering and defense technology as Ethshar's city walls and gate towers, but it had its own grim power, certainly. Sterren was quite sure that he would not care to try and pass that wall and gate without a very clear invitation.

Of course, his escort, now numbering fifteen in all, clearly constituted an invitation.

The castle within that outer wall was vaguely pyramidal in its overall shape. Low wings, a mere two stories in height, stretched out to either side of the central mass, which stood some six stories, and was in turn topped by a great central tower whose peak was, Sterren judged, fully a hundred feet from the ground upon which the castle stood. A few turrets protruded here and there, ruining the stepped outline. Window openings were nonexistent at ground level, but grew steadily from narrow slits on the second floor to broad expanses of glass under graceful stone arches on the uppermost level of the tower.

The strip of ground between the curtain wall and the keep was entirely taken up with paved walks and close-packed patches of garden; Sterren was a bit surprised to see no inner line of defense there. The gap between Ethshar's walls and its outermost street, he knew, was carefully kept clear of trees and permanent structures of any sort, to allow for the deployment of troops and military equipment in the event of siege or assault; in times of peace, such as the past two centuries, this area filled up with the city's criminals and homeless. Semma Castle had no equivalent of this infamous Hundred-Foot Field.

He had little time to look at the gardens, though. As soon as the last of the company had passed the outermost gate the trumpet fanfare ended with a final flourish, waiting guards slammed the outermost pair of the heavy doors, and servants in red and yellow garb leapt forward to take charge of the horses. Sterren was quickly lifted from the saddle and lowered to the ground by half a dozen of the men in his escort, as his mount was led to the stables beside the castle's inner gate.

This assistance was welcome, since he suspected he would be too stiff, after so long in the saddle, to have dismounted under his own power.

He was whisked past the stables and into the castle proper. The main door was, like the outer gate, equipped with a full range of defenses, but on foot, and alerted by the intervening greenery, he looked a little more closely this time and saw signs of disuse — dust on the hinges, a spider-web across one of the overhead openings. Forty years of peace, he guessed, had had an effect.

He had expected the party to stop and disband once

they were all inside, perhaps leaving him in the charge of servants, or a guard or two, but instead the whole contingent marched on down a broad, marble-floored central corridor. The soldiery kept him carefully centered in the group.

"Where are we going?" Sterren demanded, in Semmat.

Lady Kalira glanced toward the commander of the honor guard and whispered a question Sterren could not catch. The soldier nodded in reply, and Lady Kalira called back to Sterren, "The king is waiting to meet you."

"The king?" Sterren wasn't certain he had heard the word correctly; he did know its meaning, as it had come up in discussions with Alder.

"Yes, the king, His Majesty Phenvel, third of that name, by right of succession king of Semma and lord of the southern deserts."

"Oh." Sterren had never met a king before, and was unsure how to react.

A pair of heavy, gold-trimmed doors swung open, and Sterren found himself swept into what he immediately identified, despite a complete lack of previous experience with such things, as a throne room. A broad red carpet stretched from the door to the base of a dias, and up three steps to the feet of a portly man in scarlet robes, seated on a large black chair. To either side of the carpet stood a small crowd of people, all well-dressed, of all shapes and sizes.

Lady Kalira stopped at the foot of the dias; the soldiers stopped at the same instant she did, and gracefully stepped away to either side, with the exception of Alder and Dogal, bringing up the rear, who remained on the carpet.

Sterren, not having known what was coming, took a step or two forward before he stopped himself, coming uncomfortably close to walking into Lady Kalira's back.

Kalira bowed deeply, going down on one knee before her sovereign. Hesitantly, and awkwardly, since he had never made such an obeisance before, Sterren copied her actions.

Lady Kalira rose, and Sterren stood again.

The hall was almost, but not quite, silent; Sterren could hear a steady hiss of whispering among the watchers.

"Your Majesty," Lady Kalira said, "may I present your servant Sterren, Ninth Warlord of Semma." She gestured toward Sterren and stepped aside, turning so that she stood on the edge of the carpet, her back to the audience and able to speak to either monarch or Ethsharite.

Thinking some action was called for, Sterren bowed again, from the waist this time, wishing somebody had seen fit to coach him a little.

"Hello," the king said.

"Hello," Sterren replied nervously. He tried to judge the king's age, and guessed it at something over forty, but almost certainly still short of sixty.

"Are you really Tanissa the Stubborn's grandson? It's hard to believe."

Sterren, still unfamiliar with the language, needed a moment to puzzle that out and phrase a response. This was not the sort of question he had expected from a king in what he took for a formal audience. "Yes, I . . . Yes, your majesty, I am," he replied. He was grateful that Lady Kalira had provided him, in her introduction, with the correct form of address.

"I never met her," the king said, "but I heard about her when I was a boy, especially from her brother — your great-uncle, that is, the old warlord. She ran away with that merchant a couple of years before I was born. And you're really her grandson, are you?"

Sterren nodded.

"There's no need to be shy, lad," the king said, smiling. "After all, we're all family here."

"We are?" Sterren asked, puzzled.

"Oh, certainly; didn't you know? You're my seventh cousin once removed. I looked it up." He gestured expansively, taking in the crowd of observers. "And these," he said, "are the collected nobility of Semma. And all of us, lad, are descended from Tendel the First, first king of Semma."

"You are?"

"You, too, lad," Phenvel corrected him, gently.

"I am?"

"Yes, indeed; I'm in a direct male line, of course, and you descended from the second son of Tendel the Second, rather than the first son. You're also descended from a couple of Tendel the First's daughters — the nobles here tend to marry back into the family."

This came as something of a shock to Sterren, once he had puzzled out exactly what had been said, and at first he simply didn't believe it. A king, one of his ancestors? All these people his relatives? He was in the habit of thinking of himself as having no family at all; to find himself in a room crowded with his distant relations was more than he could absorb. He could imagine no reason for the king to lie about it, however.

"Oh," he said.

"That's one reason you're here, straight from your journey. We all wanted a look at you, our long-lost cousin."

"Oh," Sterren said again. This whole situation was beginning to seem unreal. Oh, the castle was real enough, and the people — he could smell them, as well as see and hear them, and he'd never heard of an illusion that detailed — but the idea that they were really the ruling class of one of the Small Kingdoms, just a few leagues from the edge of the World, and that he was one of them, a hereditary warlord, seemed so completely absurd that for a moment it was easier to believe the whole thing was a gigantic joke of some kind.

An uncomfortable silence fell, to be broken by Lady Kalira.

"Your Majesty," she said, "I believe that our new warlord is weary from his journey, and overwhelmed by meeting you. Nor has he eaten since dawn."

This was not strictly true, since Sterren's party had finished breakfast well after sunrise, but it was close enough.

"Of course," the king agreed. "Of course. Take him to his room, then, and let him recover himself. We'll speak with him more when he's rested and has eaten." He waved a hand in dismissal.

Lady Kalira bowed, and Sterren imitated her again. Then she motioned for him to follow, and led the way to the right, through the crowd to a door, and out of the throne room. Alder and Dogal followed discreetly.

They emerged into a corridor, where Lady Kalira turned left and led the way up curving stairs. Sterren's stiff legs protested, but he followed her.

At the second floor she kept going, and Sterren followed without question.

At the third floor he paused, hoping she would change her mind, but she kept on climbing. He suppressed a moan.

At the fourth floor he considered asking how much further they had to go, but couldn't think of the right words in Semmat.

At the fifth floor he was panting heavily.

At the sixth floor the staircase ended, and he breathed a sigh of relief as Lady Kalira led him down a passageway — and then she reached another staircase and started up again. He balked.

Alder and Dogal came up behind him and did not stop; he yielded, and hurried on, up into the tower.

After just one more flight, on the seventh floor, they left the staircase and headed down one more short passage, to an iron-bound door. Lady Kalira turned a large black key in the lock, and then swung the door open to reveal the room beyond.

"This is your room, as the warlord," she announced. She stood back to let him enter. "It was your great-uncle's for almost twenty years, and his father's — your great-grandfather's — for half a century before that."

Sterren stepped in cautiously.

He was in a large, airy chamber, one side mostly taken up by three broad, curtainless, many-paned windows. Thick tapestries, slightly faded but still handsome, hid the stone walls. A high canopied bed stood centered against one wall, with a table on either side, a wardrobe beyond the left-hand table and a chest of drawers to the right. Opposite the bed was a desk, or worktable, flanked by tall bookcases jammed with books and papers. A chair was tucked away in each corner of the room; counting the one at the desk, there were five in all.

Sterren turned, and discovered that the wall around the doorway was covered with displays of weapons — swords, knives, spears, pole-arms, and a good many he could not put a name to, even in Ethsharitic. He wondered if he, as warlord, was expected to learn to use them.

The weapons were all dusty. In fact, everything was covered by a layer of dust — the desk, the books, the papers, everything. The air was full of the dry, dusty smell of disuse. It was plain that nobody had been living in the room recently.

Hesitantly, he crossed to the windows and looked out. He judged the angle of the sun and decided he was looking almost due north.

The view was spectacular; he could see the castle roofs

below him, hiding his view of the outer wall and most of the surrounding village. Beyond that he could see a few houses — and then the plain, rolling on into the distance, spotted with farmhouses, orchards, and various outbuildings, marked off into individual holdings by hedges and fences. He saw no roads, however; what traveling was done here was apparently done straight across country.

To the right he thought he could see, out near the horizon, the farms and grasslands fading into desert sand; somewhat to the left of center he thought he might be seeing the peaks of distant mountains somewhere beyond the horizon.

He turned back to the doorway, and saw that Lady Kalira and the two soldiers were still standing in the corridor. He had a sudden vision of the door slamming, trapping him inside.

"Aren't you coming in?" he asked.

Lady Kalira nodded and stepped in.

"What did you wait for?" he asked.

"I would not enter your private chamber without an invitation, Lord Sterren," she replied.

Baffled by this pronouncement, which clearly implied that he had some authority and was not merely a prisoner, it took Sterren a moment to realize that Alder and Dogal were still waiting in the hall. He looked at Lady Kalira.

She looked back, paying no attention to the soldiers. "May I sit down?" she asked.

"Yes," Sterren said in Ethsharitic, again caught off-guard by her sudden deference. He corrected himself, repeating it in Semmat, as he remembered his escort waiting for him, back out on the plain.

Maybe they were serious about calling him a lord.

She pulled a chair from a corner and sat. Sterren considered for a long moment before lowering himself cautiously into the chair by the desk.

The healing salve on his saddlesores was working; he could sit with only mild discomfort.

"You must have questions," Lady Kalira said. "Now that we're safely home, maybe I can answer them."

Sterren stared at her for a moment, still puzzled, and then smiled crookedly. "I hope so," he said.

Five

"Everything in this room is yours," Lady Kalira said. "This, and the position of warlord, are your inheritance from your great-uncle Sterren. Nothing else; everything he owned when he died is right here, or was given, at his request, to others."

Sterren struggled with that for a moment, and carefully phrased a question.

"How did he give anything to me? How did he know I . . . I was alive, when he hadn't seen my grandmother for so long?"

"Oh, he didn't know you existed, but he had no choice in the matter," Lady Kalira said, waving the question away. "Semma has very clear and definite laws on the lines of succession. This room and its contents were his as the warlord, not his, personally, so he had no say about who would receive them, nor who would receive the title. If people were allowed to influence successions it would result in all sorts of intrigues — and frankly, we have too much of that even as it is."

"Succession? Intrigues?"

Lady Kalira explained the words as best she could, and eventually Sterren thought he understood.

"But why *me*?" he asked. "Isn't there anyone here who could be warlord?"

The noblewoman snorted in derision. "Your ancestors," she said, "were about the worst line in the whole family at providing enough heirs. It doesn't help that warlords tend to die young, in battle."

That statement, when the unfamiliar terms had been defined, did little to help Sterren's peace of mind, but he made no comment.

"After you," Lady Kalira continued, "the next heir is the old warlord's third cousin — your third cousin twice removed. That's only the seventh degree of consanguinity. You're an heir in the third degree of consanguinity. That's a pretty big difference. And besides, you're young and strong . . ."

Sterren took this as flattery, since he knew he was relatively scrawny.

". . . and she's past fifty. If she had a son — well, that would be the eighth degree, but it might do. Unfortunately, her only child is a daughter. Unmarried, even if we allowed inheritance by marriage instead of blood."

An attempt to explain the new words this time was unsuccessful until, exasperated, Lady Kalira rose and crossed to the desk, where she found a sheet of paper, a pen, and ink, then leaned over and began drawing a family tree.

Sterren, still seated, watched with interest as she ran down the history of Semma's nine warlords.

The first, Tendel, was the younger brother of King Rayel II, born almost two hundred years ago. His son, also named Tendel, followed him, and a grandson after that, but this third Tendel managed to get himself killed in battle early in the disastrous Third Ksinallionese War, before he got around to marrying and siring heirs. His brother Sterren inherited the title as Fourth Warlord, only to get himself killed three years later in the same war.

This first Sterren had been kind enough to produce five children, though three of them were daughters, and the younger son died without issue. The elder son succeeded as Fifth Warlord. His only child became Sixth Warlord, and in turn produced only one son, the eventual Seventh Warlord, before meeting a nasty end after losing a war.

Sterren, Seventh Warlord was only twenty-one when he inherited the title, and lived to be seventy-three. He was something of a legend. He broke with tradition, and instead of marrying a distant cousin married an Ethsharitic woman he found somewhere.

They had three children, though the second one, Dereth, died in infancy. The eldest, Sterren, eventually became the Eighth Warlord — and the youngest, Tanissa the Stubborn, ran away with an Ethsharitic trader in 5169 and was never heard from again.

She, of course, was Sterren of Ethshar's grandmother. And since her brother never did get around to marrying or producing children, that made Sterren the Ninth Warlord.

The next-closest heir was Nerra the Cheerful, a grand-daughter of the Fourth Warlord's eldest daughter — not exactly an obvious choice.

Lady Kalira put aside the sketchy geneaology after that and continued her explanation without further prompting. Sterren listened politely, following the unfamiliar words as best he could.

When it had become clear that old Sterren was finally dying the royal genealogist, unaware of Tanissa's son and grandson, had needed over an hour simply to determine who the heir should be.

He had noticed the notation in the records of Tanissa's elopement, and had reported it, along with his conclusions, to the king and his advisors. After considerable debate Agor, the castle theurgist, had been called in; he in turn had called up Unniel the Discerning, a minor goddess, who after much coaxing had, in her turn, called upon Aibem, a more powerful god, who had, finally, informed everybody that although Tanissa was dead, her grandson was still alive and well.

After that, of course, Lady Kalira and her little entou-rage had been sent to find Sterren and bring him back to Semma, and they had done just that. Lady Kalira, who was not anywhere in the line of succession for warlord, had gotten the job because she was the heir presumptive to her cousin Inria, Seventh Trader. Inria, eighty years old, could not have made the trip herself.

When Lady Kalira had finished, Sterren nodded. "And here I am," he agreed. "Now what do I do?"

"I would think that would be obvious — you're to take command of the army and defend Semma."

"Defend Semma?"

"Protect it from its enemies," she explained.

"What enemies?"

"*All* enemies."

"Semma has enemies?"

"Of course it does, idiot! Ksinallion, for one, and Ophkar, for another."

Up until that moment, Sterren had entertained a vague hope that his unwanted new job would turn out to be a sinecure, with a title and pay and no duties. He suppressed a sigh of disappointment.

It came as especially bad news that *both* Semma's larger neighbors were considered enemies — but at least, he told himself, he hadn't arrived in the middle of a war.

"Do you think that . . . that a war may come soon?"

Lady Kalira grimaced. "Much too soon," she said, "from the look of you, and what I've seen in the barracks of late."

Had his knowledge of Semmat been good enough for the job, Sterren would have made a retort about being glad to relinquish his position as warlord, which he hadn't asked for in the first place, if she thought someone else could do better.

Instead, he asked, "What do I do now? Today?"

"Well," Lady Kalira said, looking about the chamber, "I suppose you'll want to settle in here, maybe clean up a little. I'll have Dogal fetch water and something to eat; I don't suppose that you'll want to come down for lunch. You'll be expected to eat at the High Table at dinner, of course, to talk to His Majesty and meet some of the people here — the princes and princesses, for example — but I think you can leave all that until dinner. For this afternoon, I would recommend that you take some time to learn the situation here — talk to your officers, maybe look over the barracks, that sort of thing. You're the warlord; you must know more about it than I do."

Astonished, Sterren said, "But I was never a warlord before!"

"It's in your blood, isn't it?"

"Not that I ever noticed," Sterren replied.

Lady Kalira ignored that, as she turned to the doorway and called, "Dogal, go down to the kitchens and get wash water and something for Lord Sterren to eat, would you?"

Dogal bobbed his head. "Yes, my lady," he said, and then quickly departed.

"Alder, here, will help you unpack, if you like," she suggested.

Sterren nodded absently. Alder stepped into the room, carrying the bundle of possessions that Sterren had collected from his room back on Bargain Street. He deposited it upon the bed and began untying it.

"My officers, you said," Sterren said. The phrase carried an impression of power and authority, and he felt a sudden surge of interest.

"Yes, of course," Lady Kalira replied.

"I suppose I should meet them, talk to them."

"Yes."

The thought of all those stairs came to him, and he asked, "Could you send them up here?"

"Of course, Lord Sterren," Lady Kalira said, with a faint bow.

The bow startled him. Lady Kalira noticed his surprise, and explained, "Lord Sterren, I think I really should tell you that as warlord, now that you have accepted the position and that the king has acknowledged you, you outrank me. In fact, you are now one of the highest-ranking nobles in Semma. Historically, the warlord and the foreign minister are equal in rank and second only to the king and his immediate family, with all others — steward, treasurer, trader, all of them — your inferiors."

"Really?"

"Really."

Sterren mused on that for awhile, wondering just what such an exalted rank would actually mean in terms of power, privilege — and responsibility. He almost forgot Lady Kalira was there until she reminded him.

"My lord?" she asked.

"Ah," Sterren said, startled. "Yes?"

"Lord Sterren, I'm tired and hungry, too. If you have no more questions, may I have your leave to go?"

Startled anew, Sterren stammered. "Of course," he managed at last.

Lady Kalira curtseyed, then turned.

"Send up my officers," Sterren called, "when I'm done eating."

He was sure she had heard him, but she said nothing as she slipped out of the room.

He stared after her for a moment.

The switch from her role as exasperated jailer to one of deferential subordinate was curiously unnerving. He was not accustomed to having *anyone* defer to him. He had always settled for simple tolerance, which was all a tavern-gambler or street brat could reasonably ask.

There was something very seductive about the thought of a woman unable to leave his room until he granted permission. Admittedly, the aging and irritable Lady Kalira was not herself seductive in the least, but the *idea* of such power certainly had its appeal.

But it came with the job of warlord, with all the unknown hazards and duties that must surely imply. War meant swords and blood and death and killing, and he wanted no part of it.

But Semma had been at peace since twenty years before he was born. Maybe he could defend it without fighting any wars, as his immediate predecessor, the great-uncle he had never known, had.

"My lord," Alder said, startling him from his muddled thoughts, "shall I hang this in the wardrobe?" He held up one of Sterren's old tunics.

"Yes," Sterren said. He took a sudden interest in his belongings, seeing that everything went somewhere appropriate, and that he knew how the room was arranged. It was becoming clear that, barring the unforeseen, he was going to be staying for quite some time.

He was unsure, now, whether that was good news or bad.

Six

He pushed away the plate and stood up.

Alder looked up, startled, and began, "My lord . . ."

"Oh, go ahead and eat," Sterren said crossly. He was already getting tired of the strange new deference paid him. Alder had just started to eat, but he was obviously ready to leap up and follow orders, should his warlord care to give any.

His warlord did not. His warlord was feeling very much out of place. His moods kept swinging back and forth. This room, and title, and rank were all very well, and could be a lot of fun — but they also seemed to be permanent and involuntary, which could be tiresome, quite aside from the accompanying responsibilities and risks. It was clear, despite the submissive gestures from Alder and Lady Kalira, that he was still something of a prisoner; if he tried to just walk out of the castle, and head back toward Ethshar, he was quite sure that Alder or Dogal or both would follow him, and probably stop him before he got out of the village.

And he was tired of seeing Alder and Dogal, after several days spent traveling in their close — *very* close — company.

At least Lady Kalira was gone, and he would be meeting other people soon.

Of course, that, too, had both its appealing and frightening aspects. These people were barbarians, not Ethsharites; he was sure that he was not what anybody expected in a warlord, and he had no idea just how the Semmans might deal with his shortcomings. That mention of summary execution, back in the tavern on Bargain Street, had stayed with him, always somewhere in the back of his mind.

Dogal and Alder had eaten in turns, and Dogal was now guarding the door, keeping Sterren's officers, who had arrived a moment earlier, waiting in the hall.

"Dogal," Sterren called, "send them in."

Dogal said nothing, but stepped aside and allowed the three waiting men to enter.

Each in turn stepped into the chamber, bowed, spoke, and then stepped aside to make room for the next.

"Anduron of Semma, Lord Sterren," said the first, with a graceful bow and a jingle of jewelry. He was tall and sturdy, richly dressed in blue silk, perhaps thirty years old — certainly much older than Sterren. Like every Semman Sterren had yet seen, he was dark-haired and deeply tanned. Sterren thought he detected a family resemblance to the king.

He also detected, more definitely, a trace of scent, something vaguely flowery.

"Arl of the Strong Arm," said the next, bobbing his head. He was shorter, but Sterren guessed his weight to be no less than Anduron's, and his age was probably similar. He wore a red kilt and red-embroidered yellow tunic, and smelled of nothing but leather and sweat.

"Shemder the Bold," said the third, without ceremony. He fell between the others in height, but clearly weighed less than either of them, being thin and wiry, and was younger as well, surely no more than twenty-five — but still older than Sterren. His garb was similar to Arl's, but more ornate and better-kept, and Sterren could detect no odor at all.

These three were more or less displaying the forms of deference due a superior, but it was obvious they did not really feel any of the respect those forms implied.

Lady Kalira had been subtler in her contempt.

"I'm Sterren of Ethshar," Sterren replied, bowing in his

turn. He pronounced "Ethshar" correctly, refusing to yield to the Semman usage. After all, he thought resentfully, Semmat did use the TH sound — just not in combination with SH.

"Your pardon, my lord," said Anduron, "but would it not be more proper to call yourself Sterren, Ninth Warlord of Semma?"

Anduron's words were smoothly spoken, and Sterren would have liked to make a graceful reply. His limited knowledge of the language forced him to make do with, "I guess you're right. I'm still new at this." He smiled, not very convincingly.

Behind him, Alder was hurriedly stuffing the last few bites of gravy-soaked bread into his mouth.

The three new arrivals stood stiffly silent for a moment.

"Lord Sterren," Shemder said, finally, "you sent for us?"

"Yes," Sterren said. "Of course. Sit down." He waved at the chairs in the various corners. Alder was just getting up from the chair at the desk, and after an instant's hesitation Sterren settled on the foot of the bed instead of trying to maneuver behind the soldier.

The officers obeyed, bringing the chairs to a rough semicircle. Once seated, they stared stonily at Sterren.

He took a deep breath, and delivered his little speech, two of the longest sentences he had yet contrived in Semmat.

"I called you here because I am told I am a warlord now, whether I like it or not. I think I need to find out what that means, and what it is I am expected to do."

The officers still stared silently.

"You aren't making this easy," Sterren said, blinking at them.

"Lord Sterren," Shemder said, "you still haven't told us what you want of us."

"What I want," Sterren said, "is to know what I, your warlord, am expected to do. I want you three to tell me."

The three exchanged looks.

"My lord," Shemder said, "it is not our place to tell you what to do. It is your job to tell *us* what to do."

Sterren suppressed a sigh. Whether they resented the elevation of a stranger as their superior, or whether they were testing him somehow, or whether they were simply stupid or stubborn or unimaginative, Sterren had no way of knowing, but he could see plainly enough that his officers were not going to be a great deal of help.

At least, not at first. Perhaps they would adjust eventually.

"Lord Shemder . . ." he began.

"I am no lord," Shemder interrupted.

Sterren acknowledged the correction with a nod, and said, "Shemder, then, tell me your duties."

"My duties, Lord Sterren?"

"Yes, your duties." He hoped he hadn't gotten the wrong word.

"I have no duties at present, my lord; I am the commander of the Semman cavalry, not a mere guardsman."

"Cavalry?" The word was unfamiliar.

"Cavalry."

Sterren looked at Alder, who supplied, "Soldiers on horses."

Sterren nodded, filing the word away. "Cavalry. Good. You're the commander of the Semman cavalry. Do you have a particular title? Do I call you my lord, or commander?"

"*Captain*, my lord," Shemder said grimly. "You call me Captain."

"Thank you, Captain Shemder. And Captain Arl, is it?"

"Yes, Lord Sterren." Where Shemder had sounded

barely tolerant of his new lord, Arl sounded resigned and despairing.

"Captain of what?"

"Infantry, my lord — foot soldiers."

Sterren nodded politely, appreciative of Arl's trace of cooperation in explaining an unfamiliar word without forcing Sterren to ask.

"And Captain Anduron?"

"*Lord* Anduron, my lord. I am your second in command, in charge of everything that Captain Arl and Captain Shemder are not — archers, the castle garrison, supply, and so forth." He spoke with studied nonchalance, sprawling comfortably on his chair.

"Ah!" That sounded promising, especially once Alder and Lord Anduron between them had explained the unfamiliar words. Sterren wondered if he could palm off all his duties on Lord Anduron and leave himself to enjoy his position as a figurehead. Lord Anduron had a look of cool competence about him that Sterren hoped was not mere affectation. "How many archers are there?" he asked.

Lord Anduron's reply burst Sterren's bubble instantly.

"None, at present," he said calmly.

"*None?*"

"None. We've had no need of any for forty years, after all; archers aren't particularly impressive in parades or display, and bow-wood is expensive. Old Sterren — that is, your esteemed predecessor, the Eighth Warlord — allowed all the old archers to retire, and left it to me, or my father before me, to replace them, and we didn't trouble to do so. If we need archers, I'm sure we can find and train them quickly."

"Ah." Sterren tried to look wise and understanding, although he had missed several words, and was fairly certain that training a competent archer took a good deal more time and effort than Lord Anduron thought — especially if there were no trained archers around to serve as teachers. "What about the castle . . . garrison? Is that the word?"

"My lord speaks Semmat like a native, of course," Lord Anduron said. Shemder interrupted him with a quickly-suppressed burst of derisive laughter. Lord Anduron cast him a cold glance, then went on, "The castle garrison, my lord, is composed of whoever happens to be inside the castle at the time of an attack."

"I see — you mean the nobles, and the servants, and so on?"

"Why, no, Lord Sterren, of course not. One could hardly expect the nobility to soil their hands with the hauling about of gates and bars, or hurling stones, and the servants will have their normal duties to perform. No, I mean whatever villagers reach the shelter of the castle walls in time."

Sterren stared at Lord Anduron for a moment, then decided argument would do no good, most particularly in his limited Semmat. He turned his head and asked, "Captain Shemder, how many men and horses do you have?"

"Twenty men, my lord, and twelve horses," Shemder replied promptly and proudly.

Sterren realized with a shock that his escort into the castle had been most of the cavalrymen in the entire kingdom — and *all* the cavalry's horses.

"Captain Arl?"

"At present, Lord Sterren, I have sixty-five men and boys, all fully armed, well-trained, and ready for anything."

Sterren somehow doubted that the Semman infantry was ready for anything. What, he wondered, would they do in the face of an attack by the overlord of Ethshar of the Spices? Azrad VII had ten thousand men in his city guard alone. He could overwhelm Semma completely with a tenth of his soldiery, without calling on any of his more important resources — the militia, the navy, his magicians, the other two-thirds of the Ethsharitic triumvirate, and so on.

But these were the Small Kingdoms, and things were obviously different here.

The three officers all seemed very confident, certainly, and they surely knew more of the situation than he, a foreigner, did.

Even so, eighty-five men and a few frightened refugees did not seem like a very large force for a castle the size of Semma's.

"Lord Anduron," he asked, "what about magic?"

The young nobleman looked puzzled. "What *about* magic, my lord?"

"What magicians do you command?"

"None, my lord; what would I have to do with magicians?"

"Are they infantry or cavalry, then?"

"No," Arl said, as Shemder shook his head.

"Aren't there any magicians in the castle, then?" Sterren asked, truly frightened.

The three officers stared at each other. It was Lord Anduron who spoke, finally, saying, "I suppose there might be one or two. Queen Ashassa keeps a theurgist about, Agor by name, and I've heard the servants chatter about a wizard among their number. The village has an herbalist or two, and a witch, I believe, but they aren't in the castle. Lord Sterren, forgive me, but why do you ask?"

"Don't you use magic . . . Isn't it . . ." Sterren's Semmat failed him momentarily. He took a deep breath, and began again.

"In Ethshar," he said, "Lord Azrad keeps the best magicians with him. They would use their . . . their magic, if the city were attacked. Ships carry magicians, to defend against . . . against other ships, which of course have their own magicians. No one would dare a big fight without magic." He cursed himself and all of Semma for his lack of a correct title for Azrad, and the words for "spells," "pirates," and "battle."

For several long seconds the room was absolutely silent. Then Shemder spat a word that Sterren had never heard before.

"Lord Sterren," Lord Anduron said, "we do not use magic in war here."

Lord Anduron's tone was flat and final, but Sterren could not stop himself from shouting, "Why *not*?" In his thoughts, which were in Ethsharitic, his phrasing was a good bit more colorful.

"It isn't done. It never has been."

Sterren stared at him for a moment. "I see," he said at last. He blinked, and then said, "If you will forgive me, I am tired from my journey. I need to rest." In truth, what he felt a need for was time to digest the situation. "Go now, and I will speak with you again later. Perhaps after dinner. I would like to . . . to look at the soldiers."

"Review the troops?" Arl suggested.

"I think so," Sterren agreed, nodding. He stood up.

The other three leapt up as well. Each in turn bowed, and then left the room.

Lord Anduron bowed deeply, and swept out; Arl bowed stiffly, and marched out; Shemder bobbed his head, and stalked out.

Sterren stared after them, then burst out, in Ethsharitic, "What a bunch of idiots!" He had been willing to give them the benefit of the doubt in regard to the numbers and preparedness of their forces, but to so completely and arbitrarily rule out the use of magic in warfare was ridiculous!

What would guard them against treachery? How could they know what the enemy was planning? Who would heal wounds? Sending soldiers out to fight with nothing but swords and shields was *truly* barbaric.

And most importantly, what would they ever do if they fought an enemy who did not bother with such scruples?

Obviously, they would lose, and lose quickly and decisively.

He could only hope that nothing like that happened while he was warlord. His duty, Lady Kalira had told him, was to defend Semma, but some things were indefensible.

An Ethsharitic obscenity escaped him.

"My lord?" Alder inquired, startled by the outburst.

"Nothing," Sterren said. "It's nothing." His initial amazement at the idea of fighting a war without using magic was beginning to fade, and another thought struck him. "What was that that Shemder said, about using magic to fight?"

Uncomfortably, Alder asked, "You mean that word, *gakhar*?" He shifted uneasily.

"Yes, that's it." Sterren saw Alder's discomfort, but declined to let him off the hook; he stared inquiringly.

Reluctantly, Alder said, "It means a . . . a person of no culture, a person not fit to be among ordinary people."

Sterren considered that, then stared after the vanished Shemder the Bold.

"You mean *he* called *me* a barbarian?" Sterren was dumbfounded. He wasn't sure whether to laugh or scream with rage at the unbelievable insult of being called a barbarian by people such as these, but after a moment laughter won out.

Alder stared at him, puzzled and amused, but not particularly displeased with his new warlord.

Seven

The clothes in the wardrobe did not fit him; Sterren, Eighth Warlord had obviously been considerably larger than was Sterren, Ninth Warlord. Not that he had been anything like Alder or Dogal, but he surely had the advantage of a few inches over his great-nephew, both in height and circumference.

Even so, Sterren thought that he would do better to wear something from the wardrobe, belted up tight, than to try and get any more use out of his own tattered garments. He was to eat dinner with the king, at the High Table, and he had not a single tunic left that had neither patches nor major stains.

Furthermore, he saw that all his clothes were cut differently from the prevailing mode in Semma. The local style was looser, more flowing, but with more fancywork to it.

He picked out an elegant black silk tunic embroidered in gold, and a pair of black leather breeches — black seemed to be the predominant color in the collection, and he guessed it had something to do with the office he held. It seemed an appropriate color for a warlord.

Of course, it might just be that his great-uncle had liked the dramatic, or had had a morbid streak, but in any case, black clothes might not look quite so oversized on him.

He would, he thought with a sigh, have to alter all the clothes, take them in to fit him.

No, he wouldn't, he corrected himself, brightening up; he was an aristocrat now! He could find a servant to do that. The castle probably had a tailor somewhere.

He pulled the tunic over his head and looked in the

flaking, yellowed mirror that hung in the back of the wardrobe.

He shuddered. The tunic almost reached his knees; he looked like a little boy.

He pulled on the breeches, then began adjusting belts and fabric.

By tucking in the top of the breeches and folding under the cuff on each leg he was able to make them fit, though they were still rather baggy in spots. The tunic was less cooperative, but he finally contrived an arrangement of two belts, one under and one over, that pulled the hem up to a height he could live with. The embroidered sleeves he had to roll up.

He was studying his appearance critically when someone knocked on the door.

"Who is it?" he called, unthinkingly using Ethsharitic.

"What?" someone answered in Semmat. The voice was female, young and female.

"Sorry," he called, switching to Semmat as he adjusted his belts. "Who is it?"

"The Princess Lura, Lord Sterren," Alder's voice replied.

Sterren whirled around and stared at the door. A princess? He glanced down at himself.

He looked foolish, he knew, but he would have to face this soon enough. He pursed his lips, and decided not to put off the inevitable. "Come in," he called.

The door swung open and Sterren looked up to see who was there, but at first he saw no one. Then he let his gaze drop.

"Hello," Princess Lura said, smiling up at him. "You look funny in those clothes; don't you have any that fit?"

Sterren was not particularly fond of children, but Lura,

who he guessed to be no more than nine, at the most, had an irresistable grin.

Besides, she was a princess. He smiled back, and it was only slightly forced.

"No," he said, "I'm afraid I don't. The clothes I brought with me are all worn out."

"Can't you get new ones?" she demanded.

"I haven't had time," he explained.

"Oh, I guess not." Her gaze dropped for a moment, and an awkward silence fell, to be quickly broken when she raised her eyes again and said, "I wanted to meet you. I never met anybody from Ethshar before."

Sterren noticed that she pronounced "Ethshar" correctly, even when speaking Semmat, and nodded approvingly. "I can understand that," he said. "I must seem . . . um . . . I must be like . . . I guess you haven't." His Semmat vocabulary had failed him again. He hastened to cover over his slip. "I never met a princess before."

"No?"

He shook his head. "No," he said.

"Not even back in Ethshar?"

"Not even in Ethshar. There's only one princess in all of Ethshar of the Spices, and I never met her."

Actually, technically, there were no "princesses" at all, but Azrad VII's sister, Imra the Unfortunate, was a reasonably close approximation. Sterren had no idea what her correct title would be in Semmat; in Ethsharitic she was simply Lady Imra.

"Oh, we have lots of princesses here!" Lura announced proudly. "There's me, of course, and my sisters — Ashassa doesn't live here any more, she's in Kalithon with her husband Prince Tabar, but there's Nissitha and Shirrin, still. And there's my Aunt Sanda. That's four of us, not counting Ashassa."

Sterren nodded. "Four's a good number, I guess," he said, smiling foolishly.

Lura's expression suddenly turned suspicious. "I'm not a baby, you know," she said. "You don't have to play along with me."

"I'm sorry," Sterren said, dropping the false smile, "I didn't mean to . . . to do as if you were a baby. Um . . . how old are you?" He looked a little more closely at her face. He could not tell her age with any certainty, but he noticed a resemblance to her father, the king.

"Seven," she said. "I'll be eight in Icebound. The ninth of Icebound."

"I was born on the eighth of Thaw, myself," Sterren said.

Lura nodded, and another awkward silence fell. The two of them stood there, looking at each other or glancing around the room, until Sterren, desperately, said, "So you just wanted to meet me because I'm from Ethshar?"

"Well, mostly. And you *are* the new warlord, so I guess you're important. Everybody *else* wants to meet you, too, but they didn't come up here, I did. My sister Shirrin was scared to, and Nissitha says she doesn't have time for such foolishness, but she's just trying to act grown-up. She's twenty-one and not even betrothed yet, so I don't know why she's so proud of herself!"

Sterren nodded. Lura obviously loved to talk — another resemblance to her father, he thought. He wondered if he had finally found someone who would tell him everything he wanted to know about Semma Castle and its inhabitants; certainly, Lura wasn't reticent.

On the other hand, how much would she actually know? Gossip about her sisters was one thing; a warlord's duties were quite another.

"Are you *really* a warlord?" she asked, breaking his chain of thought.

"So they tell me," he said.

"Have you killed a lot of people?"

Sterren shuddered. "I've never killed *anyone*," he said, emphatically.

"Oh." Lura was clearly disappointed by this revelation. She did not let that slow her for long, however.

"What's it like in Ethshar?" she asked.

Involuntarily, Sterren glanced out the broad windows at the endless plains to the north. "Crowded," he said. He pointed out the window. "Imagine," he said, "that you were on the top of the tower at *Westgate*, looking east across the city. The eastern wall would be halfway to the . . . to where the sun comes up, and everything in between would be streets and shops and houses, all crowded inside the walls." He didn't know any word for "horizon," and hoped Lura would understand what he meant.

Lura looked out the window, and asked, "What about farms?"

"Outside the walls, never inside."

She looked skeptical, and he saw no point in arguing about it. "You asked," he said with a shrug.

She shrugged in reply. "You're right," she said, "I did. When are you coming downstairs? Everybody's waiting to meet you."

"They are?"

"Well, of *course* they are, silly! Come on, right now; I know *Shirrin* wants to meet you, especially."

"She does?" Even when he remembered who Shirrin was — one of Lura's sisters, and therefore a princess — Sterren could not imagine why she would particularly want to meet him.

"Yes, she does. Come on!"

Sterren glanced helplessly around at the room. He had no idea what his position was relative to this little terror of a princess; certainly, she must outrank him, but would her youth affect her authority to order him about?

He couldn't be sure of that. Reluctantly, he followed her as she marched out of the room.

Once in the hallway, Alder and Dogal fell in step behind him, and together the four of them tramped down the six flights of stairs to the door of the throne room. He stopped there to catch his breath while Lura waited impatiently.

They did not enter the throne room, but turned aside at the last moment and headed down a short corridor and through an unmarked door of age-darkened oak. Beyond was an antechamber, panelled in smoke-stained wood and furnished with heavy velvet-upholstered benches; Lura led Sterren directly through this, and through another door.

This gave into a sunny little sitting room, and as Sterren entered, Lura leading him by the hand, he glimpsed the inhabitants leaping to their feet.

He found himself facing two women and a girl a few years younger than himself, all richly dressed, all standing and staring at him.

"Shirrin, look who I found!" Lura announced.

The girl blushed bright red and glanced about as if looking for some way to escape. Seeing none, she stared defiantly back at Sterren, her cheeks crimson.

The older woman looked reprovingly at Sterren's guide. "Lura," she said, "watch your manners."

The younger woman simply stood, silently gazing down her nose at Sterren. It was quite obvious that she had noticed his attire and didn't think much of it.

Or maybe she didn't think much of him in any case; Sterren couldn't be sure. He had the distinct impression, however, that the woman would have sniffed with disdain if sniffing were not perhaps a trifle vulgar.

He smiled politely.

"Hello," he said. "I'm Sterren of Ethshar — Sterren, Ninth Warlord, they call me."

"My lord Sterren," the older woman said, smiling in return, "what a pleasure to meet you! I'm Ashassa, formerly of Thanoria, and these are my daughters, Nissitha," with a nod toward the younger woman, "and Shirrin," with a nod toward the blushing girl. "Lura you have already met, I take it."

"Yes," Sterren said, "she introduced herself." He realized, with a twinge of dismay, that he was speaking to the Queen of Semma, and had presumably just come barging into the royal family's private quarters.

At that thought, he glanced around quickly.

The room was pleasant enough; a floor of square-cut white stone was partly covered by brightly-hued carpets, and white-painted paneling covered the walls on three sides. The fourth side was mostly window, the glass panes arranged in ornate floral patterns and the leading picked out with red and white paint. Several couches stood handy, all covered in red velvet, and a few small tables of white marble and black iron were scattered about.

Nothing was extraordinarily luxurious, however. Sterren had seen rooms of similar size and appointments, though never in any style quite like this one, back in Ethshar.

The queen was nodding. "I'm afraid Lura can be somewhat impetuous," she said. "Of course, we've all been looking forward to meeting you, our long-lost cousin."

"A very *distant* cousin, of course," Nissitha interjected, with a meaningful glance at Sterren's tunic.

"Lura said that you wanted to meet me," Sterren acknowledged. "She mentioned Shirrin in particular, though I don't . . ."

He was interrupted by a shriek from Princess Shirrin. The red had faded somewhat from her cheeks, but now it flooded back more brightly than ever, and she turned and ran from the room.

Sterren stared after her, astonished.

Lura burst into giggles. Nissitha stared down at her youngest sister in clear disgust. The queen's expression shifted to polite dismay.

"Did I say something wrong?" Sterren asked, hoping he hadn't just condemned himself to a dungeon or worse.

"Oh, no," Queen Ashassa reassured him. "Or at least, not really. It's Lura's doing. And of course, Shirrin's being foolish, too. She's thirteen, you know, a very sensitive age, and Lura's doing her best to embarrass her. Don't let it worry you." She turned to Lura and said sternly, "Lura, you go apologize to your sister!"

Lura's giggling suddenly stopped. "For what?" she demanded, "I didn't do anything!"

"Do as I say!" the queen thundered, pointing.

Lura knew better than to argue any further; she marched off after Shirrin.

"I'm sorry, my lord," the queen said when Lura had closed the door behind her. "Those girls love to tease each other. You see, Shirrin's all full of romantic stories about Ethshar and warlords and lost heirs ever since our theurgist, Agor, first told us about you, and Lura's been making fun of her for it."

"Silly things," Nissitha remarked, "getting worked up over nothing!"

Sterren was at a loss for a reply. "Ah," he said.

"Well, then, my lord," Queen Ashassa said, "as long as

you're here, Lura was quite right, we've all been eager to meet you and talk with you. You must understand, none of us have ever been more than a few leagues from this castle; my ancestral home in Thanoria is only six leagues or so, and that's the furthest any of us have traveled. Ethshar seems unspeakably exotic. Do sit down, and tell us something about it!"

Sterren glanced at his guards, but Dogal and Alder were being steadfastly silent. Seeing no polite way to refuse, he reluctantly and delicately seated himself on one of the velvet couches, while Queen Ashassa and Princess Nissitha settled onto others, and asked, "What can I tell you?"

Princess Nissitha's expression plainly said that he couldn't tell her anything at all, but Queen Ashassa asked, her tone sincerely interested, "Is it true that the city of Ethshar is so large that you can't see from one end to the other?"

"Well," Sterren said, considering the question, "it would depend where you were standing. I suppose from atop the . . . the lord's castle you could see the city walls on both sides. But mostly, it's true."

The overlord's palace was not really a castle, but his limited Semman vocabulary did not include a more suitable term.

The queen asked more questions, and Sterren did his best to answer; gradually, as the topics ranged from the city's size to the recently-begun overlordship of Azrad VII to wizards and other magicians, Sterren found himself relaxing and enjoying the conversation. Queen Ashassa, despite her royal title, was a pleasant enough person.

Princess Nissitha never said a word, and eventually rose and glided haughtily away.

After a time, a servant entered quietly and announced that dinner was ready. Queen Ashassa rose, and for a moment Sterren thought she was going to offer her arm, to be escorted in to the meal, as he had seen ladies do in Ethshar.

Either Semman etiquette was different, or the difference in their stations as queen and warlord was too great; Ashassa marched off on her own, leaving Sterren to follow in her wake.

The dining hall, Sterren discovered, was the throne room where the king had first received him. Trestle tables had been set up and covered with white linen, and chairs brought from somewhere to line either side. A smaller table stood upon the dias, crossing the T, with a dozen chairs behind it.

As yet, almost all the chairs were still unoccupied.

Queen Ashassa took a seat at the high table, near the center; Sterren, recognizing that the high table was a position of special honor, guessed that it was reserved for the royal family and headed for a seat at one of the long tables.

A servant caught his elbow.

"My lord," the servant whispered, "you sit on the king's right." He pointed to the high table, indicating a chair two spaces over from the queen's.

Sterren froze, suddenly overcome with fright at the idea of sitting up there and eating in full view of dozens, maybe hundreds of people, in his ill-fitting clothes, with his simple Ethsharitic manners that were surely foreign to these barbarians with their noble trappings. The servant pushed gently at his elbow, and reluctantly, he allowed himself to be prodded forward, up the steps onto the dias.

He seized control of his dignity once he reached the top step, and marched on to his place unaided.

The princesses, he saw, were taking their seats on the queen's side of the table, to his left. To his right, a young man of roughly his own age and with a resemblance to the royal family took a seat two places over. Another, perhaps a year younger, took the seat just beyond that. A mutter of conversation filled the room, but Sterren, with his still-poor grasp of Semmat, could not catch any of it.

Then the king entered, followed by an entourage of soldiers and courtiers. Silence fell. Everyone who had been seated rose; Sterren followed suit a bit tardily. The courtiers gradually peeled away from the group and found seats at the long table as the party progressed up the length of the hall, but they remained standing by their chairs.

King Phenvel reached his place and sat, and his guards took up unobtrusive positions along the back wall. He nodded politely, and the rest of the company sat as well.

That was the sign for the meal to begin, and the low mutter of conversation resumed. It quickly built up to considerably more than a mutter, and was punctuated by the occasional clash of cutlery as diners sorted out their tableware.

The knives and forks appeared to be silver, and Sterren wondered what they were worth.

As yet, he had nothing to eat with them, so he let his own implements lie undisturbed on the tablecloth.

The noise level was roughly that of a busy but well-behaved tavern, and Sterren found that somewhat startling. He had somehow expected a roomful of aristocrats to eat in dignified silence.

That, he realized, was foolish. People were people, regardless of titles.

Other people continued to drift in and take seats, as the king exchanged a few pleasantries with the queen. Sterren looked about the room, feeling a little lost.

A middle-aged man sat down to Sterren's right and smiled at him.

"Hello," he said, "I'm Algarven, Eighth *Kai'takhe*."

"Eighth what?" Sterren asked before he could catch himself.

"*Kai'takhe* . . . Oh, you don't know the word, do you? Let me think." The fellow blinked twice, frowning, then smiled again, and said, in Ethsharitic, "Steward!"

"You speak Ethsharitic?" Sterren asked eagerly, in Ethsharitic.

Algarven smiled. "No, no," he said in Semmat. "Just a few words."

"Oh," Sterren said, disappointed.

He suddenly remembered his manners, and introduced himself.

"Oh, we all know who *you* are," Algarven assured him.

Somehow, Sterren did not find that reassuring.

"Here, let me tell you who everybody is," Algarven said. He began pointing.

"You know the king and queen, of course. There to the queen's left is the treasurer, Adréan."

Adréan was a plump man of perhaps fifty, making him a decade or so older than Algarven; he wore a heavy gold chain around his neck, and his tunic was an unusually ugly shade of purple.

"Beyond him, that's old Inria, our Trader. If she were a little younger, she'd have been the one to go and fetch you."

Inria was an ancient, toothless hag, wearing black velvet and grinning out at the inhabitants of the hall.

"And then there are the three princesses, Nissitha, Shirrin, and Lura . . ."

"I met them this afternoon," Sterren remarked.

"Ah! And did you meet the princes?" Algarven turned to the other side and gestured at the four youths there, ranging in age from a young man of perhaps eighteen to a boy of ten or eleven.

"No," Sterren admitted.

"We have here Phenvel the Younger, heir to the throne, and his brothers Tendel, Rayel, and Dereth."

"A fine family," Sterren said.

"The king certainly hasn't shirked his duty in providing heirs, has he?" Algarven agreed. "And his father didn't, either; down there at the first table, those three on the end here, that's the elder Prince Rayel, and Prince Alder, the king's brothers, and his sister, Princess Sanda. Another brother, the elder Tendel, got himself killed seven years ago in a duel."

"Ah." Sterren could not think of anything further to say, and was saved from the necessity of inventing something by the sudden arrival of servants bearing trays of food — breads, fruits, meats, and cheeses.

From then on, the meal was simply another meal; Sterren forgot his exposed position on the dais, forgot his improvised garb, and set about filling his belly.

Between bites he continued to make polite conversation with both the steward Algarven and King Phenvel himself, but this largely consisted of simple questions and required little thought. Any time he found himself at a loss for words he simply reached for another orange or buttered a roll.

By the end of the meal he felt fairly comfortable with the royal family and his fellow lords. They were, after all, just people, despite the titles, and he was one of them.

When he reflected on this, he was amazed at himself for accepting his situation so readily.

Eight

The barracks adjoining the castle gate was reasonably tidy, but Sterren would not have applied the word "clean" to it. The cracks between the stones of the floor were filled with accumulated black gunk, and cobwebs dangled unmolested in the less-accessible corners of the ceiling. Various stains were visible on the whitewashed walls; some of them, particularly those near the floor, were very unappetizing.

He had certainly seen worse, though; his own room, back on Bargain Street, had been only marginally better.

His belly was pleasantly full, and his head very slightly aswim with wine, and he decided not to pick nits.

He had come directly from the dining hall out to the walls to make this inspection of his troops and their lodging, so as to get it over with. His main purpose, he reminded himself, was to see what sort of men he was supposed to command, not to criticize anybody's housekeeping.

But still, it seemed to him that a really first-rate group of soldiers would keep their quarters in better shape.

He did not bother to look in the cabinets or kit-bags at each station, nor under the narrow beds. He would not have known what to look for, and besides, it seemed like an invasion of the soldiers' privacy. He glanced at the bunks, each with one blanket pulled taut and another rolled up to serve as a pillow, and could see nothing to comment on.

He walked on through to the armory, where a fine assortment of weapons adorned the walls and various racks. He reached out at random and picked up a sword.

It came away from the rack only reluctantly, and left a little wad of rust behind. The area of blade that had been hidden by the wooden brackets was nothing but a few flakes of dull brown rust, and the leather wrapping on the hilt cracked in his grasp. Grey dust swirled up, and he sneezed.

Behind him, he heard some of his men shuffling their feet in embarrassment. He carefully placed the sword back on the rack.

He should, he knew, reprimand somebody for the incredibly poor condition of the sword, but he was unsure who, specifically, to address. Furthermore, even if he was the warlord, he was also a foreigner and a mere youth and not even particularly large. The soldiers were all considerably older and larger than himself. He knew that his title should give him sufficient authority to berate them all despite being so thoroughly outweighed and outnumbered, but he could not find the courage to test that theory.

Maybe later, he told himself, when he had settled in a bit more, he could do something about it.

Even as he thought it, he was slightly ashamed of his cowardice.

"My lord," someone said, "*these* are the weapons we use for practice." A hand indicated a rack near the door.

Sterren picked up another sword. This one was in far better shape, without a spot of rust, the grip soft and supple — but the blade, he saw, was dull.

Well, it was only a practice blade. You wouldn't want to kill anyone in mere practice, would you?, he asked himself. He nodded and returned the weapon to its place.

He wished he knew more about swords and other weapons. He had no idea what to check for.

The rust, however, was obviously a very bad sign.

He turned back to face his men.

All of them, as he had noticed before, were larger than himself, but not all were mountains of muscle like his personal escorts, Alder and Dogal. In fact, the majority seemed to be pot-bellied or otherwise running to fat. He mentally compared them to the city guards he had seen back in Ethshar, strolling the streets to keep the peace, or rousting the beggars from Wall Street, or carousing in the taverns.

The Royal Army of Semma did not fare well in the comparison. Ethshar's guardsmen came in all sizes, but they all had a certain toughness that this oversized bunch did not display. Guardsmen might be fat, but they were never soft.

Much of Semma's soldiery looked soft.

Sterren suppressed a shrug. Things were different here. Whatever duties these men had, they obviously didn't require the sort of ruggedness that was needed to maintain order in the world's largest, richest, and rowdiest city.

Alder had told him that Semma had been at peace for fifty years; Sterren hoped that that was not about to change.

If it did, though, and all he had to fight with was this pitiful handful of men, well, Semma wasn't *his* homeland. He could always surrender.

Couldn't he? It occurred to him that he had no idea what the customs were in the Small Kingdoms regarding prisoners of war.

He walked from the armory back into the barracks, and noticed something he had missed before. One of the bunks had been moved. It had been shoved up against a wall, so that the space between that bunk and the next was twice the space between any other two. As further confirmation, half the floor in the widened space was cleaner and lighter than the rest of the barracks floor.

His curiosity was piqued. "You," he said to the nearest soldier, "slide that bunk out from the wall, would you?"

The soldier glanced at his mates, who all somehow managed to be looking in other directions.

"Come on," Sterren said, using the phrase Lady Kalira had used when urging her horse onward.

The soldier stepped forward, moving slowly as if hoping for some miraculous reprieve, and pulled the bunk out, back to its original position.

In doing so, he uncovered several lines of chalk drawn onto the dirty planks.

Sterren recognized the lines immediately, and grinned. He suddenly saw that he had something in common with these oversized barbarians.

"Three-bone?" he asked, in Ethsharitic.

The soldiers looked blank, and he puzzled out a Semman equivalent and tried that.

One soldier shook his head and replied, "No, double flash."

His companions glared at him, too late to hush him. Sterren waved their displeasure aside. "What stakes?" he asked. "And do you pass on the first loss or the second?" He had picked the word for gambling stakes up from Dogal during the journey from Ethshar. Double flash was not his favorite dice game, by any means — he would greatly have preferred three-bone — but it was certainly better than nothing.

A friendly game was just what he needed to help him feel at home.

It would also serve nicely to get to know some of his men, and perhaps to build up a little money that the other nobles would know nothing about. That could be very useful if he ever decided to leave.

He still had his purse, and the winnings from his last night in Ethshar. He pulled out a silver bit. "Will this buy me a throw?"

Feet shuffled, and someone coughed.

"Well, actually, my lord . . ."

"For now, just call me Sterren, all right?"

"Yes, my lord. Ah . . . Sterren. We usually play for copper."

"Good enough; can someone make change? And who's got the dice?"

Coins and dice emerged from pockets and purses, and a moment later Sterren and three soldiers were crouched around the chalked diagram, tossing copper bits into the various betting slots. Any further inspection was forgotten.

When the dice were passed, Sterren felt the familiar thrill of competition — but the sense of calm oneness with the dice that he usually felt was absent.

He dismissed it as an effect of the unfamiliar surroundings, and proceeded to throw a deuce, losing his turn.

It was well after midnight when Sterren wearily climbed back up to his room in the tower. His purse was lighter by several silver bits — the equivalent of over a hundred coppers. His luck had been consistently bad.

Whatever talent or charm had kept him alive and solvent in the taverns of Ethshar obviously had not worked in this alien place.

He wondered, as he hauled himself up the dimly-lit stairs, if it would ever work again. If it didn't, he would have to give up dice for good.

Now, *that* was a really terrible thought!

He thrust it aside as he reached the top, and saw Alder standing by the door of his room. As he walked down the short stretch of corridor and into his room he ran over the rest of the day in his mind.

It had certainly been an eventful one.

He hoped he never had another like it.

Alder opened the door and followed him into the room. As Sterren stood yawning, the big soldier lit a candle on the desk, and stood awaiting orders.

Nine

Sterren stretched, thought for a moment, and then shooed Alder out. When the door had closed behind Alder's back he took a moment to make sure all his belongings were stashed where he could find them. That done, he lay down on the great canopied bed and tried to sleep.

His blood was still pumping hard from the excitement of the game, the shock of losing so badly, and the long climb up the stairs from the barracks, all coming at the end of an extraordinarily long and bewildering day; sleep was slow in coming. He was still lying awake when he heard a quiet knock on his door.

"What is it?" he called.

The door opened partway, and Alder stuck his head in.

"There's someone here who wants to see you," Alder said apologetically. "He says he has business with you."

"At this hour?"

Alder explained, "He's been stopping by regularly all evening, but you weren't in before."

That was true enough. "All right," Sterren said, "what kind of business?"

"He won't say. Something about settling an account your great-uncle left, I think."

"Settling an account?" That did not sound encouraging at all. "Who is it?"

Alder considered before replying, "He's a traveling merchant, I think — if that's not too grand a word for him. He deals in trinkets and what-not. I don't know his name, but I've seen him before. He really *did* deal with the old warlord."

"Trinkets?"

Alder explained, "This and that. Little things."

Sterren considered telling Alder to get rid of this uninvited visitor, but his curiosity got the better of him; what had the old warlord had to do with a traveling dealer in trinkets? Why was the merchant so eager to see him that he had not been able to go to sleep at a reasonable hour and leave the business, whatever it was, until morning?

"Send him in," he called, as he sat up on the bed.

Alder ducked back out of sight, and a moment later another man slipped in through the half-open door, then carefully closed it securely behind him.

He was short and dark, his hair greying, and he looked as if he had been fat once, but was not eating well lately. He wore a greasy brown tunic and even greasier grey breeches; his boots were well made, and also well worn. Despite his clothing, his face and hair were clean, and he had no objectionable odor.

After closing the door he checked the latch carefully, then turned and made a polite but perfunctory bow.

"Hello, Lord Sterren," he said. "Allow me to introduce myself. I'm called Lar Samber's son. As your guard said, I'm a dealer in trinkets and oddities, and the occasional love charm or poison."

Sterren nodded an acknowledgement, but before he could say anything, Lar continued, "And I'm sure you're wondering what old Sterren had to do with me, and what this account is I want to settle. That wasn't really my reason for coming here. I have another business besides my trading, you see — or rather, I trade in a product less tangible, but more important, than beads and gewgaws. Your greatuncle was my only customer, and the only person who knew about it." He paused, eyeing Sterren, his face curiously expressionless.

Sterren nodded expectantly. "Go on," he said.

Lar hesitated for the first time.

"I don't know you," he said.

"I don't know you, either," Sterren pointed out.

Lar nodded slowly. "True enough, and it's not as if I have a choice." The merchant hesitated again, but only briefly. "I'm your chief spy," he burst out hurriedly. "I deal in information. Naturally, this is a secret, one that your great-uncle kept well; nobody else in Semma ever knew, until now. I'm trusting you with my life, my lord, by telling you this."

His face remained oddly blank even as he said this; if he felt any great anxiety over the risk he was taking, it did not show.

Sterren puzzled over the word "spy" for a moment, then smiled, and pointed to a chair. "Sit down," he said, "and tell me about it."

Lar's face did not change as he took a seat, but Sterren was sure he was relieved.

He was relieved himself; it was good to know that his predecessor had had spies, and had not relied entirely on his three officers and their men.

A thought occurred to him; Lar was a traveler and a dealer in information. "Do you speak Ethsharitic?" he asked.

Startled, Lar admitted, "Some. Not much. Mostly I speak Ophkaritic, Ksinallionese, Thanorian, and Trader's Tongue."

Sterren had never even heard of Thanorian, but he didn't let that worry him. Instead, he burst out with a string of questions in his native tongue.

Lar had to repeatedly ask him to slow down, and several times the conversation switched back into Semmat for a time, or slipped into a pidgin of the two languages that they improvised on the spot. Even so, Sterren was able to communicate more freely than he had in days.

Unfortunately, what Lar had to communicate was not encouraging.

Both Ophkar and Ksinallion were planning to invade Semma.

Somehow, although he had been trying to convince himself war was unlikely, this news did not really surprise Sterren at all.

This impending invasion was not really a secret; in fact, the suspicion that it was being planned had been responsible for the urgency of Lady Kalira's mission to Ethshar. The aristocrats of Semma were confident that they could survive a war — if they had a warlord.

So they had sent for Sterren.

Lar, however, did not stop his revelations at the mere fact of the coming war; he went on to detail the reasons for it, and also the reasons it had not yet begun.

The underlying reasons were simple enough: Ophkar and Ksinallion both wanted Semma's land and wealth and people. For three hundred years, Ophkar and Ksinallion had been bitter enemies; they had fought six wars in that time. In the first, Ophkar had captured the Ksinallionese province of Semma; in the second, Ksinallion won it back. It was during the Third Ophkar/Ksinallion war, in 5002, that Semma, under Tendel the Great, had rebelled against the cruel yoke of Ksinallion and asserted its independence, siding with Ophkar and leading to an Ophkarite victory.

Five years later, when Tendel died, Ophkar invaded Semma and attempted to annex it. Semma survived by enlisting Ksinallion's aid.

From then on, Semma's policy was to maintain a balance of power between Ophkar and Ksinallion by siding with whoever was weaker at any given time, playing the

two off against each other in order to maintain its independence. Tendel's son and heir, Rayel the Tenacious, had
understood that; it was only when he was old and ill that
matters had gotten out of hand, and a war with Ksinallion
resulted in 5026. His successor, Tendel II, known as Tendel
the Gentle, reigned for twenty-two years without ever letting the balance slip.

He was followed by Rayel the Fool, who only lasted
nine years, six of them spent fighting Ophkar — and losing.

Phenvel I, also called Phenvel the Fat, had done much
better; no wars were fought during his twenty-one years on
the throne.

The idea of the balancing policy was beginning to fade,
though, as the kings of Semma forgot how precarious their
position actually was; Phenvel II, Phenvel the Warrior,
fought Ophkar for seven years of his seventeen. Admittedly,
he *won* — the only time Semma ever single-handedly defeated Ophkar — but seven years of war could not have
been pleasant. Many stories of the horrors of that Third
Ophkar/Semma War were still told.

And the resulting weakness was largely responsible for
Ksinallion's victory over Semma in the Third Ksinallion/
Semma War, during the reign of Rayel III. He earned the
name Rayel the Patient by waiting eleven years, carefully
building up his forces and waiting until the time was right,
before he launched his counter-attack and won the Fourth
Ksinallion/Semma War.

Even that victory was probably a mistake; it laid the
groundwork for the disastrous defeat Rayel IV suffered in
5150, in the Fifth Ksinallion/Semma War. Only Ophkar's
threat to come in on Semma's side had prevented Ksinallion
from annexing Semma outright.

That was Rayel the Tall; he was followed by Rayel V,
Rayel the Handsome, whose death brought about the nego-

tiated peace at the end of the Sixth Ksinallion/Semma War, establishing the present borders. That had also been the Sixth Ophkar/Ksinallion War.

Tendel III had been called Tendel the Diplomat because he managed to talk his way out of war several times in his twenty-four year reign; he was an expert at playing Ophkar and Ksinallion off against each other, and even bringing in their other neighbors: Skaia, Thanoria, Enmurinon, Kalithon, even little Nushasla, far to the north, at Ksinallion's farthest extreme. None of those bordered on Semma, but the threat of a two-front war was surprisingly effective. Ophkar had no desire to fight Skaia or Enmurinon; Ksinallion preferred peace with Kalithon and Nushasla; and Thanoria served as a threat to both.

But then Tendel III died, in 5199, and his son Phenvel III came to the throne.

Lar hesitated to characterize his sovereign unfavorably, but from his mutterings about inbreeding and "other interests" it was plain to Sterren that the merchant considered the king an idiot.

Fortunately, Phenvel III had had the services of a few people who were *not* idiots, notably Sterren, Seventh Warlord, and Sterren, Eighth Warlord. Father and son had kept up the policies of Tendel III, using diplomacy, threats, saboteurs, and whatever else was necessary to keep peace.

King Phenvel had made this difficult, with his arbitrary insults directed at both his larger neighbors. When Prince Elken of Ophkar asked for the hand of Princess Ashassa the Younger, Phenvel had instead sent her to Prince Tabar of Kalithon. When King Corinal II of Ksinallion offered a treaty on trade routes, Phenvel had first ignored it, then sent an envoy to Ophkar asking if they cared to make a better offer. When a secret envoy came from Ophkar to discuss the possibility of war with Ksinallion, Phenvel publicly announced the whole affair; when Ophkar reacted with protests and Ksinallion offered an alliance, Phenvel had dismissed the whole thing as a foolish joke.

There had been other incidents, as well, and now, for the first time in three hundred years, Ophkar and Ksinallion had arranged an alliance against Semma, considering Phenvel III a mutual foe.

While they lived, the warlords had prevented such an alliance, but with the death of the Eighth Warlord, all the elaborate network of checks and treaties had collapsed. Enmurinon and Kalithon and Thanoria and Nushasla and Skaia were no longer involved; despite the web of intermarriages that had allied them to Semma, they all refused to make any further promises. Phenvel's mother had come from Enmurinon, his wife from Thanoria; a daughter was a princess in Kalithon, and an aunt had been queen in Nushasla. Still, Semma was on its own. Phenvel had somehow offended every single one of his foreign relatives.

Sterren's spirits sank steadily as he listened to all this.

"Why aren't the Ophkaritic and Ksinallionese armies already here?" he asked.

Lar sighed, and explained that the only reason the armies of Ophkar and Ksinallion had not yet invaded was that they were still settling how the booty and conquered territory were to be divided. Lar and his like — he employed several people himself, and was fairly sure that old Sterren, Eighth Warlord had had some others in his own employ — had done their best to delay these negotiations, bringing up potential difficulties, picking at nits, losing messages, and so forth, and had managed to hold things off this long. The coming winter rains would presumably provide another short breathing space, but in the spring both armies would surely march.

And it was Sterren's job, as warlord, to hold them off indefinitely, or if possible to defeat them outright.

"How am I supposed to do that?" Sterren demanded.

Lar shrugged. "I wish I knew," he replied. "I really do."

Ten

As usual, the off-duty soldiers were playing dice in a corner of the barracks. Sterren sighed at the sight.

His dismay was partly due to the fact that despite his best attempts at speech-making, his repeated talks about how important it was that Semma's chosen defenders do all they could to get themselves ready to fight had obviously had no effect on how his men spent their leisure time.

It was also due, however, to the knowledge that he didn't dare join the game. Since arriving in Semma, his once-notorious luck at dice had deserted him completely.

He had been embarrassed to discover that without that edge, he was actually a very poor gambler. Whenever he played, he lost steadily.

At least he now knew, beyond question, that he had indeed picked up a trace of warlockry in his brief apprenticeship; nothing else could explain how he had flourished for so long back in Ethshar. Wizards and witches had been unable to detect any magic in use — but wizards and witches knew nothing about warlockry.

It was slightly odd, perhaps, that he'd never been caught by a warlock, but maybe warlocks took pity on him, or chose to protect one of their own, no matter how feeble his talents.

And his talent had to be warlockry, because no other form of magic was so dependent on location. He knew that much. Wizardry and witchcraft and sorcery and theurgy and demonology and herbalism and all the others worked equally well almost everywhere, or so he had heard — though there were those who complained that so much wizardry had been used in the city of Ethshar of the Spices that its residue fouled the air and weakened subsequent spells.

Warlockry, though — a warlock's power depended on how close he was to the mysterious Source of the Power that all warlocks drew on.

Nobody knew exactly where the Source was, or what it was, because nobody who went to find it ever came back, but every warlock knew that it was somewhere in the hills of Aldagmor, near the border between the Baronies of Sardiron and the Hegemony of Ethshar. It supposedly called to warlocks who grew strong enough to hear it, and lured them away — and since all warlocks improved with practice, that meant most of them heard it, sooner or later, and if they stayed within range they were eventually drawn away to Aldagmor. This was referred to as the Calling, and it was invariably accompanied by weird, frightening dreams and other strangeness, and it was something that warlocks did not talk about to outsiders; it frightened them, and admitting that warlocks were afraid of anything was not in the best interests of the art. Sterren only knew about it because his former master had explained it, in lurid detail, in trying to discourage him from his apprenticeship.

Even warlocks, though, even those who had heard the Calling and woke up every night with nightmares about it, did not know what the Source was. Nobody knew what it was, or why it should be in that particular place.

Some people theorized that that spot was the exact center of the World, and that the Power was a gift of the gods, but others maintained that the Source was something from outside the World entirely, a mysterious *something* that had fallen from the heavens on the Night of Madness, back in 5202, when warlockry first emerged. Sterren had been a babe in arms on that night when half the people in Ethshar woke up screaming from nightmares they could never remember, and when one person in a thousand or so was suddenly transformed, forever after, into a warlock, able to move objects without touching them, to kill with a thought, to start fires with a mere gaze.

Whatever the Source was, whatever the Power was, Sterren had never had more than the faintest trace of it, and here in Semma, dozens of leagues to the southeast of Ethshar and almost that much farther from Aldagmor, which lay well to the north of the city, even that trace was gone.

In fact, in two sixdays of careful investigation, Sterren had been unable to find any evidence that anyone in all of Semma had ever heard of warlockry, or ever had any trace of the Power at his or her command. Nobody could provide him with a Semmat word for "warlock" or "warlockry." Nobody even remembered anything about a night of bad dreams, twenty years before, and Sterren had always thought that the effects of the Night of Madness had been worldwide.

Warlockry was totally, completely unknown in Semma.

Sterren had had to give up playing dice.

Watching the men toss down their coins on the betting lines, totally ignoring the presence of their warlord, he also gave up any hope of successfully defending Semma against the armies of Ophkar and Ksinallion with the forces at his disposal.

Lar had brought another report the night before; Ophkar had two hundred men under arms, Ksinallion two hundred and fifty.

Semma had ninety-six. And that was after Sterren had had calls for volunteers posted in all the surrounding villages. Furthermore, although fifteen or twenty of them took their role seriously, the rest seemed to think being a soldier meant nothing more than an excuse to go drinking and wenching in exchange for a few hours a day of marching and weapons drill — or, in the case of the cavalry, riding and weapons drill.

Sterren knew that war was coming. Lar knew that war was coming. Lady Kalira and a dozen other nobles knew war was coming. The rest of the castle's inhabitants, including the king, refused to worry about it.

Princess Shirrin apparently believed that war was coming, but thought that it was all very exciting, and that Sterren, her valiant warlord, would save the kingdom by single-handedly slaughtering the foe, as if he were some legendary hero like Valder of the Magic Sword. At least, that was what Princess Lura reported her sister's thoughts to be; Shirrin herself still found it impossible to say more than a dozen words in Sterren's presence without blushing and falling into an embarrassed silence.

She hadn't actually run away from him for more than a sixday, though, and he had seen her, several times, watching him and his men from a window, or around a corner.

Princess Nissitha deigned to speak to him on occasion, now, but still obviously considered him far beneath her.

He sighed again. His life was not going well.

He had carefully broached the subject of defeat to Lady Kalira one night, in the castle kitchens, when both of them had been drinking.

"You don't want to think about it," she had said, very definitely.

"Why not?" he had replied.

"Because if you lose a war you'll be killed."

"Not ness . . . ness . . . necessarily. Surely you don't expect the army to fight to the last man . . ." he began.

"No, you silly Ethsharite, that's not what I mean." She had glowered at him.

"What do you mean, then?" he asked, puzzled.

"I *mean*," she said, "that for the last century or two it's been traditional for a victorious army to execute the enemy's warlord, as a symbolic gesture. You can't go around killing off kings; it sets a bad precedent. And you don't want to slaughter anyone useful, not even peasants. But a defeated warlord isn't any good to anybody, and he might go around plotting revenge, so he gets beheaded. Or hanged. Or burned at the stake. Or something." She hiccupped. "Your great-great-grandfather, the Sixth Warlord, got drawn and quartered, back in 5150."

Sterren, who up to that point had been more or less sober, had proceeded to finish the bottle, and a second one as well.

He had no desire to die, but he was beginning to run out of alternatives. He still saw no way to escape from Semma; his door was always guarded, as was the castle gate, and any time he set foot outside at least one soldier accompanied him. He had not tried ordering his escort away; it seemed pointless.

Even if he did lose an escort and make a dash for it, he would probably be caught and brought back long before he could reach Akalla of the Diamond and get out to sea — and that was assuming he could *find* Akalla despite the lack of roads, maps, guides, and landmarks.

Chances of escaping back to Ethshar looked slim, and a failed escape attempt would mean execution for treason. That made it too dangerous to risk.

If he stayed, however, he would wind up leading his pitiful army into battle and inevitably being defeated. If he survived the battle, which was certain to be a rout and probably a bloodbath, he would still be executed by the victors.

He could not imagine any strategem whereby he could win, with his ninety-six men against more than four hundred. A purely defensive war would take longer, perhaps —

the castle could probably hold off the invaders for a month or two, at least — but a long siege would not put the enemy in a very favorable frame of mind, and Semma had no friends who might come to lift a siege, nor much hope of outlasting the foe.

Sterren wished he had some way of coaxing his native Ethshar into aiding Semma; Azrad's ten thousand guardsmen would make short work of these silly little armies that the Small Kingdoms fielded.

When Azrad VII had come to power a little over a year before, however, he had inherited from his father, Azrad VI, a long-standing policy handed down in unbroken line from Azrad I against interfering in the internal squabbling of the Small Kingdoms. On the rare occasions when an army from Lamum or Perga or some other little principality had strayed across the border into the Hegemony it had been quickly obliterated, but Ethsharitic troops were never, ever, sent into the Small Kingdoms themselves.

Sterren leaned against the whitewashed stone wall of the barracks and told himself that he needed a miracle.

Well, he replied silently, every Ethsharite knows that miracles are available, if one can pay for them.

Miracles were available in Ethshar, though, in the Wizards' Quarter, not in Semma.

The only magician of any sort that the royal family put any trust in was Agor, the castle's resident theurgist. Other than a glimpse or two of that rather confused and confusing fellow, Sterren had not as yet encountered a single magician worthy of the name during his stay in the Small Kingdoms.

He hadn't been able to do much looking, of course; his duties, and his desperate attempts to train his "army" into something useful, had not left him the free time to go wandering about investigating village herbalists and the like.

It was always possible that some eccentric hermit was

lurking in a hut somewhere out there, a hermit with sufficient magic to defeat both would-be invaders, but how
could Sterren locate him, if he existed?

Well, how had the Semmans located *him*, when they
needed a warlord?

They had asked Agor, of course.

And Agor might actually be quite a good theurgist, for
all Sterren knew. He might be all the miracle-worker Sterren needed.

Sterren glanced again at the dice-players, at the unmade
bunks, at swords lying about unsheathed and dropped
carelessly anywhere convenient, and decided that it was
time he spoke with Agor. He had tried acting like the warlord he was supposed to be, and had gotten nowhere; now,
thinking like the Ethsharite he had always been, it was time
to call on a magician. When all else fails, hire a magician —
that was sound Ethsharitic thinking!

He turned and marched out the door of the barracks.

He knew exactly where he was going, for once. Princess
Lura had pointed out the theurgist's door to him a few days
earlier. Agor made his home in a small room in one of the
smaller towers, far above the barracks, but a level below
Sterren's own more luxurious quarters.

Sterren stood in the corridor for a minute or two, gath-
ering his courage, before he knocked.

"Come in," someone called from within.

He lifted the latch and stepped in.

Agor's chamber was hung with white draperies on every
side, covering all four walls. Two narrow windows were
left bare, and provided the room's only light — but given all
that white and the sunny weather outside, that was plenty.
The chamber smelled of something cloyingly sweet — in-
cense, perhaps? Sterren was unsure.

A few trunks, painted white and trimmed with silver,

stood against the various walls. A plump featherbed, also white, occupied one corner.

In the center of the room, seated on a greyish sheepskin that had probably been white once, was Agor himself, a rather scrawny fellow of thirty or so, with a pale, narrow face and a worried expression.

He wore white, of course — white tunic worked with gold, and off-white breeches. His feet were bare. A scroll was unrolled on the floor in front of him.

"Yes?" he asked, looking at Sterren in puzzlement.

"I'm Sterren, Ninth Warlord," Sterren said. "You're Agor, the theurgist?"

"Oh, yes, of course, my lord. Yes, I'm Agor. Do come in!" He gestured welcomingly.

There were no chairs of any description, so Sterren rather hesitantly seated himself on the stone floor, facing the theurgist.

"So you're Sterren," Agor said. "I'm glad to meet you. I take a special interest in you, you know; I was the one who found you." He smiled uncertainly.

"I know," said Sterren, while inwardly wondering just what sort of special interest the other was referring to. After all, in the dozen days since his arrival in the castle, Agor had not bothered to say as much as a single word to him, and had apparently not even bothered to get a look at him, since he had not immediately recognized him.

He knew he should say more, but found himself unsure how to begin. He knew he wanted a miracle that would keep him from getting killed as a result of the coming war, but he did not know how to ask for it.

He didn't really know just what sort of a miracle he wanted. He did not really want *anyone* to get hurt or killed.

He was still thinking about this when, after a slightly

longer-than-comfortable silence, Agor asked nervously, "What can I do for you, my lord?"

Sterren resolved to simply present the situation to Agor and then see where the discussion went. Perhaps a way out of his quandary would appear.

"Well, first, you can promise me that anything I tell you won't be repeated outside this room," he replied.

"If you wish it so, my lord."

"I do. Ah . . . tell me, have you taken any interest in Semma's military situation?"

"No," the theurgist immediately answered. "Would you like me to?"

This response caught Sterren off-guard, and his tongue stumbled over his answer.

"I . . . that . . . I mean, that's not . . ." He paused, caught his breath, and tried again.

"What I meant was, are you aware that Semma is in very serious danger?"

"No," Agor replied calmly. "Is it?"

"Yes!" Sterren collected his wits, and continued, "This is what I don't want you telling anyone. A war with both Ksinallion and Ophkar is coming, and soon. I expect both of them to attack as soon as the mud dries in the spring. And we don't have a chance of defeating them; we're out-numbered four to one, and our army is in terrible shape, and I'm the warlord, but I have no idea at all how to run a war, or even how to get these damn soldiers to take it seriously!"

"Ah," Agor said, his face blank.

"Yes," Sterren said.

"So you expect to lose a battle? Do you want me to try and get a god's blessing on our troops, is that it? I don't suppose that would violate the ban on using magic to fight wars."

"No! Or at least, not just that, though I suppose it couldn't hurt." He paused, considering. "Would it really help?"

"No," Agor said, without an instant's hesitation. "I've explained this to everybody before, but I suppose you weren't here. The gods don't approve of war or fighting, and they won't have anything to do with it. They don't take sides."

"I don't approve of it, either! Are you sure they wouldn't be willing to take into consideration that we're being attacked, that we don't *want* to fight?"

"It wouldn't matter. The gods swore off war after they wiped out the Northerners two hundred years ago, and they don't change their minds easily. Besides . . ." This time Agor *did* hesitate, but at length he said, "Besides, can you tell them that we did nothing to provoke an attack?"

"*I* didn't do anything!"

"But did anyone?"

Sterren remembered what Lar had told him about King Phenvel's behavior. "I suppose so," he admitted.

"Then the gods won't help. At least, not directly."

That reminded Sterren of his original intention in visiting Agor. "But they might indirectly?" he asked.

"Oh, certainly. It might seem odd to a layman, but the fact is, the gods tend to be very careless indeed about the long-term consequences of their actions. You could probably get a great deal of useful advice from them, as long as it's not overtly military."

Locating a powerful wizard would hardly be overtly military, but Sterren decided to check out other possibilities first. He asked, "Could they, perhaps, do something to stop Ophkar and Ksinallion from attacking? Start a plague, or something?"

Agor was visibly shocked by the suggestion. "A plague? My lord, how can you think such a thing?"

"Could they?" Sterren persisted.

"No, of course not! My lord Sterren, I am a theurgist, not a demonologist! The gods are *good*; they do not do evil. Plagues are the work of demons!"

Sterren's cynicism, drummed into him by years on the streets of Ethshar, came surging to the fore. "The gods don't do evil?" he inquired, sarcastically, remembering that he, himself was in Semma, facing eventual execution, because of a god's interference.

"Well," Agor said, "not *directly*. Sometimes their actions can have evil consequences, for some . . ."

"I would think so!"

". . . but they won't start a plague, or anything else like that."

Sterren considered this.

Agor was probably right. After all, he was a theurgist, and surely he knew his business. All his life, Sterren had heard from priests and theurgists and even laymen that the gods were benevolent, that they did not approve of any sort of destruction or disorder, that the evil in the World was due to demons or human folly.

It was probably true.

Or if not, at least it was probably true that he, Sterren of Ethshar, would be unable to get the gods to take his side in the upcoming war.

"All right," he said, "we'll forget that idea, then." Another thought popped into his head, though, and he asked, "Might they protect us from the invaders? Stop the war somehow, or at least provide us with what we need to withstand a siege? You say they don't like war; could they prevent this one?"

"Excuse me, my lord, but wouldn't that violate the traditional ban on magical warfare?"

"What if it did?" Sterren snapped, his frayed temper breaking. "*I* never agreed to any such ban, and I'll be killed if we lose this war! I'm no Semman, and I think it's a stupid tradition."

"Ah," the theurgist said, nodding. "I see."

"Does breaking the ban bother you?"

"Well, not really; it's none of my business."

"Then, can the gods do something to prevent this war?"

Agor hesitated, and chewed his lower lip for a moment before replying, "Well, maybe . . ."

"Maybe?"

Agor blinked uneasily and shifted on his sheepskin. "Well, actually, my lord, they . . ." He stopped, visibly unhappy.

"They what?" Sterren urged.

"Well, actually, my lord, some of the gods would probably be glad to do that sort of thing, but . . ."

"But *what*?"

"Well . . ." Agor took a deep breath, then let it out and admitted, "But I don't know how to contact them."

Eleven

Sterren stared at the bony theurgist, who stared back miserably.

"What do you mean, you can't contact them?" Sterren demanded. "Aren't you the royal theurgist here?"

"Yes, my lord, I am."

"Are you a fraud, then?"

"No," Agor said, with a touch of wounded pride visible through his dismay, "I'm not a fraud; I'm just not a very good theurgist."

"You aren't?"

"No, I'm not. Ah . . . do you know anything about theurgy?"

"I know as much as most people, I suppose," Sterren said, glaring.

"But do you know anything about how it actually *works*?" Agor persisted.

"No, of course not!"

Agor nodded, as if satisfied with Sterren's answer. "Well, my lord," he said, "it's like this. A theurgist is just a person with a natural talent for prayer, who has learned how to pray in such a way that the gods will actually listen."

"I know that," Sterren said sharply.

"Well, anybody can pray, of course, but the odds are that the gods won't hear, or won't answer. Have you ever wondered, my lord, why the gods don't listen to everybody, but they *do* listen to theurgists?"

"No," Sterren replied flatly. This was not strictly true, but he didn't care to be sidetracked.

"Well, it's because of the prayers we use. We learn them

as apprentices, just as other magicians learn their spells. The gods are too busy to listen to *everything*, but there are certain prayers that catch their attention, just the way certain sounds might catch *your* ear, even in a noisy place — the rattle of dice, for instance."

Sterren realized that Agor really *had* taken an interest in him; coming up with that particularly appropriate example could not have been a coincidence. His annoyance faded somewhat. "Go on," he said.

Agor continued, "Some people are better at some prayers than others. I don't know why, they just are — just as some people are better at drawing pictures, or singing."

Sterren nodded. He knew, first-hand, that some people had a talent for warlockry, while others, like himself, emphatically did not, and he could see no reason other magicks, such as theurgy, should be any different.

"There are many, many gods, my lord. I only know the names and prayers for nineteen of them; that was all my master knew, and all he could teach me during my apprenticeship. It's not a bad number, really. Many of the best theurgists only know a dozen or so specific prayers, and I've never heard of anyone who knew more than perhaps thirty, unless he was also dabbling in demonology — except we don't call those prayers, we call them invocations or summonings."

"So you can ask nineteen different gods for help, but *only* those nineteen?"

"Yes, but really, not even all those. You see, as I said, some people are better at some prayers than others. Some gods are just harder to talk to, too. And I know nineteen names and prayers, but I can't get all nineteen of them to listen to me. Or at least, I never have. Maybe I learned a syllable wrong somewhere, or maybe they just don't like me, but I can't get all of them to listen."

Sterren saw where this was leading. "How many *do* listen to you, then?" he asked.

"Usually, three," Agor replied nervously.

Sterren stared. "*Three*? Out of nineteen?"

"I *told* you I'm not really a very good theurgist," Agor said defensively.

"How did you ever wind up as the royal magician, then?"

"The royal magician to the court of King Phenvel III of Semma? Of *Semma*, my lord? You're from Ethshar; you know better. If I were any good, would I still be here?"

"I suppose not," Sterren admitted.

"I was born in Semma, but I ran away from home when I was twelve, and served my apprenticeship in Lumeth of the Towers. I couldn't make a living there, though, and I didn't speak anything but Semmat and Lumethan, so when I got tired of starving in Lumeth I came back here, where there wasn't any real competition. They don't care if I can only talk to Unniel, Konned, and Morrn, because nobody else here can talk to *any* of the gods!" A trace of pride had crept into Agor's voice.

"Unn . . . Who were those, again?"

"Unniel, Konned, and Morrn. Unniel the Discerning is the goddess of theurgical information, Konned is a god of light and warmth, and Morrn the Preserver is the god of genealogy."

"I never heard of any of them," Sterren said.

"And how many gods *have* you heard of by name?"

"Not many," Sterren admitted. Laymen virtually never bothered with names, since only theurgists could count on getting a specific deity's attention. Usually prayers were directed to categories of gods, or just any god who might be listening, to increase the chances of reaching *someone*.

Sterren realized he could not name a single god, other

than the three Agor had just mentioned — and he didn't think he could pronounce two of those. Konned was easy enough, but the diphthong in Unniel and the R sound in Morrn were very alien indeed.

"So, could any of those three help us?" he asked.

"I don't see how," Agor replied. "Morrn is completely useless; all he does is keep track of family trees. If you need to know your great-great grandmother's childhood epithet, or when your third cousin was born, he can tell you, but that's it. He's been very useful to me, since all the nobility of Semma are obsessed with family, but a war is completely out of his area."

"And Konned?" Sterren did not care to try pronouncing Unniel.

"Well, if you make a regular sacrifice to him, he'll provide you with supernatural light at night, brighter than any candle, and he'll keep you warm in the winter, so we don't have to worry about freezing during a siege — but that's about it. And freezing isn't very likely in Semma anyway."

"And . . ."

"Unniel's our best hope, I suppose. She knows everything there is to know about all the other gods, and sometimes she can be coaxed into carrying messages to them; I found you by having her call her brother Aibem for me. I know a prayer for Aibem, but I can never make it work right, so when I really need him, sometimes I can get him through Unniel. Aibem is a god of information; I've never found anything he doesn't know, but getting him to tell me what I'm after is usually like trying to catch a black cat in a dungeon at midnight. Unniel can also talk to the dead, sometimes — not all the dead, just certain ones, and I have no idea why."

"Information? Couldn't Unn . . . Unniel or Aibem tell us how to avoid the war, then?"

Agor shrugged. "I don't know," he said. "Maybe." He sighed. "It's too bad I could never get Piskor the Generous to answer; she provides food and water and advice, and that would be ideal if we're besieged, wouldn't it?"

"It would help, certainly," Sterren agreed.

They sat in moody silence for a moment, thinking.

Sterren considered what he had just been told, and decided that he did not care to rely on the gods for help.

That meant returning to his original intent of locating a really powerful magician and somehow buying a miracle. Agor, it appeared, did not qualify.

"So, Agor," he said, "are there any other theurgists in Semma?"

"No," Agor answered. "It's too bad, because I wouldn't mind having someone to talk theurgy with."

"What about other magicians? Do you know of any?"

"Oh, certainly! When I first got the job here, naturally I looked over the potential competition. It turned out I had nothing to worry about." Sterren suppressed a groan at this news. Agor continued, "There are a few village herbalists, of course, and a couple of local shamans who seem to be more fraud than anything else. There are two wizards in the whole kingdom; one's here in the castle, where he helps out in the kitchen, and the other's in a village to the east. The one here in the castle used to be the other's apprentice, I think."

He paused, thinking.

"I don't remember exactly how many witches there are; four or five, I'd say. None of them are in the castle."

"What about sorcerers, or demonologists, or warlocks, or thaumaturges, or . . . or anything?"

"Well, demonology is illegal, of course, and I haven't found any outlaw demonologists, but I suppose one could be hiding somewhere. The gods can't see demons, usually. Sorcery is illegal, too, I suppose because the Northerners used to use it so much, and I know for certain there aren't any sorcerers."

"And warlocks?" He used the Ethsharitic word, since he had never heard a Semmat term.

Agor looked puzzled. "What's a warlock?" he asked.

"Another sort of magician," Sterren explained. "We've had them in Ethshar for about twenty years now."

Agor shrugged. "I never heard of them," he said.

That accorded well with Sterren's suspicion that warlockry did not work in Semma, that the Power in Aldagmor was too far away. Quite aside from his losses at dice, surely, if warlockry were possible, there would be warlocks.

"Anything else?" he asked.

"Not that the gods would tell me about. Believe me, I've asked them."

Sterren nodded. No mysterious hermits, then. He could not help asking, "You're absolutely sure there aren't any you've missed?"

"I could have missed a demonologist, and maybe one of these warlock things you mentioned, but that's all."

"How good are the two wizards? And the witches?"

"My lord Sterren, the younger wizard is working in the castle kitchens, lighting fires and entertaining the cooks; how good do *you* think he is? And they always say you can judge the master by the student."

Sterren did not entirely believe that particular proverb, but he admitted that the older wizard could not be much of a miracle-worker. "What about the witches?"

"Well, my lord, none of them ever gave me any competition for the post of royal magician; does that tell you enough?"

Sterren had to agree that it did. He stared at the gleaming silver hasp on a nearby trunk, trying to think what else he could ask.

"My lord Sterren," Agor said, after a thoughtful pause, "do you really mean to use magic to fight this war?"

Sterren started. "Of course I do!" he shouted. "How else am I going to get out of this alive?"

"In that case, my lord, I don't think you'd want Semman magicians in any case. They've all been raised in the tradition of using no magic in war. Wouldn't it make more sense to get your magicians from somewhere else?"

"I suppose so, but where?"

"Ethshar, of course."

"Of course," Sterren said sarcastically. "Except that I'm not allowed to go back there!"

"Really? Well, then you could send somebody. But are you really sure you aren't?"

Sterren opened his mouth, and then closed it again.

Because of the way he had arrived, he had *assumed* that he would not be allowed to leave Semma, but nobody had ever actually *said* that. And certainly, there were all the magicians he could ever need in the Wizards' Quarter of Ethshar of the Spices.

Not that they would be eager to go gallivanting off to Semma to get involved in something as nasty and unpleasant as a war. He would need a powerful incentive.

Gold would work just fine, of course.

Sterren didn't have any gold himself, but Semma's royal treasury contained a good bit of the stuff. As warlord, his officers had assured him that he had access to the treasury for legitimate military expenses. He didn't even need the treasurer's cooperation; as warlord, he outranked the treasurer.

However, he *did* need the king's permission for any expenditures out of the ordinary.

Sterren realized that it was time to speak to the king.

Twelve

His Majesty Phenvel III looked distinctly bored, but Sterren pressed on with the speech he had prepared, trying not to stumble over any of the unfamiliar words. He had picked up a few choice Semmat phrases from Agor and Lar, and did not want to ruin their effect by mispronouncing them.

"It seems clear," he said, "that if Semma has won so many of its wars, and yet neither treacherous Ophkar nor perfidious Ksinallion has ever resorted to magic to defeat us, then Ophkar and Ksinallion cannot have many magicians available. If they had magicians, surely they would have used them rather than admit defeat! Therefore, they will be unable to counter whatever magic we use. One really good wizard could probably turn the tide of this next conflict — a competent demonologist might be even better, if one could bring oneself to deal with such dark forces . . ."

"No demons," the king interrupted.

"Your Majesty?"

"No demons, no demonologists," Phenvel said, emphasizing his words with a wagging finger. "No sorcerers, either. We'll use good, clean magic if we need to use magic at all."

"Oh, we *do* need to, your Majesty," Sterren replied quickly. "I swear that my own inexperience and the sorry state that my poor senile great-uncle left the army in leave us no other choice." He mildly regretted insulting his dead relative, but after all, the man was dead, and he really *had* left the army in sad shape.

"All right," the king said. "But no demonology and no sorcery. Is that clear?"

"Oh, yes, your Majesty!" Sterren grinned with sudden relief. Up until that moment he had thought the king was not listening, and would reject the whole idea out of hand.

"It might be entertaining to have some real magic around here," Phenvel said. "Agor's all very well, with his lights and voices, but I'd like to see something new. Do you think you can find a wizard who can fly? I've heard that some of them can do that; is it true?"

"Oh, yes, your Majesty," Sterren assured him. "I've seen it myself, in Ethshar's great . . . in Ethshar." That was true enough. He had meant to say that he had seen wizards fly in the Arena, but he didn't know the Semmat word. He had also seen his warlock-master fly. It was not a particularly rare or valuable talent.

"Good. Find a magician who can fly."

Sterren nodded. He knew better than to argue, though he could see little military value in the ability to levitate.

"Yes, your Majesty. Then may I have a letter of credit against the treasury, to show that I . . ."

"No letter!" Phenvel snapped. "Do you think I'm a fool, to give you free run of my money like that? No, I'll give you a pound of gold and a few jewels — I understand that wizards like jewels. That should be enough, I should think."

The bottom dropped out of Sterren's stomach, but he did not dare argue at this point, for fear the king would change his mind and cancel the whole project.

A pound of gold, though, would barely buy a single untraceable death spell back in Ethshar, let alone magic on a scale to be of real military value. Powerful wizards did not work as cheaply as the pitiful village witches and herbalists out here on the edge of the World.

So much for borrowing against the entire royal treasury to hire a squad of hotshot magicians from the Wizards'

Quarter! He would be lucky to find one really good wizard at that price; more likely he would have to settle for a few failed apprentices.

"I do like the idea of getting a few new magicians around here," Phenvel mused, "I really do. But no sorcerers, and no demonologists, not even a little one."

Sterren nodded again. The king was repeating himself, but that was hardly unusual. Nobody had ever dared point out such little slips, so the king made them frequently.

He was trying to phrase a request to be excused, when Phenvel said, "You'll need to have a guard along, of course, and I think Lady Kalira should accompany you. Does that suit you?"

"Very much, your Majesty," Sterren lied. He had hardly dared admit it even to himself, but he had had the idea of taking this opportunity to simply vanish in the streets of Ethshar in the back of his mind right from the start. Guards would make that much more difficult — but perhaps no more difficult than buying the services of a competent magician for a pound of gold and a few nondescript gems.

It appeared he was still doomed.

At the very least, though, he would be able to revisit his homeland before he died. He had been fighting off homesickness for the last day or two, ever since the possibility of returning to Ethshar had begun to seem real.

"Good," the king said. "You're excused, then, and I wish you a safe journey."

Sterren bowed, and backed out of the audience chamber.

In the corridor outside he straightened up, brushed at his cut-down black tunic, and then stood, staring stupidly at the door, for a good three minutes.

What was he supposed to do now? Just turn and go? How was he to collect the gold and gems, or find Lady

Kalira? Who was to choose the guards he would take with him?

Kings were not much on detail work, he supposed. It was up to him. Unless someone told him otherwise, he assumed that he would have to organize the expedition himself.

He glanced around. The only people in the antechamber with him were the two doorkeepers, and he knew better than to ask one of them to leave his post.

Sterren had no servants of his own, and always felt uneasy ordering the castle servants about, since they always seemed to have plenty of work to do without running his errands, but he was the warlord, commander of the Semman army, and his soldiers never seemed to do anything at all unless he was there egging them on. He headed for the barracks.

As usual, half a dozen soldiers were dicing in the corner. The barracks was otherwise empty.

"You men!" he called.

Two of them looked up, without much interest.

"Settle up, the game's over. Right now."

The two glanced at each other, and two more looked up, startled.

"Now!" Sterren bellowed.

Reluctantly, the game broke up, and the six men came sloppily to attention, facing him.

"All right, you, Kather — go find the Lady Kalira, and tell her I must speak to her as soon as possible. Let her choose the time and place, but make plain that it's very urgent, and then come back here immediately and tell me what she said."

Kather stood silently, accepting this.

"Go!"

Startled, Kather nodded. "Yes, my lord," he muttered,

as he started off.

"You, Terrin," Sterren said to the next, "go find the Lord Treasurer, and tell him that I need a pound of gold and a dozen of the finest gems in the treasury, no later than dinnertime tonight, by the king's express order. Arrange a time and place for me to pick them up. If he needs to check with the king first, I have no objection, so long as he's quick about it. If he doubts your authority, bring him back here to speak to me."

Terrin, having learned from Kather's experience, essayed a quick bow, said, "As you wish, my lord," and departed.

Sterren looked over the remaining four. He knew them all slightly, but only slightly, and did not think much of any of them.

"Gror," he said, choosing the best of the lot, "I need a party for a voyage to Ethshar — a peaceful expedition, recruiting aid for the coming war. Who would you suggest?"

"Uh . . ." Gror blinked. "My lord, I . . . I don't know."

"You could call for volunteers," another soldier, Azdaram by name, suggested.

"I could," Sterren agreed.

He considered the idea.

He almost immediately saw an obvious drawback, and prepared to discard the whole notion.

Then he caught himself.

The problem with calling for volunteers was that he might well wind up with men only interested in a diversion from the tedious life of a Semman soldier. It was entirely possible that some of them would desert at the first opportunity . . .

He stopped his chain of thought at that point and backed up.

They might desert. The guard intended to keep *him* from deserting might themselves desert.

That might not be good for Semma, but it would, on the other hand, be a gift from the gods for him, personally. If his escort were to vanish, he could easily lose himself in the streets of the city, and leave Semma to fend for itself.

It probably wouldn't do much worse without him than with him, really. He was hardly a great warlord, after all.

He tried to think what would happen if the guards *did* desert, and he, too, slipped away.

What would Lady Kalira do? What would the others, back here in Semma do — the king, the queen, the princesses, his officers and men, even Agor the theurgist?

Well, the officers and men would presumably go out, fight, and lose. Some would die, the rest surrender. Semma would probably be divided up between Ophkar and Ksinallion, and the royal family sent off into exile somewhere. Agor would almost certainly find employment elsewhere, without much difficulty.

That wasn't so awful, was it? It seemed that a few soldiers were going to die anyway, no matter what happened, so he refused to worry about that. As for exiling the royal family, it was hard to imagine King Phenvel in exile, but on the other hand, it was hard to imagine him doing much of anything. He seemed born to be an incompetent monarch; the only way he could survive the way he was was if other people had no choice about putting up with him.

Princess Shirrin would find exile terribly romantic and exciting, Sterren was sure. Princess Lura would think it was fun. Princess Nissitha would be mortified. Queen Ashassa would take it calmly in stride.

The young princes he didn't know well enough to say, but he suspected they would rather enjoy a change of scene.

As for divvying up Semma, would anyone but the deposed aristocrats care? In his sixnights in Semma he had never seen any sign that the peasants cared a whit which king they paid taxes to.

There might be practical problems in slipping away, though. Lady Kalira would be in Ethshar when he deserted, and she would probably try to track him down. She might even succeed, eventually — though surely not before the war was lost.

What if she found him?

Well, it was obvious that the aristocracy of Semma would not be at all happy with Sterren, Ninth Warlord. He would, beyond question, be guilty of treason under their laws. In all probability, any Semman noble who ever found him would try to kill him on sight.

That was not really a very appealing long-term prospect, but then, he didn't have to stay in Ethshar of the Spices. He could move on to Ethshar of the Sands or Ethshar of the Rocks, or even head north to the Baronies of Sardiron. The nobility of Semma would not be likely to find him; the World was a big place.

The Small Kingdoms would be too dangerous, though; the Semman aristocracy, all two or three hundred of them, were likely to scatter through the region, sponging off various relatives and allies.

He'd want to take a new name, of course.

It occurred to him that the Semmans knew his true name. That was awkward. That meant that they would always be able to find him if they could afford a good wizard, or even a very good witch. Warlocks didn't use true names; neither did sorcerers, so far as he knew.

Theurgists sometimes did, and the Semmans were familiar with theurgy. That was how they had found him in the first place.

And worse, couldn't demonologists use true names?

If the Semmans were determined to track him down and kill him, and had the sense to hire magicians, they could do it.

Desertion looked considerably less appealing than it had a moment before.

On the other hand, Semmans weren't accustomed to magic, and if Sterren could keep the gold and gems with him when he slipped away, perhaps he could buy himself some decent magical protections.

Could a true name be changed?

He didn't really think it could, but he didn't know.

He realized he was standing there looking stupid in front of his four men, and he cut off his thoughts abruptly.

"All right, then, I'm calling for volunteers — do any of you four want to sail to Ethshar?"

The four looked at each other, and then one by one, answered.

"No."

"No, my lord."

"I don't think so."

"Not really. Not *sail*. I don't trust boats."

Sterren was not surprised.

"All right, then, I want all four of you to separate and go find my other soldiers, all of them, and ask for volunteers. Then meet me back here, with the volunteers. And if you don't find enough volunteers, I'll take you four, instead. Understood?"

"Yes, my lord," they chorused raggedly. One by one, they straggled away on this unwanted errand. One of them, Arra Varrin's son, thought to bow as they headed for the stairs.

Sterren watched them go, and pretended not to hear the grumbling that began as soon as they were out the door.

When they were out of sight, he sank down onto a convenient bed and began thinking, planning, and weighing possibilities.

Could he really slip away in the streets of Ethshar?

Did he want to?

Which death was more certain — commanding a grossly-outnumbered army, or being an escaped traitor?

That was a very hard question to answer, and it was one he had to consider carefully. He had no interest in dying.

He had plenty of time to consider the question, of course. He would have the entire journey to Akalla, and then the voyage across the Gulf of the East, to decide what to do and make his plans.

Of course, he knew he might never have a chance to slip away — his soldiers might not desert, he might be closely watched at all times. Still, he also knew he would be thinking about an escape all the way to Ethshar.

Thirteen

As the rooftops of Ethshar grew slowly nearer Sterren leaned on the ship's rail and stared at them hungrily. He could smell the city as well as see it, a scent of smoke and spices with an undertone of sewage, a wonderfully familiar odor that he hadn't smelled in far too long. He had never realized, until this moment, that the city *had* a distinctive odor — he had never left the city until being dragged off to Semma, so the smell had always been there, unnoticed.

Now, though, he knew that he had missed that smell during his absence, that to him that scent meant home, as the salt spray of the ocean or the hot rotting-grass smell of Semma never could.

To his left, Dogal the Large — Dogal d'Gra, that is — sneezed.

To his right, Alder the Very Large — Alder d'Yoon — said, "May the gods keep you well!"

Dogal snuffled in reply, wiped his nose with the back of his hand, and then spat at the ocean below.

Alder, apparently interpreting Dogal's response as a negative one, said, "Well, at least we're finally here. Not much longer now before we're off this damned boat."

"Except that we've got to sail back," Dogal muttered.

"But going back, the wind should be with us, rather than against us," Alder said.

Sterren took no part in the conversation, but he thought that it was certainly true that the wind had been against them. He understood now why Lady Kalira, on her previous voyage to Ethshar, had bought herself a storm from the weather-wizards in Akalla of the Diamond, and why she had wanted to spend two-thirds of his meager hoard of treasure on another one for this trip — after, of course, she had used up most of her own resources in hiring a ship that would sail when and where she wanted, rather than one that would treat the Semman party as ordinary passengers.

Sterren had absolutely forbidden wasting their funds on a storm; the little gold he had would not really be enough as it was, he was sure. He had refused to listen to any argument from Lady Kalira; it was easy enough to simply stop thinking in Semmat, so that her words became meaningless noise. His mind was made up.

Of course, he had not realized that the prevailing winds of the season were from the northwest, and that it would take their chartered ship a month and a day to tack up the Gulf of the East to Ethshar of the Spices. To make any progress to the northwest at all against the cold, steady autumn wind, they had had to beat back and forth, zigzagging across the Gulf from one side to the other.

The only good thing about the delay was that it had given him considerable time to practice his Semmat.

Sterren was heartily sick of the cramped shipboard life and the ship's constant wallowing and rolling, and his feet were almost itching at the thought of walking on dry land again.

The fact that the land in question was his homeland, and that he might yet have a chance to slip away to freedom, made waiting all the harder.

Of course, he might *not* have a chance to slip away. Lady Kalira, when informed of the expedition, had insisted on bringing the two soldiers she most trusted, Alder and Dogal, and had gotten royal backing for this demand. Sterren had had no choice but to yield.

He thought that Alder and Dogal liked him, at least slightly, but he was also quite certain they would not willingly let him desert and leave Semma to its fate.

This was unfortunate, since the other four in the party might well desert, themselves. They were genuine volunteers — Kendrik, Alar, Zander, and Bern were their names, and Sterren was not impressed with any of them.

He knew Kendrik's type from his gambling days; the man was obviously convinced that he was smarter than anybody else, and only needed the right opportunity to make himself rich, famous, and powerful. Semma certainly didn't provide many such opportunities, Sterren had to admit — but he suspected that Kendrik wouldn't find them in Ethshar, either, because he wasn't anywhere near as clever as he thought he was.

People like Kendrik had been among the most generous suppliers of Sterren's funds before his abrupt departure from Ethshar's taverns — but they were also bad losers and very likely to accuse him of cheating. Sterren didn't like Kendrik any better than he had liked those old opponents.

Alar appeared to have volunteered just because somebody asked him. He was easy-going, not too bright, and highly suggestible. Sterren suspected that he had wound up a soldier at somebody else's suggestion, and that he might well desert along with one of the others because he wouldn't see any reason not to, until it was too late.

Sterren might have suggested it to Alar himself, if Alder and Dogal hadn't been present. Once they were ashore he might well make a few suggestive comments in Alar's hearing. For now, though, he was keeping Alar close at hand. He didn't really like the poor fool, but such people could be useful to have around — they could be talked into doing all the unpleasant tasks one inevitably encountered.

Zander had joined the army to get away from a boring life as a peasant farmer. He had volunteered for this trip to get away from a boring life as a soldier in Semma Castle. Ethshar, whatever its flaws, certainly wouldn't look boring to him, and he could easily decide against returning to his boring old homeland.

Sterren thought Zander was pretty boring, himself.

Bern was a mystery; he had said nothing beyond the necessary minimum for politeness ever since he answered the call for volunteers. Sterren had absolutely no idea what to expect from Bern — desertion, loyalty, insanity, anything might be possible.

Alder and Dogal, of course, had not volunteered. Alder might have, given a choice, but Dogal was clearly fed up with travel after his previous journey, and would greatly have preferred to have stayed home, where he had a friendly understanding with one of the cook's more attractive female assistants, and where he didn't have to worry about seasickness or foreign languages and customs.

Alder was a bit more adventurous, and seemed genuinely, if inexplicably, fond of Sterren. Sterren suspected it might be an emotion similar to what one might feel toward a stray puppy one had taken in; after all, Alder had found Sterren, and taught him Semmat, and helped him settle into his job as warlord.

Lady Kalira would never have volunteered; on her previous journey she had discovered, to her surprise, that she hated travel, and hated Ethshar. Neither one fit her romantic preconceptions; the stories never mentioned seasickness, rude sailors, smelly crowds, and all the other inconveniences she had encountered. Furthermore, she thought the whole idea of using magic to fight a war was revolting. She did, however, have a powerful sense of duty, which accounted for her cooperation, such as it was. The king had sent her, and she did as her sovereign ordered.

She had surely heard the call from the lookout when the city came into view, but she was ignoring it, staying in her cabin below.

To some extent, Sterren thought he could sympathize with her, but at the sight of the city spreading across the World before him, its smell in his nostrils, he found his eyes filling with tears, and felt a swelling in his chest as if he were about to burst.

He swallowed, and to distract himself, he called to a sailor who was hanging from the forestay, "Hey, there! Where will we tie up?"

The sailor glanced at him, but shook her head.

Sterren realized he had spoken in Semmat, since Alder and Dogal had been speaking it.

"Where will we tie up?" he called in Ethsharitic.

"The Tea Wharves," the sailor called back. "Near the New Canal!"

Sterren was unsure exactly where the Tea Wharves were, but he knew the New Canal — which, despite its name, was about four hundred years old; it was new only in comparison to the Grand Canal, which was no longer particularly grand, but had been there for centuries before the New Canal was dug.

The New Canal divided Spicetown from Shiphaven, in the northwest corner of the city. The Wizards' Quarter was near the southeastern corner. Sterren's party would need to do some walking, it appeared.

That was no problem; it might provide more opportunities to escape from his escort. If there was a crowd at the Arena, for example, he could easily become separated "accidentally." The Arena was directly on the way, too; Arena Street was certainly the best route to the Wizards' Quarter from either Shiphaven or Spicetown.

That assumed that he actually wanted to slip away. After a month of debating that with himself, he still hadn't really decided.

It would seem an easy enough decision to make, really —

life as a fugitive in his homeland, or near-certain death in a nasty little kingdom in the middle of nowhere — but whenever he thought he had settled on escape he kept finding himself reconsidering, thinking of what might happen to the people he had come to know in Semma. Would Princess Lura wind up starving somewhere? Might Nissitha and Shirrin be raped by their victorious enemies? Would Alder and Dogal and all the soldiers he had diced with get themselves killed in a futile defense?

None of this, he told himself, really ought to be any responsibility of his — he hadn't volunteered to be warlord.

Still, he *was* the warlord, like it or not, and abandoning Semma to its fate seemed wrong.

Of course, *not* abandoning Semma might get him killed, and that seemed even worse.

Perhaps, he thought with sudden inspiration, he could hire his magicians, and *then* disappear into the city streets. Semma could still win its stupid war, but he would be free and home. True, he would be guilty of treason under Semman law, but surely, nobody would go to all that much trouble looking for him under those circumstances. The Semman nobility would have no very strong reason to hold a grudge against him if he won their war for them, whether he was present at the time or not.

And if his magicians *didn't* win — and given his estimate of the purchasing power of his available funds, that seemed likely — at least he would have made an honest effort, and would be no worse off than if he had deserted before recruiting anybody.

He would have *tried*, and if the Semman princesses were still raped or murdered, if the Semman army was still slaughtered, he would have done the best he could.

He liked that approach. He would carry through on his promise, hire the best magicians he could — and then, if the opportunity arose, he would escape on the way back to the ship.

That shouldn't be too difficult, he thought. He smiled and blinked away the tears of homesickness.

He would hire magicians — but how did one go about hiring magicians for something like this?

His smile vanished again as he realized that he had no idea at all.

To buy a love spell or a curse, to cure warts or foresee the future, he knew exactly what to do. He would take his money to the Wizards' Quarter and pick a likely magician by reading the signboards.

None of the signboards had ever advertised "Wars won," though. How would he know which magicians to approach? Trial and error would not work; there were hundreds of magicians in the Wizards' Quarter, and asking each one in turn would take years. Most surely wouldn't be interested.

Recruiters of various sorts always worked in the city's markets, particularly Shiphaven Market and Westgate Market, calling out their offers to the passing crowds; anyone who wanted to take up a career as an adventurer, or any other particularly hazardous and messy job, could go to the markets and pick from several options.

But there was no market in the Wizards' Quarter. There was Arena Plaza, but Sterren had never seen a recruiter there. The nearest true market was in Southgate — and Sterren had never been there at all. The taverns and gaming in Southgate were organized, and freelancers like himself were not welcome.

Or would Southmarket, by the reservoir, be closer to the Wizards' Quarter than Southgate? He had passed through there once. He didn't *remember* seeing recruiters, but he could not be absolutely sure they hadn't been there.

And there was always Eastgate Market, and Hempfield Market, and Newmarket, and Newgate — he had gambled in inns and taverns near all those, at one time or another, before settling back into his home turf around Westgate and the two Merchants' Quarters. Those other markets had no recruiters, generally, and weren't particularly close to the Wizards' Quarter, but should he rule them out completely?

For the first time, Sterren began to see the city's immensity as a serious drawback.

He blinked, shook his head, and reconsidered.

None of the various markets seemed exactly right, but pretty obviously, Shiphaven Market would be the best if he decided to go that route. It was the traditional place to recruit people interested in traveling by sea, after all, and it would be closest to the Tea Wharves, wherever they might turn out to be. That would mean less walking through the city streets, but on the other hand, Shiphaven Market was always crowded, was not too far from his old stamping grounds, and was surrounded by places to hide.

He didn't know all those places as well as he might, since he had usually avoided Shiphaven in order to avoid drunken sailors who might be prone to violence, or ships' officers who might stoop to kidnapping to complete their crews, but he thought he could manage to find something.

But would there be any magicians around Shiphaven Market?

The Arena Plaza was certainly much closer to the Wizards' Quarter, and he thought he remembered a signboard there that he could post a message on — that was a second possibility that did not deserve to be discarded out of hand.

For that matter, simply asking around in the Wizards' Quarter, or walking the streets calling for volunteers, might produce results. Perhaps he could inquire after ambitious near-term apprentices, or even journeymen. The magicians surely gossiped among themselves, and would know who might be desperate enough for work to be interested in such an adventure.

And what's more, there was no reason he couldn't try all three approaches.

He smiled again. That would certainly be reasonable, and would call for a good, long stay in Ethshar, with visits to two of the most crowded places in the city — Shiphaven Market and Arena Plaza. The Wizards' Quarter was less crowded, but full of nooks and crannys and odd little byways where a person could easily lose sight of his companions.

That seemed very promising indeed.

As the city loomed before him, heart-twistingly familiar, his resolution to stay until he had hired magicians evaporated. He decided instead that he would take any opportunity to escape that arose, because any opportunity might be the last.

If the opportunity never came at all, he would live with that.

He was a gambler, after all. He was accustomed to accepting what the gods of luck sent him and making the best of it. If his luck let him slip away, he would; if he never got a chance, he would go through with the hiring of magicians and play out his role as warlord.

He could see the docks ahead, now, and the mouth of the New Canal. Three wharves projected out at an angle, across a band of mud, a few hundred feet to the left of the canal; the ship seemed to be headed directly for them, and he guessed that these were the Tea Wharves.

That was the Spicetown side, but getting across to Shiphaven would be easy enough. Spicetown had no market square; the spice merchants did their bidding right on the docks. Shiphaven Market would still be the first stop in the search for magicians.

This expedition, he thought, might even be fun.

Fourteen

Sterren stopped walking and pointed. "That's the New Canal," he said, speaking loudly to be heard over the wind, "and Shiphaven Market's just the other side. That's where we want to start looking."

Lady Kalira glanced at the row of shops on the opposite bank and sniffed. "I don't see any market over there," she said, a trifle petulantly.

"It's not right on the canal, it's a few blocks in." In truth, Sterren was not at all sure how far it was; he was not overly familiar with this part of the city, and had never before needed to get from Spicetown to Shiphaven Market. "Are you still sure we should start looking immediately, and not find ourselves a good meal or a place to sleep?"

"We can sleep on the ship," Lady Kalira replied, irritated. "And eat there, too, if we have to. Now, where's this market?"

"How do we get across?" Alder asked. "Is there a bridge?"

Sterren had to think for a minute. "Well, there is on the Upper Canal, which turns off this one — or maybe it's on the New Canal right before the Upper Canal turns off, I'm not sure."

"Boats," Kendrik pointed out. "There must be boats going across."

"Of course there are," Sterren said, although he hadn't known there were until he saw what Kendrik had spotted: A small, flat-bottomed boat, obviously unfit to leave the calm waters of the canal, tied up to a dock on the opposite side. A man lay dozing in it, and some rotting fruit rinds were bumping gently against one gunwhale. Looking around, Sterren saw that a similar dock on the near side jutted forty feet out into the canal and had a space on one side where just such a boat could readily tie up.

"A ferry, that's what it is," he added, as he led the way down to the dock.

He hoped it actually was a ferry; if not, he knew he was going to look very foolish.

"I don't understand why we're doing this," Zander muttered as he followed his warlord down the cobbled slope.

"Because Shiphaven Market is where people recruit for foreign adventures; I told you all that," Sterren retorted, as his feet hit the first planks.

Zander was not silenced. "Is it always this cold?" he asked, pulling his tunic tighter at the throat.

"No," Sterren and Lady Kalira replied, simultaneously.

Sterren was not particularly pleased with the cold and wind, or with Zander's whining. Both acted as deterrents to desertion. The immense size of the city did, as well; Sterren, being a native and accustomed to it from birth, had not realized how intimidating it must be to a foreigner, newly arrived from the rural openness of Semma, to find himself surrounded by a seemingly endless maze of walls and streets.

Even the rich city smell that he found so comforting probably seemed like an alien stink to the Semmans.

He was rapidly losing hope that all four of his volunteers would desert, but if even one did, he thought he could send the others after him, while he and Lady Kalira supposedly continued his recruiting mission. That might provide sufficient opportunity for his own escape.

He came to the end of the dock, stopped, and waved an arm above his head.

"*Hai!*" he called, shouting at the top of his lungs in

order to be heard over the wind. "Over here!"

The man in the flat-bottomed boat looked up, startled out of his doze, and saw the party on east side. He sat up, then stood, and picked up a long-handled oar.

Sterren could feel Lady Kalira's impatience as they stood and watched while the ferryman casually used the blunt end of the oar to push off from the dock, and then began paddling his way slowly across the canal, fighting the steady breeze that wanted to push his ungainly craft out to sea. The gap between the two docks was a good forty yards, Sterren judged, and it took several long minutes for the boat to cross it.

When it drew near, the ferryman stopped rowing, reached down, and came up with a coil of rope. He threw one end of it up onto the dock.

Alder, with admirable presence of mind, caught it and began hauling the boat in.

The other end of the rope was secured to the boat's blunt bow, and in a moment that bumped up against the battered end of the dock.

"Bunch of barbarians, is it?" the ferryman muttered in Ethsharitic. "I can't take you all at once!" he called aloud.

The Semman soldiers spoke no Ethsharitic, and were all crowding forward toward the boat. "Wait!" Sterren called. "Not all at once! You'll . . . you'll . . ." He could not think of a Semmat equivalent for "sink," "swamp," or "capsize."

He didn't need one; the soldiers got the idea, and stopped pressing.

In his native tongue, Sterren called to the boatman, "Yes, they are a bunch of barbarians, but I'm stuck with them. How many can you take?"

"How many of you are there?" the boatman asked, eyeing the little mob.

Sterren did a quick head-count to make sure he hadn't forgotten anyone, then answered, "Eight, in all."

The boatman considered, and said, "I can take four each time, easily enough. Two trips will do it, then. I'll give you a cut rate, too — six bits the lot."

Sterren was not at all sure that was actually a cut rate, but he paid no attention. Here, sent by the gods, was a chance to split the party. He turned to Lady Kalira. "He says he can only take four at a time," he explained. "I'll go on ahead with Zander and Alar and Bern, say, and then he'll come back for the rest of you."

"Oh, no!" she replied. "No, I stay with you! You, me, Alder, and Dogal go first, and the rest can follow."

"My lady, need I remind you that I am in charge here, and not you? This is my city, and I am your warlord . . ."

"This is your city, all right," Lady Kalira interrupted, "and that's exactly why I'm staying with you."

Sterren opened his mouth to argue, and then caught sight of the expression on Alder's face.

It was not an easy expression to describe, having something of resignation, annoyance, and doubt in it, but Sterren knew immediately that it meant Alder didn't trust him any more than Lady Kalira did. He closed his mouth.

"All right," he said after a moment, "we'll go first, then those four." He pushed his way past the soldiers, and climbed down into the boat. "My lady, if you will?" he said, turning back and offering a hand.

Lady Kalira accepted his aid, stepping down into the boat. She settled on one of the seats in the bow.

Dogal followed, and then Alder with the bowline, and Sterren, prompted by the ferryman's gestures, settled the two of them amidships, while he sat in the bow beside Lady Kalira.

"Oars are on either side," the ferryman pointed out from where he stood in the stern.

Sterren translated, and Alder and Dogal each took an oar as the ferryman reached over them with his own long oar and pushed them away from the dock.

It took the Semman soldiers a minute to get the hang of rowing, but even so, the trip west was much quicker than the ferryman's solo trip east had been.

Once across, they clambered quickly ashore.

The ferryman waited, and once they were all safely on the dock he said, "That'll be six bits. I don't get the others until I see the money."

Sterren did not bother to translate this for the others; he just pulled the money from his purse and tossed it to the ferryman, who caught it deftly.

Then the foursome had to stand on the western dock and wait while the ferryman returned for the other soldiers.

It was only then that Lady Kalira realized that none of the other four spoke even a single word of Ethsharitic, or even Trader's Tongue. The ferryman did his best to make himself understood in both languages — bits of his shouting carried across the water — but the four Semmans were very slow indeed to find places in the boat and cast off successfully.

Sterren watched the others carefully, glancing back now and then at the city streets behind them, but he saw no opportunity to make a dash for shelter. He waited, unhappily, until the party was reunited.

The north wind was chilly, and Dogal was shivering badly by the time the others scrambled up out of the boat. Even Sterren felt the cold.

"This way," he said, with no idea whether it was the right way; he just wanted to get moving and out of the wind.

He led the way up away from the canal, past a cross street, around a sinuous bend, and through two three-way intersections.

Then he stopped, trying to figure out where he was.

The other seven, all close behind him, nearly trampled him.

He looked about. The others followed suit.

They were obviously in Shiphaven. Most of the people in sight on the streets wore the blue kilts and white tunics of sailors. Two chandlers' shops were in sight, and a cooper's as well. A red-haired woman sat on the balcony of a nearby brothel, but wore a heavy shawl wrapped about her against the wind. She called a greeting, judging the soldiers to be potential customers; Kendrik in particular stared at her greedily.

Sterren did not recognize the street. He considered stopping one of the sailors strolling by, but rejected the idea immediately; he would not admit so easily to being lost in his native city.

Even over the clatter of passing feet and the whistle of the wind in the nearby eaves, he could hear voices ahead and to the left. "This way," he said, marching on.

The Semmans followed, Alder and Dogal close on his heels, Lady Kalira just behind, and the others trailing along.

The next intersection was another cross street, and he turned left, to find himself looking directly at Shiphaven Market, two blocks away.

He recognized the street, then; he was on East Wharf Street. He still could not identify the one he had followed from the canal, however.

"There you are," he said, pointing, "Shiphaven Market!"

He was rather proud of having led the party successfully through an unfamiliar part of the city, but none of the Semmans seemed impressed by his accomplishment. None of them realized, of course, that this part of the city was unfamiliar.

In fact, he wondered if it had really sunk in yet that the city was big enough that he wasn't familiar with all of it.

"Good," Lady Kalira snapped. "Let's go find a wizard and get back to the ship, before we all freeze."

"Doesn't have to be a wizard," Sterren began, but Lady Kalira's glare discouraged him from saying any more. He marched on.

The market was not crowded, probably because of the weather, Sterren guessed. The foul winds would have kept down the number of ships reaching the harbor, with goods to sell or vacancies in their crews to fill, and the cold would discourage the casual browser. He doubted he saw much more than a hundred people milling about.

One of them, however, was unmistakably a wizard, complete with crimson robe and an assortment of well-filled pouches and sheathes on her belt. Another, tall, thin, and pale and wearing black, might well be a warlock.

Sterren suddenly began to think that his presence here was a mistake. What did he want with magicians? All he wanted was to be left alone. He stopped walking.

"Come on," Lady Kalira said, and Alder reached out for his elbow.

He walked on into the market square, found a quiet spot, and then stopped again.

"Now what?" Lady Kalira demanded.

Sterren was overcome with irrational fear — stage fright, although he had never encountered that term for it. He knew that the time had come to call out his recruiting pitch, but he could not bring himself to speak.

Inspiration struck. "You tell them what we want," he told Lady Kalira.

"*Me?*"

"Yes, you; as your warlord, I demand it."

"But my lord, I don't speak Ethsharitic!"

In his panic, Sterren had forgotten that.

Reminded of it, a sudden inspiration struck him, and before he could lose his nerve again he raised his hands and shouted, "People of Ethshar! These barbarians think I'm going to give a recruiting speech for them, but the truth is that they're holding me prisoner against my will! I ask that you summon the city guard!"

"Wait a minute," Lady Kalira said, hauling down one arm, "what was that you said?"

"I said . . ."

"You didn't say anything about magicians, and I heard you say something about the city guard, I think."

Sterren saw that doubtful expression on Alder's face again, and saw his hand fall to the hilt of his sword. He cleared his throat.

"Just warming up," Sterren said. He looked about, and realized that nobody else had paid any attention to him, anyway. The wind had apparently carried his words away unheard — or perhaps they had been taken for a joke, or a stunt to attract attention.

He looked over his own party, and for the first time he noticed that Kendrik was gone.

He smiled, but decided not to point this absence out.

Not yet, anyway.

For now, it would clearly be safer to behave himself and seriously try to recruit magicians; his chances of slipping away might well improve later on.

He turned back toward the center of the square and shouted in Ethsharitic, "Magicians needed! Magicians needed! I represent his Majesty, King Phenvel the Third of Semma, and I am here to hire fine magicians of every school to aid the royal Semman army!"

"That's better," Lady Kalira muttered, recognizing the familiar names.

A young man stopped to listen as Sterren continued, "Excellent pay! Comfortable accommodations! An opportunity for glory and honor in a worthy cause! Magicians of every sort are needed!" He found himself getting into the spirit of the occasion; it wasn't really all that different from the times he had had to talk a losing opponent out of retaliation.

"You think you're going to find decent magicians here, at this time of year?" the young stranger asked, smirking.

"Shut up," Sterren answered conversationally. "Magicians!" he called.

The listener snorted.

A middle-aged couple in fine clothing wandered up to listen.

"We need magicians! Payment in gold and gems, all expenses to be borne by the royal treasury!"

The red-robed wizard approached, and then the tall man in black.

"You, wizard," Sterren asked, beckoning, "would you be interested in a trip to Semma, the jewel of the Small Kingdoms?"

The wizard smiled wryly and turned away.

"*I* might be," the man in black answered.

"Are you a magician, sir?" Sterren asked.

The man in black raised a hand, and a thick swirl of dust rose up from the hard-packed ground of the market, spiralling upward before him, ignoring the wind that should have scattered it across the marketplace. The dust gathered into a ball the size of a fist, hung there in the air for an instant, and then burst apart and vanished, whipped away on the breeze.

"I'm a warlock," said the man in black.

Fifteen

After an hour's harangue, Sterren gave up. His throat was sore, his voice giving out, and he had lost the crowd's interest completely.

The warlock had stood by, waiting patiently the whole time. He had neither committed himself to the venture nor turned it down, had not demanded to know more, but had simply waited.

A black-haired woman with a runny nose, about Sterren's own age and wearing a purple gown with stains that resembled those one might acquire sleeping in the Hundred-Foot Field, had also turned up, claiming to be a wizard, and she had actually volunteered. She had been more concerned with Sterren's guarantee that she would be fed for as long as she was in Semma's employ than in the particulars of the job, or the payment offered.

The sun was low above the rooftops on the western side of the square. "Time for dinner," Sterren said in Semmat, turning to Lady Kalira. "Don't you think so?"

"I suppose," she said.

She had spent much of the hour wandering about the market, looking at the goods offered for sale, but she had not bought anything. Sterren suspected that she had been too embarrassed by her poor command of Ethsharitic — if you could call her dozen or so phrases "command" — to try to haggle in that language, and the local merchants, while likely to speak several tongues, would not be likely to know anything so obscure as Semmat.

Of course, Lady Kalira spoke Trader's Tongue, Sterren remembered, and most of the merchants could probably handle that, but perhaps she didn't realize it. Or maybe language had nothing to do with it, and her funds were running low. That might be inconvenient, since he had hoped that her purse would be there to fall back on in an emergency.

Whatever the reason, Lady Kalira had returned, empty-handed, a few minutes before.

Dogal and Alder had stayed close at hand throughout Sterren's pitch; even while speaking he had watched for a chance to slip away from them, but had not seen one.

The same could not be said of Alar, Zander, and Bern, all of whom had wandered off. Zander and Bern had returned; Alar, as yet, had not, nor was there any sign of Kendrik.

Sterren switched back to Ethsharitic and asked the warlock, "Would you care to join my companions and myself for dinner, and perhaps discuss the job further?"

The warlock nodded casually.

"Is there somewhere around here where we can get a decent meal," Sterren asked, "or should we head down to Westgate?"

"This is not my part of the city," the warlock replied.

Sterren hesitated, and thought better of asking him any further questions, such as which part of the city was his, and why wasn't he in it. Instead, he turned to the wizard, a questioning look on his face.

Before he could speak, without a word, she pointed to a tavern on the north corner of Flood Street, where a faded signboard depicted a golden dragon.

"Good enough," he said, as he led the way.

"Wait a minute," Lady Kalira objected. "What about Kendrik and Alar?"

Sterren stopped. "My lady," he said, "Kendrik deserted before we even reached the market; I last saw him among the . . . the . . ." He paused, and then resorted to using the

Ethsharitic word. ". . . the *brothels* on . . ." He paused again, sighed, and said, "*East Wharf Street*," in Ethsharitic. Switching back to Semmat, he continued, "Alar wandered off some time ago, and I have no idea where he has gone, and I don't want to either search for him, or wait for his return."

"But you can't allow desertion!"

"I can't allow myself to starve, either, or perish of thirst."

A look at Lady Kalira's face let him know that that was not going to be sufficient. "All right," he said, capitulating, "Zander, you and Bern go find Kendrik and Alar. Then meet us at that inn, there." He pointed to the Golden Dragon. "If we aren't there, go back to the ship. It's at the . . ." He stopped. He wished he knew the word for "wharf" in Semmat, but he didn't, and besides, if these two asked for directions in Semmat, nobody would know what they were saying. "*Tea Wharves*," he said in Ethsharitic, then asked in Semmat, "Can you say that?"

"Why should we say it?" Zander asked.

"In case you get lost," Sterren explained.

The concept of "getting lost" was not one Zander, born and raised on an open plain, thought of the same way a city boy like Sterren did, but looking at the maze of streets Zander saw the sense in it. He said, "Oh."

"*Tea Wharves*," Sterren repeated. "Try it."

Zander struggled to wrap his tongue around the unfamiliar syllables. The resulting mess was not recognizable.

"Bern?" Sterren asked.

"Tea Wharves," Bern said, in accented but perfectly intelligible Ethsharitic. Sterren peered at him suspiciously.

"You don't speak Ethsharitic, do you?"

"No, my lord," Bern replied.

"Zander, try it again. *Tea Wharves*."

Zander managed to produce something almost adequate this time.

"Good enough, I suppose. Work on it while you're hunting for your comrades."

Zander nodded; Bern didn't bother. Together, they turned and marched back into the market crowd.

Sterren watched them go, neither knowing nor caring whether he would ever see either of them again.

He had gotten rid of four of his seven unwanted companions, he thought; he was more than halfway to freedom!

"This way," he said, leading the way to the Golden Dragon.

The tavern was less than half full, and they found a table readily, not far from the door. Sterren, after some consideration, decided that neither facing the door nor sitting with his back to it would be best for slipping away; he sat with his right side toward the door, his back to the open room.

Lady Kalira sat opposite him, against a wall; Alder took the chair to his right, back to the door, and Dogal to his left, facing the door. The warlock sat between Alder and Lady Kalira, the wizard between Dogal and Lady Kalira.

Sterren took the opportunity for a look at his two recruits.

Both were thin, but the wizard's slenderness appeared to be due to borderline malnutrition, while the warlock was simply built that way. The wizard wore her hair in long black ringlets that trailed halfway down her back, and even in her present tattered and dirty condition they were still showed signs of having been combed not too long ago. Her face was rather drawn, her eyes brown and anxious; if she were clean, smiling, and better-fed, Sterren thought, she would be attractive, possibly even beautiful.

She sniffled, and dabbed at her nose with a stained cuff.

The warlock was clean and looked as if he was as well-fed as he cared to be, but he was definitely not smiling. His lined, narrow face was fixed and expressionless, his mouth a thin line, his pale green eyes unreadable. His hair, black with the first traces of grey, was cut short, barely covering his ears. Sterren guessed him to be over forty; how much over he had no idea. He might have been handsome once, but now, Sterren thought, he was merely striking.

As soon as they were seated, even before the serving maid could reach them, the warlock said, "I notice that in an hour's speech, you never once specified the nature of the employment you offered."

Caught off-guard, Sterren agreed, "I suppose I didn't."

The wizard was staring hungrily at the approaching tavern girl, and Sterren used that as an excuse to change the subject. "My lady," he said in Semmat, "what shall we have, and at whose expense?"

"You brought us here," Lady Kalira said, "you pay for it. You wanted dinner, we'll have dinner. What was the man in black saying?"

"He asked a question about our offer. Wine with your meal?"

Lady Kalira nodded.

Sterren glanced at each of the remaining soldiers in turn, and each nodded. "Wine would be welcome," Alder said.

Sterren nodded back, then switched to Ethsharitic and asked the wizard, "Would you like wine with dinner?"

The serving maid had reached the table, heard this final question, and saw the wizard's nod.

"We have several fine vintages," she said. Her tone made it a question.

Sterren said, in Ethsharitic, "The three barbarians wouldn't appreciate it, and I can't afford it, so I do hope my two guests will forgive me if we have the regular house wine, and whatever you have for the house dinner tonight, rather than anything special. That's for all six of us, unless . . . ?"

He looked questioningly at the warlock, who made a small gesture of acquiescence with one hand. The wizard said, "That would be fine."

The tavern girl departed.

"The nature of this proposed employment?" the warlock said.

Sterren had carefully avoided being specific in his marketplace spiel, for fear of frightening off prospects, but he realized that the time for prevarication was past.

He sighed. "I'm the hereditary warlord of one of the Small Kingdoms, a little place in the far south called Semma. I didn't want the job, but I'm stuck with it. Semma is on the verge of war with two larger neighbors, and we're doomed. The army is absolutely pitiful and badly outnumbered. We don't stand a chance unless we cheat. In the Small Kingdoms, at least in Semma's neighborhood, they don't use magic in their wars; it's considered dishonorable or something — it's cheating. Well, I'm ready to cheat, because otherwise I'll be killed for losing. So I'm here looking for magicians who can help us win this war. It shouldn't take much, since there's so little magic there and the soldiers will never have fought against magicians before." He looked at the warlock, hoping that he wouldn't dismiss the idea out of hand.

"A war?" The warlock's tone was calm and considering.

Sterren nodded, encouraged that the warlock had not rejected the idea out of hand. He glanced at the wizard.

She had hardly listened; her attention was on the door to the kitchen. It was an interesting door, with the skull of a small dragon mounted so as to form the top of the frame and the dragon's lower jaw serving as a door-handle, but Sterren suspected the poor young woman was far more interested in what would be coming through that door than in the decor that gave the tavern its name.

The wizard caught his eye, and turned back to him.

"I don't care what the job is," she said, sniffing and brushing a stray ringlet back over her shoulder. "If it won't get me killed outright and you pay in gold, I'll take it." She hesitated, then wiped her nose and asked, "It won't get me killed outright, will it?"

"I certainly hope not," Sterren said. "If we win, it won't, but if we lose, you'll probably have to flee for your lives." He shrugged. "Fleeing shouldn't be difficult; it's wide-open country, and the kingdoms are so small it should be easy to get safely across a border before they can catch you."

The warlock nodded. "You say Semma is far to the south?"

Sterren nodded again. "About as far to the southeast as you can get, really; from the castle's highest tower you can see the edge of the World, on a clear day. I've seen it myself." He stared at the warlock, a suspicion growing in the back of his mind.

He had not really had time to consider his two prospective employees, but now he did.

Warlockry was virtually unknown in Semma. He had no way of knowing for certain whether it would work there at all, and he was quite sure it would be far less effective than it was in Ethshar. A warlock, therefore, would not be his preferred sort of magician.

On the other hand, this particular warlock seemed very interested in going south.

Sterren could guess what that meant. This particular warlock probably wanted to get as far away from

Aldagmor and the Power's Source as he could. He might have already had the first warning nightmares that meant he had pushed his warlockry to dangerous levels.

Warlockry, as Sterren knew from his aborted apprenticeship, drew its power from a mysterious Source located somewhere in the Aldagmor region, a mountainous area far to the north of Ethshar, on the edge of the Baronies of Sardiron. A warlock's power varied as the inverse square of the distance from this thing. A warlock's power also increased with use; every spell a warlock cast made the next one a shade easier. Most magic worked that way, of course; most skills of any kind did. The effect was rather extreme with warlockry, however, because warlockry, unlike all other magic, also directly counteracted fatigue; magic not only didn't tire a warlock, it revivified him, without limit.

Except that there *was* a limit. When a warlock's power reached a certain level, he began to have nightmares. From then on, every further use of warlockry caused more and worse nightmares, which could make life virtually unbearable.

Eventually an afflicted warlock wouldn't even need to be asleep to suffer these hideous visions, and in the end, every warlock ever known to have reached this point had died or vanished. Those who did not commit suicide were often seen wandering north, toward Aldagmor, usually flying — but then were never seen again.

This was known as the Calling, because that was what the nightmares seemed to be — a horrible, supernatural summons of some kind that would draw a warlock either to Aldagmor or death — or both.

What most warlocks did is, when the first nightmare hits, to move south or west, further from Aldagmor, and give up warlockry for good. The smarter ones would have been charging exorbitant fees in anticipation of this, and could to retire in comfort.

Sterren guessed that *this* warlock had pushed his luck, and had had considerably more than *one* nightmare, so that he was now desperate to get as far from Aldagmor as possible, as quickly as possible.

Whatever his reasons, the warlock might be either a great stroke of luck or utterly worthless, depending on just what power *did* remain to him in Semma, so very far from Aldagmor.

Bringing him along would be a gamble, but after all, Sterren had always been a gambler.

If any warlock could be of help in Semma, one already touched by nightmare, on the verge of the Calling, would surely be most likely. The Calling only came when warlocks reached the height of their power. In fact, one theory was that the Calling was something the gods used to remove warlocks who were becoming *too* powerful, who might damage the gods' plan for the World.

A lesser warlock would not be worth bothering with, but a really powerful one might be. He would surely be greatly weakened, but he would also be something that nobody in Ophkar or Ksinallion would ever have seen before.

"Nightmares?" Sterren asked quietly.

For the first time since Sterren had first seen him in the market, the warlock's calm expression changed; he let a flicker of surprise at Sterren's knowledge show. Then, slowly, he nodded.

Sterren smiled slightly. He knew that the Calling gave the warlock reasons for coming south far more important than a pound of gold.

That meant he would probably work cheap, far cheaper than his level of power might otherwise justify.

"You'll be coming, then?" Sterren asked.

The warlock nodded again.

Sterren turned to the wizard. "And you?"

"What's the pay, exactly? Are meals included?" Her voice shook a little. She looked at Sterren as she wiped her nose on her sleeve again.

The serving maid chose that moment to return with a tray holding six plates of stewed vegetables, tainted with only the smallest trace of mutton. A bottle of red wine and half a dozen stacked mugs were included, as well.

Sterren and the two Semman soldiers distributed the plates, while the warlock sent the cups floating through the air to the appropriate places. At a gesture, the cork sprang from the bottle's neck, and the bottle then settled itself in front of Lady Kalira.

Startled, she picked it up, and only after a moment's hesitation did she begin pouring.

Sterren threw the warlock a puzzled glance. If he had reached the threshold of nightmare, didn't he realize that every additional use of warlockry would increase his danger? At least, that was what Sterren's master, Bergan the Warlock, had said.

The warlock saw the look, and smiled slightly. "In honor of our imminent departure for more southerly climes," he said, raising his cup as if in a toast.

The others probably thought it *was* just a toast, but Sterren knew what the warlock meant. After keeping his magic in check — for hours, days, sixnights, even months? — he was allowing himself a little freedom, secure in the knowledge that he would soon be sailing away from whatever waited in the mountains and valleys of Aldagmor.

Sterren put that out of his mind and turned to the wizard. "The pay," he explained, "will include meals, and a hammock aboard ship, and a room in Semma Castle —

possibly shared with others, but a bed of your own, at any rate. You'll need to learn some Semmat, I'm afraid; virtually nobody there speaks a word of Ethsharitic. If we win our war, then the magicians involved, as a group, will be paid ten rounds of gold, and a dozen choice gems — I can show them to you later, if you like, but not in a tavern like this. How this payment is to be divided up is yet to be determined; either the magicians can decide amongst themselves, or King Phenvel can divide it up as he deems appropriate. Would that suit you?"

She nodded, sniffling.

"If you don't mind my asking, just what magic do you know?" Sterren inquired. Obviously, she knew no spells to keep a cold away.

"Wizardry, of course," she said.

That was no surprise, but Sterren knew well that wizards came in a wide range of skills and power. "Much wizardry?" he asked.

"Well . . ." She hesitated, then admitted what her soiled clothes and empty belly had already made obvious. "No, not really. A few spells."

"Not just tricks, though, I hope," Sterren said, knowing he was prodding her on what was surely a sensitive subject.

"No, real spells!" she snapped. "I am Annara of Crookwall, and I am a full journeyman in the Wizards' Guild; I served my six years as apprentice, and I learned what my master could teach me!"

Her flash of pride vanished as suddenly as it had appeared. "That wasn't much, though," she admitted, nervously tugging her hair back from her face.

That was no surprise. Sterren nodded and poured himself wine.

As they ate, the warlock and the three Semmans said nothing, while Sterren and Annara made polite small talk.

Sterren inquired about her upbringing in Crookwall, while she, in turn, asked about Semma, and was surprised to learn that he was a native of Westgate, rather than some-place more exotic.

After the meal had been consumed, Sterren leaned back in his chair and looked across at Lady Kalira as he tried to decide what to do next.

"Well, my lord," Lady Kalira said, seeing his attention focused on her, "you have two magicians here, do you not?"

Sterren nodded.

"Is that sufficient, then?"

Sterren guessed at what the Semmat word for "suffi-cient" meant. He glanced at Annara, who would give no details of her abilities beyond admitting to "a few spells," and then at the warlock, who had as yet given no name, who might well be totally powerless in Semma.

"No," he replied immediately, before even considering his own hopes for escape. "These two may help, but neither of them can provide any assurance of winning."

"Then you plan to try to recruit more?"

Sterren nodded.

"My lord, are you sure you have no other intentions?"

He picked up her phrase to ask, "What other intentions might I have?" He eyed her cautiously.

"Delay, perhaps."

"*Baguir?*" He did not recognize the word. He guessed it to be something like "escape," but could not be certain. "What's *baguir?*"

"To put off, to stall, to hold back, to go slowly; I don't know the Ethsharitic."

That was not the reply Sterren had feared and expected. "Delay?" he asked. "Why should I want to delay?"

"I would not know, my lord, but your refusal to pur-chase any magical assistance in sailing hither, and your insistence that two magicians are not enough, would seem to imply that you are certainly in no hurry about this foolish, disreputable business."

He picked up her phrase again, without any very clear idea what it meant, save that it had a strong negative connotation. "This disreputable business may save Semma, my lady."

"Not if you continue to delay."

"I'm not delaying! Why should I?"

"Well, my lord, it has occurred to me, in my more cynical moments, that if you can stretch your visit to this, your homeland, long enough, perhaps the war in Semma will be fought and lost before our return, and you can retire to a comfortable exile here."

Sterren stared at her. That possibility had never occurred to him.

A very tempting possibility it was, too.

He glanced quickly to either side, at the two other Semmans, the only ones in the tavern who could understand this Semmat conversation.

Alder looked seriously upset; Dogal was calmer, but eyeing Sterren suspiciously.

"I am not delaying," Sterren insisted.

"Then tell me, my lord, just how much longer we must remain here, and how many magicians you think to find."

"My lady Kalira, I've only just started! One hour in a . . . in one market is nothing! If we could find one magician I could be sure was powerful enough, that would be all we need; without that one, I think half a dozen might serve. To find the right ones, though — I have no way of knowing how long it will be!"

Lady Kalira sighed. "My lord Sterren, let us speak frankly," she said. "You know that despite your rank, I was sent here as your gaoler, to make sure that you did, in fact, return to Semma before the spring, when invasion is all but certain."

Sterren noticed Alder turn to stare at Lady Kalira as she said this; he had obviously not realized either that Sterren was still under suspicion by anyone but Dogal and himself, nor that an invasion was imminent.

"You have managed to lose four of the six men set to guard you, though I am not sure how . . ."

"They may come back," Sterren interrupted.

Lady Kalira held up a hand. "Yes, they may, but at present they are not here. Let me continue." She glared at him.

"Go on," Sterren said.

"As I was saying, you have very cleverly disposed of two-thirds of your escort already, and acquired two of the magicians you sought, to confuse matters and perhaps, for all we know, to deceive the two guards remaining. We have no very clear idea what you have been discussing with them throughout this meal, since we don't know Ethsharitic; you could have been planning your escape, with their connivance, under our very noses."

Sterren wished he had been bold enough to try it.

"Now, you are demanding an effectively unlimited opportunity to stroll about the city, looking for a chance to slip away and hide from us in a city you know far better than we could ever hope to. I am sorry, but as your unwilling gaoler, I can't allow it. We must set a term, at the end of which we will depart this place and sail homeward with all due speed. I would suggest that by noon tomorrow we be under way."

Sterren sat back and used a fingernail to pick the last remnants of his supper from between his teeth as he considered this.

"I see what you mean, my lady," he said at last, "and I truly do understand. I do not suppose that you would accept my word that I will not escape, or delay until it's too late." To his own surprise, he realized that he really would be willing to give his word, and that he would keep it, as he always had. Semma was not really as bad as all that, and the idea of his soldiers being slaughtered was not an appealing one. If he could just find the right magic, he was sure he could win the war. It was a challenge, a gamble, and he wanted to meet it head-on. He wanted to see if a little magic really *could* change a sure defeat into victory.

And after it was over, maybe *then* he could desert.

"No, my lord," she said, "I'm afraid I couldn't accept your word. After all, despite your noble ancestry, and your apparent good intentions, what are you really but a merchant's brat, brought up in the streets, accustomed to cheating at dice to earn your bread? How much honor can I expect from such as you?"

Sterren smiled wryly, to hide how much Lady Kalira's clinically-exact description hurt him. "More than you might think," he said. "But if you will not take my word, there is little I can do to make you believe me." He sighed. "Until noon, though, is not enough. If you could give me three days . . ."

He let his voice trail off.

"Three days?" It was her turn to sit back and consider.

"Today is the twenty-first of Snowfall," she said. "You will agree, then, that we must all be aboard ship by nightfall on the twenty-fourth, ready to set sail with the next tide?"

Sterren nodded. "Agreed," he said.

"You'll promise not to attempt escape?"

"You said that you can't accept my word, but all the same, I'll give it. I won't try to escape before nightfall on the twenty-fourth of Snowfall."

"All right," she said. "Three days, and then we drag you back to the ship."

Sixteen

By morning the month of Snowfall was living up to its name. It was snowing, and Sterren decided that Shiphaven Market was not going to be worth another visit. Instead, he left Annara and the warlock aboard ship while he, Lady Kalira, Alder, and Dogal all set out in the early gloom for the Arena and the Wizards' Quarter.

None of the other four soldiers had turned up yet, and that meant Lady Kalira was in a very bad temper. Sterren made no attempt at conversation as he led the way up Warehouse Street, through Shortcut Alley to North Street, and on out of Spicetown.

As they neared the Grand Canal, however, the overlord's palace gradually became visible ahead, and Sterren noticed all three Semmans staring at it.

They weren't being quite attentive enough to encourage escape, and besides, he had promised not to, but he did venture to remark, "Pretty, isn't it?"

"Is that where the wizards live?" Lady Kalira demanded.

Startled, Sterren said, "No, of course not! That's Lord Azrad's . . . ah . . . castle."

"How far to the magicians, then?"

"Well, North Street forks ahead and we go left on . . ." He hesitated, and then switched to using Ethsharitic for place names. ". . . on the *Promenade*, and then on the other side of the *Palace Plaza* we take *Arena Street*, and then it's about a mile to the *Arena*, I guess."

"You're joking!"

"No, I'm not."

"A *mile*?"

"About that."

"I will never get over the size of this city," Lady Kalira said, more to herself than to Sterren. "What a mess!"

Sterren did not consider his home city a mess, but he knew better than to say anything. They made the rest of the journey in silence.

The streets were almost empty because of the snow, and the city's normal odor was largely suppressed by the pale-gray blanket that covered the rooftops and most of the streets, but the scent of spices, wood-smoke, and charcoal was still strong. The mansions of the New City were silent and elegant, the snow hiding much of the damage time had done them; even the slums of the outer Arena district were quieter and less offensive in such weather.

They passed Camp Street, and then the Arena itself, and came to the plaza just south of the main entrance.

There, to the right of the rampway into the Arena, was the message-board that Sterren had remembered, a six-foot-high wall of rough pine planks weathered grey, fifteen feet long, plastered over its entire surface with faded and torn bits of paper, parchment, and fabric.

Sterren had written up his notice the night before, aboard ship, but he realized as he looked for a place to put it that he had not thought to bring any tacks or nails. With a shrug, he found a notice that had been attached with unusually long cut nails, announcing an estate auction that had taken place a sixnight before, and he rammed the corners of his own message over the blunt ends of the nails.

Satisfied, he read it over again.

"Magicians," it said in large letters at the top, and then continued in smaller writing below, "Employment opportunity for magicians of every school. The Kingdom of Semma is recruiting magicians for government service for a term of several months, but not to exceed one year. Room and board furnished, and transportation both ways, as well as payment in gold and gems. To apply, or for further information, contact Sterren, Ninth Warlord of Semma, aboard the *Southern Wind*, now docked at the Tea Wharves in Spicetown. Final application must be made by nightfall, 24 Snowfall, 5221."

He stepped back, and realized that his fine, big page was almost lost amid the jumble of paper and cloth.

There was, however, nothing he could do about it.

He looked at some of the other messages on the board, wondering what they were all about. One caught his eye immediately.

"Acclaimed prestidigitator seeks part-time employment. Leave message with Thorum the Mage, Wizard Street."

Sterren was unsure exactly what a prestidigitator was; some sort of magician, surely! "Part-time employment" — that wasn't exactly what he was offering, but still . . .

Thorum the Mage, he told himself, on Wizard Street. That wouldn't be too hard to find.

He was about to start looking for more notices when he was reminded of his companions by the sound of feet shuffling in the slush.

"*Hai*, you three," he said. "Come here and help me read these! Some of them are from magicians looking for work! I should have come here in the first place, instead of bothering with Shiphaven!"

Dogal shook his head. "I can't read," he said.

Lady Kalira and Alder started forward, but then Alder stopped. A moment later, as she got close enough to make out the messages, so did Lady Kalira.

"We can't read them, either," she said. "They're all in Ethsharitic."

"Well, of course they . . ." Sterren let his voice trail off as he realized that he was the only one present who could read

Ethsharitic. He turned back to the board and drew a deep breath, then let it out in a sigh.

"I'll read them, then," he said.

Two hours later he felt he had covered the board adequately. Snow, meanwhile, had attempted to cover Alder and Dogal; Lady Kalira had taken shelter in the arched entrance of the Arena.

"Doesn't this stuff *ever* stop falling?" Dogal asked.

"Of course it does!" Sterren retorted, instinctively leaping to the defense of his native city.

"And then what happens to it?" Alder asked. "What do you people do with it all?"

"Nothing; it melts, of course," Sterren said. "This isn't Sardiron, where it piles up all winter."

"Well, how would we know that?" Alder replied angrily, his temper obviously shortened by the long, cold wait.

"From experience, of course. Haven't you ever seen . . . seen it before?" He could not think of a Semmat word for "snow."

Alder and Dogal both stared at him, startled. "No, of course not!" Alder replied.

"How could we have seen it before?" Dogal asked.

It was Sterren's turn to be startled. "Oh," he said. "Doesn't it . . . I mean, don't you have this stuff in Semma?"

"No," Alder answered.

"It doesn't fall in the winter, like this?"

"No, it rains in the winter in Semma. We don't have snow."

Sterren noted the word for later use, and then dropped the subject. "Oh. Well, I have a dozen messages here from magicians looking for work, and I want to follow up on them, before I forget any names. Come on."

The "dozen" was actually fifteen, though there was some overlap in the message drops they used.

With much grumbling, the soldiers came. Lady Kalira emerged from the entryway and joined the party as Sterren led them back out to Arena Street and on to the southeast, toward the Wizards' Quarter.

Five blocks took them to Games Street, a thoroughfare that Sterren remembered well, even though he had rarely played there. The times when he tried it had all been remarkable enough to stay very clear in his memory.

And Games Street, of course, marked the line between the indeterminate streets between the Arena and the Wizards' Quarter, where various performing magicians made their homes, and the heart of the Wizards' Quarter proper, where virtually all the city's magic shops were clustered.

In fact, just one more block south on Arena brought them to Wizard Street. There was no marker, but it was unmistakable. "TANNA the Great," advertised a signboard at the corner, "Wizardry for Every Need, Love Charms a Specialty." Peculiar odors mixed with the inevitable smell of woodsmoke — the city's famous spices had been left behind a mile to the north, but here there were strange new scents that might have been spices, or herbs, or something else entirely.

Two doors down on the right was a signboard announcing the presence of Thorum the Mage, which was one of the names Sterren had memorized. He headed directly for it.

Two hours later they took a break for a midday meal, and bought bits of beef fried in dough from an open-front shop between two gambling halls on Games Street. They ate in silence, leaning against a wall, as snow drifted by and Sterren, between bites, considered what he had learned.

For one thing, he now knew what a prestidigitator was — little more than a charlatan, really. A great deal of magic appeared to be fraudulent. Never having had money to spend on spells and amulets, he had never had occasion to find this out.

Other magic, of course, was completely real and authentic and could be enormously powerful.

Unfortunately, while the frauds would often work cheap, for the more serious magicians a pound of gold would not pay for a sixnight's work, let alone the month or more that might be necessary for a trip to Semma and back with a war in the middle.

He had been turned down by two witches, two theurgists, a wizard, a warlock, and someone who called himself a thaumaturge, a term Sterren was not familiar with.

On the other hand, he had turned down a prestidigitator, an illusionist, a sorcerer whose talents seemed genuine but hopelessly inappropriate for the job at hand, and an herbalist.

Not all of these were from the advertisements at the Arena; the theurgists and the sorcerer had turned up on their own while Sterren and his party were discussing matters with Thorum the Mage, a pleasant old fellow who, thanks to his central location, made a significant income as a message center and referral service, in addition to what his wizardry brought him.

The morning, Sterren had to admit, had been a washout. He chewed his last bite of dough, pulled his coat collar tighter, and stared longingly through the snow at a dicegame visible through a tavern window on the opposite side of the street.

He wished that he could just go back to playing dice, and thinking entirely in his native tongue, without having to switch languages every few minutes, without worrying about wars or wizards or warlords or warlocks, hereditary duties and summary executions. He wanted to forget that

Semma had ever existed, forget that he had ever met any of the inhabitants of that silly little kingdom.

He couldn't, of course. Semma was real, and somehow or other he had the misfortune to be its warlord now, rather than just a tavern gambler.

Joining that game across the street was a tremendous temptation, but a glance at Lady Kalira's sour expression convinced him that it wasn't even worth asking if he could take a few minutes to replenish their finances.

He sighed, swallowed the last traces of his meal, and said, "Come on."

The three Semmans looked at him, uncomprehending.

"Oh, come on," he said, in Semmat this time.

They came.

Seventeen

The afternoon was more successful than the morning. For one thing, the snow stopped and the sun came out, which improved tempers all around.

For another, the neighborhood grapevine was working for them now, and when they checked back in at Thorum's they found a young witch, eager for adventure in foreign lands and willing to work cheap.

Another cooperative and promising witch turned up a few stops later, and then a sorcerer by the name of Kolar, whose collection of talismans included a few that clearly had some military usefulness — and, fortunately for Sterren, not all that much commercial value, so that Kolar was willing to accept Sterren's offered job.

All three of these individuals were instructed to report to the chartered ship, the *Southern Wind*, by midday on the twenty-fourth.

At the next stop an argument broke out. The magician in question here was ready and willing to take the job, but Lady Kalira recognized the emblem she wore at her throat.

"She's a demonologist!" she said. "We can't take a demonologist!"

"Why not?" Sterren demanded. "She can probably do more for us than the rest put together! Demons *love* war! They created it!"

"And that's one reason that using a demonologist is too dangerous!" the Semman aristocrat shouted.

"That's ridiculous!"

"It is *not* . . ." Lady Kalira began; then she caught herself, and continued with enforced calm, "It is not ridiculous, my lord Sterren. And in any case, the reasons do not matter. If I might remind you, His Majesty specifically forbade the inclusion of sorcerers or demonologists. Are you going to defy a royal edict? Might I point out that the penalty for doing so is entirely up to the king's discretion, even to beheading, for a member of the nobility?"

Sterren opened his mouth to argue, and then stopped.

Phenvel III was more than a little foolish, and prone to whims. For all Sterren knew, he really might order Sterren's execution if he was angry enough, and only think better of it after it was too late.

And he *had* specifically forbidden demonologists and sorcerers.

Sterren had forgotten that for a moment. He had not made the connection when he hired Kolar — Kolar the Sorcerer.

"Oh, damn," he said.

He apologized to the demonologist, a woman by the name of Amanelle of Tirissa, and led the way back to the house where Kolar rented an upstairs room.

When that little problem was dealt with, Sterren continued with his search.

When the sun was below the rooftops and the shopkeepers began lighting the torches out front, he called it a day and headed back toward Spicetown, the Semmans trailing along behind him.

He didn't even think about trying to slip away. The quest for magicians had caught his interest.

It was full dark well before they reached the wharves, and Sterren had to ask directions twice before locating the *Southern Wind*. He was asleep within seconds of falling into his hammock.

That was the twenty-second of Snowfall.

On the twenty-third, once again, the day was spent in the Wizards' Quarter, recruiting. Word had gotten around, however, and this time Sterren was able to sit at Thorum's table, drinking cheap ale and making jokes with old Thorum about the Semman barbarians he was saddled with, while candidates presented themselves.

The Semmans sat idly by, wondering what Sterren and the fat old wizard found so funny.

The weather was warmer, too, and the snow had melted away completely by mid-afternoon.

Even the now-familiar walk back to the ship seemed easier, especially since Sterren took care to set out well before dark. Lady Kalira brightened considerably when she discovered Alar aboard the vessel, waiting for her, apologetic about both his own extended absence and having completely lost track of Kendrik, Bern, and Zander.

Sterren thought he was a fool for coming back, but did not say so.

Sterren did not bother to leave the ship on the twenty-fourth, but instead began the preparations for the journey back to Akalla of the Diamond.

He had found no chance to slip away, and he was not at all sure he would have taken it if he had. Princess Lura's grin and Shirrin's blush lurked in the back of his memory, and he did not want to leave them defenseless.

When the ship sailed on the evening tide, she had aboard her Sterren, Lady Kalira, Alder, Dogal, and Alar, of the original party of eight; the other three had never turned up. Sterren hoped that they would get by, stranded in a foreign city where they didn't speak the language or know the customs. They had chosen to desert, but they had not necessarily known what they were getting into; life in Ethshar was much more complex than their simple existence back in Semma.

Perhaps, he thought. Alar was not such a fool after all.

In addition to Sterren and the four Semmans, the *Southern Wind* carried the warlock, who had still not given a name; Annara, the journeyman wizard; three witches, named Shenna of Chatna, Ederd of Eastwark, and Hamder Hamder's son; and a wizard who called himself Emner of Lamum. All but the warlock were young, beginners who had not yet found places for themselves, though none of the others were quite so young as Annara and Sterren himself.

Sterren had turned down assorted frauds and charlatans, and given in to the royal fiat against sorcerers and demonologists; he had talked to several theurgists, only to be told that they could not help with anything to which the gods objected as strongly as they objected to war. No other warlocks had turned up once the amount of the pay was known. A few of the more obscure or minor sorts of magician had turned up, such as oneiromancers and herbalists, but after much discussion had not stayed.

Still, Sterren had half a dozen assorted magicians.

He hoped it would be enough.

He wished he knew more about magic.

He *did* know a little, of course. He had taken an interest in the arcane arts as a child.

It was only a little, though, not much more than a few characteristics of the major varieties.

He knew something more than a minimum about warlockry, of course, from his brief stay with old Bergan. He knew it used no spells or incantations, but only the warlock's will, to guide and shape the Power it drew upon. The only differences between what one warlock could do, and what another could do, depended on the relative level of imagination and expertise in manipulating Power.

The other magicks did not appear to operate that way at all. For example, theurgists and demonologists used rote formulae to summon superhuman beings, as Agor had explained to him, and those beings were specialized and individual.

To a warlock, Power was Power, at least until the nightmares began, and there were no formulae — or at least, so Bergan had told him, and Sterren had no reason to doubt his old master.

That meant that Sterren's warlock would be able to do as much as *any* warlock in waging war; there were no special spells or formulae he had to know.

Wizards, on the other hand, carried formulae to bizarre extremes; where theurgists and demonologists just used words and songs and signs, wizards needed an incredible assortment of ingredients for their spells — dragon's blood and virgin's tears and so forth. Wizardry seemed to have no logic to it whatsoever.

And Sterren, accordingly, had no idea at all what his two wizards were capable of. Annara had a small pouch of precious ingredients for her spells; Emner had a large travelling case jammed full of jars and boxes for his. Neither would specify what spells he or she could perform. A demonstration would be meaningless; spells that proved beyond doubt that their wizardry was authentic and powerful would not mean that they knew any spells that would stop Ophkar or Ksinallion.

Witches fell somewhere in between. Witches used rituals, chants, trances, and so forth, but could improvise them apparently at will, and did not require the arcane substances that wizardry called for. Witches had individual spells, but seemed to be able to modify them far more readily than wizards could. They had specialties, but almost any witch could tackle almost any piece of witchcraft — though naturally, a specialist in a given field could outperform a novice.

Witchcraft was versatile and adaptable — but limited. It

just didn't do anything as impressive as the other magicks. No witch ever moved a mountain or flattened a city — but wizards had reportedly done both. Warlocks could call up storms, shatter walls, strike foes dead with a glance, set the very ground ablaze; wizards seemed to be able to do absolutely anything if they could find the proper spell; but witches were far more limited. A witch could light a fire in an instant, but only in a proper fuel. A witch could open a locked door, but not shatter one. A witch could predict a storm, but not bring one.

What use his three witches would be in battle Sterren was not quite sure, but he thought they would be far better than any ordinary warriors.

Sorcerers, with their prepared talismans that could be used instantly, seemed much like wizards, though perhaps a little less impressive. He wondered what Phenvel had against them.

Herbalists might be very useful if the war was lost, for treating the wounded, but unless one were to poison Ophkar's water supply, Sterren could not see much use for an herbalist in battle. the various other specialties likewise seemed too narrow in scope. What good was an oneiromancer, for example, if nobody happened to have any dreams?

So he had his three witches, his two wizards, and his nameless warlock, and ninety-three fighting men.

He hoped it would be enough.

After all, his life depended on it.

Part Two

War

Eighteen

Sterren stood shivering beside the right-hand draft horse and stared miserably through the rain and gloom at the distant glow of the campfires and the looming black shape of Semma Castle. The mare's breath puffed up in clouds from her nostrils, and Sterren could smell her sweat. Raindrops pattered heavily on the old wagon that he had bought in Akalla, on the driver's seat he had just abandoned and on the hooded heads of the six magicians huddled in the back. The four Semmans, on their own mounts, were clustered nearby.

"I thought they'd wait until spring," he said again.

Lady Kalira replied, "We all did. They always waited before." Her tone was flat and dead. Sterren was grateful that she was not castigating him for refusing to buy a storm to speed their journey; it was bad enough that he was cursing himself for it.

"I guess one of their warlords must have as little respect for tradition as I do," he said resignedly.

"Or maybe," Alder suggested, "they heard you were gone and figured that it would be a good time to attack, when you weren't there to lead us."

"More likely they found out he was fetching these damned magicians, and they wanted to take the castle before they could get here," Dogal muttered.

Sterren ignored that, and tried to think what to do.

A selfish part of him suggested turning around and heading back to Akalla. After all, through no fault of his own he had been cut off from the castle and its defenders. If he left, who could say he had failed in his duty?

He glanced up at Lady Kalira, sitting astride her horse.

She could, for one, and he could accuse himself, as well. He had gone and fetched magicians to fight his war; well, here he was, here were his magicians, and here was the war — a little sooner than he had expected, perhaps, but so what?

All he had to do was figure out how to use the magicians he had hired. He had to at least make the attempt after coming this far, he told himself.

If he tried and failed, if the castle fell anyway, then he could flee in good conscience, and even Lady Kalira could not fault him.

First, though, he had to try to defeat the enemy.

But how was he supposed to do that with his six sorry magicians?

"What do we do now?" Annara called from the wagon in Ethsharitic, echoing his own thoughts. She glanced at the deserted farmhouse off to the party's left, as if expecting monsters to leap from it at any minute.

"Are you sure it's really the enemy besieging the castle, and not just a festival of some sort?" one of the witches asked in the same tongue; Sterren did not see if it was Hamder or Ederd, and could not yet distinguish them by voice.

He did not bother to reply to the witch, but after a moment he told Annara, "That's up to you people. This is what I hired you for, after all — to fight this stupid war. I'd say that your first job is to break the siege." He did not say *how*, of course, since he didn't have the faintest idea how to go about it.

"In the *rain*?" Shenna of Chatna wailed.

The other two witches shushed her.

"Don't tell me to shut up!" she shouted. "I'm cold and I'm wet and I don't like this place and I wish I'd never come here!"

Hamder and Ederd exchanged unhappy glances; then Ederd, in the rear of the wagon and out of Shenna's sight, raised his hands in a curious embracing gesture.

Shenna abruptly fell silent, but her expression was still one of abject misery.

The Semmans watched all this uncomprehendingly; none of them had picked up much Ethsharitic in the twelve days of the return voyage, and the magicians had not had time to learn much Semmat. All six magicians had preferred relying on Sterren as their translator to struggling with the unfamiliar tongue, and as a result he now saw the wisdom of Lady Kalira's ban on Ethsharitic during his own first voyage south. He had been forced to learn Semmat in order to make himself understood; the magicians were picking up a few words — at least, some of them were — but only as a sideline, not as a matter of survival.

Forbidding the crew to speak Ethsharitic, or refusing to use it himself, would not have made much difference, since the six magicians had each other to talk to. Besides, he hadn't noticed the problem until after they reached Akalla of the Diamond. Once he *had* noticed, he had thought he could safely leave it until the party reached Semma Castle.

And now, of course, it was too late, and they might never reach the castle at all.

He had just said that breaking the siege, if siege it actually was, was up to the magicians. Shenna's outburst, however, had not been followed by any suggestions from any of the others. They were all waiting for him to tell them what to do.

He suppressed a sigh. What had he done, he wondered, to deserve this? Why did *he* have to be in charge?

Sterren observed the witches silently for a moment, then beckoned to Hamder.

The young witch clambered over the side of the wagon, dropped to the mud, and splashed over to the shelter of the farmhouse eaves. Sterren joined him there.

"Witches can read minds, can't they?" Sterren asked.

Hamder hesitated. "Sometimes," he admitted.

"Well, right there two leagues ahead of us are a few hundred minds, I'd say, and I'd like to know what some of them are thinking and planning. I'd like to be sure just who we're facing, for one thing; is that both Ophkar and Ksinallion there, or did one of them decide to get the jump on the other? If one of them tried a sneak attack, then maybe we can swing the other over to our side after all, despite King Phenvel."

Hamder looked distinctly unhappy. "My lord Sterren . . ." he began.

"Oh, forget the 'lord' stuff, when we're speaking Ethsharitic!" Sterren interrupted. He had grown accustomed to hearing the title in Semmat, but it still sounded silly in Ethsharitic.

"Yes, my . . . yes, sir. As I was saying, I doubt I'll be able to learn much. None of those people out there are going to be thinking in Ethsharitic."

Sterren stared at him. "*Thinking* in Ethsharitic?"

"Yes, sir. After all, people do tend to think in words, or at least the same concepts that we use words for, and those are different in different languages."

"So you can't read minds unless you know the right language?"

Hamder nodded, then stopped himself. "Well, there are exceptions. If you're up close to someone, and paying close attention, you can usually start to pick up the underlying concepts after awhile. In fact, that's how we witches learn other languages so quickly . . ."

"You learn other languages quickly?"

"Of course! Witches are famous for the gift of tongues!"

"I haven't heard you speaking Semmat."

Hamder's mouth opened, then closed. "Oh," he said. After a moment's pause, he asked, "Were we supposed to? I didn't think there was any hurry."

"It might have been nice," Sterren pointed out. "I don't particularly enjoy translating back and forth for everybody, especially when I don't know Semmat all that well myself, yet."

"Oh." Hamder was obviously embarrassed. "I'm sorry, sir."

"Never mind that." Sterren brushed it away. "Can you tell me anything about whoever's around all those campfires, or can't you?"

"I . . . I . . . I don't know, sir. Probably not, from this distance."

"You have my permission to go closer, witch."

Hamder glanced at the distant campfires, then back at Sterren. "Ah . . . could it wait until morning? They're liable to be a bit nervous at night . . ."

Sterren sighed. "They're presumably fighting a war; they're liable to be a bit nervous any time. But never mind, at least for now." He started to turn away, then paused.

"The other witches — I assume that they would give me the same answers?"

"I think so, sir — but I can't be certain. We do have our specialties."

Sterren nodded and waved in dismissal. Hamder sloshed away, back to the wagon; Sterren stayed where he was and gestured for Emner, his second wizard, to join him.

Emner slid from the wagon and slogged up beside him.

"You're a wizard, right?"

Emner nodded, cautiously.

"Wizardry can do just about anything, right?"

"Given the right conditions, the right materials, and the right spell," Emner replied judiciously, "wizardry appears to be capable of *almost* anything."

"But you, yourself, are limited in what you can do, I suppose."

"Yes," Emner answered immediately. "Very limited."

Sterren nodded. "Over there," he said, waving an arm in the direction of Semma Castle, "it appears that there is a hostile army besieging the castle that I hired you to defend. I don't *know* what the situation is, but that's how it appears. Is there anything you can do about it?"

Emner considered this carefully. He gazed thoughtfully at the distant campfires, then looked up at the sky. He moistened a finger and held it up to check the wind, then scanned the eastern horizon.

"I don't know," he said, finally. "I know a few spells I thought would be useful in a war, but I don't see how any would help in the present situation. If the wind were behind us, I could levitate and drift over that way, with a magical shield under me in case I were spotted, to see what's happening — but the wind's awfully light, and from the north, and I'd need to go east. I don't have a spell for directional flight. I know a spell that can stun a man, and make him somewhat suggestible, so that if we could catch someone alone I might well coax truth from even a reluctant tongue, but I can't think . . . Hmm . . ." His voice trailed off.

Sterren waited patiently, and after a pause Emner continued, "I have another spell. I never thought it would be any help, but it might serve here, after all. I can make a stone or a stick whistle, from a distance — hardly a valuable talent, I'd have said, and I certainly chafed at being forced to practice it as an apprentice. Now, though — perhaps I can lure someone over with a whistle, stun him, and question him."

Sterren nodded, considering. "You're sure you can do that?"

Emner hesitated, then said, "Reasonably sure."

"Could Annara do it?"

"No." Emner did not hesitate at all this time.

"Why not?" Sterren asked, genuinely curious.

Emner blinked, and then slowly replied, "I am not sure it's my place to say."

"Oh, go ahead," Sterren said, annoyed.

Emner paused, as if thinking out his words in advance, and then said, "I suppose you know that Annara had been sleeping out in the Hundred-Foot Field, and hadn't eaten for two or three days when you found her."

"I suspected as much," Sterren acknowledged.

"Well, it's so," Emner said. "She told me, as a fellow Guild member. Naturally, I was curious about how she came to be reduced to that, and she was glad to have a chance to discuss her situation with a fellow wizard. It seems that although she is a true wizard, and served the full apprenticeship required by the Guild, and was initiated into the Guild's mysteries, she never managed to master more than a handful of simple spells. Her master only knew a dozen or so, and she found herself unable to manage some of those — including the ones that provided most of his small income. The spells she *did* learn — well, they're real enough, and they have their places, but they aren't exactly *marketable*. There isn't any demand for them, as a rule. And I can't see how they could be of any use at all in the present situation."

"You didn't think your own could help, at first. Perhaps I should ask Annara directly; after all, she's surely more familiar with the possibilities of her magic than you are."

Emner shrugged. "Maybe. We've agreed to trade spells, and better both our positions, but to be honest, I think I agreed to that as much from pity as from my own self-interest. Her spells . . . Well, for instance, what use is there to an invisibility spell that only works on transparent objects?"

"Transparent objects?"

"Yes, transparent. Water, ice, glass, and so on."

Sterren nodded. "I see your point. It's an interesting idea, though, that invisibility spell. What if you were to make weapons out of glass, and then enchant them?"

Emner considered that. "I'm not sure how it works, but you're right, that might be interesting. Hard to parry a glass sword, I suppose — but easy to break one."

"I was thinking of glass arrows. You wouldn't know where they're coming from."

Emner nodded slowly.

"Well," Sterren said, after a moment's silent thought, "that's not doing us any good right now, is it? We don't have a glassmaker's oven at hand. Thank you for your help, wizard, and if you would go back and send me the warlock, I'd appreciate it."

Emner bowed slightly in acknowledgement, then trotted back to the wagon and hauled himself back aboard.

A moment later the warlock strode up beside Sterren. He wore a heavy black cloak and hood against the rain, and had it pulled well forward, hiding his face completely. Sterren found himself speaking to an oval of black shadow.

"How do you feel?" he asked.

"Terrible," the warlock replied, through clenched teeth.

"Oh?" The warlock had been complaining of head-aches and constant fatigue since the third day aboard ship. He had also taken to sleeping long hours — he was always the first to retire at night, and the last to awaken. The morning after leaving Akalla he had had to be hoisted into the wagon still half asleep, and had almost fallen out twice since then.

But at least, Sterren thought, there had been no sign of nightmares.

"My head feels like it's going to burst."

"Oh." Sterren made a sympathetic noise. "Ah . . . are you aware of the situation here?"

"No."

Sterren waited for a moment, expecting him to go on.

"No?" he said at last.

"No. Should I be?"

"I think so, yes."

"All right, then, what's the situation?"

"Well, over there is Semma Castle, which is what we all came here to defend. And all around it there appear to be campfires, and what look like tents, sentries, siege machinery, and so forth. What's more, judging by this house behind us, and the others we passed in the last league or two, the peasants in the area appear to have fled their homes. I would assume that what we see here are the armies of Ophkar and Ksinallion, besieging the castle, but I am not actually certain of that. I called you up here in hopes you might be able to help me settle the matter."

"You want to know if those are really the armies you think they are?"

Sterren nodded. "That's right."

The warlock snorted. "How the hell should I know?" he demanded.

"You're a warlock, aren't you?" Sterren asked calmly.

"That's right, I'm a warlock — I'm not a damned mind-reading witch, or a wizard with a scrying spell, or a sorcerer with a crystal ball, or a theurgist with a god whispering my ear, or even a demonologist with an imp to run my errands!

I can *do* things — or I could back in Ethshar, anyway — but I don't have any way of knowing any more about what's out there than you do."

"Do you have any way of finding out? Could you fly over and take a look around, perhaps?"

The warlock was silent for a long moment, the only sounds the patter of the rain and the snuffling of the horses a dozen paces away.

"I don't know," he said at last. "I know how to fly, certainly, but I'm so *weak* here . . ." He took two steps away, and then stood, arms raised, hood thrown back, face up.

He seemed to shudder, from his head right down to his muddy boots; his cloak flapped suddenly, although there was no more wind than a moment before.

Then he toppled over backward into the mud.

Sterren hesitated, then decided against lending aid.

The warlock got to his feet under his own power, then glared at Sterren and shook his head.

"No," he said, "I can't fly here."

Sterren nodded. "All right," he said. He turned back to face the rest of the party, where the others had watched the warlock's pratfall in puzzled silence.

"We'll stay here until morning!" he called, first in Ethsharitic, and then in Semmat, pointing at the empty farmhouse.

"Then what?" Lady Kalira called back to him.

Sterren glanced over his shoulder at the dozens of campfires that ringed the castle. "Then we find out who those people are," he said.

"And if they're the enemy?" Lady Kalira demanded.

"Then," said Sterren, "we attack!"

Nineteen

Shenna's shriek awoke Sterren from a sound slumber; he sat up quickly, looking around for the source of the scream.

Everyone else was roused as well, and the other two witches reached her first. After an exchange too quick for spoken words, Hamder turned and called, "Sterren! Shenna says that someone was prowling around the house we're in, and saw us!"

Sterren was still not really thinking. "Who was it?" he asked.

"I don't know!" Shenna replied. "I didn't see him."

"Then how do you know he was there?" Annara asked.

"I had wards set, and he tripped one, wizard!"

"Well, if he didn't know we were here before, he certainly does now, the way you screamed," Emner said.

Ederd and Hamder frowned at that; Shenna chose to ignore it. Sterren said nothing, but mentally filed it away for future reference that the witches and the wizards did not appear to like each other much. He wasn't sure if it was a personal matter, or something inherent in the two arcane disciplines.

"Did anyone else have any wards, or other spells, set to warn us of intruders?" Sterren asked.

"I don't even know what wards *are*," Annara announced.

"I wouldn't brag of it," Ederd snapped.

Sterren raised a hand for silence, just as Lady Kalira demanded in Semmat, "What's going on?"

"The witch . . . her magic heard something," he said.

Alder, who had been watching the magicians, heard this and immediately headed for the nearest window, approaching it carefully, then peering around the frame, out into the rain.

Dogal took a window on the opposite side, and after a moment Alar headed for the door. The fourth side of the room was the wall separating the main room from the kitchen; the warlock, seeing what the soldiers were doing, slid quickly through the curtained doorway, presumably to look out the kitchen window.

"There's someone running off toward the castle," Dogal announced. "A soldier, I guess — he's wearing a red kilt and a sword, anyway."

"What army?" Sterren asked.

Startled, Dogal replied, "How should I know?"

Sterren, not fully awake even yet, could not think of a Semmat word for "recognize" or "identify," so after a moment's mental fumbling he just said, "What uniform?" He had certainly had to learn *that* word in order to function as warlord.

"I can't tell Ophkar from Ksinallion," Dogal said, "or from Shan on the Desert or anywhere else, for that matter. It's not Semman, though."

Alder had crossed the room during this exchange, and was squinting after the fleeing figure. Lady Kalira came up behind Dogal, as well.

"Looks Ksinallionese to me," Alder said. Lady Kalira nodded agreement.

"Not Semman?"

"Oh, no," all three agreed. "Not Semman!"

Sterren sighed. "We'd better get out of here, then," he said.

Nobody argued, and in five minutes the party had collected its belongings and retired to the porch, where the horses were waiting.

In another five, the Semmans were all mounted, the

draft horses were hitched up, and Sterren and the magicians were all settled in the wagon, moving unhappily out of their shelter into the thin morning drizzle.

"Which way?" Hamder asked.

That, Sterren had to admit, was a very good question. With a shrug, he pointed north. "That way," he said. He shook the reins, and the wagon led the way across a muddy brown cornfield.

After a few minutes he reined in his horses and held up a hand to signal the Semman outriders. They gathered into a little knot at the center of what was probably a pasture in the summer, but was now mostly more mud.

The others all stared at him expectantly, hunching against the thin misty rain.

Sterren hesitated, unsure of what to say.

"Well," he said at last, in Ethsharitic, "here we are in Semma, and that's the Ksinallionese army over there, and maybe the Ophkarite army as well. Your job is to drive them out of Semma. Go right ahead."

The magicians glanced at one another, then back at Sterren, for a long moment before Hamder asked, "How?"

"How should I know?" Sterren said, irritated. "You're the magicians, with all your secrets."

"But you're the warlord," Annara pointed out, "and you're the boss; you hired us, now tell us what to do."

Sterren had dreaded this, and here it was. "I don't know anything about it," he said. "I was forced into this stupid job, and I don't know any more about fighting a war than you people do."

"In that case," Hamder said, "I think we may all be in very serious trouble."

"Why don't we just go home?" Shenna asked. "We can't do anything here! Look at all those people!"

In point of fact, the besieging armies were invisible from

where Sterren's party happened to be at that moment, but nobody bothered to correct her. Sterren had told them, on board ship, that they would be facing armies totalling about four hundred and fifty men.

"Not a one of those soldiers," Sterren pointed out, "knows anything about magic. Not one! They've probably never even seen any magic; it's all scarce as fish fur in this part of the world!"

"Well, we aren't exactly Fendel the Great," Annara retorted.

"No, but you're magicians, and you all agreed to come here and fight this war. Now, let's fight it! You, Emner, last night you were telling me you could levitate, and that you have a shield spell and a way of dazing people?"

"Felshen's First Hypnotic Spell," Emner replied, "and Tracel's Levitation, and Fendel's Elementary Protection. But I'll still just be one man against an army, and Felshen's won't kill anyone, or make them give up the fight. I can harass them, I suppose, but . . ."

"But nothing!" Sterren interrupted. "You're forgetting the effect it will have on their morale to have a genuine wizard attacking them! These soldiers have never conceived of using magic to fight a war; you'll terrify them!"

Emner looked doubtful.

Sterren was growing desperate. "Listen, I don't expect you to destroy an army overnight, but this *is* what you all agreed to do, what you came here for, the reason we fed you all and transported you here and even clothed some of you." (Annara had owned only a single tattered purple robe; Lady Kalira had provided her with a decent change of outfit while aboard ship, so that she could clean and repair the gown, with fabric, thread, and needle provided by Lady Kalira. She was wearing her own purple again at the moment, but she knew who Sterren meant.) "I think you'll find that it's not as hard as you expect. Remember, it's not just the eleven of us here; we have an army of our own inside that castle over there, with three fine officers who I'm sure will take advantage of any opportunity we give them." Sterren was not at all certain of anything of the sort, and actually expected his three officers to fumble every opportunity, but he knew better than to admit that. "Those people in the castle, hundreds of them, including dozens of innocent women and children, are depending on us!"

That was most likely true; he could easily picture Princess Shirrin, watching from the castle windows for the triumphant return of her warlord hero. She probably expected him to ride up on a white charger, banners flying and trumpets sounding, rather than driving a battered Akallan haywagon.

"I can set some traps," Annara admitted grudgingly. "At least, while my supplies hold out. I'll need some wax. And parchment, if you have any."

"There!" Sterren said. "That's more like it!" He looked at the others expectantly.

"If one of these witches or the warlock can push me once I'm airborne, I can levitate and go see what's happening, or take messages into the castle," Emner said.

The witches glanced at each other, but it was the warlock who said, "I ought to be able to manage that much. You're weightless when you levitate, aren't you?"

"Well, not really, not with Tracel's," Emner admitted. "There's another levitation spell that makes you weightless, but I never got the hang of it."

"Well, I can try it, anyway," the warlock said.

"We can probably help," Hamder volunteered, "as long as you're in sight."

"You can do a test run," Sterren suggested.

That elicited a round of nods.

"We can . . . well, *I* can pick off enemy soldiers, strangle them at a distance, if we can find them away from the main camp," Ederd said.

"Or drop rocks on them," Hamder said.

Shenna wrinkled her nose in disgust, then admitted, "I can poison their water. Without touching it. I think." She hesitated, and then repeated, "I *think*. It's a lot easier to just make their food go bad, if you can find out where they keep it and it's not sealed in anything."

All eyes fell on the warlock, who shrugged and said, "I don't know how much I can do, here, but I'll do what I can. Strangling from a distance — I might be able to do that. Easier, for me, to just stop hearts."

A moment of uneasy silence followed this announcement.

"There!" Sterren said, breaking it. "You see? This shouldn't be as bad as all that! There's a lot we can do, and they won't have any way to fight it, or even know what's going on!"

A couple of the magicians nodded glumly. Nobody argued. Nobody displayed any enthusiasm, either.

Sterren decided to settle for what he could get. Enthusiasm might come later. A lack of resistance was enough to start with.

"What's going on?" Lady Kalira asked, in Semmat.

Sterren sighed and told her.

Twenty

Two days later, in a barn roughly a mile and a half northwest of Semma Castle, two of the witches were straining, watching or listening or using some other sense Sterren couldn't guess at. The Semmans and the other magicians were waiting for something to happen. For himself, Sterren didn't expect to know anything about it until the witches told him.

Both witches started suddenly, but that was nothing very new. They often reacted to unseen events while in perceptive trances.

Even with that warning, the bang a second or so later came as a complete surprise. Sterren had been quite sure he wouldn't hear it.

For that matter, he hadn't expected the spell to work. Annara had been so very pessimistic about her abilities ever since he first met her that he had, he realized, given up on ever getting any use out of her.

He glanced over at her, and she looked as surprised as he felt. "Gods!" she said, "I made it as big as I could, but that must have been *huge*!"

Sterren had to agree with that. According to what the witches had gleaned from the minds of passing soldiers, Sterren and his band were presently almost a mile from the Ophkarite warlord's tent, and that was where the false message had presumably gone. An explosion that could be heard for a mile would have to be much larger than what they had expected.

Ederd suddenly emerged from his trance. "I thought you'd like to know," he said without preamble, "we just killed the general's secretary — I mean, the warlord's. We didn't get the warlord himself."

"*Killed* him?" Annara squeaked.

Ederd nodded. "You don't want the details," he said, "but I'm sure he's dead. Didn't hit anybody else, though, and although there were plenty of sparks, the tent didn't catch."

Sterren looked at Annara with new respect. "Good work," he said.

"But the Explosive Seal isn't supposed to *kill* anybody!" she protested. "At worst, it's intended to . . . well, to blow their hands off. Usually it just burns them a little."

"Well, maybe you got something wrong, then," Sterren suggested.

"I don't think so," Ederd replied. "He was holding the parchment up to his face, studying the seal. I think he suspected something."

"Oh . . ." Annara looked sick.

"What's going on?" Alder asked, in Semmat.

"We just killed the . . . the . . . a helper to the Warlord of Ophkar," Sterren told him.

"Helper?"

"The man who writes and reads for him."

"His aide?"

"I guess so."

Alder grinned broadly. "Well, it's a start," he said.

"This magic may do some good after all," Dogal admitted grudgingly.

Sterren nodded, but he doubted that they would be able to use that particular stunt again. The enemy was warned.

Well, maybe they would find other ways to use the Explosive Seal. Could it be put on tent-flaps, perhaps? Or saddles, to detonate when the cavalry unsaddled their horses?

And could the enemy really afford to ignore sealed messages?

They hadn't ignored this one. Hamder's witchcraft had convinced the sentries that he was telling the truth, despite the total lack of confirmation; they had accepted him as an Ophkarite courier despite his lack of uniform, his unfamiliarity with the Ophkaritic language, and the fact that he had approached, on foot, from entirely the wrong direction. Even though he had only been able to pick a dozen or so words of the language from their minds, he had managed to make them absolutely certain that the parchment they accepted was an urgent message from the king of Ophkar that must be delivered to their warlord immediately.

Not a bad stunt at all, and Sterren had made sure Hamder knew how impressed everyone was. He regretted that Hamder wasn't in the main room to thank again.

And now Annara had come through, as well; Sterren had not expected the seal to do any real damage.

He hoped that Emner and Hamder would be equally successful.

Even as that thought crossed his mind, Shenna dropped out of her trance and announced, "Hamder's bringing the wizard back, but I don't know why."

Sterren answered, "Thanks. I'll go ask."

He got up from the floor, brushed himself off, ambled across the room, and mounted the ladder to the hayloft.

Hamder was sitting cross-legged in the open loft door, staring fixedly out toward the castle. Sterren looked over his shoulder and saw a small black dot growing larger in the distance.

"What's happening?" he asked.

The witch ignored him. Sterren glanced down just as Hamder's breath came out all in a rush, and he toppled over sideways into the hay.

"I can't do it any more," he said in a breathy whisper.

Sterren could see, now, that Hamder had completely

exhausted himself. He leaned forward and peered at the distant figure of Emner, drifting helplessly above the enemy armies.

"Maybe the warlock can fetch him back," he said.

Hamder had no breath to reply, but he managed a feeble nod.

Sterren turned and clambered back down the ladder, then headed for the corner where he had last seen the warlock.

The black-robed Ethsharite was still there, crouched down and muttering to himself. He did not glance up as Sterren approached.

"We have a problem," Sterren said. "Emner's drifting out there, and Hamder's exhausted."

The warlock shook his head, then winced; it was obvious he had another of his headaches. "Get one of the other witches," he said. "I've been experimenting; I can't move anything as massive as a person, not even when he's levitating."

"They're busy; are you sure?"

The warlock looked up at Sterren, then rose to his feet. "Do you have any string?" he asked.

"I don't know," Sterren replied. "Why?"

"Because if you did, I might be able to lift one end of it up to him, and he could just pull himself in with it. But I know what I can do, and I can't move him. You'll need to get one of the other witches."

Sterren sighed, and went to get one of the other witches.

That trick with the string, though — that might be useful. He wanted to remember that.

He sighed again, remembering the high hopes he had had for his warlock. The fellow was turning out to be pitifully feeble. He could levitate a few pounds at a time, light small fires, open locks — but that was about it, and he was almost constantly sick with his ferocious headaches.

The headaches worried Sterren somewhat. He had never heard of warlocks getting headaches. Ordinarily, warlocks were the epitome of health and vigor, able to heal themselves, able to obliterate any diseases that attacked them, drawing strength from the Power — at least, until the nightmares started. Even then, they stayed physically healthy, except perhaps for some minor adverse effects of not sleeping.

The nightmares had stopped for this one, but the mysterious headaches might well be worse than the nightmares. Since the headaches had started the warlock even seemed to have more grey in his hair.

Sterren had heard of warlocks who fled south when the nightmares began, but he had never heard anything about headaches.

Shenna was back in trance, but Ederd was taking a break, leaning back against a pile of straw. After all, the excitement was over, the explosion had gone off; Shenna could keep an eye on things by herself for the moment.

"Ederd," Sterren said, "you'll have to take over with Emner; Hamder's worn out."

"Is he all right?" Ederd asked, getting quickly to his feet.

Sterren was not completely sure whether Ederd meant Emner or Hamder, but it didn't really make much difference. "I think so," he replied.

Ederd was already at the ladder and climbing.

Sterren looked around the interior of the barn.

Alder and Dogal were sitting on one side, chatting quietly in Semmat. Lady Kalira and Alar were talking nearby. Shenna was sitting cross-legged in the center of the floor, and the warlock was in his corner, leaning against a wall.

Annara was doing something with her belt-dagger and a bucket in another corner. Ederd and Hamder were up in the loft, fetching Emner back from scouting mission.

It was a shame Emner knew no Semmat, and Sterren could not be sure anyone in the castle spoke Ethsharitic or Emner's native Lamumese; otherwise, he could have used the wizard to establish contact with the besieged Semmans. Nobody else in the party could levitate that far; the witches could, working together, get one of their number a good way off the ground — but only for a very short time, nowhere near long enough to propel him or her all the way to the castle ramparts. The warlock had been able to fly in Ethshar, but here he was unable to lift himself so much as an inch.

It occurred to Sterren for the first time that he could send written messages back and forth — even if his own Semmat was limited, especially in writing, Lady Kalira was fluent and literate.

That was something to keep in mind — but then, what would he say in a message? And Hamder had half-killed himself hauling Emner about on his scouting trip; getting him in and out of the castle would be a major project.

The whole project of winning the war was turning out to be more work than he had hoped. His magicians, while willing enough once they got started, seemed unable to think for themselves, and needed to be told what to do almost every step of the way. He had thought at first that he could turn them loose and sit back and wait for victory, but instead he found himself plotting and planning constantly.

He wondered why he bothered. He had made his gesture; why didn't he just pack up and go home to Ethshar?

There was Lady Kalira, of course, and the three soldiers, who might try to stop him, but he thought that he could slip away if he tried, take a horse — or all the horses, to prevent pursuit and give him something to sell in Akalla to pay for passage — and make a dash for it.

The longer he stayed here, the more likely he was to be captured or killed outright by the invaders. He wasn't really doing Semma much good; only one enemy soldier dead so far, after two days!

There were all those people in the castle depending on him, but how much good could he really do them?

He thought it over, very seriously, and decided he didn't know why he was staying.

Maybe he *would* flee, in a day or two.

But not yet.

Twenty-One

He had still not fled by the twenty-first of Midwinter, 5220. In two sixnights of war, Sterren and his little band had settled down into a calm routine. Each day, Sterren and the magicians would pick away at the enemy, using whatever stunts and devices they could come up with, while the four Semmans would scout out a new hiding place. Sterren did not think it would be safe to stay in the same place two nights running, and it made the Semmans feel useful.

He still had just the four Semmans with him. None of them had deserted — if it would have been desertion, under the circumstances — and no one else had turned up who cared to join Sterren's guerrilla band.

So far as Sterren knew, no one had been able to slip out of the castle, and if anyone had, he might well have other plans, in any case.

Occasionally a peasant who had fled when the invaders arrived and taken shelter with friends or relatives not too far away would wander by to see if it was safe to go home, but these people always left immediately once they saw that the invading army was still there. None of them ever volunteered to help Sterren and his crew.

Sterren got the impression from these strays that most of the peasants who had lived in the village and surrounding farms were now lurking quietly just beyond the horizon, waiting for the war to be over and refusing to get involved with a struggle that they saw as being the aristocrats' affair and none of their business.

Lady Kalira denounced them as unpatriotic cowards; Sterren and the three soldiers were less condemnatory. After all, what could a few unarmed peasants do?

Even the three Semman soldiers weren't doing much. It was the magicians who were waging the war, and the Semmans did nothing but run errands.

Annara had become quite expert at the Explosive Seal, and had successfully booby-trapped books, tent-flaps, and even a pair of boots.

Actually, she had not ensorcelled the tent-flaps themselves, merely the leather ties that laced them shut. The witches had found it very difficult to put the laces back without disturbing the seals.

She had not managed to do a saddle; the horse had refused to stay sufficiently still.

The spell had four noticeable drawbacks.

First, it took half an hour, and any interruption during that time, Annara insisted, could be disastrous. She needed to be left strictly alone for the full time. That meant that someone had to stand guard over her, and that she could not be moved quickly if an emergency arose. So far, no emergency had arisen, but Sterren worried about it all the same.

Second, she had to have whatever she was putting the seal on right there in front of her, which meant that somebody had to steal it away from the enemy, and then put it back again later. Emner and the witches had been able to do this, using Emner's levitation spell or the witches' little mind-twisters, but it was very risky, especially when cautiously putting sealed tent-ties back in place.

Third, the spell required a drop of dragon's blood for each seal, and Annara had only had a tiny vial of the stuff, perhaps a dozen drops in all. Emner was no help; when asked, he said, "I never use the stuff. None of my spells need it, and it's so expensive!"

Sterren knew it was expensive, and was amazed that Annara hadn't sold hers long ago, but she explained, "With it, and my other things, I'm a wizard and I can work magic.

Without my supplies, I'm just another charlatan. And besides, if you hadn't turned up when you did, I *would* have sold it. I just wasn't that desperate yet."

Fourth, and finally, the seal was visible. It came out either red or black — Annara was unable to explain why it should be one or the other, rather than always the same, but it seemed to vary at random between the two.

The seal itself was made of wax, and when Annara used clear beeswax from a supply found in an abandoned kitchen, she was able to enchant the stuff with Eknerwal's Lesser Invisibility so that the wax could not be seen at all — but even then, the trace of dragon's blood remained visible, shaped into a strange rune, and nothing could be done to hide it.

That hadn't helped the owner of the boots, who started to put them on in the dark and lost his right hand and foot. It hadn't helped the lieutenant who opened the first book, who had taken the rune to be mere ornament and lost an eye and three fingers, as well as the book. The first enchanted tent-flap laid a soldier up with serious burns from shoulder to fingertip.

The owner of the second enchanted tent-flap, however, had been more cautious, and had carefully not disturbed the rune. He slipped into his tent from the back, crawling in the mud, and had then taken the tent down entirely and moved it well away from camp before poking at the flap with a stick.

The resulting explosion burned the tent to ash, but injured no one.

After that, the enemy knew what to look for, and the use of the Explosive Seal changed somewhat. Annara no longer bothered with the Lesser Invisibility, and instead of seriously trying to injure anyone, she put the seal in places where it would have maximum nuisance value.

For example, with all three witches standing guard,

convincing the few late-night passersby that Annara either wasn't there or had every right to be there performing her arcane ritual, she sealed the wheel of a water-cart to its axle hub. The seal blew the wheel off, terrifying the horses, when it came time to haul the next load.

The warlock pointed out that one of the witches could have done the same damage with a hammer, but Sterren thought the demoralizing effect was worth the special effort.

He took the hint, though, and later sent the witches around breaking spokes and cutting ropes.

The Ksinallionese army's financial records were found with a seal on them, and a messenger was sent home to fetch another copy, since no way could be found to open them without incinerating them.

Two more tents were sealed and had to be taken down and detonated.

All in all, Annara was earning her keep. So were the witches who helped her.

Emner, with his levitation spell, had provided excellent scouting reports, locating the enemy's headquarters tents and counting the soldiers present (which turned out to be about three hundred, not the full four hundred and fifty). He had stunned a few sentries when the witches needed a distraction, and had made life miserable for a few of the enemy for several hours by enchanting a cockroach to sing "Spices in the Hold," an old sea chanty, loudly and off-key for hours on end. That had only stopped when one of the soldiers, more by luck than skill, stamped on the roach.

That the roach was dead, Emner explained, made no difference, as far as Galger's Singing Spell was concerned, but a hard tap on the enchanted object was the signal to stop. If somebody happened to step on the dead insect again later, it would start singing again.

Unfortunately, nobody happened to step on the dead roach.

In addition to helping the wizards, the witches had pulled off several little tricks of their own. Shenna had spoiled a hundredweight of meat and a wagonload of vegetables, so that at least for a few days the besiegers ate less than the besieged. Sentries had acquired the habit of disappearing, and turning up dead in entirely the wrong place — so much so that for the last three nights there had been no sentries at all.

Only one water-cart's load had been poisoned; Shenna found it to be far more difficult than she had thought. Furthermore, the result had a discernable odor and a nasty taste, so that no one would take more than a tiny sip before spitting the stuff out.

The warlock had not worked closely with the others. He preferred to slip away by himself and pick off random enemy soldiers. He did not need them to be nearby and isolated, as the witches did. Also, where the witches' victims turned up stranged or stabbed, the warlock's simply fell over dead, without warning, without a mark on them, in the midst of their friends and companions.

This had created a good deal of near-panic. The witches reported picking up snatches of conversations about curses and demons.

Unfortunately, the enemy officers had not allowed this to get out of hand. They had even launched a counter-propaganda campaign, arguing that this demonic activity indicated that the evil Semman king had joined forces with powers of darkness and had to be stopped, now, before he became more powerful.

The success of this argument was in doubt, but as yet the invading army seemed to be holding up. Sterren had no reports of desertion or mutiny.

There were certainly casualties, though. All in all, Sterren counted forty-one dead and seven injured among the enemy as a direct result of the magicians' efforts, and in addition they had created considerable disorder. He was pleased. Forty-eight men were a significant part of the besieging army — and Sterren had not lost a single person! His people had been spotted, on occasion, but so far they had always escaped.

He had managed to establish communication with the inhabitants of Semma Castle, too. Although the warlock could not lift or push a person that far, and the witches could only do so by utterly exhausting their reserves, the warlock could, and did, send messages written on parchment sailing over the enemy's encirclement and into the castle, to drop into the courtyard there.

In reply, the people in the castle would run a green banner up on the west ramparts, and hang their own message beneath it on a string. The warlock could usually retrieve this without too much trouble.

Thus, Sterren knew that the castle's inhabitants were far from comfortable. They were horribly overcrowded, as over a hundred peasants had taken shelter within the walls when the invaders arrived, in addition to the usual dense population — and those peasants also added heavily to the food consumption, of course, since none of them had brought any significant amounts of food with them.

Fortunately, the winter stores had been safely inside the walls when the invaders came. Even with all the additional mouths to feed, the castle had plenty of food and water, enough for at least another month.

In addition to the crowding and worry attendant upon any siege, the attackers had siege machines in use that dropped flaming bundles into the castle every so often, and at other times hurled heavy stones through windows or even through roofs. The stable in the western courtyard had been burned to the ground one night when a watchman dozed off at his post. A dozen windows had been smashed, and holes punched through three roofs. Five people had been killed outright, a score injured, and a great many were ill — overcrowding made isolation impractical and hygiene more difficult, and diseases of various sorts were getting out of hand. Lice were a nuisance, too.

Sterren's three officers were apparently unable to organize a very coherent defense, and any thought of a sortie was abandoned when they could not agree on who would lead it.

That, somehow, did not surprise Sterren in the least.

And finally, the enemy was trying to undermine the castle walls, and the defenders could not agree on what to do about it. A few hastily-trained Semman archers had forced the attackers to stay under shelter, but that was easy enough, given the village outside the gate; crude galleries had been built connecting some of the houses and shops, so that enemy sappers could approach without exposing themselves to arrows.

With all this in mind, on this particular day, the twenty-first of Midwinter, Sterren had resolved that it was time to do something about the siege machines. The sappers were a more serious problem in the long term, but the siege machines would be easier to get at, and were doing more harm to the morale of the besieged.

Their shelter, at the moment, was a partially-burned farmhouse to the northeast of the castle, and it was there, on the morning of the twenty-first, that Sterren gathered his entire band into a circle on the floor of the main room.

"Emner," he said, "tell me about their siege machines."

Emner shrugged. "What can I tell you? They're siege machines."

Sterren glared. "How many are there? What kinds? Where are they?"

Emner coughed, embarrassed. "Oh," he said. "Well, I'd say they have about half a dozen in all, mostly trebuchet catapults, but also a mounted ram. The ram's in the village; the others are arranged in a ring around the castle, spaced out pretty evenly."

"What's a trebuchet?" Annara asked. Sterren was pleased — partly because it meant she was paying attention, but mostly because now he didn't need to ask himself, and show how little he knew.

"Well, it's like a big lever on a frame; there's a heavy weight on one end, usually a big box filled with rocks, and on the other end is a sling. There's a rope attached to the sling end, and the rope winds around a drum at the bottom of the frame. You wind the rope around the drum, and it pulls the sling down and the weight-box up. You load whatever you want to throw into the sling, release the rope, the weight falls, and whap, the sling flies up and throws whatever you put in it. Depending on what weight you use, it can toss up to, oh, three hundred pounds, I'd say, over a castle wall from safely outside archery range. Anything heavier than that and the frame's likely to break."

Sterren nodded; whatever his other faults, Emner was good at descriptions. Sterren felt he had a good, clear picture of how these catapults worked.

That didn't mean he knew what to do about them.

"Is there some way we can burn them all?" he asked.

The witches looked at each other, while Annara and Emner blinked and shrugged.

"What sort of wood are they?" Hamder asked.

"Um . . . ironwood, I think. Maybe oak. Something very hard and strong," Emner replied.

"I can't kindle *that*," Shenna said. "Sorry."

"Not me," Ederd said

Hamder shook his head.

Sterren looked at Annara.

"I don't think so," she said. "All I have that can burn things is the Explosive Seal, and that generally won't set anything more than paper or oilcloth on fire. And besides, I meant to tell you, I only have enough dragon's blood left for one more seal, and not a very big one, either."

That was unpleasant news; the Explosive Seal had been one of their best resources. He turned to the four Semmans, who were huddled against one wall, looking bored.

"Does anyone in the castle," he said in Semmat, "have . . . ah . . . from an animal that makes fire . . ." As he spoke, he was vaguely aware that the witches were whispering with Emner about something.

"A dragon?" Lady Kalira asked. "There are dragons in the mountains north of Lumeth of the Towers, but they've never come this far south."

"Not the whole dragon, just the . . . the stuff. Red stuff. From inside." Sterren knew he had heard the Semmat word for "blood," but he could not think of it.

"Blood? Dragon's blood?" Alder asked.

"Yes! Blood. Dragon's blood."

"I never heard of anybody who had any," Lady Kalira replied. "Why? Is it good for something?"

"Annara needs it for her magic."

The four Semmans looked at one another, then back at Sterren. "Sorry," Alder said.

Sterren sighed, and switched back to Ethsharitic. "About these catapults . . ."

"From Emner's description, they're too big for us to

move," Hamder said. "Especially if it's really ironwood."

"It takes ten men to move one, even with the wheels," Emner explained.

"And witches may use magic instead of arms and legs and backs, but they aren't any stronger than Ophkarite or Ksinallionese soldiers, even so," Shenna said.

"Can you break them, somehow?"

Shenna and Hamder started to glance at each other, but Ederd flatly stated, "No. Not if they're as strongly made as Emner says."

Emner shrugged apologetically. "They need to be strong to heave rocks that big," he said.

"All right," Sterren said, "the witches can't do anything. What about you, Emner?"

"I can make them whistle or sing, but that's all. I'm sorry." He spread his hands in a gesture of helplessness.

Sterren turned to Annara, but before he could speak, she said, "Not without more dragon's blood, and probably not then."

That left the warlock.

"I don't know," he said. "I can't burn the frames, nor break them outright, not in my present condition, but I might be able to break some of the ropes, or do some other damage. I don't have the straight lifting power these witches have here, but I believe I can do subtler things — crackings and frayings and twistings — that they cannot."

"Crackings?" Emner looked thoughtful, and said, "If you could crack the main crosspiece, the lever, while they were preparing to fire, the whole machine would probably come apart under the strain."

"That would be perfect," Sterren said.

The warlock shrugged. "I can try," he said.

"Good," Sterren replied. "And you will."

Twenty-Two

"Will this do?" Sterren asked, pointing.

The warlock crept up beside him and peered over the ridgepole. "I think so," he said. "I can see the structure from here, anyway."

Sterren nodded. "Good," he said, "because we can't find anywhere better that's half this safe."

The warlock glanced at him. "Why did you come with me, then, if it's dangerous?" he asked.

Sterren was not really sure himself. He shrugged, and said, "I get tired of just hearing reports. I wanted to see some of the action for myself." He did not really want to think about that any more; it only reminded him just how dangerous his situation actually was, perched on a rooftop a hundred yards from an enemy camp. He changed the subject.

"How's your head today?"

"Better — or at least different," the warlock said.

"Different? How is it different?"

The warlock hesitated, and said, "Maybe I'm just getting used to it."

It seemed to Sterren that his mysterious black-clad companion was being unusually talkative today, and he decided to try to take advantage of that to get a few answers to mysteries that had been bothering him.

"You know," he said, "I never heard of warlocks having headaches like yours. That's not what the stories say happens when you move south."

"I never heard of it, either," the warlock said. "I don't understand it."

"It *is* somehow related to your magic, isn't it?" Sterren asked.

"Oh, I would say so." He hesitated, and then continued, "You're a warlock yourself, aren't you? I thought I could see that, before we got so far south and I lost my finer perceptions."

"Not really," Sterren admitted, "I failed an apprenticeship."

"Ah, that would explain it entirely! It took me a long time, you know, to decide that you were one — you didn't *act* like one, but you seemed to know the art, and I could feel *something* in your mind. I thought you were just keeping it secret, for some reason."

"No," Sterren said, "I might have a trace of the Power, but I'm not really a warlock. I won more than I should at dice, back in Ethshar, but that's all."

The warlock nodded. "Then you wouldn't know," he said.

"Know what?"

"What it feels like to use the Power."

"No," Sterren agreed, "I don't know. What *is* it like?"

"Well, it's hard to explain. It's as if something — not someone, because it clearly isn't human, but *something*, perhaps a god or a demon or something we don't have a name for — is whispering in your mind, and you can't understand anything it's saying, you can't be sure it's words at all, but you can pull strength from it all the same, you can take the sound of the whisper and reshape it and use it to feel and shape and change the world around you. Do you understand?"

Sterren almost thought he did. He nodded, and said nothing.

"And after you've used warlockry a lot, the whisper is always there, *always*, whether you're listening or not, using the Power or not, awake or asleep. It's a constant background, and it gets a little louder each time you draw on it.

And it's trying to tell you something, but you don't know what."

He paused, and then said, "You know about the night-mares."

It was not a question, but Sterren nodded again.

"The nightmares are when the whisper begins to make *sense*. You still can't make out the words, still can't tell what it's trying to tell you, or what's whispering, but you catch bits of it, little bits and pieces of images. And you can't shut them out; the whisper is always there, it won't go away, and those images seep into your mind little by little." He shivered.

"And when you came south?" Sterren prompted.

"When I came south," the warlock said, "the whis-pering faded away. It was wonderful at first; I could forget the little glimmers of meaning I'd been catching, and the nightmares stopped. I couldn't hear the whisper at all. But then, when we headed inland, I started to hear *buzzing*."

Startled, Sterren stared at him. "Buzzing?" he said.

"Humming, buzzing, something like that. It's not really a sound, it's a source, a mental sensation, like the whisper — but this one isn't a voice, isn't an intelligence at all, it's a mindless drone, like a beehive or a millstone. And . . . well, have you ever lived somewhere where you hear some un-pleasant noise *constantly*? A *loud* one? It gives you a head-ache." He sighed. "But after awhile, you get used to it, and in time, you don't even notice it any more. I expect that in time I won't notice this any more. At present, I'm still con-stantly aware of it, but my head doesn't hurt any more."

Sterren nodded.

He thought he understood the analogy the warlock made, and had an idea what it must feel like — but he had no idea what could be causing the "buzzing" the warlock described.

But then, nobody knew what the Aldagmor Source was, either. Presumably there was another, different one somewhere near Semma, one that had never created its own magicians the way the Aldagmor Source had back in 5202, but which warlocks could perceive.

"If it's like the Source," he asked, "can you draw Power from it?"

The warlock looked at him, startled. "I have no idea," he said. "I haven't been able to so far; it doesn't *offer* Power the way the Source does. But it . . . I don't know." He chopped his words off short and stopped speaking.

Sterren decided not to push the matter. He peered over the farmhouse ridgepole and said, "I think they're getting ready to load. It looks like pitch. A ball of pitch. I suppose they'll light it right before they release."

The warlock stared. "Yes," he said.

"Can you crack the beam?"

The warlock didn't answer; Sterren glanced over, and saw his jaw clenched with strain, his eyes narrowed.

Sterren shaded his eyes with a hand, and stared at the trebuchet. Was the beam starting to bend a little more than it should, perhaps?

He shifted, squinted, stared harder.

The catapult exploded. One moment it was there, the crosspiece bending only slightly, and the next instant the entire superstructure was gone, lost in a spreading cloud of red-hot debris. The great wooden bucket of stones that served as the counterweight crashed to the ground and shattered, the ball of pitch burst into flame and rolled back onto the crew that had just loaded it, and the framework simply vanished in the burst of glowing fragments. The earth shook, and a tremendous rolling roar reached the two men on the rooftop.

Sterren gaped, and clung desperately to the thatch as the building swayed beneath him.

A long moment later, burning splinters began to rain down about him, spattering onto the thatch. The scent of burning reached his nose, and he began sliding quickly backward down the slope.

He stopped at the edge and looked back up the slope.

The warlock was still lying there on the roof, but nothing touched him; fragments that might have struck him instead swerved aside as they approached.

"Gods," Sterren said, "what happened?"

The warlock turned and grinned down at him, by far the broadest smile Sterren had ever seen on that dour face. "Can't you guess?" he said. "It was your idea, you know."

Sterren shook his head.

"I've tuned into the buzzing; I'm drawing power from it. I'm as powerful as I ever was!" He rose upright, in a totally unnatural manner; his hands and knees never moved, but his body simply swung up unsupported. Once standing, he lifted further, up into the air. His black robe spread into great flapping wings, and he laughed triumphantly. "Sterren," he called, "there are no voices! It's just power, nothing but power!" He laughed again, and thunder rolled overhead.

The warlock looked up at the sound, and without warning, a bolt of lightning flashed down, and incinerated the remaining fragments of the catapult.

The lightning was not the natural blue-white; it was a fiery orange-red. Warlock lightning. Sterren had heard of it, but never seen it.

Another bolt struck off to the left, destroying another catapult; then a third, and a fourth, and a fifth, and the enemy's long-range arsenal was gone.

The wind was rising, and Sterren decided that a roof

was not a good place to be. He was unsure how completely the warlock was actually controlling this sudden storm, and did not care to risk a miscalculation — or even a deliberate attack, since after all, he hardly knew the warlock. He slid down until his feet caught on the ladder they had used to climb up, and then descended quickly.

Thunder boomed again, and this time even the thunder was clearly unnatural — it was great rolling laughter.

It was recognizably the warlock's voice.

He hurried around the corner of the house, and was in time to see the wind sweeping soldiers off their feet, knocking them flat to the ground.

Then the wind stopped, and the braver Ksinallionese — Sterren had learned the different uniforms, and could see no Ophkarites on this side of the castle — got to their feet again.

The thunder-voice spoke again, in words this time.

"Go home!" it roared. "This land is under the protection of Vond the Warlock! To stay here is to die!"

Then, again, laughter rolled across the plain.

Sterren saw the enemy milling in confusion at first; then a mounted officer panicked and spurred his horse to a gallop, bound north toward Ksinallion.

Panic spread like a wave through the besiegers, rippling out from that fleeing lieutenant, and in minutes the entire army was in full flight, pursued by howling unnatural winds.

Their morale had been deteriorating for days — men dying mysteriously, explosive booby-traps scattered about, strange figures flying overhead invulnerable to arrows. This supernatural storm and voice like an angry god was more than these frightened soldiers could take. Individually or in groups, they broke and ran, bound for their homes.

Sterren did not blame them in the least for running. He

stood and watched, smiling happily, as the storm swept on around the castle, driving the besieging army away from every side.

He had won the war. He and his six magicians had defeated fifty times their number. He was safe from execution by either side. In fact, he would be a hero to the Semmans.

He looked up at the warlock, hanging in mid-air, his black robe transformed into immense black wings that gave him the appearance of a hovering hawk, and waved triumphantly.

Vond, as the warlock had called himself, returned the wave. Thunder rumbled about him, and clouds gathered thickly overhead, ready to burst.

Sterren looked at the distant castle. The inhabitants had a celebration coming. They were saved.

At least, Sterren corrected himself, they were saved from Ophkar and Ksinallion. He supposed they would now have to deal with Vond — he would presumably want to stay here permanently, away from the whispering of Aldagmor. Having so powerful a warlock around the place might well change a few things. He might not be satisfied with the handful of gold and gems he had been promised. At the very least, Agor would probably be displaced as royal magician in short order.

But, Sterren thought, his grin returning, that wasn't *his* problem.

He remembered the peasants whose only interest in the siege was knowing when it would be over, so they could go home, regardless of who won. They probably wouldn't care about anything Vond did, either. It wasn't *their* problem.

King Phenvel might have a problem. Agor might have a problem. Any number of other people might have problems.

Right now, Sterren felt as if he had none at all.

Vond probably felt the same way, Sterren thought, and a tiny little thought poked its way into his mind, like a pin working into a quilt.

If the warlock thought his problems were gone, he was wrong; he definitely had a very real problem.

Sterren looked up, wondering if Vond knew.

The storm broke suddenly, and sparkling blue rain spilled heavily down, soaking him instantly. He looked up, blinking, and saw Vond hanging in the sky, cloak spread, head thrown back, laughing wildly as the sheets of rain parted before him, leaving him untouched and dry.

Twenty-Three

Eventually, of course, Vond landed again. Sterren was stubborn enough to wait for him.

He was not stubborn enough to wait out in the rain, though. He ducked into the little farmhouse and tried in vain to dry off, glancing out the windows every so often to see if Vond had tired of playing with the storm.

The clouds were rained away completely somewhat before sunset, but the warlock stayed aloft, whipping the winds back and forth, sending sprays of sand and rock hither and yon. The besieging armies were long since gone, leaving behind scattered bits of equipment and trash, strewn across a sea of mud.

Sterren saw no bodies, but he suspected a few might be out there. He noticed that much of the village surrounding Semma Castle had been flattened, not just the sappers' ramshackle structures or the lightly-built shops, but the solid original houses as well.

The sun was down, and the last light fading, when the warlock finally settled to earth.

"*Hai*," Sterren called from his shelter, "congratulations!"

Vond turned, spotted him in the window, and bowed. "Thank you, my lord," he said. He smiled. "Gods, that felt good! To be able to let myself go, use all the power I wanted, without worrying about those damned nightmares — it was wonderful!"

Sterren did not bother going around to the door. He hoisted himself up into the window, and was about to drop down on the outside when he felt an invisible grasp close about him and pull him gently free of the frame.

He floated gently over, and found himself hanging in the air in front of the warlock.

This was disconcerting, but not particularly uncomfortable. Sterren flexed a little, and found he could move freely, but that no matter how he moved he remained floating in the same spot, a couple of yards from the warlock's face.

"Hello, there," he said.

"Hello," Vond replied, grinning broadly.

Sterren shifted, getting a bit more comfortable in his unnatural elevation. He considered carefully exactly what he ought to say, and finally just asked, "What happened?"

"Well," Vond said thoughtfully, "I'm not sure of all the details. Somehow, though, I tapped into the buzz, and then I had all the power I wanted, all at once." He waved at the desolation on all sides, displaying his handiwork.

Sterren nodded, contemplating the wasteland. "And you aren't worried about nightmares?" he asked. "What if this new source is just like the one in Aldagmor, in the long run?" While the warlock had been reveling in his new power, Sterren had spent much of the storm considering the various possibilities, and he felt that it would be unfair to not point the many possible dangers out to Vond.

Vond shook his head. "It isn't. It can't be. I'd know."

Sterren didn't reply, but the warlock read his doubting expression.

"You think I'm being reckless, don't you? Don't worry, Sterren, I'm not. I tell you, I *know* this new source isn't like the old. Whatever the Source in Aldagmor is, it's conscious, or at least run by a conscious entity — I've known that since I was an apprentice. We warlocks always have a vague feeling of contact, of communication, when we use our magic, and besides, surely the nightmares and the Calling to go to Aldagmor are *sent* by something."

Sterren nodded. He had to admit that much.

"Well," Vond said, "*this* power source does *not* seem to be conscious — it's just raw power. When I used the Aldagmor source, as I told you, it was like listening to a whisper, hearing it but not catching the words. Using this new source like listening to the hum of a bee — there *are* no words, just sound."

"But if that's so, then why aren't there any warlocks here already, drawing on this source?" Sterren asked. "They don't even have a word for warlock in Semmat!"

"I can only guess," Vond said.

"Guess, then," Sterren said.

Vond waved dramatically. "Warlockry, my dear Sterren, first appeared on the Night of Madness, back in 5202 — you know that. That was when the Source first appeared in Aldagmor. It created warlockry, all at once; warlocks appeared spontaneously, hundreds of them. It was . . . well, it was as if the thing let out one shout, to get people listening, and then its voice died away to that whisper I keep talking about."

Sterren nodded.

"Well," Vond continued, "this *new* source never shouted. There's no telling what it is, or how long it's been there, but it could mean a whole new existence for warlocks, because if it's not conscious, then it won't cause any nightmares or compulsions, now, will it?"

"I don't know," Sterren said, "and neither do you. Maybe it's just sleeping. Maybe the one in Aldagmor was just sleeping there, all along, until it woke up in 5202, and this one could wake up tomorrow."

"Or it could sleep for another thousand years, if you're right," Vond said, "but you aren't. I can *feel* it, I tell you; this new source is *dead*, not just sleeping. It was never alive and never will be. It's totally mindless."

"You're the one taking the risks," Sterren said, "so it's none of my business, really, but Vond, I wouldn't put that much faith in it if I were you. How do you *know* it isn't sleeping? You *can't* know. Your feelings could be wrong."

Vond shook his head. "No, you don't understand what it's like. I can use the power itself to tell me whether it's conscious, sleeping, alive, dead, whatever. It's mindless, empty — like a . . . a running stream, or a millwheel grinding."

Sterren was still uneasy, but saw no point in further argument on that particular subject. Vond was clearly not eager to consider any negative aspects to his situation just now, and after all, anything Sterren could say would be mere guesswork. "I hope you're right," he said.

"I *know* I'm right," Vond replied.

"If you are," Sterren said, nettled by Vond's certainty, "then why hasn't anybody found this thing before? Even if it never made its own warlocks, the way the Aldagmor source did, there have been warlocks for twenty years, and you can't be the first one to ever come south."

"I may be the first one to ever come *this far* south," Vond replied.

Sterren conceded the point, but said, "Even so . . ."

Vond cut him off. "Maybe," he said, "I'm somehow different. Perhaps I'm unique, the only warlock who can use this new source — it *is* a bit different, after all, and I might never have . . . have listened to it, if you hadn't suggested it."

"Did you ever think you weren't like other warlocks before this happened?"

"No, not really. I was getting very powerful, of course. The power increases with use as one becomes attuned to it, better able to listen in to the Source, as it were, and I'd been listening very closely for quite some time. Lord Azrad hired me to dredge the harbor last year, you know, and I did it single-handed, and . . . well, after that, the whisper was more of a mutter, and then . . . well."

"The nightmares," Sterren said.

"Eventually, yes. And then you came along, and here we are."

Sterren decided to stop looking for flaws. For one thing, he had not even mentioned what he saw as the most likely long-term problem, but seeing how easily Vond had hauled him out the window, he had a certain uneasiness about the warlock's new power, and he thought he might someday *want* Vond to have problems.

Not that he had any intention of telling the warlock that. "And so here you are with this new source of magic," he said, smiling. "Congratulations!"

"Yes, isn't it wonderful? I was straining hard, trying to listen to the old Source, to draw enough power to crack that beam, and I was ignoring the buzz, and then I thought about what you said and tried to listen to the buzz, too, and then it wasn't a buzz anymore, it was something entirely different, something that I could draw power from, and it was *close* and *strong* and I was more powerful than I ever was back in Ethshar!"

"It's close?" Sterren asked. He had somehow assumed that the buzz came from somewhere beyond the edge of the World, and was a good distance away.

"I think so — in that direction." He pointed off vaguely northwest — but then, Sterren thought, almost the entire World lay to the northwest of Semma. This new source was not beyond the edge of the World, but that didn't really narrow it down much.

The two men looked at each other, glanced around at the storm-blasted plain, and then simultaneously started to speak. They stopped, and Sterren gestured for Vond to speak first.

"I'd say the war is won," the warlock said. "Now what do we do?"

"I'd say," Sterren replied, "that we go to the castle and collect our rewards."

Vond nodded. "Sounds good to me," he said.

"We'll want to get the others," Sterren pointed out.

"That's no problem," Vond said, "I'll bring them." With that, he rose again into the air and began soaring toward Semma Castle.

Sterren, quite without any action on his part, sailed along close behind, and he glanced back to see other figures being swept up and carried along in similar fashion — he spotted Annara by her distinctive purple robe, and Lady Kalira by her red gown, and Alder and Dogal by their size and armament. The other five were just black dots at first.

A moment later they were all standing at the castle gate, ranged in two neat rows, Sterren and Vond in the front row center. An unearthly glow of Vond's making played across them all and lit the area a pale gold.

A sentry peered timidly over the ramparts above.

"*Hai*," Sterren shouted, remembering at the last minute to use Semmat, "it's I, Sterren, Ninth Warlord, and my comrades! Open the gate!"

The soldier hesitated. "But, my lord," he said, "the invaders . . ."

"The invaders are gone," Sterren replied. "The war is over!"

The sentry glanced uneasily out across the ruins of the village, where Vond's storm had indeed ripped away every trace of the sappers' shelters and most of the other buildings as well. "They're really gone?" he asked.

"All of them," Sterren assured him. "The war is over. We won."

"Sterren," Vond said, speaking Ethsharitic, "I can open the gates."

"I know," Sterren replied in the same tongue, "but let's be polite about it. Give them another five minutes."

"Five minutes, then."

Sterren switched back to Semmat and said, "The magician who made the storm is becoming impatient. He says in five minutes, if the gate is still closed, he'll smash it to pieces."

The sentry immediately said, "Yes, my lord. I'll have it open in a moment."

It took about a minute and a half before the gate swung wide, and Sterren thought he saw disappointment on Vond's face as the whole party marched in.

Part Three
Warlock

Twenty-Four

Sterren was uneasy even before he led his victorious little squad into the throne room. They had been kept waiting in the antechamber considerably longer than he had expected. Most of the party had taken it well — after all, the Semmans were used to their king's foibles, and the others had not known what to expect — but Vond seemed noticeably impatient.

Sterren found that he really did not like the idea of being around someone as powerful as Vond when he got impatient.

He marched into the throne room neither meekly nor belligerently, but with the best approximation of calm assurance that he could manage, and found Vond on his right hand, sweeping forward a few inches off the floor, while the others straggled along behind rather haphazardly.

As he marched in, while he kept his face turned straight forward, toward the king, as protocol demanded, his eyes were flicking back and forth, taking in as much as he could of the people gathered there.

The soldiers who stood in ragged lines on either side mostly looked either bewildered or bored; Sterren suspected that not a one of them really knew what was going on. Behind them, he could see a significant percentage of the castle's noble population, and he tried to read their expressions without letting his own interest show.

He saw a wide variety of emotions — puzzlement, delight, anger — but the dominant reaction to the arrival of Semma's warlord and his party appeared to be poorly-suppressed fear.

That did not bode well.

Remembering the violence of the warlock's storm, however, Sterren could not say it was an unreasonable reaction.

He spotted the king's children huddled to the left of the throne; The faces of Lura and Dereth were alight with excitement. Nissitha's mouth was drawn up in her usual expression of polite distaste.

Shirrin's expression was unmistakably wide-eyed adoration.

Sterren stopped at the appropriate distance from the throne and bowed.

Vond stopped beside him, and condescended to dip his head slightly. Sterren saw this from the corner of his eye, and was relieved; it was not a bow, but at least it was something. He had worried that Vond would go out of his way to antagonize Phenvel, with Sterren caught in the middle. Given how frightened most of the Semmans looked, and how easily fear might turn to anger, he very much wanted to avoid any open antagonism.

"So you're finally back!" the king said, and Sterren's hope for peace and amity faded.

"We returned as quickly as we could, your Majesty," he said, his tone as ingratiating as he could manage — which was quite ingratiating indeed, as he had had years of practice with creditors and innkeepers. "The wind was not in our favor."

"You had magicians with you, didn't you?" King Phenvel demanded.

"Only on the way back, your Majesty, and none of them could . . . could turn the wind," Sterren explained.

The king stared at him, then snapped, "Are you trying to tell me that little breeze we had today was *natural*?"

Sterren blinked. "Oh, no, your Majesty," he said. "That was the . . . the work of Vond the Warlock." Sterren gestured at the warlock. "However, it's a spell he . . . it's new, a spell he had not . . . um, not learned yet during our journey." He wished he knew Semmat better. Even what he did know was somewhat rusty, since he had mostly been using Ethsharitic for the last few sixnights, talking far more to the magicians than to Lady Kalira and the three soldiers.

Furthermore, the obvious hostility was making him nervous, so that he was forgetting some of what he *did* know.

Vond recognized his name and bowed slightly in acknowledgment.

"Ah," the king said. "So he found some way to study the arcane arts while hiding from the invaders, rather than fighting?"

Sterren was shocked at this snide question, with its implications of cowardice and incompetence. "Your Majesty," he replied, "Vond defeated the armies of Ophkar and Ksinallion, almost by himself."

"And took his own sweet time doing it, too! I suppose he thinks he'll be getting more money out of me by making it look hard, but he won't, and neither will any of these other sorry specimens you've dragged back here. One storm, and the enemy ran! The gold and gems I gave you are too generous for such a sorry performance!"

Sterren could think of no reply to this. He did, however, find himself sympathizing with the rulers of Ophkar and Ksinallion who had ordered the invasion.

"Besides," the king continued, "the war is hardly over merely because we won a battle. I'll need to send ambassadors to arrange a peace and settle terms, won't I? If you'd gotten a surrender, instead of a rout, I could have given terms to the warlords and saved some time."

This hardly struck Sterren as a major problem, but he managed to avoid saying anything disrespectful by saying nothing.

"And furthermore," the king said, "what about the

mess you people left? Half the village is ruined, there's mud everywhere, and all that wind blew tiles off half the roofs and took the banners right off the flagpoles. I went up to the tower and looked, and it looks awful! And I don't suppose any of your magicians would dirty their hands with cleaning it up! No, don't say anything, warlord, I won't ask them to; I'll have my people see to it. You can pay your magicians and send them home now; we won't be needing them around here any more."

He waved a dismissal, but Sterren found, to his own astonishment, that he was not willing to be dismissed yet. "Your Majesty," he said, trying hard not to clench his teeth disrespectfully, "I did not start this stupid war. I ended it, as quickly as I could. I had . . . had hoped that you would . . . would show more . . ." His Semmat failed him completely.

"Gratitude?" Phenvel practically sneered. "Gratitude, for doing the job you were born to? Warlord, if you had fought the enemy properly, with sword and shield, I might be more respectful, but to bring in wizards and witches is hardly a courageous act. It's the doing of a merchant, not a warlord, and what I expect from someone three-quarters Ethsharitic, not a true Semman at all!"

"Not for me!" Sterren said, outraged, "I don't want anything for me! For them, the magicians! They left home to come here and fight for you!"

"I didn't ask for them," King Phenvel retorted. "And they've been paid. And who the hell are they all, anyway? A ragged-looking bunch, I must say!"

Sterren stared at the king's slippered feet and forced himself to calm down. When he was once again in control of himself, he said, "If I might present them, your Majesty?"

"Go ahead," the king said, with a nonchalant wave.

Sterren gestured to his right. "Vond the Warlock, late of Ethshar of the Spices." He switched to Ethsharitic, and said, "Vond, this is his Majesty, Phenvel, Third of that Name, King of Semma."

Vond bowed, mockingly.

Sterren ignored the mockery and turned.

"Annara of Crookwall, journeyman wizard," he said.

Annara curtseyed deeply. The king nodded politely.

"Shenna of Chatna, witch."

Shenna, too, curtseyed, moving more briskly than gracefully. Her skirt was so thoroughly soaked that this sent a spatter of mud onto courtiers at one side of the hall.

"Chatna," said the king, "where is that?"

"In the Small Kingdoms, my lord," Shenna said, in slurred Semmat. "Just inland of Morria, near the Gulf of the East."

Sterren was startled, both by this information and by Shenna's use of Semmat. He had assumed Chatna to be an Ethsharitic village somewhere, and had not realized that Shenna had bothered to pick up any of the local language during her stay in Semma.

Not that she knew it well, since she had used entirely the wrong title.

He gathered his wits quickly, and continued with the introductions, hoping that Phenvel would not criticize the error in protocol.

"Ederd of Eastwark, witch. Emner of Lamum, wizard. Hamder Hamder's son, witch."

Each bowed in turn.

"Lamum?" Phenvel asked.

"A kingdom on the Eastern Highway, your Majesty," Sterren replied, before Emner could react. "Just across the border from the Hegemony of the Three Ethshars." He was pleased that he had remembered that bit of trivia.

"Sterren," Vond said, during the momentary lull while the king absorbed the introductions, "what the hell is going on?"

Sterren ignored him long enough to ask, "Your Majesty, may I translate your words to the magicians? Most of them speak no Semmat."

Phenvel waved a hand. "Go ahead," he said.

Sterren turned to Vond and said quickly, "He's been making an ass of himself, complaining that we took too long to get back here and too long to break the siege and that the storm damaged the castle and he'll have to have his people clean up the mess it left. I don't know why he's in such a foul mood; he's been gratuitously insulting to all of us, particularly you and me. I think it might be because he's scared to death of you."

He noticed that Annara and Emner were listening closely, and added, "He's probably scared of *all* of you. Magic is scarce around here."

"I suppose that means no more pay and no big celebration," Emner said.

"I'm afraid not," Sterren agreed.

"Ah," Vond said, "I'm not really surprised. That's rather what it sounded like. Has he said what he expects us to do now?"

"He expects you to take your pay and go home. I haven't yet mentioned that you may not want to."

The warlock shrugged. "You don't need to tell him; he'll see for himself soon enough. Do you think you could arrange us some rooms for the night, though? It's getting late."

"I was planning on it; dinner, too."

"Good." The wizards nodded agreement, and Sterren turned back to the throne.

"Your Majesty," he said, "I ask a favor of you. These six magicians have fought for you. Please, give them food and shelter here for a few days, to rest, after their efforts. We ask no more than that."

Relief flashed quickly across the king's face, then vanished. "Granted," he said. "We have dined, but I'm sure the kitchens can provide for you, and my chamberlain will find accommodations. You may go."

Sterren bowed, and started to back out.

"Wait a minute," the king said, holding up a hand, "Lady Kalira, didn't you take six soldiers with you?"

"Yes, your Majesty," Lady Kalira replied.

"I see only three now, and I had asked to see your full party; what happened to the others? Wounded? Killed?"

"Deserted, your Majesty, while we were in Ethshar."

"Deserted?" King Phenvel said, aghast.

Lady Kalira nodded. Sterren, hearing the king's tone, wished she had lied a little.

"Warlord, I am not pleased at all. Three desertions!"

Actually, he sounded as if he were quite pleased. Sterren guessed that he was happy to have something with which to rebuke his warlord, should the occasion arise.

Sterren started to phrase a reply, and then thought better of it. Pointing out that desertion spoke worse of Semma in general than of his performance as warlord would only make trouble. "Yes, your Majesty," he said. He looked up and met Phenvel's eyes. He was not ashamed of any part of what he had done. After all, he had won the war, or at least the battle, whatever Phenvel might say.

The king met his gaze for a moment, then turned angrily away. "All right, then, you may go!"

Sterren bowed, and he and the magicians went, bound for the kitchens and dinner.

Twenty-Five

The long climb to his chamber, after the long and bewildering day, was exhausting, and Sterren fell into his bed and lay staring at the canopy for only a moment before falling asleep.

During that moment he thought about the conversation in the kitchens, held as the magicians ate the best meal they had had in sixnights.

The kitchens, and for that matter the corridors and halls, were full of peasants who had taken shelter in the castle during the siege, but the magicians had had no difficulty in establishing their right to privacy. A wave of Vond's hand had sent the refugees scurrying, leaving the new arrivals alone.

They had discussed the division of their pay. Everyone conceded that Vond deserved the lion's share, but the other magicians felt that they, too, had contributed something, that their demoralization of the enemy had made the warlock's triumph easier.

Vond had said almost nothing during this, but had nodded calm acceptance when Sterren proposed that each of the other five be paid one full gold piece, and that Vond receive the other five and all the gems.

Sterren had gone on to apologize for the poor reception the king had given them, and all six had been wonderfully understanding. Shenna had made a few bitter remarks, but had carefully not directed them at Sterren.

Vond had said nothing, then.

The conversation had shifted to whether or not they should all head directly back to Ethshar. The wizards and witches discussed various ideas without reaching any conclusions.

Vond had stated simply, "I'm staying here," and said nothing more.

The party had broken up not long after that, and servants had escorted the magicians to rooms in the south wing. Sterren had wearily ascended to his own room in the tower. His last sight of the warlock was not reassuring; Vond was clearly very much awake, unlike the rest of the party, and was looking about intently as he followed the footman down the crowded passage.

Vond's entire manner worried Sterren, but he was too tired to really think about it. He closed his eyes and slept.

It seemed just a moment later that a distant rumble awoke him. He blinked, and saw sunlight pouring into his chamber, and realized it was mid-morning.

The rumble sounded again, and he felt the bed shift slightly beneath him, and he realized that bright, unobstructed sunlight was pouring in. The rumble was not thunder.

He sat up, startled.

The rumble sounded again, and despite the trembling of the bed he thought it came from outside. He slid from the bed and crossed to the window.

The view had changed since last he saw it. The castle roofs were spattered with broken tiles and shards of stone, wood, and tile. The outer houses of the village were gone. The rolling countryside was no longer a neat patchwork of farm and field, sprinkled with houses and barns, but a great expanse of mud and wreckage, strewn with all manner of debris.

And directly before him, a half-mile or so away, a black-robed figure was hanging in mid-air, arms spread wide, cloak flapping like wings, and below him the earth itself was splitting open. The sandy mud had washed back to either side, forming a deep pit easily a hundred yards across — and not just the mud, but the clay beneath, down to the hard bedrock.

Then the rumble came again, and as Sterren watched an immense block of that bedrock rose up into the air toward the hovering warlock.

The block was rectangular, and by comparing it to Vond — for the flying man could hardly be anybody else — Sterren judged it to be about ten feet high, fifteen feet long, and five feet thick — give or take a foot or three in any dimension.

The block hovered for a moment, then slid sideways through the air, and then dropped to the ground.

The rumble sounded again, and again, and again, and another block lifted into the air, slid sideways, and landed on top of the first. The cutting and lifting went more quickly this time.

A third and a fourth were added to the stack, and the cutting was just beginning on a fifth when someone pounded loudly on the door.

"Lord Sterren?"

Sterren started for the wardrobe, but then realized he had never undressed the night before. He still wore the same tattered and mud-stained garments he had worn through the storm and the audience with the king.

This was not the time to worry about neatness, he decided. He changed direction and crossed to the door.

"Yes?" he called.

"My lord, the king wishes to see you immediately."

Sterren was not surprised. He opened the door, and found himself facing a very worried-looking messenger boy. "I'm here," he said. "Come on."

A few minutes later he found himself facing a very worried Phenvel III in the royal family's private sitting room, the king's expression an odd contrast to the warm sunlight and bright, cheerful furnishings. The only other people present were the messenger boy and a worried valet. Another rumble ran through the castle as Sterren made his formal bow.

"Warlord," the king demanded, "what the hell is your magician doing out there?"

"I don't know, your Majesty." Sterren would have been far more expressive in Ethsharitic; in Semmat he had to stick to the simple statement of fact.

"Is this something to do with the war?" the king demanded peevishly. "Do you expect another attack? I thought you said the enemy was beaten!"

"I don't know, your Majesty," Sterren repeated.

"Why not? He's your damn wizard!"

"He's a warlock, your Majesty, not a wizard," Sterren explained wearily, "I hired him for a job. I don't own him. He does as he pleases."

"What in hell is a warlock?"

"*He* is, your Majesty. A kind of magician unknown here in Semma. Until now."

"All right, he's a warlock," the king said, "What's he *doing*?"

"I don't know, your Majesty," Sterren admitted.

"Well, damn it, go find out!" The note of fear in King Phenvel's voice was obvious.

Sterren bowed. "As your Majesty wishes," he said.

He departed quickly, before the king could change his mind or impose stupid conditions. He was curious himself.

He did not bother with any sort of preparations or cleaning up; he marched directly from the royal apartments out of the castle, ignoring the peasants huddled asleep on the corridor floor, pausing only to ask the man at the gate, "Did the black-robed magician come through here?"

"No, my lord," came the reply. "He flew over the north wall."

Sterren nodded and marched on.

The outside air was cool, but wonderfully fresh and clean. The ruined market at the castle gate, however, was not clean at all.

Travelling by air, he quickly concluded, was a major advantage. As he picked his way through the wreckage of the village he wondered how he and his party had ever gotten to the castle gate without so much as tripping over a broken beam.

Then he realized that Vond had been with them, more or less leading the way. He had undoubtedly cleared a path.

Sterren had been following an old road, but now he stopped and looked around.

Sure enough, a path had been cut directly through the village, straighter than any street there had ever been, from the gate out toward the farm where he and Vond had climbed the rooftop to spy on the Ksinallionese trebuchet. He clambered across a smashed pottery shop to reach it, and then followed it easily out into the open fields beyond.

Once clear of the ruins of the village, he turned north and headed toward Vond, who was still hanging in the sky, stacking up immense blocks of stone.

A bird sang cheerily somewhere nearby, and a gentle breeze rumpled Sterren's hair as he walked.

He was perhaps halfway to the edge of Vond's pit when the warlock stopped cutting slabs and turned to a low rise nearby — not that there were any real hills, other than the one covered by Semma Castle; this little bump in the ground was one of the higher elevations in the area. It also had the distinction of somehow having avoided being churned into mud by armies and storms; the top of it still bore a large patch of brown grass.

With a deeper, louder rumble than any that had come before, the top of the hillock lifted up and flattened out. The rumble continued for several minutes, and the ground shook wildly; Sterren stumbled and fell to all fours. The birdsong stopped abruptly.

He watched, and realized that Vond was filling in underneath the patch of grass, pulling soil and rock from all sides, building himself a rectagular mound of earth with the grassy area on top.

It took several minutes; then, abruptly, the rumbling and shaking stopped. The rectangular mound stood like a giant block.

Vond eyed the mound critically, and then made a few adjustments, hauling tons upon tons of rock and sand to prop this corner or that edge up a little farther.

That done, he then levelled out the area around his raised rectangle until it was as smooth as a well-laid floor for at least fifty feet on all sides.

Sterren watched this without moving.

When the warlock was satisfied, the slabs of stone that he had quarried earlier began lifting from their piles and drifting over to the mound, settling in on all sides, walling it in with solid stone.

Sterren stood and marched on as this proceeded.

He got within shouting distance within another few minutes, but merely stopped and watched at first.

The stone slabs were being set upright against the sides of the mound, then pressed in at the base until they stood exactly vertical. When one was in place, the next would fly over to join it. Sterren could not be sure — he was still a couple of hundred feet away — but it appeared that the seams between stones were somehow being welded shut, so that the rectangular mound was soon surrounded by what amounted to a single solid piece of rock.

When that casing was done, more slabs were laid horizontally around the outside, their inner edges butted up flush against the base of the retaining wall.

The operation was thunderously loud, of course; anything that slapped tons of stone about like building blocks had to be. During a lull, however, when the next slab was just beginning its flight toward the construction site, Sterren called, "*Hai*! Vond! Hello!"

Vond glanced over, saw him, and waved.

Sterren waved back.

Vond held up a hand, signalling Sterren to wait. The slab continued along its path, fell in neatly next to its predecessor with a resounding crash, and then with much grinding and hissing was pushed tightly into place against the wall.

That done, the warlock dropped from the sky until he hung a foot or so off the ground, five feet in front of Sterren.

"Good morning," Sterren said.

Vond nodded a polite greeting.

"Pardon me for asking so bluntly," Sterren said, "but what are you doing?"

"I'm building a palace," Vond replied.

Sterren looked at the stone construction. "A palace?" he asked.

Vond turned and followed his gaze.

"Well," he admitted, "it doesn't look like much yet, but I've just started. I want it on a hilltop, but there aren't any around here, so I'm going to build my own. It seemed stupid to build a hill, and then dig half of it back out for the crypts, so I'm building the crypts now, and then I'll put the hill up around them."

"Oh," Sterren said. "Oh, I see; that piece in the middle, the rectangle with the grass on top, that'll be a courtyard, right?"

"Yes, exactly!" Vond smiled broadly.

"And you'll have cellars on all four sides, and then the palace on top of the cellars, and then you'll pile up the dirt and put a hill around the whole thing?"

"Yes, exactly!" Vond repeated. "What do you think?"

"Seems like a lot of work," Sterren said.

"Oh, no," Vond protested, "it's fun! After all, I'm a warlock; the more magic I use, the better I feel. It's not like other magicks that tire people out, or like ordinary work; it's invigorating! And I'm pretty much all-powerful now, you know."

Sterren nodded. "Ah . . . I don't know if it's any of my business," he said after a moment's hesitation, "but I don't know how well this is going to go over with the local people around here. After all, you're tearing up several small farms here, and I don't suppose that the peasants who lived here are gone for good. Most of them probably just ran to the castle or to some relative's house, and will be back as soon as they hear that the war's over, and they're likely to be pretty upset about this."

Vond shrugged. "Too bad," he said. "What can they do about it?"

Sterren blinked at this callousness, and said, "You're still mortal, aren't you? Somebody might put a knife in your back."

"Ha!" Vond said derisively. "Let them try! Don't worry about me, Sterren. It'll take more than any of these barbarians can do to kill *me*."

"You're sure of that?" Sterren asked, genuinely curious.

"Oh, yes," the warlock replied confidently.

Sterren looked over the beginnings of Vond's palace and remarked, "I don't suppose old King Phenvel is going to like this much, either."

"I don't expect him to," Vond retorted. "That's why I'm doing it — well, one reason, anyway."

"What's another?"

Vond grinned. "For one thing, it's fun! Haven't you always wanted to live in a palace and have everything at your beck and call? I have — and now I can! Warlockry's just about limitless, you know; nobody's ever found anything it can't do. It's just that we've all always been so scared to use it, because of the nightmares and the whispering and the Calling. Well, here, I don't have to worry about those! I have the power without the limits! Old King Phenvel can go bugger a goat, for all I care. I can do anything I want to here, and there isn't a damn thing he can do about it."

"For your sake, I hope you're right," Sterren said. "I'd feel awful if you got killed because I brought you here and you misjudged the situation."

"I haven't misjudged anything! It's that old fool of a king who misjudged, telling me to take my lousy jewelry and go home. You know why I want a hill, Sterren? So it'll be higher than his. I could have taken his castle away from him — and I might do it yet, if he goes on bothering me — but I thought it would be more fun to just outshine him completely, build a palace bigger and higher and more beautiful than his castle ever was. After all, his is something of a dump, really — sloppy and crowded and not much to look at."

Sterren nodded. "I can understand being annoyed at him," he agreed, "but don't you think you're overreacting?"

Vond considered this for a few seconds, and then said, "No. I mean, if it weren't going to be fun, that would be different. It's not as if I have anything better to do, or anywhere else to go. I'm stuck here, and I might as well make the best of it. Getting back at Phenvel for being such a fool is just a little extra, not the real reason."

"I can see that," Sterren admitted. He hesitated, and then asked, "What do you plan to do when the palace is finished?"

"Live in it, of course."

"I mean, do you have any long-range plans?"

Vond shrugged. "I hadn't decided. I expect to collect a few concubines, spend some time decorating the palace, collecting treasures to go in it, that sort of thing."

"I see," Sterren said. He hesitated, and then plunged on. "So, at least so far, you weren't planning to conquer Semma, or anything like that?" He hoped fervently that he hadn't just presented Vond with an appealing idea.

No, he decided, he was certain that anyone in Vond's position would have thought of it already.

Vond laughed. "Don't be silly," he said. "I've *already* conquered Semma. They just don't know it yet!"

Twenty-Six

Sterren stayed and chatted with Vond for several more minutes, but he could see that the warlock was eager to get back to his palace-building, and he knew that the king would be growing ever more impatient.

He was not looking forward to facing King Phenvel, but he knew he would have to sooner or later, and he decided he might as well get it over with. He told Vond farewell and started back toward the castle.

He had gone scarcely a dozen steps when he paused and considered.

Did he really have to go back to the castle at all? Couldn't he just turn and head overland to Akalla, and back home to Ethshar? After all, if Vond had conquered Semma, then presumably, he was no longer the hereditary warlord, and King Phenvel no longer had any authority over him — or anybody else, for that matter.

It occurred to him for the very first time that royal power and authority were simply a matter of belief, of common consent to an arrangement. There was nothing inherent in Phenvel of Semma that gave him the power of life and death over his subjects; that power existed only because the people of Semma *believed* it existed. His castle guards and his courtiers obeyed him because they believed he was the rightful ruler of the land, and others obeyed because those guards and courtiers enforced his wishes.

If the guards ever decided that Phenvel was just a crazy old man, then he would *be* just a crazy old man.

Vond's power, on the other hand, was quite real. He might not have any hereditary title or special cachet of authority, but he could easily make anyone obey him by using his warlockry. He needed no guards or courtiers. When he said that he had already conquered Semma, Sterren could accept that — who could defy him?

And wasn't that the true definition of power? Vond could do anything he pleased, and no one could prevent it. Phenvel could do what he pleased only so long as people believed in his authority as king.

Vond's power seemed much more substantial.

This, Sterren guessed, would soon make the warlock's conquest an accepted fact. Phenvel had offended Vond, and now Vond was making plain just who really held power in Semma. Surely, Phenvel's power would collapse quickly once it became obvious that he could do nothing against Vond. His authority would be destroyed, and the whole elaborate structure of hereditary nobility would undoubtedly collapse with it.

Sterren would no longer be warlord.

He could just turn now, and go home.

But on the other hand, it was a long trip, and he was in no particular hurry. The situation in Semma had gotten very interesting, and he was curious about how it would turn out.

He was interested, also, in what might befall some of the people in the area.

He walked on, toward the castle.

The gatekeeper let him in without discussion, and he headed directly for the royal apartments.

He was admitted immediately. Queen Ashassa and the two younger princesses had joined the king; Princess Lura grinned at him, and even Princess Shirrin managed a tentative smile.

The instant Sterren had completed his formal bow King Phenvel demanded, "Well? What's he doing out there?"

"He says he's making a castle, your Majesty," Sterren replied. He did not know the Semmat for "palace," and was unsure what other verb might be most suitable for "building."

"Making a castle?" Queen Ashassa asked, puzzled.

"Yes, your Majesty," Sterren said.

"What do you mean, making a castle?" the king demanded.

"I mean, your Majesty, that he is taking stones, very large stones, and putting them together into a . . . a castle. I don't know the right words to make it clearer."

"A *real* castle, or just an image of some kind, a model?"

"A real castle, your Majesty. He says he will live in it."

"That's ridiculous. *This* is Semma Castle, and I am king! No one else may build a castle in my realm!"

Sterren did not waste time answering that.

"Go tell him to stop!" the king demanded.

Sterren hesitated. "I can tell him," he said, "but he won't stop."

"Well, *make* him stop! This is all your fault, after all; you're the one who brought all these infernal magicians here! We've never needed a lot of fancy magicians in Semma, and we got along just fine until you brought this whatever-it-is who's not a wizard here!"

"Your Majesty, your army was . . . the enemy had at least three men to each one of yours. Magic was . . ."

"Oh, stop arguing! You go tell him to stop what he's doing and put everything back the way it was!"

"Your Majesty . . ."

"Go! Do it!"

Sterren went.

He nodded politely to the man at the gate, and followed the clear path through the ruined village once again.

Vond saw him coming.

"Oh, hello," he said, "I didn't expect you back so soon."

Sterren shrugged as he looked over the half-built crypts. "The king sent me," he said. He strolled out onto one of the stone slabs.

"Oh?" Vond said.

"Yes. He wants you to stop what you're doing and put everything back the way it was."

"I daresay he does."

"He ordered me to come tell you to stop."

Vond nodded. "Go ahead, then."

"In the name of Phenvel, King of Semma, stop building your palace and put everything back the way it was!"

"No. You can go back and give him that answer. Was there anything else?"

"Not from him. I was wondering, though — don't you think it might get rather lonely, out here in this palace?" He waved at the cellars, which now covered a wide area around the "courtyard" and had a partially-completed outer wall around most of two sides.

Vond looked down at his elaborate stone box.

"Maybe at first," he admitted, "a little. But I expect other warlocks will come along, once word gets out about the new source of power here."

"You expect word to get out?"

Vond looked momentarily disconcerted for the first time since he drove off the invading armies.

"Of course," he said, "but if it doesn't, I'll send messengers back to Ethshar. You know, I hadn't thought about that — we're really way out here in the middle of nowhere, aren't we?"

Sterren nodded. "If you go up about a hundred feet and look over that way," he said, pointing south, "you ought to be able to see the edge of the World."

Vond sighed. "I've always lived in Ethshar, back in the middle of things, where you can't keep a secret if you try. I hadn't thought about how the news would spread; I just took it for granted."

"I don't think you can, here."

"Well, I'll send messengers. I expect people will notice when I start building an empire, in any case."

"Oh," Sterren asked, "are you planning to build an empire?"

"Oh, I think so," Vond said. "Isn't it sort of traditional, for conquerors? Besides, Semma is so *tiny*! If I want to put together a decent harem I need more to choose from, for one thing!"

"What did you have in mind?" Sterren asked cautiously.

"Well, to start," Vond said, "I was planning to conquer Ophkar and Ksinallion; that should be easy enough, since I've already routed their armies. After that, I thought I'd see how far I could go before I start to hear that whisper out of Aldagmor again. I'm not stupid, Sterren; I won't be sailing off to Ethshar where the nightmares will get me. Even so, I ought to be able to put together half a dozen of these silly little kingdoms, don't you think?"

Sterren had to concede that the warlock probably could, indeed, rule everything in the area. After all, he had lost contact with Aldagmor and started getting his headaches back in Akalla, which meant that Akalla, Skaia, Ophkar, and Semma would almost certainly be well within his grasp, and probably Ksinallion and several other kingdoms as well.

Not that any of those kingdoms amounted to much of anything.

"And you don't think you'll get lonely, or bored?" he asked.

"Why should I?" Vond snapped. "I can have as many people around as I want, just by ordering it! And beautiful women — there must be some, even here. Men in power always attract beautiful women."

"But they'll all be scared of you. You won't have anyone you can talk to just casually, as an equal — or even near-equal. And what will you *do* with this empire?"

"I'll just sit back and enjoy it, of course! I'll live the good life. And other warlocks will hear about it and will come to live here; I'll have my own court, and all the nobles will be warlocks, and we'll rule because we deserve to, not because we were born lucky."

"What if one of these other warlocks gets ambitious and decides to take over, though?"

Vond shook his head. "It can't happen. I thought of that. But I got here first, so I'll always be the most powerful, as long as I keep using magic. Look, I was almost as powerful as a warlock could ever get, back in Ethshar — I had the nightmares pretty badly. If I'd done one or two more big magicks, I'd have heard the Calling and gone north. So nobody is going to arrive here any more powerful than I was when *I* got here. And nobody will have any special way to overtake me, because warlockry doesn't work that way. You get more power by using power, and you can only use it so fast. As long as I keep working magic, I'll always be more powerful than anyone who comes after me. You see?"

Sterren did see, and said so.

Vond nodded. "So," he said, "my empire will be a haven for warlocks — when they start worrying about the Calling, they'll pack up and come here, where they can safely use all the magic they want."

Sterren could see how this might, in fact, happen. He could see how it would be very pleasant indeed for warlocks.

He could also see how it might be very unpleasant for everybody else. Magicians elsewhere always kept each other in check, or were kept in check by natural limits on their magic. Witches and seers and sorcerers and a variety of other magicians generally had only very limited abilities. Demonology was risky, and ever more risky as it got more powerful, since demons can't be trusted. Theurgy was limited by the gods' unwillingness to interfere with the World beyond a certain level. Wizardry — well, Sterren didn't really know what kept wizards from getting out of hand, unless it was rivalry with other wizards, or something about the seemingly chaotic way wizardry worked, or maybe just the difficulty of acquiring the bizarre ingredients they needed for their spells.

Warlockry had always been kept in check by the Calling. Now Vond had found a way around that — or at least he thought he had.

Sterren suspected that Vond was being overly optimistic about that, but in light of his announced plans to build an empire, mentioning this seemed like a mistake.

He wondered what the other sorts of magician might think about all this. Might the rumored-to-exist Wizards' Guild resent the presumption of a warlock establishing an empire?

They very well might, Sterren thought, and he almost said as much to Vond, but then he caught himself.

Why should he do Vond any favors? The man was about to enslave an entire section of the Small Kingdoms to avenge a slight from a foolish old man — and for the fun of it. It was true that he and Sterren had been comrades in arms, as it were, but that hardly took precedence over common decency.

But on the other hand, would Vond be any worse than Phenvel? He might turn out to be a perfectly adequate ruler.

Sterren had no way of knowing. He decided to wait and see. Meanwhile, he would keep any possible threats to Vond's usurped authority to himself, in case he needed them later. That included both the Wizards' Guild and what

Sterren thought was a basic flaw in Vond's logic about his safety from the Calling.

For one thing, he could not be completely certain that either threat really existed.

"*Hai*, Sterren!" Vond called. "Did you fall asleep or something?"

Sterren realized that he had been standing motionless, absorbed in thought, for several seconds. "No," he called. "Just thinking."

"About what?"

"Oh," he said evasively, "what an empire of warlocks would be like."

"Well," Vond replied, "I hope you'll stay around and find out! I owe you a favor, Sterren, for bringing me here. You treated me well and fairly, and it was your suggestion that helped me tap into the new source. Oh, I think I might have latched onto it eventually by myself, but you made it easier. You know, you've got a tiny bit of warlockry yourself; you could be one of the rulers of the empire!"

Sterren shook his head. "I don't have any warlockry. Not here, anyway."

"It's there, Sterren, it's just attuned to the Aldagmor Source, not the new one. I can fix that. I can let you hear the new one, at least as well as you ever heard the Aldagmor one."

"I doubt that. I've got no aptitude for it."

"Don't be silly; you lived off it for years, didn't you?"

"I never affected anything but dice, and I didn't even know I was doing that! Some magic!"

"But it should be different here; after all, I think we're only ten leagues from the source itself."

That caught Sterren's interest. "Ten leagues?"

"I think so; I can feel it, you know, and sort of measure . . . there aren't words for it in Ethsharitic. We warlocks haven't worked them out yet. But yes, I'm pretty certain the source is ten leagues that way." He pointed to the northwest; Sterren noted the exact direction as carefully as he could, for future reference.

"Ten leagues or a hundred," he said, "I don't think I'll ever be much of a warlock."

"Don't argue with me!" Vond snapped. He gestured at Sterren, and Sterren blinked.

Something had happened; he could feel it in the back of his head.

"There!" Vond said. "I've adjusted your brain a little; now you can hear the new source!"

"I don't hear anything," Sterren said.

"I don't mean hear, with your ears! I mean you're a warlock. You can draw power from it. Here, catch this without touching it!"

Vond pulled a clear, shiny object from the air in front of him, and tossed it at Sterren.

Sterren threw up his hands to ward it off, and at the same time, in the back of his mind, thought to himself that maybe he *was* a warlock, maybe he could catch it, control it as if it were the dice he had guided back in Ethshar. He tried to think of it that way, to imagine what it would feel like to move something without touching it.

Then the little sphere shattered on the stone at his feet.

He looked down, bent over, and picked up a sliver. It was ice; it melted away in his hand.

"I *tried*," he said.

Vond was glaring at him in disgust. "I know you did. I felt it. And I guess you were right; you're no warlock!"

"Where did you get the ice?" Sterren asked, looking at the water on his fingers.

"I pulled it out of the air; it's easy, for a real warlock."

"Oh," Sterren said, oddly impressed. He had seen Vond

cutting out huge slabs of bedrock without tools, but some-how pulling ice out of the air seemed even more unnatural. "Can you do it again?"

"Of course I can!" Vond said, clearly affronted.

"I only meant . . ." Sterren began.

"Oh, go away!" Vond snapped. "I'm tired of all your questions, and I've got a palace to build! You go tell those people in that castle that I'm in charge now, and when I finish the palace I'll tell them what I want from them."

Sterren started to say something, and thought better of it.

"Go!" Vond thundered — literally, as the air about him flashed crimson and the word sprang up from the ground.

Sterren went.

Twenty-Seven

"I wouldn't worry too much," Sterren said. Princess Shirrin blinked at him. She and her father were the only two Semmans present; the queen and Princess Lura had gone elsewhere, and at the moment the servants all happened to be out of the room.

"Oh, you wouldn't, would you?" said King Phenvel.

"No, I wouldn't," Sterren repeated. "You can't do anything about him. You're just going to have to live with it. He's not . . . not . . ." Sterren groped unsuccessfully for a Semmat word approximating "malicious," and gave up. "If you don't anger him," he said, "he won't hurt anybody."

"But he's a usurper, a traitor!" the king shouted.

Sterren shrugged. He didn't consider it treason, since Vond was Ethsharitic, but he had to admit that the term "usurper" was accurate enough.

"All right, warlord," King Phenvel said. "If you were king of Semma, how would *you* deal with him?"

"I'd surrender," Sterren said immediately. He didn't know the word for "abdicate."

Shirrin let out a little squeak of dismay, which the two men ignored.

Sterren didn't point out that if he were king of Semma, he would abdicate in any case, regardless of whether or not an all-powerful warlock were causing trouble. Being king did not look like an enjoyable occupation.

"Oh, go away," Phenvel growled.

Sterren bowed, and retreated.

With his duty fulfilled for the moment, he headed directly for the kitchens; he had not yet broken his fast, and his stomach was beginning to cramp with hunger.

He was not particularly surprised to find the two wizards and three witches already there, seated along the benches around two sides of a low table. The presence of Princess Lura, perched atop a high stool, was somewhat less expected, but not a great shock.

He greeted them all politely, and then asked one of the cooks' helpers to find him something. ". . . a stale bun, a lightly-chewed bone, whatever comes to hand."

She laughed. "Don't worry, my lord, we can always see what the dogs wouldn't finish!"

"Oh, excellent! Do that, please!"

The servant hurried off, and Sterren settled onto a chair near a large chopping block that could serve him as a table, facing the others.

"Hello, Lord Sterren," Princess Lura said. "What's your crazy magician doing?"

"Oh, I don't think he's *crazy,*" Sterren replied.

"What *is* he doing?" Shenna asked, in Ethsharitic. "I woke early this morning, but he was already up and gone. I'm not sure he slept at all."

"I've heard warlocks don't need much sleep," Emner remarked.

"Speak Semmat!" Lura demanded, in Semmat.

"I'll translate anything important," Shenna promised, in lightly-accented Semmat better than Sterren's own. "And if I don't, then Hamder or Ederd or Sterren will. But Annara and Emner here don't *know* any Semmat."

"Well, I don't know any Ethsharitic, and this is my daddy's castle!"

"But we're not talking to your daddy; we're talking to each other," Shenna pointed out. "I promise, Lura, I'll translate."

"That's your Highness Princess Lura, to you," Lura corrected grumpily.

Sterren looked at Lura for a moment, trying to decide whether he should say anything, and decided he shouldn't.

"Well?" Emner asked, using the Ethsharitic word.

"He's building a palace," Sterren said in his native tongue. "He's appointed himself dictator of Semma and plans to build an empire run by warlocks."

Shenna hesitated, and then translated this to Lura as, "The crazy magician is building a palace so he can be a king, too."

"Why would he want to do that?" the princess demanded.

Sterren answered in Semmat, "He thinks your father wasn't very nice to him."

Princess Lura looked baffled. "But Daddy is rotten to *everybody*!"

"*I* know that," Sterren said, "but Vond isn't used to it. His feelings were hurt."

"*That's* pretty silly," Lura declared.

Sterren shrugged. "I guess so," he said.

"What was that about?" Annara asked, in Ethsharitic.

Sterren sighed. He saw the kitchen maid approaching with a well-stocked platter — despite the threats, it was heavily loaded with dried fruit, slices of mutton left from breakfast, and assorted breads — and decided he didn't want to deal with explanations just then. "Look," he said in Ethsharitic, "I want to eat something, and I get confused dealing with two different languages. Could you people wait awhile?" He switched to Semmat, and said, "I want to eat now. Your Highness, could I come to your family quarters later and answer your questions then?"

The little princess looked at Sterren, and then around at the magicians. "Oh, all right," she said. She slid from her perch and stalked off.

Sterren and the five magicians managed not to laugh at

her retreating figure. The warlord made it a little easier for himself by stuffing a pastry in his mouth; he found it hard to laugh with a mouthful of flaky crust.

When Princess Lura was safely out of earshot and the edge had been taken off his hunger, Sterren leaned back in his chair and began talking, answering the magicians' questions.

With a little prompting, he explained about warlockry; of the five, only Ederd knew anything about it at all. He described what was known of the Aldagmor source, and the Calling, and Vond's discovery of a secondary source ten leagues to the northwest of Semma, and he reported what Vond had said of his intentions.

When he had finished, the five looked at one another.

"I think I'll go home," Shenna said. "It doesn't look that safe around here." Hamder nodded in agreement.

"I must admit that if warlocks are going to be running things around here, they won't have much use for witches," Ederd agreed, "but I think I'd like to stay for a little while and see what develops."

Sterren nodded approvingly. His own attitude was very similar.

"Suit yourself," Hamder said. "I'm going home."

"Me, too," said Shenna.

Emner and Annara were obviously uncertain of their plans. They were eyeing each other doubtfully.

"One of us should stay to keep an eye on things, I think," Emner said at last, "and the other should go contact a Guildmaster."

Annara nodded. "You better go," she said. "I don't know any Guildmasters."

"I'm not sure I do, any more," Emner said.

"Well, you go, anyway," Annara insisted.

Emner nodded.

"What's this about Guildmasters?" Sterren asked.

Annara and Emner exchanged quick glances.

Emner cleared his throat. "I suppose you've heard of the Wizards' Guild," he said.

Sterren nodded.

"Well," Emner explained, "Guildmasters are the officers of the Wizards' Guild. This is all more or less secret, you understand, but it's not one of the *big* secrets; we won't be punished for telling you."

"You think your Guild will want to do something about this?" Sterren asked. He hoped for some facts to back up his earlier theorizing.

Emner spread his palms. "Who knows? They might, though, and if we didn't tell them about it, and they found out later, it wouldn't do our standing any good, that's certain."

"They probably won't do anything," Annara said. "They generally don't like to interfere with non-wizards. But they like to know what's going on. And sometimes they do intervene, eventually. Usually they wait a minimum of ten years, to see what's going to happen. The Guild has been around a long, long time, and it's a pretty patient organization."

"How do you know all this?" Hamder asked.

"We're members of the Guild, of course," Emner said. "You can't be a wizard if you don't join. They kill anyone who tries, usually in some spectacularly horrible way."

"How do you join?" Hamder persisted.

"When you sign on as an apprentice, you're initiated into the Guild before you're taught your first spell," Annara explained. "All through your apprenticeship, you'll get lessons about the Guild, as well as about wizardry itself. Not that they really tell you much. How the Guild actually works is all secret. There are Guildmasters, and there are rumors of an Inner Circle within the Guildmasters, but we don't . . . well, at least *I* don't know whether there's really an Inner Circle, or who gets chosen to be a Guildmaster, or anything else about how the Guild operates. I just know that if you break a Guild rule, you die, and I know what the Guild rules are, and what I can and can't tell outsiders."

Emner nodded. "It was the same for me," he said, "even though my master's old master was a Guildmaster himself, until he died."

"So you intend to inform the Wizards' Guild of Vond's plans," Sterren said. "Then what?"

Emner and Annara exchanged glances. "Then I go home," Emner said, "if the Guild will let me. And I'll buy a dream-spell or a messenger-spell and let Annara know what the Guild wants her to do, if anything, if they haven't sent a message already."

"And what does the Guild do?"

"I have no idea," Emner said.

"Most likely," Annara said, "they'll argue for several months, maybe years, and give the problem time to either go away by itself or develop into something serious. My master always said that was how they worked."

Emner nodded. "My master never said, but it sounds right."

Sterren turned to Ederd. "Is there a Witches' Guild?"

The three witches exchanged glances. "Not really," Shenna said. "There are two rather loose organizations, the Brotherhood and the Sisterhood, but they're nothing like what Annara described. At least, the Sisterhood isn't. I never joined either one, but I was invited by the Sisterhood once. I turned it down; I didn't like the rules. They swap spells and recipes, and talk shop a lot, and they have an emergency fund for when a member's in trouble, but they've got a lot of regulations about not competing with each other and not keeping secrets from the group and a whole bunch of other stuff that I didn't want to put up with."

"The Brotherhood's even looser," Ederd said. "I was a member for a year, but I got tired of paying dues for nothing, and I quit."

"I never even heard of it," Hamder said.

Ederd looked at him curiously. "Your master never mentioned it?"

"No, she didn't," Hamder said, glaring back.

"Is there a Warlocks' Guild?" Shenna asked. "You seem to know a lot about them, Sterren."

"I failed an apprenticeship," he said. "If there is a Guild, I didn't get far enough to find out about it. I don't think there is, though; warlocks tend to be pretty anti-social. And they don't have the history wizards and witches do; they haven't even lasted twenty years yet."

"I wonder about the sorcerers?" Hamder said.

"And the theurgists?" Annara added.

"You could ask Agor about them," Sterren said. "He's a theurgist here in Semma, though he isn't a very good one."

"I'll do that," Annara said. "Where do I find him? I think I'd like to talk to him about all this, and see what he thinks we ought to do about Vond out there."

Ederd nodded agreement. "Good idea."

Sterren shrugged. "I can show you his room, but there's no hurry."

"Speak for yourself," Hamder retorted. "I intend to get out of here today, in case somebody gets Vond mad and he decides to squash this whole castle."

"Me, too," Shenna said.

"I don't think he'll do anything like *that*," Sterren said.

"All the same," Emner said, getting to his feet, "the three of us who are going probably ought to go, without wasting any more time. If you don't mind, Sterren, I'm going to go pack my things." He turned to Annara. "I have that spell you wanted written out; I'll trade it for the Explosive Seal any time it's ready."

"I don't know how to put all of it in writing; I'd better come show you," Annara said. She rose, and together the two wizards departed.

"Excuse me, my lord," Hamder said, as he, too, stood up, "but I think the wizard's right. I'll go pack."

Shenna just nodded without saying anything, as she and Hamder left.

That left just Sterren and Ederd.

"Well," Ederd said, "I suppose I'll go look around the castle, see if I can find a window with a good view of the warlock's palace, and let you eat in peace." He rose.

Sterren nodded. "If you like climbing stairs, my chamber in the tower has a great view. Tell the guards I said you could go in."

Ederd bowed, and left.

Sterren ate.

Twenty-Eight

"Ten leagues to the northwest, you say?"

Sterren nodded. Queen Ashassa looked thoughtful.

"That would be Lumeth of the Towers," she said. "Perhaps near the Towers themselves."

"Maybe it *is* the Towers!" Princess Lura said.

The queen nodded. "Maybe it is," she agreed. "Certainly, nobody knows what they're for, and generating this magic you describe seems as likely an explanation as any."

Sterren glanced at Nissitha and Shirrin, but as usual, they said nothing. Nissitha stared at him disdainfully, and Shirrin, whenever she saw him look in her direction, looked quickly away. The adoration he had seen so often in her face seemed to be gone, now, replaced by a ferocious disappointment.

Prince Dereth, age eleven, watched carefully, but said little beyond occasional expressions of wonder.

Nobody replied to the queen's comment, and when the silence began to lengthen uncomfortably, Sterren asked, "Is there anything else, your Majesty?"

"Just this, Lord Sterren. You know this man Vond, and you know something of his magic. What would you advise us to do?"

Sterren frowned slightly. He could only give one answer, but he knew it was not one that the queen would like.

"Nothing," he said. He would have liked to have said more, explaining his reasons, but the effort of making himself understood in Semmat was too much. He had been talking all morning, save when he was walking back and forth between the castle and Vond's building site, and he was tired of it. He left his answer a single word.

"You think he could defeat our entire army, if you marched against him?"

"Yes, your Majesty — easily." Sterren did not bother to point out that the warlock had already defeated the much larger armies of Ophkar and Ksinallion; the queen knew that.

Ashassa eyed him for a moment, then nodded slightly. "All right, Lord Sterren," she said, "you may go."

"Thank you, your Majesty." He rose, bowed, and backed out of the room.

Once in the corridor he paused, unsure where to go.

The three departing magicians might well have already left, and he had no idea where to find Annara or Ederd — unless Annara had tracked down Agor, in which case she might not appreciate any interruptions. The climb back to his own room was too much to face immediately.

Well, there were always his duties as warlord; he had not seen anything of his troops since returning from Ethshar save vague shapes moving on distant battlements, or guards at various doors. He headed for the barracks.

As he walked, he reviewed his own thoughts about Vond and the unexpected turn of recent events. He had not had a chance to sit down and think about it, but in the course of the morning's several discussions, he had reached several conclusions.

The warlock's plans had several good points to them, in truth. Uniting several of the Small Kingdoms, and putting an end to their stupid little wars, would hardly hurt anyone or anything except the egos of the conquered rulers. Most of the people affected would be peasants, who would acquire a new ruler, and who would no longer have to worry about having their farms looted and burned, their wives and daughters assaulted by invading soldiers.

That assumed, of course, that Vond actually could build and hold his empire as easily as he believed he could, but Sterren thought it was a very reasonable assumption. As Vond had pointed out, warlockry without the Calling was virtually limitless, and right now, at least, he was free of the Calling. Magic was scarce and feared in this region. Who could effectively oppose him?

The local nobility would find themselves deprived of their traditional powers and perquisites, but Sterren found himself untroubled by that prospect. Life was inherently uncertain, always a gamble; why should kings and nobles be exempt from that uncertainty? The lot of them could go elsewhere and find ways to survive, he was sure, or could presumably find places for themselves under Vond's rule; even a warlock could not do everything himself, and would surely need experienced administrators to handle the details of governing.

The question was, what else would Vond do, beyond uniting the kingdoms and dispossessing the nobility?

That, of course, Sterren did not know. Vond had spoken of concubines — that might mean abduction and rape, or it might just mean accepting offers. He was setting himself up as an absolute ruler, but did that mean only that he would expect his orders to be obeyed, or that he would treat everyone else as mere slaves, to be beaten or killed at whim?

Benevolent despot or brutal tyrant — the difference would lie in Vond's personality, and Sterren simply did not know the man well enough to guess which he would become.

If he became a tyrant, then what? If he turned out benevolent, then Sterren would leave well enough alone, but what if he became a tyrant?

Walking out and heading back to Ethshar was a possibility, but somehow it did not seem like a very appealing one. After all, Sterren had to admit that he had brought Vond here.

He had had no way of knowing what would happen, of course. Nobody could have known about the new power source in Lumeth. Still, intention was not always as important as results. He had never intended to lose when he played dice, but that hadn't put food in his mouth when he *did* lose. One had to live with the results of one's actions, whether those results were planned or not.

If Vond were a tyrant, what then?

There was the Wizards' Guild, of course, lurking somewhere in the background, but what Annara and Emner had told him of the Guild was hardly very inspiring. Slow, cautious, not eager to interfere — that did not describe an organization that would efficiently remove a tyrant.

There was assassination. Sterren had discussed the possible assassination of the kings of Ophkar and Ksinallion with Lar Samber's son, his inherited spy, and thought he had a good idea of what would be involved. Semma had no history of assassination, no one trained in assassination; he could send his soldiers or Lar's spies, but they would probably fail and either die or be captured in the attempt. They might also be traced back to him, their warlord. Against a mere king, Lar judged the odds on a first attempt no better than one in five, and getting steadily worse with each attempt as the target took ever stronger counter-measures.

Lar had hinted at knowledge of an organization of professional assassins, but Sterren had the clear impression that this group, if it actually existed, did not operate anywhere near Semma. Furthermore, if he had understood Lar's hints, they were very expensive, very secretive, and generally not easy to deal with. They were not so much a gang or a guild as a cult; the name Demerchan had been mentioned once.

That might be worth pursuing if all else failed, but it did not look promising.

He could try to reason with Vond, of course; Vond considered him a friend and ally. Perhaps he could sway the warlock, keep him from becoming a tyrant in the first place.

He would have to try that.

There was one other possibility, one that he had seen almost immediately as the inevitable solution. He considered it as he opened the barracks door. It was a solution that would take care of itself, eventually, but which he could either hurry or hinder.

Vond thought he was free of the Calling, but if Sterren understood the situation correctly, Vond was missing a vital point.

He shoved the whole question to the back of his mind as someone shouted, "It's the warlord! Three cheers for Sterren, Ninth Warlord!"

A ragged cheer broke out, and Sterren froze in the doorway.

He looked over his men, astonished by this display of enthusiasm. He had been so concerned with Vond that he had forgotten that it was only a day ago that the invading armies were sent fleeing. These soldiers didn't care about any warlocks; they were happy to have the siege broken, the catapults and battering ram destroyed, their constant duties on the walls at an end, and the methods used did not worry them at all. They were spontaneously applauding *him*, Sterren of Ethshar, who had brought them this easy victory.

He smiled and raised his hands in triumph for a moment. The cheering died down, and as men sank onto their bunks he spotted the three hunched backs in the corner.

The gamblers had not let a mere warlord interrupt their dice game.

"Thank you for your . . . your welcome," Sterren stammered. "I'm happy to be back! You did well!" He hesitated, looking at the listening faces and unsure what more to say.

He shrugged, and said, "What's the game back there? Can I play?"

Startled laughter broke out, and then applause; someone grabbed his arms, and a moment later he was in the corner, the dice in his hand.

"It's three-count, bet on the low roll," someone said.

Sterren nodded. He knew the game.

"Your turn, my lord," someone else said, as coins rattled onto the stone.

He shook the dice and tossed them. To keep the dice and win the coins on a first roll, he needed to roll three ones. If anything else came up, he had to pass the dice and the coins stayed. Three-count, the primitive ancestor of Sterren's favorite three-bone, was usually a long, slow game, with a good many small bets changing hands rather than a few large ones; it was something played by bored people eager to waste time, rather than serious gamblers, and Sterren had never played much.

He watched as the dice bounced from the wall and rolled across the floor. The first landed showing a single pip; the second bumped it, but did not tip it over, and it, too, showed just one pip when it came to rest.

The third bumped the toe of a soldier's boot and stopped, showing one pip.

Laughter and applause sounded again, as Sterren picked up his winnings.

Nobody was laughing half an hour later, when Sterren had won some sixty copper bits in one of the shortest games of three-count ever seen.

The soldiers scattered, leaving him standing there with a full purse in one hand, the dice in the other. He stared at the bits of polished bone.

His talent was back. Vond's attuning had worked, and he was drawing luck from the Lumeth source.

He wondered whether he should be pleased.

Twenty-Nine

The peasants were being evicted from the castle, and Sterren stood atop the wall and watched as they went unwillingly out the gate into the wreckage that had been their village.

These were the people who had run for the shelter of the castle walls when the banners of the invaders first appeared on the horizon; the gates had been shut and barred well before the enemy armies came within bowshot, leaving the stragglers to flee in all directions. The people who had reached the castle were not the bravest, and had been in no hurry to venture back out into the World.

King Phenvel, however, had had enough of the crowding and inconvenience, and at dinner the previous night had announced that all peasants were to be outside the gates before noon. He had ordered Sterren and Lord Algarven, the royal steward, to see to it.

Although he did not really think that Phenvel's authority still amounted to much, Sterren had shrugged and obeyed. Vond had only begun building his palace the previous morning, and despite Sterren's warnings, the new situation had not yet sunk in. Phenvel still thought of himself as ruler of Semma, and the other Semmans still had the habit of obeying him. The castle was still his.

So now Sterren stood on the ramparts, watching his soldiers herd the peasants out the gate.

Each one, whether man, woman, or child, did the same thing upon passing the gate. Each one looked north, at the warlock's building site.

Vond's project was progressing well. He had completed his crypts, or at least the shell, in that first day, and had built his hill up around them overnight. Now he was erecting white marble walls on that base. The ground shook each time a new section dropped into place, and the roar of stone grinding against stone was almost constant.

Vond's first quarry, now closed, had yielded granite, so the marble, gleaming in the morning sun, was a surprise, and combined with the horrendous racket it was very hard to ignore.

The entertainment, for Sterren, was not that each face turned toward the palace, but in seeing what each one did next.

Some stopped and stood staring, open-mouthed, until proddings from behind forced them to move on. Others took a single glance and marched on, stolidly accepting this miraculous construction as just another event that was none of their business. A few looked, then looked away, clearly frightened, as if just looking at the palace might somehow get them in trouble. Some of the children laughed and applauded as huge stones fell into position, or pointed wonderingly at the tiny black-robed figure hanging unsupported above the high white walls.

The next thing that each peasant did, after looking at Vond's latest handiwork, was to look at the ruined village, and the reactions to that were far more consistent. Sterren could see despair plainly in the expressions and slumped shoulders of virtually all the evictees.

He had already decided, by the time the first peasant passed the threshold into the mud-soaked, debris-strewn village market, that he would order his soldiers to help with the clean-up and rebuilding. They were supposed to be men of war, and it was the war that had made this mess, so cleaning it up fell within their duties as Sterren saw them.

The last peasant was stepping unwillingly out into the mud when the roar from the north stopped.

It took a moment for the echoes to die away and silence to descend, and by then everyone had noticed the change, and every face had turned toward the new palace.

The little black shape no longer flew above the marble walls; instead, it was soaring gracefully toward them. Sterren heard a few whispers from the crowd below, but then silence fell again as they all stared at the approaching warlock.

Sterren, too, stared, wondering why Vond had stopped work at this particular moment. He hadn't finished the wall he was working on. If he was coming to force King Phenvel to surrender, it struck Sterren as rather peculiar timing.

Then he realized that from his position high above the palace, Vond would have seen the people emerging from the castle. He might even have seen Sterren on the battlements above, and recognized him.

And Sterren, after all, was warlord of Semma. The warlock might think that an attack was being organized, or a formal surrender, or some other operation involving him.

"*Hai!*" he called, waving an arm. "Vond! Over here!" He did not want the warlock to believe for even a moment that anything suspicious was going on. He could probably kill every peasant there — and Sterren, too — as easily as Sterren would stamp on an ant.

Vond waved, and a moment later he settled down onto the wall beside Sterren. The peasants below stared up at the two of them.

"Hello, Sterren," he said. "What's happening? I saw the crowd from over there." He waved toward his palace, and Sterren saw a proud smile flash across his face. "Coming along nicely, isn't it?"

"Yes, it is," Sterren agreed. Privately, he thought that the place looked somewhat forbidding; Vond had not bothered with much architectural detailing, but had used huge blank slabs of stone for most of his construction. He had not yet cut windows in them, either. The result, despite the white marble, looked more like a fortress than a palace.

Vond himself looked as human and ordinary as ever, just a smiling middle-aged man in black robes, and it was a bit hard to comprehend that he had single-handedly erected most of that fortress in a day and a half.

"What's this?" the warlock asked, waving at the market square. It was obvious to anyone that the ragged crowd milling below was no army readying for an attack.

"The king's evicting them," Sterren explained. "They took shelter in the castle during the siege, and now that the siege is over they're leaving."

"Where are they going?" Vond asked, interested.

"Here," Sterren said, waving. "They're mostly from the village here. They'll have to clean it up and rebuild, of course; I'll be sending my men out to help. I suppose some of them come from the farms, too." He couldn't resist adding, "I don't know if any of them are from the farms you've torn up for your palace."

Vond glanced at him, startled, and then looked back down at the peasants.

"Oh," he said. "But this can't be all the people from all those farms and the entire village, too! What happened to the rest? Did the invaders kill them?"

Sterren shrugged. "Some of them, probably, but a lot must have fled every which way. You remember meeting some of those. These are just the ones who got to the castle before the gate was closed; nobody's gone out to bring in the others yet."

Vond stared down at the people for a moment longer, and a good many of them stared back at him.

"*Hai*," he called suddenly, "I am the Great Vond, the new lord of Semma! You see my palace over there!"

Sterren started to protest, to grab the warlock's sleeve, and then thought better of it. After all, the warlock was speaking Ethsharitic, which none of the peasants understood, a fact that Vond had clearly forgotten.

"I am going to want servants. Any of you who would be interested in working for me, you need only walk over to my palace and wait there! You need not decide immediately; come when you choose, and I will find places for you!"

A mutter of puzzlement ran through the crowd. Nobody moved.

"I will show you, now, why I am the true ruler of Semma, and not that oaf who calls himself your king!"

Vond raised his arms, and the mud of the marketplace rippled. Stones and broken beams were thrown up, to hang in mid-air for an instant, and then fling themselves away, out of the village and into the distance. The mud itself separated into water and soil, and the water, too, was flung away.

In a moment, the marketplace was clean and dry, the dirt hard-packed beneath the peasants' bare feet, pressed down almost into pavement by Vond's warlockry.

Sterren, watching in fascination, thought that even the dirt from the peasants' clothes and faces had gone into that smooth surface, leaving the crowd noticeably cleaner.

With a rush of wind, debris rolled up from one blocked street into a ball that hung in the air, and then sailed away.

Then another street was cleared, and another, in similar fashion.

In twenty minutes, Vond had cleared out all the wreckage, leaving untouched the houses that still stood, and removing all trace of those that had been knocked down.

Unfortunately, that left only half a village, and most

of that half was missing windows, doors, roofs, or even chunks of wall.

Vond eyed the results critically, then shrugged. "It's a start," he said. He raised a hand again.

Something, perhaps a motion in the corner of his eye, made Sterren turn and look at the castle. Faces were crowded in every window, watching this spectacle.

He turned back toward the village.

The wreckage that had been sent off over the hills was coming back now, as one huge, irregular mass that hung in the air like a cloud. It was shifting its shape like a cloud, too, though far faster than any natural formation. Wood, stone, and thatch were separating out into distinct portions; everything else was being dropped into a refuse heap in a handy field.

It occurred to Sterren for the first time that there were no natural clouds anywhere in sight, which, in light of what he had been told, hardly seemed normal for winter in Semma. He wondered if the warlock was controlling the weather, keeping the sky clear to make his working environment more pleasant.

When the different materials were sorted, Vond chose a house and studied it critically.

The thatch roof and most of the shutters were gone, but it was otherwise intact. Vond waved, and masses of thatch came flying down from the cloud and piled themselves into place.

"What about the shutters?" Sterren asked.

Vond glanced at him, then back at the house. "To Hell with the shutters," he said. "I can't do everything! How am I supposed to find the right ones out of all that?"

Sterren shrugged. "Just asking," he said.

The repair work continued, as Sterren and the peasants watched.

As the day dragged on, most of the peasants settled to the ground, sitting or lying on the hard earth and chatting amongst themselves. A few leaned up against the castle walls. None dared venture out of the market.

The faces in the castle windows changed, as people tired of watching and were replaced by others. Still, Vond had a steady audience for his performance. Sterren thought he saw Princess Shirrin there almost the entire time.

Some time after noon Sterren spotted one of his soldiers and ordered that food and drink be brought out for the peasants and himself. He asked Vond if he cared for anything.

The warlock declined the offer and continued with his work.

Sterren realized he hadn't seen Vond eat anything in days, and that there was surely no food in his unfinished palace. Was he living on magic alone?

Perhaps he was. Sterren thought better of inquiring, and didn't worry about it. He watched as his soldiers distributed bread, water, cheese, and dried fruit to the peasants, and then ate his own meal, which was similar save that he drank wine.

The restoration of the village took a long time; in fact, Vond still had three houses unfinished when the sun sank out of sight and the sky began to darken.

Vond took care of that easily enough by summoning an orange glow in the sky that gave him enough light to work by.

When he had completed repairs to every house that had still stood, he lowered his arms and said, "There!"

Sterren nodded. "Very impressive," he said.

Vond leaned over a merlon and called, "You can go home, now! If your house is gone, stay with a neighbor, and I'll take care of you later!"

The crowd below stirred; some of the peasants, particularly the children, had gone to sleep, and were awakened. Nobody left, however. Nobody made any move to leave the market. They just stared up at the warlock and the warlord.

"Why are you just sitting there?" Vond shouted.

Sterren reached out and put a hand on his arm. "They don't understand Ethsharitic," he said.

Vond whirled, and stared at Sterren for a moment. Then he turned back to the market below, realization dawning.

"Oh," he said. "Oh, *damn!*"

"You might want to learn Semmat," Sterren suggested mildly.

"I'd rather they learned Ethsharitic," Vond snapped. "And if I'm going to build an empire, I don't want to have to learn half a dozen different tongues, damn it!"

Sterren shrugged. "Well, in time I'm sure you can make Ethsharitic the common language for your court, but right now, none of these people knows a word of it."

"How the hell did all these stupid little languages happen, anyway? This was all part of Old Ethshar once, you know!"

"I have no idea," Sterren said, "but they did. Maybe it was demons, or a trick by the ruling class to keep people where they belonged."

Vond glared down at the village, lit a weird shade of orange by his unnatural illumination. "I suppose I'll need interpreters," he said.

"At least for now," Sterren agreed.

For a moment, nobody spoke. Then Vond said, "You tell them, Sterren. Tell them they can go home. Tell them that if any of them want to work as my servants, they should come to my palace in the morning. I'm going home." He rose into the air.

Sterren waved a farewell as the warlock began drifting

away, then leaned over the ramparts and called, "The Great Vond has finished his work! Go home now! The Great Vond wants servants! If you want to be a servant to the great Vond, go to his castle . . ." He remembered the word for "palace" from earlier conversation, and rephrased that. "Go to his palace in the morning! If your house is not fixed, stay with a friend!"

The peasants stared up at him, and he heard someone say, "Who in the World is that?" He didn't know if the man meant him or Vond; after all, since he had gone off to Ethshar before the invasion, he had not been seen much in his role as warlord.

Then, as his message sank in, the people began scattering to their rebuilt homes and shops.

The orange glow was fading rapidly as Vond moved off toward his fortress, but both moons were in the sky to allay the darkness. Sterren took one final look at the palace, its marble walls gleaming an eerie yellow against the black sky and plain in the strange mixed light, and then climbed back down from the wall and went inside.

So far, he could hardly accuse Vond of tyranny.

Even so, he knew that the empire was doomed from the start.

Thirty

Nine days after the rout the Ksinallionese army marched back into Semma.

The exterior of Vond's palace was almost complete; only the top of the huge northwestern tower remained open to the sky, although none of the roofs had yet been tiled.

The warlock scarcely needed to worry about leaky roofs, of course, since he could keep the rain away easily enough, as he in fact had so far. Besides, Sterren thought, a leaky roof wouldn't do any harm, since there was nothing inside the palace as yet but bare stone walls and floors. He and Ederd had spent much of the previous day strolling through its empty halls and chambers, admiring the vast expanses of bare marble, as Vond explained what would eventually go where.

The warlock's half-dozen servants had watched silently from their impromptu camp in what would in time be the kitchens. They had little to do, as yet, beyond seeing to their own most basic needs. Nothing needed cleaning yet, and Vond could not be bothered to eat real meals, but simply conjured up food from somewhere whenever he got hungry. He had no wardrobe to worry about; he still wore the same black warlock's robe.

The stairways were not yet built, so the only way into the upper floors was by levitation. Some rooms had no windows as yet.

Even so, it was a very impressive job for a mere eight days' work. All the more so, because Vond had spent a day or so cleaning and rebuilding the village around the old castle.

Looking out from his tower room in the old castle, and seeing the army on the horizon beyond the new palace, Sterren wondered what they thought of this great brooding edifice that had not been there when they left, just nine days before.

For that matter, he wondered what the people of Semma thought of it.

He sighed. He should, he thought, have realized that the lords of Ksinallion and Ophkar would not give up so easily as all that. A single battle was not a war.

Well, it wasn't his problem, now that Vond had conquered Semma.

He watched as Vond appeared, rising out of the unfinished tower, his cloak spreading like wings on either side. He waited for the Ksinallionese army to be swept away.

It wasn't. Instead, Vond dropped to the ground facing it, out of sight behind the palace.

Puzzled, Sterren waited a moment for him to reappear, then turned and headed for the stairs. He wanted to see what was happening.

By the time he had saddled a horse and ridden out the gate and past the palace, it was all over. He found Vond standing atop a newly-erected stone dias in the middle of a field, and the entire Ksinallionese army spread out before him, bowing in obeisance.

Three fresh corpses lay at the foot of the dias, sprawled awkwardly, swords fallen from their hands. Another corpse lay in the dirt amid the bowing Ksinallionese, this one burnt black.

"Hello, Sterren," Vond said as he rode up.

"What happened?" Sterren asked.

"Well, these men marched up, as you see, and I stopped them. I didn't hurt them, just stopped them. Most of them couldn't understand a word I said, but a few spoke

Ethsharitic, and one of them said they wanted to parley. I think my citadel had impressed them. Anyway, that one there," he said, pointing to one of the bodies that wore an officer's uniform, "claimed to be the Ksinallionese warlord. That fellow over there," indicating a bowing survivor, "served as his interpreter. They said that they had no quarrel with me — they called me a wizard, but I let that slide, since they didn't know any better. Anyway, they said they were at war with Semma, not with me."

Sterren nodded.

"Well, I explained that I had conquered Semma, and intended to conquer Ksinallion, too, but that I hadn't gotten around to it yet, and I offered them a chance to surrender. The warlord got all red in the face, and swore he'd never surrender to a damned wizard, or something like that, and I told him that in that case, he might as well try and kill me, and we'd see what happened. So he tried, and I let him take a few stabs at me with his sword, and then I exploded his heart."

Sterren found the calm way in which Vond described this murder to be extremely upsetting, but he hid that reaction and asked, "What about the others?"

"Well, after that, there was a lot of discussion in whatever language these people use amongst themselves — Ksinallionese, I suppose it is. Then this one," he said, indicating another corpse, "tried to distract me, while that one," pointing to the final unburnt body, "came up behind me and tried to stab me. I stopped both their hearts. And while I was doing that, that one over there," he pointed to the burned remains, "fired an arrow at me. He was too far away to be sure of getting his heart properly the first try, so I fried him, instead. After that, I told the interpreter that I would now accept the surrender of anyone who cared to surrender and bow to me. And then you rode up, and here we are." He waved a hand. "I think a few at the back ran, instead, but I won't worry about it." He looked over the hundreds of groveling figures. "I think I've just acquired a palace guard," he said, smiling.

"What are you going to do about Ksinallion, then?" Sterren asked.

"Oh, I guess I'll fly there this afternoon and stage a few demonstrations, and let them surrender. I wasn't planning to start empire-building until I had my citadel finished, but I can't just leave them there after this."

Sterren nodded.

That afternoon Corinal II, King of Ksinallion, capitulated. He abdicated in favor of the Great Vond, and the Kingdom of Ksinallion became the second province of the Empire of Vond.

At least, Vond considered it the second. Sterren, who had ridden along to watch, pointed out that Phenvel had not actually surrendered yet.

Vond shrugged that off. "I'll worry about that after I finish my palace."

Two days later Vond intercepted a party of Ophkarite soldiers spying on his palace and took a break from construction to force another capitulation. He had to kill King Neran IV before Neran's heir, the newly-elevated King Elken III, would surrender and add Ophkar to the Empire of Vond.

Vond got home in time to finish tiling the roof.

That night, during dinner at the high table in Semma Castle, Phenvel finally confronted Sterren directly and demanded, "Whose side are you on, the warlock's or mine?"

"I am on the side of what's best for Semma, your Majesty," Sterren replied quietly, putting down his fork.

"What does *that* mean?"

"Your Majesty, I mean what I said."

What he actually meant was that he was in favor of whatever caused the least trouble and did the least damage to lives and property. He was not particularly concerned with any other criteria in choosing "best."

"And who do you see as best for Semma, me or the warlock?" Phenvel demanded.

"At the moment, your Majesty," Sterren said, "I see only that to argue with the warlock is to die."

"To defy me can get you killed, too, warlord!"

Sterren tensed at this threat, but forced his voice to remain calm. "Your Majesty," he said, "I don't think you want to do that. The warlock thinks me his friend, and would not like it if you killed me." He hesitated, considering whether he dared say anything, and if so how much, and then added, "Besides, I can promise you that he will not rule for long."

"Oh?" Phenvel eyed Sterren intently. "Why not?"

"I'm sorry, your Majesty, but I can't tell you that." He gestured at the crowded tables. "If someone here were to hear, and word get back to Vond, I fear what would happen." In a moment of inspiration, he suggested, "Perhaps you could ask the wizard Annara."

Phenvel looked without thinking, then realized that Annara, as a mere commoner, was not at the high table; as a rule, she and Ederd ate their meals in the kitchen with the servants.

He snorted, and turned back to his fried potatoes. Sterren was able to finish his meal in peace, and then slip out of the castle unnoticed.

He strolled through the village, with its odd empty spaces where houses had been destroyed, and down the hill, where he paused and looked at Vond's palace.

The greater moon was high in the sky, the lesser low in

the east, and the white marble seemed to almost glow in the moonlight. The five towers — one at each corner, and a much larger one over the gate in the center of the northwestern wall — stood out starkly against the starry sky. Lights shone from a few windows, but he knew that most of the structure was still empty.

He watched it unhappily.

Vond was accomplishing some impressive feats. The palace was beautiful, at least on the outside — although a bit ominous in its appearance, with its high, blank walls. The village at Semma Castle was cleaner and sounder than ever before — at least, what there was of it. Ophkar, Ksinallion, and Semma were united for the first time in three hundred years, and at the cost of only seven lives in all, counting from the day after Vond's sudden acquisition of access to the Lumeth power source.

But it all made Sterren very uneasy. He knew that it could not possibly last, and even while it *did* last, he did not trust Vond to remain as harmless as he had been so far.

He had more or less decided on a course of action already, but he was not happy with it. He liked Vond; the warlock was like a child with a new toy, or really, an entire new playroom. Still, he, Sterren, intended to do all he could to remove Vond from power in Semma, not on behalf of any foolish king, but because Vond was clearly very dangerous indeed.

What would happen if the Wizards' Guild did decide to remove Vond? A magical battle of the scale Vond operated on might lay waste to the entire area.

What if other warlocks *did* come along, and take part in ruling the empire? No matter how benevolent Vond might be — a question that was still in doubt — sooner or later, a warlock would come along who was not.

And Vond would not always be there to stop such a warlock.

Better, Sterren thought, if Vond were to go quickly, before any other warlocks arrived.

He sighed, and decided to go sleep at the Citadel, as Vond's palace was now known, rather than Semma Castle. The warlock had said he was always welcome there, though he had not yet been given a room specifically for his own use or moved in any of his belongings. Phenvel, on the other hand, was no longer making Sterren feel welcome at all.

He said nothing to the warlock of what had happened. It was only coincidence that the next day Vond came to Semma Castle, smashed every door that was closed against him to splinters, and demanded Phenvel's formal surrender of authority.

Phenvel, Third of that Name, King of Semma, agreed immediately, and the Kingdom of Semma ceased to exist, becoming instead the Capital Province of the Empire of Vond.

Thirty-One

By the first of Greengrowth in the year 5221 Vond's palace was complete, furnished inside and out. The streets of his capital were laid out and paved. His new courtiers, recruited from his three provinces, could all hold a simple conversation in Ethsharitic, and were teaching the tongue to others.

Sterren of Semma, once Sterren of Ethshar, was now Lord Chancellor of the Empire of Vond.

His reaction to Vond's announcement of this honor had been, "What's a chancellor?"

Vond had shrugged. "Whatever you like. I don't need a warlord, since I do my own fighting, and that Ophkarite warlord is in charge of my guards, but I wanted to keep you around the palace, so you needed a title. That was the vaguest high title I could think of. Make of it what you will."

Sterren had kept it vague. His primary duty, he knew, was to provide someone Vond could speak to freely. Beyond that, he set himself no definite duties, but managed to imply that he was Vond's second in command, an implication the warlock supported.

Despite his new title, he still maintained his quarters in the tower of Semma Castle, as well as in the new citadel, and had managed to retain command of what had been the Semman army. His men, or at any rate those who had not gone over to the citadel to sign up with the Palace Guard, were now the Chancellor's Guard.

All three of his officers had resigned, at different times and giving different reasons. Captain Arl had submitted his resignation two days after Vond's storm had routed the invading armies; that had been the earliest he had been able to speak to Sterren. He had done so on the grounds that his men had been inadequately prepared for battle, which meant he had failed in his duties.

Sterren suspected that Arl had expected to be asked to stay on, but he had accepted the resignation. Arl *had* failed in his duties. Besides, Sterren preferred not to have his great-uncle's officers around.

Captain Shemder had resigned when King Phenvel surrendered, refusing to serve a foreign sovereign.

Lord Anduron had finally resigned when Sterren accepted the title of chancellor, saying he no longer understood what his position was supposed to be.

Sterren had named Dogal and Alder as his aides and lieutenants, but did not replace his captains.

His soldiers seemed to accept the new order, and Sterren's place in it, readily enough. The Semman nobility were another matter. When Sterren encountered any of them in the corridors of the castle he was usually snubbed, or presented with a ferocious glare. Phenvel's son Dereth, no longer a prince, spat on Sterren's best tunic. Shirrin, upon seeing him, invariably broke into tears and ran — she obviously felt her hero had betrayed her. Nissitha sneered — but then, she always had. Even Lura seemed subdued, and told him, "I'm not supposed to like you any more, but I don't really see why."

Sterren caught whispers in the hallways, whispers he thought he was meant to overhear, whispers containing words like "traitor," "barbarian," and "coward." Mutters about his unfortunate ancestry, three-fourths Ethsharitic, were common. "Money-grubbing merchant's brat!" was one epithet he encountered often. "Blood will tell" was another favorite.

Sterren did not let any of this bother him. He had chosen his path and he was committed to it.

The only things that bothered him were Shirrin's tears, and he thought that if he could manage a moment alone with her, he would explain to her why he was doing what he was doing. She was a very pretty girl, after all, and just turned fourteen, not *that* much younger than he was himself.

But no opportunity to explain himself to her ever came along.

Every so often Sterren wondered why he didn't just leave and go home to Ethshar, but he always arrived at the same answer. He had brought Vond here, so he was partly responsible for him. He was the only one in Semma except Vond himself who knew anything about warlockry, which meant that he was the only one who could see and understand everything that was happening.

And he also thought he was a restraining influence on Vond. The warlock had no other friends or confidants at all.

Besides, now that he was no longer the warlord, there was no great hurry about getting out of Semma, and there were clearly historical events happening that were interesting to observe.

Actually, life in Semma and even in Semma Castle had not really changed that much at all. Most of the nobles still lived in the castle, undisturbed; a few had slipped away, but the majority remained, still more or less acknowledging Phenvel's authority. Admittedly, about a fourth of the servants had deserted them to work at the palace, but that did little more than reduce the crowding somewhat. For most of the castle's inhabitants, life coasted on, and they tried very hard to ignore the warlock and his palace.

Sterren noticed that peasants no longer came to the castle much. No taxes were paid to King Phenvel any more, and the castle's stores were being consumed but not replaced — taxes were now going to the warlock's citadel. This did not affect Sterren directly, since he was welcome at Vond's table, but it did not bode well for the other nobles.

Those few of the bolder aristocrats who departed had accepted that their old way of life was doomed, and had gone looking for greener pastures — "visiting" relatives in other kingdoms, or simply seeking their fortunes, like so many failed apprentices.

The nobles who lingered all seemed to think that matters would somehow right themselves, and everything would go back to what it had been before, with Phenvel once more uncontested ruler of Semma, but none of them seemed to have any idea how this would come about, and none of them, so far as Sterren could see, were doing anything to help it along.

He was helping it along, at least slightly, but he did not dare explain that, and instead he put up with being labelled a traitor.

He was not entirely sure that in a sense, he might not be betraying Semma by working toward Vond's downfall. After all, for the peasants, all the changes were for the better. Vond controlled the weather, and regulated the climate to an unheard-of evenness of temperament. Rain came when needed, usually at night, and never more than needed. When days threatened to grow uncomfortably cool the clouds would be forcibly scattered, and when the sun was hot clouds would gather. As a result, the spring planting was begun earlier than usual, and the fields were already turning green.

Vond had promised that roads and houses would be built once the palace was no longer occupying his time and energy. The peasants Sterren had spoken to all agreed that this would be wonderful, but he thought they didn't really believe it would ever happen. They were accustomed to empty promises from their rulers.

Somehow, this bothered Sterren far more than the hatred of the dispossessed nobles. He knew that Vond sincerely intended to carry through on his promises — not so much out of altruism as to enhance his own position. The ruler of a rich land accrues more power and glory than the ruler of a poor one, and the warlock knew that well.

But Sterren also knew that Vond might not have time to make his promises good.

He sat in the tower room the warlock had given him, staring out the window at the palace sprawling below him, and wondered what he should do.

He had encouraged Vond to build his citadel as lavishly as possible — big and elaborate throughout, and created entirely with magic. Not a single stone had been lifted into place by human muscle; even the carpets and tapestries, although woven by hand, had been delivered and laid or hung by warlockry. Sterren had steadily urged Vond to use as much power as possible — not that he had needed much urging. Warlockry was like a drug; the more Vond used, the more he *could* use, and the more he *wanted* to use.

And somehow, he did not see what the inevitable outcome of this would be.

Sterren thought that he, ignorant as he was of warlockry, knew what was going to happen to Vond better than Vond did himself. The warlock was having too much fun with his magic to see that in time, the Calling would find him even in Semma.

Sterren stared down at the citadel and wondered whether he should warn him. Now that the palace was complete, Vond might not throw his power around so freely.

That brought up the question, of course, of what he *would* do.

Well, Sterren told himself, he could hardly learn anything about Vond's plans sitting in his room. He headed for the door.

He had intended to go all the way down to the warlock's audience chamber, but halfway down the first flight of stairs Sterren changed his mind, and at the next landing he turned down the corridor and knocked on the first door.

It opened, and Annara of Crookwall thrust her head around the edge.

"Hello," she said.

"Hello," Sterren replied. "May I come in?"

Annara hesitated, glancing back into the room, then swung the door wide and admitted him.

Sterren was not surprised to see Agor, the Imperial Theurgist, sitting on Annara's bed. They exchanged polite greetings.

At Annara's direction Sterren found a seat by the window. He settled onto the cushion, and then fumbled about, trying to figure out how to ask what he wanted to ask.

Annara offered him a plate of honeyed cashews, and he nibbled on those without speaking, while Agor chatted in his newly-acquired and horribly-accented Ethsharitic about the delightful weather that Vond had ensured.

Sterren glanced around the room, looking for something that might serve to divert the conversation along the lines he wanted. He noticed a sparkle on a high shelf.

Something shiny was moving up there, he realized. He squinted.

A coin, a silver bit, was spinning on edge, but he had not seen anyone spin it, and it showed no signs of slowing down as he watched.

"What's that?" he asked, pointing.

The two magicians followed his finger. Annara said, "It's a spinning coin."

"How long has it been spinning?"

"Oh, three or four months," Annara replied.

"But you haven't lived here that long!" Sterren said, startled.

"I brought it with me from the castle," Annara said.

"How could you do that?"

"It's on a little card that folds up into a box for travelling," she explained.

"What's it for? What keeps it spinning?"

"It's magic," Agor said.

"I could have guessed that for myself," Sterren said sarcastically. "I mean, what's it *for*?"

"It's a very simple little spell," Annara said. "It's called the Spell of the Spinning Coin."

"And it just makes a coin spin on forever? That seems pretty pointless."

"It does do a little more than that," the wizard admitted. "Emner spun that one — I taught him the spell, as it wasn't one he knew. It will keep spinning as long as he's alive. If he's seriously ill, or badly injured, the spinning will slow down, and it may even wobble a little if it's *very* bad. If he dies, it will stop."

"Oh, I see," Sterren said. "So you would know if, say, he had been killed by bandits on the way to Akalla."

Annara and Agor exchanged glances. "It wasn't bandits I was worried about," Annara said.

Sterren nodded. "I suppose not." He hesitated, and then pushed on. He could hardly have realistically hoped for a better opening. "I see it's still spinning, and he's been gone for all these months. He must have contacted the Wizards' Guild by now."

"Yes," Annara said, flatly.

"And they haven't done anything? Have they communicated with you?"

She hesitated, then said, "My lord Sterren, why do you ask?"

Sterren blinked. "I'm curious," he said.

"You'll pardon me, my lord chancellor, but I'm not sure I care to satisfy your curiosity."

He had half-expected this reaction. "Annara," he said slowly, "I can understand your caution, but believe me, I'm not going to cause you any trouble."

"You will forgive me, my lord chancellor, if I . . ."

"Stop calling me that!" Sterren snapped. "I didn't ask for the stupid title! People keep hanging these silly titles on me, when I was perfectly happy just being Sterren of Ethshar. Look, Annara, I know you're worried that I'm Vond's spy, but I'm *not* his spy, not unless he can read my mind without my knowing it. If he wanted to know something, I suppose he could force it out of you easily enough by torture; you aren't enough of a wizard to defend yourself against him. Or if you are, you're also one hell of an actress, because you've had *me* fooled! *I* can't force anything out of you, though." He paused for breath, then continued more calmly, "If you're worried about which side I'm on, right now I'm not really on *any* side. I think I know how to either destroy the warlock, or to keep him in power for at least a while longer, and I honestly haven't decided which I want to do, or whether I should just leave well enough alone. I came here hoping for more information to help me decide. I can't force it out of you; Vond can. You can tell me now, and if I'm telling the truth it won't do any harm, and if I'm lying, Vond can come up here and convince you."

He stopped, suddenly unsure what he was saying, and whether he should be saying it.

Annara threw a look at Agor, then turned back to Sterren and said, "All right, Sterren. I don't suppose it will do any harm to tell you. I've had dreams. Some wizards can send dreams, you know, and I've had dreams where wizards tell me things. Some of them may be ordinary dreams, but I think at least some must have been sent. I don't always remember them when I wake up; there are tricks to remembering your dreams, and I'm not very good at it. All the same, I think I have an idea what the Guild is doing."

"Ah," Sterren said. "What are they doing?"

"Nothing. At least, nothing yet. They're watching the situation, using scrying spells and prophecies, and that's all. Oh, and it seems that reports of the events here are somehow not spreading very well, particularly not to warlocks, and those warlocks who do hear about the new power source are being discouraged or diverted in various subtle ways."

Sterren nodded. "You know, I had begun to wonder why not a single other warlock had turned up."

"Remember, Vond's invitations have all emphasized his own supremacy, and warlocks are not prone to play the sycophant. Even without my guildmates interfering, I suspect he would be attracting few converts."

"True enough," Sterren acknowledged. He sat for a moment, munching cashews and considering this news.

"So," he said at last, "is the Guild contemplating any more drastic action?"

"No," Annara said, after a moment's hesitation. "At least, not that they've told me about. The general non-interference policy seems to be holding good."

Sterren nodded, and as he did a thought occurred to him. He asked Agor, "What do the gods think about all this?"

The theurgist shrugged. "Like the wizards, they don't interfere," he said. "Not since the Great War."

Sterren accepted that. "One more question," he said, "and I'll go." He looked at the two magicians closely.

"For yourselves," he asked, "do you *want* Vond removed?"

Annara and Agor looked at each other.

Agor shrugged.

"I don't know," Annara said. "I really don't."

Thirty-Two

Five minutes after he left Annara's room Sterren peered around a drapery into Vond's audience chamber.

The warlock spotted him immediately.

"Ah, Chancellor Sterren!" he called. "Come in! Come in!"

Sterren obeyed, looking curiously about as he did.

He had seen the audience chamber before, of course — the rich red draperies down either side, the ornately-patterned marble floor, the luxurious red carpet down the center. Twenty-foot-high windows behind the dais let sunlight pour in from the palace's central courtyard; stained-glass medallions set in the windows painted colors on the floor, and the cut-glass bevels that edged the medallions ringed the colors with sprays of rainbows. Golden banners hung from the vaulted white marble ceiling; most were plain and unadorned, but three bore battle flags sewn onto them, representing Semma, Ophkar, and Ksinallion.

Three broad steps, alternating black and white marble, led up to the black marble dais, and above its center Vond floated comfortably in mid-air; he had not yet bothered with a throne.

That much was familiar. What was new to Sterren was the group of young women who stood at the foot of the dais.

He counted twelve of them, all young and all uncommonly attractive. Their garb varied from simple peasant homespun to the rich velvets and silks of the conquered nobility; their expressions varied from uncertainty to bold defiance. None of them were so much as whispering; the only sound was the rustle of their clothing.

"What's going on?" Sterren asked, breaking the silence.

"I'm choosing a harem," Vond replied.

Startled, Sterren took another look at the women.

"I've had my eye out for the last sixnight or so," the warlock explained, "and I'd noticed these young ladies as promising prospects, so when I had a moment, I brought them here to look over." He smiled wolfishly.

"Do they know what's going on?" Sterren asked, seeing confusion and fear on several faces.

Vond shrugged. "I told them, but I don't know if they understood."

"May I speak with them?" Sterren asked.

"Be my guest," Vond said with a wave.

"Ladies," Sterren said, in Semmat, "I am Sterren, Ninth Warlord of Semma." He did not know a Semmat equivalent for "chancellor," if one existed at all, and he was not yet comfortable with the title in any case. "Do you know why you are here?"

His reply was a babble of voices; he raised his hands for silence.

It took a moment, but the women quieted. Sterren pointed to one. "You; who are you?"

The chosen one looked back at him blankly. "*Ksinal-lioni?*" she said, with an odd accent.

Sterren picked another. "Do you speak Semmat?"

This one nodded.

"Who are you?" Sterren asked.

"Kyrina the Fair," she replied, "daughter to Kardig Trak's son and Rulura of the Green Eyes."

Sterren could easily understand how she got her epithet. She wore a simple green tunic and a brown peasant's skirt, but even so, she was easily more beautiful than the most elaborately-attired noblewoman Sterren had ever seen in Semma.

"You live near here?" he asked.

"In the village," she said, gesturing vaguely in the general direction of Semma Castle.

"Do you know why you are here?"

She shook her head, which sent a ripple through her long, gleaming black hair and wafted perfume in Sterren's direction. "No, my lord."

"How did you come here?"

She glanced at Vond, and at the other women, clearly not eager to act as spokeswoman. Nobody volunteered to take her place, and after an instant's further hesitation she explained, "Perhaps an hour ago, something like a great wind, yet not a wind, snatched me up and brought me here. I found myself in a great hall, where I could move freely, but where all the doors but one were closed and barred, and the one open door was guarded by men who would not let me leave. Another woman was there, as well, and then these others were swept in, as I was, one by one, and when we were all there, the guards led us here, using their spears to keep us together."

Sterren nodded his understanding.

"This is the Great Vond," he said, gesturing toward the warlock. "You all probably guessed that."

Several women nodded.

"You all know he now rules this land?"

Seven women, by Sterren's count, nodded. He guessed the other five spoke no Semmat.

"You know he is a warlock, a magician?"

More nods.

"He is also a man. He has brought you twelve here to choose women to . . ." Sterren paused, wishing he knew more Semmat; he could think of a hundred delicate ways to phrase this in Ethsharitic. "To warm his bed," he said at last.

That elicited not nods, but startlement, anger, fear, and at least one crimson blush.

Vond was watching all this, and, Sterren saw worriedly, looking bored.

"Sterren," he said, "I take it you've just explained why I brought them here."

Sterren nodded.

"Tell them," Vond said, "that any who wish to leave are free to go, but that those who stay, and who please me, will be richly rewarded."

Hesitantly, Sterren translated this speech into Semmat as best he could.

The seven who understood looked at one another, clearly considering the offer. Kyrina looked at the warlock carefully for a long moment, then turned and strode for the exit.

Vond waved a hand, and the great double doors swung wide to let her pass.

Another woman, a noblewoman this time, hesitantly followed her.

One of the five who did not understand Semmat seemed to catch on, and literally ran out the door.

Others followed, each after her own fashion, until five remained, three of whom spoke Semmat. The five eyed each other warily.

Sterren watched them, puzzled. Why had these five stayed? None of them was starving; in fact, two of the five were dressed very well indeed. They should not be so desperate as to choose slavery, and surely concubinage, in this case, was a form of slavery.

Perhaps, he thought, they didn't trust Vond to keep his word, and feared he would take revenge upon them if they left. Certainly, all five looked somewhat nervous.

Or perhaps they didn't see it the way he did. They might see sharing Vond's bed as a route to power and wealth. If that was it, Sterren was sure they were wrong.

Or perhaps it was just curiosity or a sexual interest in

the warlock. Sterren hadn't really given the matter much thought, but he supposed Vond was attractive enough, and there were always stories about magicians. For himself, Sterren could see no reason a knowledge of arcane skills should imply a knowledge of erotic skills, but there were always stories.

Most likely, he thought, it was a combination of all of these that kept the five of them in the audience chamber. He found that unappealing, and decided he did not care to watch any further. He started to turn away.

"Sterren," Vond said, "I need you to translate!"

He had forgotten that. He turned back, reluctantly. "Couldn't one of your servants do that?"

"You're here; they aren't. Besides, you speak Ethsharitic better than any of them."

Sterren had to admit that this was true.

"Let's start with their names," the warlock said, waving a hand at the women.

Sterren did the best he could, given that only three of the women spoke Semmat; a fourth spoke Ophkaritic, the fifth Ksinallionese. One of the Semman women knew a few words of Ksinallionese, and the Ksinallionese spoke some Ophkaritic, so that nobody was totally cut off.

And of course, gestures and facial expressions conveyed plenty of information as well.

After half an hour or so, Vond chose the Ksinallionese to take a stroll with him and become better acquainted, and Sterren escaped with a sigh of relief, while one of the palace servants, summoned by Vond's magic, escorted the other four to the apartments they were henceforth to share.

Sterren made his way out the citadel's main gate and looked down Vond's artificial hill at the surrounding countryside.

The land had turned green with spring, and the peasants

were out in the fields, tending their crops. The sky was a radiant crystal blue, with a handful of soft white clouds sailing like white-robed wizards across it.

A party of a dozen or so men was marching up the road toward the gate. Four of them were Vond's red-tunicked palace guards, and the rest were in rags.

Sterren saw to his horror that the ragged ones were in chains. Most of them looked resigned, but two or three looked terrified.

"*Hai*," he called. "What's going on?"

The foremost guard saw him, acknowledged his presence with a bow, and called back one word.

Sterren did not catch it; the guard's accent distorted his Ethsharitic beyond easy comprehension.

"What?" Sterren called back.

"Slaves!" the soldier repeated. "We bring slaves!"

"What for?" Sterren asked, as he and the guard approached each other.

The guard spread his hands in the Ksinallionese equivalent of a shrug. "The Great Vond ordered," he said.

"Where did these people come from?" Sterren persisted.

The guard hesitated; clearly, his Ethsharitic was not very good. "We go to Akalla, buy them, bring them back," he explained slowly.

Sterren stopped and stepped aside as the party marched up past him. He watched them go without interfering.

At least they had been slaves already, and not innocent peasants Vond had had enslaved.

In fact, he supposed that it was perfectly reasonable for Vond to keep slaves, but Sterren found it a little hard to accept. For most of his life he had been far more likely to deal with slavers as merchandise than as a customer. He had never quite been reduced to sleeping on the city streets, which would have made him fair game for the slavers, and he had never been caught stealing, which could also put cuffs on a person, but those had always been closer than the sort of wealth that would include buying anyone.

He had known a few slaves, either before or after their enslavement. He had never exchanged more than a few polite words with a slave-owner — except Vond.

Or, he suddenly realized, perhaps King Phenvel; some of his castle servants might well be owned, rather than hired.

He watched the slaves march into the palace.

Vond was buying slaves and acquiring a harem. Was this necessarily tyranny? After all, he bought his slaves on the market, and his chosen concubines were there voluntarily.

No, Sterren decided, it wasn't tyranny — but it wasn't a good sign, either.

Thirty-Three

Vond conquered Thanoria on the sixteenth of Green-growth, 5221. He took a sixnight or so to consolidate his conquest this time, taking care of details he had been rather haphazard about in dealing with Semma, Ksinallion, and Ophkar. He arranged for taxes to be paid into his imperial treasury, appointed provincial officials from the former royal government, selected candidates for his harem, and so forth.

That done, he conquered Skaia on the twenty-fourth.

Enmurinon went next, on the third of Longdays, followed by Akalla of the Diamond on the fourteenth. He took special care there, due to the presence of the port, and inquired after recent arrivals, hoping for word of immigrating warlocks.

He was disappointed by the replies he received, and on the nineteenth he returned to his palace in a foul temper.

He concentrated on other affairs for several days after that, building roads, tenements, and market-halls, getting acquainted with his new concubines, and dealing with his subjects.

Rather to his surprise, he found that he did not enjoy actually ruling his empire. Settling disputes, administering justice, appointing officials, and the other traditional duties of royalty were dull and time-consuming, and provided no opportunity for him to display his magic.

Sterren had been expecting this realization. He had long ago concluded that kings were no happier than anybody else. Furthermore, he had noticed that for some time now, Vond had only seemed really comfortable and alert when using huge amounts of magic, as if warlockry were an addictive drug. When the warlock finally confessed his disappointment, late one night in a quiet torchlit arcade overlooking the palace courtyard, Sterren simply nodded and agreed, without comment.

"You don't seem surprised," Vond said, irritably.

"I'm not," Sterren said. "*I* never thought ruling looked like much fun."

The warlock settled more deeply into the sling chair he sat upon. "It isn't," he growled, "but it *should* be."

"Why?" Sterren asked.

"Because I *want* it to be," Vond snapped.

Sterren made no reply.

After a moment of disgruntled silence, Vond said, "I just won't do it any more."

"Won't do what?"

"I won't deal with all these petty details — who owns what, how to punish this thief or reward that soldier, where to put the roads, how to collect the taxes, how much coin to mint — I won't do it."

"Someone has to," Sterren pointed out, "or your empire will fall apart."

"*I* don't have to. *You* do. You're my chancellor, aren't you? I just decided what that means — it's your job to take care of anything I don't want to be bothered with." Vond smiled an unusually unpleasant smile. "I'll announce it in the morning; you'll be in charge of the administration of the empire. I'll take care of what I'm good at — building and conquest."

Sterren had hoped and feared this might happen. After all, he was the only person Vond trusted. To all the native inhabitants of his empire, the warlock was something of a monster, alien and inhumanly powerful, conquering entire kingdoms in a single day; none of them could speak to him without fear, and he dealt with them, in general, with contempt. Besides, very few were really fluent in Ethsharitic, and Vond had not yet bothered to learn any other tongues. Warlockry, unlike witchcraft, did nothing at all to enhance his linguistic abilities. Warlockry was a purely physical sort of magic; it could not teach.

The other magicians were less contemptible than the ordinary citizens, but still did not provide very good company for the new emperor. From the start, both Annara and Ederd had held back visibly, refusing to speak openly with Vond, and he had noticed this reticence. Agor's Ethsharitic was an impediment, and his eccentric behavior, cultivated since childhood to add an aura of mystery, was another.

That left Sterren as Vond's only friend, the only person he could talk with as one human being to another, and despite Vond's denials, Sterren was quite sure that the warlock was miserably lonely.

He had expected other warlocks to come and join him, and was growing ever more confused and dismayed at their failure to materialize. This drove him, more and more, to talk away long hours with Sterren.

Sterren was no warlock; he was unnaturally lucky with dice, but otherwise could barely stir a cat's whisker with his magic. Still, he had known Vond when Vond was powerless, and he knew something about how warlockry functioned, and he was not cowed by the imperial might. That made him an invaluable companion.

And Sterren had guessed that it might in time make him Vond's partner in empire, as well.

Now that that guess had come true, he was ready. This was an opportunity far too good to miss. He could do far more to prevent tyranny if he were himself involved in governing.

He had seen, over the last few months, that Vond's decisions, as emperor, tended to be quick and careless. He did not concern himself with right or wrong, with what would be best for those involved, but only with what was most expedient, what would settle matters most quickly, rather than most equitably.

Now he could change that.

He had no illusions about his own governing ability, however. He knew himself well enough to suspect that he, too, would opt for expediency after a few boring days.

"I'll accept that on one condition," he said.

Vond looked at him sharply. "Who are you, to be setting conditions?" he demanded.

"I'm your Lord Chancellor, your Imperial Majesty," Sterren replied mildly.

Vond could hardly deny that, but he was not so easily soothed. "What condition?" he demanded.

"That I may delegate my authority as I please," Sterren said. "Because as I said, *I* never thought ruling looked like fun, and I don't want to be saddled with the job any more than you do. I don't mind doing a share, certainly, but I don't want to spend my days divvying up strayed cattle any more than you do."

Vond considered this. "Fair enough," he said.

The next morning Vond set out to conquer Hluroth, and Sterren set out to establish the Imperial Council.

Thirty-Four

The Chancellor's Guard came in handy on occasion; it had saved Sterren a good deal of trouble to simply tell Alder, "Take as many men as you need, but I want Lady Kalira of Semma here in an hour."

Then all he had to do was sit in his chosen room, a small study on the second floor of Semma Castle, and wait, and an hour later, Lady Kalira glared at him across the table.

"I'm here," she said without preamble. "What do you want?"

Sterren noted, with hope and admiration, that she did *not* call him a traitor or otherwise insult him.

"Your help," he said.

Her angry glare softened to curiosity. "What sort of help?" she demanded warily.

"In running the empire."

"Empire!" She snorted.

Sterren shrugged, using both the Ethsharitic shoulder-bob and the Semman gesture of spread fingers and a down-turned palm. "Call it what you like," he said. "Like it or not, the warlock *has* united several kingdoms now, I can't say how many since he's in the process of adding at least one more even as we speak, and I think I can call it an empire." He had had plenty of time to improve his Semmat in recent months, and spoke it easily now. "I didn't come here to argue about names," he concluded.

"Maybe I did, though," Lady Kalira retorted.

"I hope not," Sterren said.

For a moment neither spoke. Then Lady Kalira said, "All right, what's your offer?"

"You know Vond named me chancellor," Sterren said.

"Whatever that means," she answered, nodding.

"He's just decided that it means I'm to take care of all the administrative details that he doesn't want to bother with," Sterren explained.

Lady Kalira considered this, and then smiled. "And I suppose," she said, "that you intend to palm the job off on *me*."

"Not exactly," Sterren said, "but I admit you're close. I want you to tell me who I *should* pass it on to."

"Should?"

"Yes, should. Who could do the best job of it, and who would do the best job of it. I know I'd botch it."

"You do?" She eyed him carefully.

He nodded.

"I think you'll need to tell me a little more of what you had in mind," she said.

"What I had in mind," Sterren told her, "is an Imperial Council, a group of the best administrators we can find, who would actually run the empire. Vond isn't particularly interested in doing that, and neither am I. Besides, Vond isn't going to be around for all that long, and I don't suppose I'll be very welcome once he's gone. A group of well-respected natives would be able to keep things going smoothly, regardless of what Vond and I do."

"Why isn't he going to be around very long?" Lady Kalira asked, staring at him.

"I can't tell you that," Sterren replied uncomfortably.

"You said the same thing months ago, and he's still here," she pointed out.

Sterren shrugged again. "So far, yes," he said.

"And you still say he won't be for long?"

"He *can't* be," Sterren insisted.

"Why not?"

"I can't tell you that," Sterren said again.

Lady Kalira considered this, and then asked, "Can you tell me how long he'll be around?"

"No. Maybe a month, maybe a year or two. I don't think he can possibly last five years."

"Did you hire an assassin, or something?" she asked curiously. "The cult of Demerchan, perhaps?"

"No," Sterren said. "Why would I do something stupid like that? He isn't doing *me* any harm. In fact, he isn't doing much of anybody else any harm, either. Look at the peasants out there — they're doing just fine! Nobody's complaining except the deposed nobles, and even *you* aren't really suffering much! And here I am, on top of it all, offering you a chance to get back into running the government!"

Lady Kalira studied him closely, and then shook her head. "I don't understand you, Sterren," she said. "I don't understand you at all."

"I don't care if you understand me or not; I just want your help in putting together this council. I thought seven members would be about right — no ties in the voting that way. And I don't want it to be hereditary, exactly, since we can't afford to have any infants or incompetents on it, but perhaps members could have the right to appoint their heirs. I don't want any of the deposed kings on it, either — it wouldn't look right unless we included all of them, and I hope that you, as a Semman, will see why I don't want *that*."

Lady Kalira smiled involuntarily at this reference to her former sovereign. Sterren took this as encouragement.

"I suppose princes or princesses might be all right, but I'll leave that up to you," he continued. "I don't know much about any of the people around here; I never really got to know most of them. I'd like you to choose the people you think I really *need* to have, to start. You're welcome to take a seat on the Council yourself, if you like, and I thought maybe the steward, Algarven, would be a good choice, but I'll defer to your judgement." He hesitated, and then said, "I think we probably don't want all seven to be Semman, and in fact, I think a good mix of nationalities would be wise, but on the other hand, Semma is the capital province, so at least one or two . . . what do you think?"

"I think," Lady Kalira said slowly, "that I need to know more about the duties of this proposed council."

Sterren smiled, and said, "What would you suggest? Vond has claimed building and conquest for himself, and left everything else to me. I prefer to leave it to a council. What would you recommend?"

"You're really serious about this?"

"Oh, yes."

She sighed.

By the time Vond returned from the successful subjugation of Hluroth they had selected four of the seven councillors, and were discussing meeting schedules.

Thirty-Five

It was the ninth of Harvest, in the Year of Human Speech 5221. The Empire of Vond extended from the deserts in the east to the ocean in the west, and from the edge of the World in the south to the borders of Lumeth of the Towers in the north.

Vond had turned back before attacking Lumeth, and had returned to his citadel trembling.

"I heard the whisper there, even over the power I draw on," he told Sterren. "I'd forgotten what it was like. Foul, dark muttering in my mind — awful!" He took a deep breath, then released it slowly.

"I almost think I can still hear it," he said, "but I know it's just my mind playing tricks on me."

Sterren hesitated, then said nothing.

"Well," Vond went on, "I know where my limits are now, at any rate. I don't dare ever venture past the borders of Lumeth or Kalithon or Shassalla, but here to the south of them, I'm all-powerful."

Sterren did not argue with Vond's claim. "It's too bad," he remarked instead. "I was curious about what would happen if you got really close to the towers themselves. Aren't they the source of your power?"

Vond nodded. "I was curious, too, but I won't risk finding out. It's too bad; I'd have preferred to have control over the towers."

That had been sixnights before, early in the month of Longdays, and that unexpected defeat had been followed by more than half a dozen quick victories over the tiny port nations of the South Coast west of Akalla, victories that had extended Vond's empire as far as it could safely go.

Now, on the ninth of Harvest, Sterren stood on a balcony and looked out across the countryside.

The land was a rich green from horizon to horizon, punctuated only by roads and buildings and the bright colors of flowers; thanks to Vond's control of the weather and reworking of the soil there were no barren spots, nowhere that the earth failed to yield generously.

Straight, smooth roads paved with stone stretched out from the plaza below the citadel, leading directly to each of the towns and castles of the empire.

The village that surrounded Semma Castle still stood, but was equalled in size and far outdone in splendor by the town growing up around Vond's palace, a town built of white and gold marble, roofed in red tile. Small fountains babbled in each corner of the plaza and at several intersections, providing drinking water for anyone who wanted it, and a much larger ornamental fountain sprayed upward at the center of the plaza. Smoke and intriguing odors rose from a dozen forges and ovens.

The two villages were growing toward each other across the intervening valley, and it seemed likely that in time they would merge into a single entity.

In time, Sterren thought, this might become a real city.

Semma Castle itself still stood, but its population had dropped drastically. Over the months, as the royal treasury and the castle stores gave out, the nobility had drifted away, fleeing the Empire or, in a few cases, finding honest work. The royal family itself was still sticking it out, but most of the others had left.

The same thing, Sterren knew, had happened in all the former capitals, the castles and strongholds that had once ruled Ophkar, Ksinallion, Skaia, Thanoria, Enmurinon, Hluroth, Akalla of the Diamond, Zhulura, Ghelua, Ansuon, Furnara, Kalshar, Quonshar, Dherimin, Karminora,

Alboa, and Hend.

So far, Vond had definitely been good for the Small Kingdoms. He had dispossessed a few hundred nobles, but he had enriched thousands of peasants. He had killed a few dozen people in his conquests, but he had probably saved at least as many from starvation.

And he was doomed.

Sterren still found it hard to believe that Vond did not realize he was doomed. It was really fairly obvious. After all, *all* warlocks were doomed. Just finding a new power source would not change that. Sterren thought Vond had had enough hints when he established the northern borders of his empire, but still the warlock did not see it.

It was not just that he was unwilling to admit it, either. If that were it, he would have cut back on his use of magic, and he hadn't. He continued to lay roads, erect buildings, manipulate the weather, and at times to light the night sky in sheer celebration of his might.

Sterren had refrained from commenting, but after all these months, he was finally convinced that Vond deserved better. He deserved a warning, at the very least — a warning only Sterren could provide.

And, Sterren promised himself, he would deliver that warning.

The only catch was to figure out how to convince Vond that he, Sterren, had only recognized the danger *now*. If Vond knew that Sterren had withheld his certainty for so long he was likely to be very annoyed indeed.

Sterren did not care to have Vond annoyed with him.

He was puzzling out an approach when someone behind him cleared a throat.

He turned, and found a palace servant, a man named Ildirin who had once been a butcher's assistant in Ksinallion, standing in the balcony door.

"Your pardon, my lord chancellor," he said apologetically, "but the Emperor is meeting with the Council and desires your presence."

"Now?"

"Yes, my lord," Ildirin replied.

Sterren knew better than to argue or hesitate; Vond hated to be kept waiting. "Where?" he asked.

"In the council chamber."

Sterren nodded, stepped past Ildirin into the palace, and headed for the stairs.

Ildirin followed at a respectful distance.

The council chamber had not been designed as such; after all, when Vond built his palace he had no idea that an Imperial Council would ever exist. He had intended the room to be an informal audience chamber, where he could meet with his cronies without the full pomp of the main audience hall, but still on a business basis rather than in his personal apartments.

Save for Sterren, however, who was usually welcome even in Vond's private quarters, the warlock had no cronies. He had a council, instead, and so the informal audience chamber had become the council chamber.

The councillors could hardly be considered cronies; none of the seven liked Vond or particularly wanted to see him remain in power. All seven, however, were willing to recognize that the Empire of Vond was a reality, and that it needed governing, and all seven were very good at governing.

Ordinarily, the Council went about its business, and Vond went about *his* business, and the two had as little to do with each other as possible, communicating with each other only through Sterren. For Vond to meet with the entire Council was unheard of.

Sterren hurried down the stairs, the wide sleeves of his

velvet tunic flapping at his sides, and marched across the broad hallway at the bottom. The great red doors at the inner end of the hallway led into the audience chamber; the black doors at the outer end led out to the plaza. He ignored them both, and headed directly for the small rose-wood door that nestled unobtrusively in one corner.

His hand on the latch, he hesitated. He rapped lightly, then opened the door and walked in.

The seven councillors were seated at the table where they carried out most of their deliberations, three to a side. Their chairwoman, Lady Kalira, usually sat at the head of the table; today she was at the foot, and the Great Vond floated cross-legged at the head. He was only slightly higher than if he had been using a chair; his knees were below the polished wood of the table-top.

"Ah, there you are!" Vond said when he saw Sterren step into the room.

"Here I am," Sterren agreed. "What's happening?" He looked about for somewhere to sit, or even somewhere better to stand, and spotted an unused chair. He turned it to face the warlock emperor, and asked, "May I sit?"

Vond waved permission. As he did, he caught sight of Ildirin peering in the doorway.

"I see you found him," the warlock said. "Now go see if you can find us something appropriate to drink; I ex-pect we'll be doing a lot of talking, and talking is thirsty work."

Ildirin bowed and vanished, closing the door behind him.

"Now," Vond said, "I suppose you all want to know why we're here, so I'll get right to the point, which is that am I not at all sure I like this 'Imperial Council' of yours."

Sterren did not like the sound of that, and decided that perhaps Vond was not in a mood to hear bad news today.

He wondered whether he could somehow convey an anonymous message to the warlock.

The councillors glanced at one another, and some at Sterren, but after a second or two all eyes came to rest on Lady Kalira.

She accepted her silent appointment as spokeswoman, and rose.

"Your Imperial Majesty," she said in her accented Ethsharitic, "we serve at your pleasure. If you wish us to stop, we will stop, we will be glad to stop."

Two or three heads bobbed in agreement; nobody indicated by even the slightest gesture or sound that he might think otherwise.

"Don't be so quick to resign, either," Vond snapped. "I know I need *somebody* to run things; I'm just not sure I want *you*, and I'm not sure you've been running things the way I want them run."

"We serve at your Imperial Majesty's pleasure," Lady Kalira repeated, bowing her head.

Her Ethsharitic had improved greatly over the past several months, Sterren noticed. Recognizing that it was the new language of government had driven her to study it far more seriously than mere curiosity had before.

"That's what you say here," Vond said, "but I hear otherwise elsewhere. I hear whispers that you're plotting to overthrow me, to restore the old monarchies. After all, you're all aristocrats yourselves; why should you accept a commoner like me as your emperor?"

Lady Kalira started to say something, but Vond held up his hand to stop her.

Sterren wondered suddenly just what sort of whispers Vond had actually been hearing. Was it whispered rumors that had upset him, or was there another sort of whisper entirely that was getting on his nerves?

Then he forgot about that, as Vond turned and addressed him directly.

"So, my lord chancellor, why is it you chose only the old nobility for your council?"

The question itself was easy to answer, so easy that Sterren wondered what Vond was really after.

"Because, your Majesty," Sterren said, "no one else in your empire has had any training or experience in governing."

"And you did not see fit to train them?"

"No, your Majesty, I didn't; I was trying to set up something to handle governing *now*, not at some indefinite future time. Besides, I don't know any more about governing or training peasants to govern than you do."

"It wouldn't have to be peasants; couldn't you find merchants or tradesmen? Running a country can't be that different from running a business."

Sterren had some serious doubts about Vond's statement, but he ignored it and answered the question. "I didn't try to find tradesmen, because I didn't see anything wrong with using nobles who already know the job. Besides, there aren't that many tradesmen around here; it's not exactly Ethshar. I mean, in Semma, they had a Lord Trader — how much of a merchant class could there be, in a case like that?"

"You didn't see anything wrong with using the nobles I threw out of power?"

"No, I didn't!" Sterren answered. "What are they going to do? You'd kill anyone who got out of line, and they know it." He gestured at the councillors, reminding Vond that they were listening.

"They could stir up discontent," the warlock suggested.

"Why should they? Listen, Vond, I don't think you appreciate what these people have done here. I picked the most competent people I could, without worrying about where they came from. Each of them agreed to help run the empire because they could see that it was here to stay, and each one of them was labelled a traitor by his friends and family because of that! They put up with that because they want to see their people — nobles, peasants, merchants, everybody — ruled fairly and well. If your empire ever *did* fall, and the old kingdoms were restored, they'd probably all be hanged for treason for having helped you!"

"You think so?" Vond said, his expression unreadable.

"Yes, I think so!" Sterren snapped.

At that point Ildirin entered quietly, bearing a tray that held a full decanter and a dozen wineglasses. He proceeded around the edge of the room to the emperor, who court etiquette required be served first.

"And I don't suppose," Vond said, "that you might be trying to put the nobility back in power, leaving me just a figurehead!"

"Why would I want to do that?" Sterren asked, genuinely puzzled.

Vond accepted a glass of wine. "Because you're a noble yourself, of course, Sterren, Ninth Warlord!" He drank.

Sterren's mouth fell open in astonishment. One of the councillors giggled, then quickly suppressed it. Ildirin silently poured wine.

"*Me?*" Sterren said at last. "I'm an Ethsharitic merchant's brat! I'm no noble; my grandmother ran away from home, and I don't give a damn who her father and brother were. I'm no more a part of the old nobility here than you are!"

Vond's expression stopped him, and he corrected himself, "Well, not *much* more. I didn't *know* I had any noble blood." He glanced at the councillors, and said, "Besides, if I were trying to restore the old nobility, wouldn't I have put kings and princes on the council, instead of these people?"

"Kings would be a little obvious," Vond pointed out, "and you *did* put a few princes in here, didn't you?"

"I did?" Sterren looked at the councillors again, and recognized Prince Ferral of Enmurinon.

"Oh," he said. Defensively, he added, "Only one. Out of seven."

"So far," Vond said.

Ildirin had served all the councillors now, and approached Sterren with a filled glass. He waved it away; it appeared he needed his head clear if he was going to keep it.

"So far," Sterren said, "and forever. I don't choose new councillors; I don't know who can handle the job and who can't. I let each councillor choose his own successor."

Ildirin, still holding the glass he had intended for Sterren, looked around the room and noticed that the emperor's glass was empty. He stepped back and started gliding silently along the wall, back toward Vond's place at the head of the table.

"Oh, I *see*!" the warlock said, sneering. "*You* won't put any kings on the council, but if these seven name kings as their heirs, and then retire, there's nothing *you* can do to stop it!"

"Don't be silly," Sterren said, and he heard someone gasp quietly at his audacity in addressing the warlock emperor thus. "The Imperial Council serves at *my* pleasure, as well as yours, your Majesty. I can dismiss any councillor any time I please. So can you, just as you can dismiss me as your chancellor. And I assure you, I'd dismiss any king or queen, and probably whatever fool named him as heir."

"Ah, you would? Why?"

"Because we don't want the old royalty back in power. We don't want one councillor, by virtue of his former station, to perhaps sway the rest of the council unduly. We don't want to confuse the peasants by restoring a king to any semblance of authority."

"That's right," Vond said, accepting the full wineglass from Ildirin. "We don't want any of that. I'm sure the peasants resent me, consider me a usurper . . ."

Algarven, once royal steward of Semma, coughed suddenly, choking on a sip of wine. Vond turned to glare at him between sips from his own fresh glass.

"Excuse me, your Majesty," Algarven said, as soon as he could breathe and talk again, "but the peasants . . . why would you think the *peasants* resent you?"

A flicker of uncertainty crossed Vond's face.

"I've overthrown their kings," he said.

"Forgive me, your Majesty," said Berakon Gerath's son, once royal treasurer of Akalla of the Diamond, "but so what? What did the old kings ever do for the peasantry? You've built roads and houses, put an end to wars, and even done what seemed impossible and regulated the weather. With all this, your taxes are no higher than the old. Believe me, your Majesty, the peasants don't mind at all that you've replaced the old kings, though they do worry a bit about the inevitable price for this bounty."

Vond handed his empty glass to Ildirin, who struggled a moment to balance everything on the tray before he could accept it. Vond threw him an annoyed glance.

"All right," Vond said, "forget the peasants. You say nobody here wants the old kings restored, but you have a prince on the council; what happens when his father dies?"

"Your Majesty," Prince Ferral said quietly, "my father has been dead for five years now. You deposed my elder brother, not my father."

"All right, then," Vond said, as Ildirin fumbled with the decanter, "what happens when your brother dies?"

"Nothing much, your Majesty. He has children, and other brothers older than myself. I am eighth in the line of succession."

Vond glared, and reached for a glass of wine just as Ildirin started to hand him one. Their arms collided, and the wine spilled down the emperor's chest, staining the golden embroidery on his black robe an ugly shade of red.

The warlock stared down at the spill for an instant, then shrieked, "You *idiot*!" He waved an arm, and Ildirin was flung back against the marble wall.

The crack as his spine broke was clearly audible to everyone in the room.

Vond waved again, and the servant's head was crushed, the bones shattered, leaving the skin a limp sack. Blood gushed from his nose and mouth as he died.

The corpse fell heavily to the floor and lay in a pool of gore.

Sterren and the councillors stared in shocked silence. The tray that held the decanter still stood on the table. Vond smoothed his robe, but did not seem overly disturbed.

Sterren knew, as he stared at the corpse, that he would not be warning Vond of anything.

Thirty-Six

Little was accomplished in the remainder of the meeting. The presence of Ildirin's body cast a pall over the conversation, and Vond seemed to have spent his anger. In the end, he agreed to let the Imperial Council continue as it had been, with the understanding that it existed entirely by his sufferance, and that he had the right to dismiss any member at any time, and to overrule any decision.

None of this had ever been in any question, as far as Sterren and the councillors were concerned, but nobody was foolish enough to point this out.

Afterward, Sterren took a long walk.

It was obvious that Vond was losing control. The magnificent buildings, the prosperous empire, the thriving crops had all served to hide this; Ildirin's gruesome death had dragged it out into plain sight.

Not only was any thought of a warning gone, Sterren was now convinced that he had to do all he could to destroy Vond quickly.

That night Vond ate dinner in the Great Hall, with Sterren at his right hand. As often as not he ate in his private apartments, if he bothered to eat meals at all, but on this particular occasion he held a formal dinner, with himself, Sterren, and the Imperial Council at the high table and the rest of the imperial household arrayed along three lower tables.

"You know, your Majesty," Sterren remarked as he chewed a bite of apple, "you haven't done any really *spectacular* magic lately."

Vond looked at him. "Oh?"

"I mean, early on, you conjured up that storm to rout

the armies of Ophkar and Ksinallion, and you quarried and assembled the stone for this palace in a few days, and so forth, and lately, you haven't done anything much more impressive than laying pavement stones. Oh, that's certainly *useful*, and so is regulating the weather, and all the rest, but you haven't done anything really *showy* in months."

"You don't consider lighting the night sky showy?"

Sterren pretended to consider that. "Well, I suppose," he admitted, "but it's not *new*. Everybody's used to it now."

"And why should I want to be showy?" Vond asked.

"To impress people, to remind everybody what their emperor is capable of. If you got the awe you're due, you wouldn't need to worry about disloyalty, and we could avoid unpleasantness like that meeting this morning."

Vond nodded.

"Besides," Sterren added, "I thought you liked using your magic as much as you could."

"I do," he said. "In fact, I've been getting irritable lately, and nervous, and I wonder if it might be because I haven't been doing enough. The power's there to be used, after all. It's always there in the back of my head, and I feel it so very clearly now . . ." His voice trailed off.

Sterren nodded encouragingly.

"What would you suggest?" Vond asked.

"Oh, I don't know — move a mountain, maybe?"

Vond snorted. "I'd need to build one, first; there *are* no mountains in the empire. Besides, where would I put it?"

Sterren waved that away. "Not a mountain, then. Well, the edge of the World lies a few leagues to the south of here; could you do something with that?"

"Like what?"

"Oh, peel it back and see what's underneath, maybe. I've heard theorists argue about what holds the World up and keeps it from falling into the Nethervoid. Or maybe just go see what lies beyond the edge, and bring back a piece."

"There isn't *anything* beyond the edge, is there?" Vond asked.

Sterren shrugged. "Nobody knows," he said.

Vond considered that, clearly intrigued.

Nothing more came of it that night, but the following morning, the tenth of Harvest, Sterren awoke not in his own bed, but hanging in mid-air, just outside the open window of his room.

"Good morning!" Vond called from above him. "I thought you'd like to come along to the edge of the World and see what it's like!"

Sterren looked up nervously. This was not really what he'd had in mind. "Good morning!" he called in reply. "I hope you slept well!"

Vond frowned.

"Actually," he said, "I didn't. I dreamt . . . well, I don't know exactly what I dreamt, but it wasn't pleasant, whatever it was." The frown faded. "Never mind that, though," he said. "We're off to the edge!"

Sterren concealed his lack of enthusiasm for the venture, and rolled over in mid-air so that he could see where he was flying.

They sailed quickly past Semma Castle, and across the few leagues of farmland beyond, into the empty southern desert.

Sterren would have watched the scenery, but there wasn't any; below and to either side he could see nothing but mile after mile of sand spattered with tough, patchy grass.

Behind him he could see the towers of Semma Castle and the Imperial Palace gradually shrinking.

And ahead he could see nothing. The edge of the World was wrapped in yellow haze.

Sterren had seen that haze from the tower, but had assumed it was just windblown sand, or glare from sunlight reflecting off the edge itself. To his surprise, he could now see that it was neither, but a sort of very thin golden mist. It would have been almost invisible in any imaginable confined area, but here it seemed to go on forever. He could look through the golden mist, but all he saw beyond it was more golden mist, and still more golden mist, until eventually it added up to opacity. If there were anything beyond the mist, he could not see it.

And of course, nobody had ever suggested that anything existed beyond the edge of the World, except perhaps Heaven, where the gods lived, and that was more usually thought to lie somewhere above the sky.

He had nothing to provide him with any scale, but Sterren thought he must be seeing literally hundreds of miles of nothing but that yellow haze.

Vond called down to him, "What is that stuff?"

"How should I know?" Sterren called back.

"Do you think we can get above it?"

"I have no idea!"

"I'm going to try." With that, Vond began to rise, pulling Sterren up with him.

They ascended for what seemed like hours, and eventually, the golden mist thinned still further — but so did the air about them. The blue sky above turned darker and darker, and grew steadily colder, until Sterren was shivering so badly that he could scarcely shout his protests to the warlock.

They had, indeed, come to the top of the yellow fog, but they had been unable to see over it or through it; all they had seen was a seemingly-infinite expanse of golden haze, stretching on before them forever, while behind them all the Small Kingdoms were laid out, the central mountain-chain curving down between the rich green coastal plain and the paler, drier eastern lands. The ocean appeared on the western horizon, the burning sands of the great deserts on the eastern, and still they saw nothing to the south but golden haze.

When they could see the haze on the eastern horizon, beyond the desert, wrapping around the southeastern corner of the World, even Vond gave up.

Sterren had been ready to give up long before; unlike Vond, he had no supernatural power source to warm him or gather in air. Frost had formed on his face and hands and he was having serious trouble breathing by the time Vond finally began descending.

When they had once again reached the warm, thick air of the everyday world, the warlock remarked, "I'd never gone that high before. It's quite something, isn't it?"

Sterren's frozen muscles had not yet thawed; he could not answer.

They landed, and Vond stepped forward to the edge while Sterren waited atop a small dune.

The edge looked like an ordinary cliff; it was not particularly straight or even, but just a place where the dunes ended in a drop-off.

What made it unique was that it extended as far as Sterren could see in both directions, and that he could see nothing at all on the other side except that infinite golden mist.

Vond stood atop that cliff, looking down.

"I can't see anything," he called back, disappointed. "Just that damned haze."

Sterren stepped cautiously forward and peered over, still several feet back.

Like Vond, he could see nothing but the yellow mist.

"Wait here," the warlock said. He rose into the air and drifted forward.

Almost immediately, he stopped and flew back. He turned to Sterren and said, amazed, "There's no air! I couldn't breathe. And that yellow stuff smells horrible, and it burns your throat. And I still couldn't see any bottom. The mist just goes on forever!"

Sterren looked up and down.

"What holds it back, though? Why does the mist stay on that side, and the air on this side?"

Vond looked up and down, as Sterren had, and then shrugged. "It must be magic," he said. "Wizardry, maybe."

Sterren shrugged. "I never saw magic do anything *this* big."

"The gods must have done it," Vond said, in sudden enlightenment. "The tales say they brought the World out of chaos, don't they? That yellow stuff must be chaos!"

That did not sound right to Sterren. The story he had heard was that the World had been a bit that was left over, unnoticed, when the universe split into Heaven and Hell. The gods had found it later, and helped shape it, but they hadn't created it out of chaos.

Besides, why would chaos be yellow? Why would it be any color at all?

He didn't think that there were any explanations for the golden mist; it was just *there*, and they would have to accept it.

"Now what?" he asked.

Vond looked about, considering. "I don't think I want to fool around with that stuff," he said. "If it *is* chaos, it's dangerous."

Sterren was not about to argue with that; he said nothing.

"What if I were to fold back the edge, here? That might even be useful; if the magic that holds that stuff back ever fails, a wall here would be a good second line of defense."

Again, Sterren was not inclined to argue, although he thought Vond was talking nonsense. He could not help balking at the immensity of the idea, however.

"Fold it *back*?" he said, his voice cracking.

"Sure!" Vond said. "I'll need to see how thick it is, though."

"How thick *what* is?"

"The World, of course!" He bent over, and Sterren watched as a narrow hole appeared in the sand before him.

The loose sand did not slide down to fill it in. Vond stared down into it for several minutes, and Sterren settled down to sit on a dune and watch.

At last, Vond straightened up. "I can't find the bottom," he said. "I went down well over a mile, I'm sure." He shrugged. "Well, I'll just peel back the top layer, then, and fold *that* up." He looked about, calculating, and his gaze fell on Sterren.

"Oh," he said, "I'd better get you out of here. This may be messy."

"All right," Sterren said, greatly relieved but trying not to show it.

In an instant, he was airborne again, flying at a fantastic speed back toward Semma, moving so fast that once again, as he had at high altitude, he had trouble breathing.

Breathless moments later, he landed, stumbling, on a village street, in the shadow of the walls of Semma Castle.

Thirty-Seven

Even over the intervening distance, low rumblings occasionally reached the village. From his perch in the castle tower Sterren could see huge chunks of sand and rock shifting in the distance, but he could make out no details.

After dark the noise continued, and an eerie orange glow lit the southern skies. The glow seemed to wax and wane erratically, and occasional sparkles of red or pale blue light rippled across it.

Sterren was very glad he hadn't used another of his ideas and suggested that Vond go fetch the lesser moon out of the sky; folding back the edge of the World was quite terrifying enough.

By noon on the eleventh of Harvest the job was complete; where once the edge of the World had been marked by a distant line of gold, now it was marked by a distant line of black that Sterren assumed to be stone, and a tiny black dot was approaching that could only be Vond, returning.

Sterren decided that the tower of Semma Castle was not where he wanted Vond to find him; he headed for the stairs.

He passed Shirrin in the sixth-floor hallway, and almost stopped to talk to her. She stared at him for a moment while he hesitated, then turned and ran, and he continued down the stairs.

When he got back to the Imperial Palace Vond was already there, sitting on air in the audience chamber with the great red doors opened wide.

Sterren paused in the entryway, unsure whether to speak to the warlock, or to slip upstairs unnoticed. Vond settled the matter by calling, "Oh, there you are, Sterren!"

Sterren strolled into the audience chamber, trying to look casual. "How did it go?" he asked.

"Oh, well enough," Vond said, smiling. "The sand wouldn't hold together, of course, so I pulled up a sheet of bedrock. It's about fifty feet thick and fifty yards high, and only the gods know how long." He stretched, and added, "It felt *wonderful*, using all that power!"

Sterren smiled back, hoping the warlock would not see how false the smile was. "I could see the difference from the tower," he said.

Vond nodded. "It doesn't look like much from this distance, though."

"True enough, but it can be seen, and when people realize what it is, think how impressed they'll be. Their emperor has turned up the edge of the World itself! The concept is more powerful than the appearance on this one."

Vond nodded. "But I'll want to do something flashy next time, something everybody will *see*. You think about what it might be, Sterren; I like your ideas." He paused, and frowned. "Right now, though, I think I might take a nap. I didn't sleep at all last night, while I was working, and my head is buzzing, as if the walls themselves were talking to me." He waved an arm about vaguely.

Sterren nodded, and watched silently as Vond drifted off toward his private chamber.

Vond still did not realize what was happening, Sterren thought. He wondered how long it would take, and when Vond would catch on.

He strolled aimlessly out of the audience chamber into the entrance hall, where the rosewood door of the council chamber caught his eye. He crossed to it, hesitated, and then opened the door and peered in.

The chamber was empty. All sign of Ildirin's sudden demise had been scrubbed away.

Sterren wondered how the other servants had received word of Ildirin's death. Who had told them, and what had they been told? How many had decided to leave?

He closed the door, and thought for a moment.

The weather was beautiful, of course, as it always was in Vond's empire — but that might not last. He decided to enjoy it while he could. The courtyard held a magnificent flower garden.

He was sitting on an iron bench, feeling the sunlight warm on his face and letting the scent of roses fill his nostrils, when Vond screamed.

The scream came not just from the warlock's throat, but from the air around him, from the palace walls, and from the stone of the earth itself; everything vibrated in rhythm. The stones groaned, so deeply that the sound was more felt than heard, while the air shrieked and even the leaves of the garden whistled piercingly.

The scream had no words; it was shapeless terror given voice.

The echoes were still fading, the air still humming, when the window of Vond's bedchamber exploded outward into the garden, spraying shattered glass in every direction; Sterren ducked and covered his head with his arms as shards rattled down on all sides.

When the last tinkling fragment had settled he looked up and saw Vond hanging in the air above him. The warlock wore only a white tunic, and his face was almost equally white. His eyes were wide and staring, his hands trembling.

"Sterren!" he called. "*Sterren!*"

Sterren said quietly, "I'm here."

Vond heard him, and looked down. He plummeted from the sky, and landed roughly on the gravelled path, falling to his knees and only catching himself from falling flat on his face with one outstretched hand.

He looked up at Sterren, and said, "The nightmares, Sterren, they're back!"

Sterren nodded. "I thought so," he said.

Vond's expression changed suddenly. Sterren's calm cut through his fear and released anger and uncertainty. "You *thought* so?" the warlock demanded.

Sterren blinked and said nothing.

Vond rose to his feet, using warlockry rather than hands and legs. "Just *what* did you think? I had a nightmare — how would you know anything about that?"

Sterren hesitated, trying to phrase an answer, and Vond continued, "It was just a nightmare! It wasn't . . . wasn't *that*. It couldn't have been. It was just a nightmare, my mind playing tricks on me."

"No," Sterren said, shaking his head and marvelling that even now, Vond could not accept what was happening.

"It was an *ordinary* nightmare," Vond insisted. "It *must* have been! That thing in Aldagmor is still out of range. It *has* to be! I haven't been using it! I've been getting power from Lumeth!"

"No," Sterren repeated. He was horribly aware that Vond was on the verge of complete panic, and could lash out wildly at any time and strike him dead instantly. "No, it almost certainly *does* come from Aldagmor."

"It *can't*," Vond insisted.

"Of course it can!" Sterren answered, annoyed at Vond's stubborn refusal to understand.

"But *how*?" Vond insisted. "I'm out of range here!"

Sterren shook his head. "Nowhere is really out of range; you know that. When you first came here, before you learned to use the Lumeth source, you could still draw on Aldagmor. Not much, but a little. Don't you remember? You couldn't fly, but you could stop a man's heart."

"But that's apprentice work! Apprentices don't get the nightmares!"

"You're no apprentice any more. Don't you see? You've been drawing so much power from Lumeth, you've become so powerful, so receptive to warlockry, that the Aldagmor source can reach you. Receptivity isn't that selective. After all, your receptivity to Aldagmor was what let you use Lumeth in the first place. They're the same thing; the more sensitive you are to one, the more sensitive you are to both. The Lumeth source is closer, so you can draw far more power from it, but you still hear the Aldagmor source, too."

"But I *don't*!"

"You *do*. You told me so yourself. You couldn't enter Lumeth of the Towers, and you've been complaining for days about whisperings and buzzings in your head; didn't you realize what they were?"

Vond paused, his expression shocked.

"No," he said at last, "I didn't. But they . . . you're right, I was hearing Aldagmor. I wasn't *listening*, since I had Lumeth, but I was hearing it. Why listen for a whisper when you can use a shout?" He focused on Sterren again.

"You *knew*!" he said accusingly. "You *knew* this was coming!"

Sterren did not dare to reply.

"Why didn't you *warn* me? I . . ." Realization dawned. "Gods, you *encouraged* me!" Vond exclaimed. "*You* — it was *your* idea to fold up the edge of the World!" Fury seethed in Vond's eyes, and Sterren expected to die then.

He didn't.

"*Why didn't you warn me?*" Vond screamed.

"I was going to," Sterren answered, truthfully. "Really, I was. But then you killed Ildirin, and hardly even noticed, and I . . . I thought you were becoming too dangerous.

Besides . . ." He took a deep breath, and continued, "Besides, would you have believed me?"

Vond's face, though still pale, was calm as he forced himself to consider this question. He sat down on the bench beside Sterren.

"No," he admitted at last. "No, I wouldn't have."

"Besides," Sterren said, "I had no idea how much longer you had, how much power you would have to use before . . . before this."

Vond nodded. "No other warlock ever came close to the power I had," he said wistfully. Sterren noted his use of the past tense. He had already resigned himself to the situation.

"So," Vond said, "I'm back where I was when you found me in Shiphaven Market, back in Ethshar — I've had my first nightmare, passed the brink. I need to either get farther from Aldagmor, or to stop using my magic and live with the nightmares, or else I'll hear the Calling and . . . and do whatever the Calling makes one do."

Sterren nodded.

"I can't get any farther away, can I?"

"We're not at the edge of the World," Sterren pointed out. "Not quite."

"But from here to the corner there's nothing but sand and grass and desert. It's not worth it. I can't even build anything to live in; it would use too much power."

"You could use your hands," Sterren suggested.

Vond snorted derisively. "I don't know how," he said.

"You could just stay here, go on as you have, and go out in a blaze of glory. After all, the Calling isn't *death*, is it? It might not be so bad."

"No," Vond said flatly. "I don't know what it is, but anything that sends those nightmares . . . No. I escaped it once, and that just makes it worse now." He shook himself, and said with sudden resolution, "I'll give up magic. I don't need it now; I'm an emperor. I can live as I please without it!"

Sterren nodded. "Of course," he said.

But he knew Vond could never do it. After using warlockry in such prodigious amounts for months, using it for his whims for years, could Vond really give it up?

Sterren did not believe it for a minute.

Thirty-Eight

Vond walked into the audience chamber, climbed the dais, and settled uneasily onto the borrowed throne. He looked down at Sterren.

"How do I look?" he asked.

"Fine," Sterren said reassuringly.

"It's not very comfortable," the warlock said, shifting slightly and looking down at the throne. "And it doesn't really go with this room."

"Phenvel's bigger than you are, and he leaned back more," Sterren pointed out. "As for the looks, maybe we can drape something over it later."

Vond nodded. "What did the servants say when you told them to fetch it?"

"I used some of the slaves you bought from Akalla, and they didn't say anything. It's not their place to question direct orders."

The warlock nodded again. "That's good," he said, in a distracted way.

After a moment of uncomfortable silence, during which Vond tried to find a more comfortable position and Sterren simply stood and waited, Vond asked, "What do you think they thought at the castle? Did anybody object?"

Sterren shook his head. "I sent half a dozen of my guards along. Nobody objected. They may be wondering about it, but they can't do anything. You're the warlock emperor, remember — you're all-powerful. Nobody knows anything's changed except the two of us."

Vond smiled, a twisted and bitter expression. "They know. Half of Semma must have heard my scream."

"They *don't* know," Sterren insisted. "They don't know

why you screamed. They don't know anything about war-lockry. Nobody in the entire empire knows anything about warlockry except you, me, and maybe a few traders and expatriates from the north."

"They'll guess, when they see me sitting in this thing."

"They won't."

Vond shook his head, but stopped arguing.

"Should I open the doors, now?" Sterren asked.

Vond waved a hand unhappily. "Go ahead," he said.

Sterren marched down the length of the audience hall to the great red doors and rapped once on an enamelled panel.

The doors swung in, propelled by two palace servants apiece — another reminder of Vond's unhappy condition, since he had always moved them magically before.

In the hallway beyond waited a dozen or so petitioners. These were the ones who had been sent on by the Imperial Council or various servants and officials as being outside the council's purview, with valid reasons to see the Great Vond himself.

There was no bailiff, usher, or doorkeeper to manage the presentations; Vond had always taken care of that himself, using his magically-enhanced voice to direct people. As Sterren looked over the uneasy little knot of people he thought to himself that a great many things would have to change if the empire was to run smoothly.

"All right," he said, "how many groups do we have here? Please, divide yourselves up, spread out, so I can see what the situation is."

The petitioners milled about in confusion; clearly, several had not understood his Ethsharitic.

He repeated the instructions as best he could in Semmat, and waited while the group sorted itself out into smaller groups.

There were five petitions, it appeared — one group of

four, a group of three, two pairs, and a single.

"Who speaks Ethsharitic?" Sterren asked.

One hand went up in each group; the single, unfortunately, just looked blank. Sterren asked him in Semmat, "Do you speak Semmat?"

He nodded. "Yes, sir," he said.

That, Sterren thought, would have to do.

He decided to start with the largest group and work down; it seemed fairest to keep the fewest possible waiting.

"All right," he said, pointing, "you four, come on in."

The Ethsharitic-speaking spokesman for the foursome led his party into the audience chamber, down the rich red carpet as the doors swung shut behind them, to stand before the dais. Sterren watched them closely, to see if they seemed aware that anything was out of the ordinary.

They did not. Apparently, either nobody had told them that the Great Vond had no throne and always conducted business floating in the air, or they had dismissed such tales as exaggerations.

They went down on their knees before the emperor and bowed deeply.

"Rise," Vond said.

His unenhanced voice seemed horribly weak to Sterren, a thin little sound that was almost lost in the great stone chamber.

The petitioners did not seem to notice anything odd. They rose.

Their spokesman took a cautious step forward and waited.

"Speak," Vond said.

"Your Imperial Majesty," the petitioner said, "we have come here as representatives for many, many of your subjects who grow peaches. This year, thanks to the fine weather you have given us, we have a very large, very fine crop — and it is all ripening at once, so fast that we do not have time to harvest it. We . . ." He hesitated, glanced at Sterren, who looked encouraging, and then continued, "We have seen you light the sky at night. Could you do this again? If you could light the sky above our trees, we could harvest by night as well as by day, and we would not leave fruit to ripen and rot on the tree before we can get to it. I . . . we understand that you have other concerns, but . . ."

"No," Vond said flatly, interrupting the petitioner.

The spokesman blinked. "No?" he said. "But your Majesty . . ."

"No, I said!"

"May I ask why . . ."

"*No!*" Vond bellowed, rising from the throne — not by magic, but standing naturally upon his own feet. His voice echoed from the walls.

A breeze stirred the warlock's robes, in a closed room where no natural breeze could reach. Vond felt it, and looked down at the swaying fabric of his sleeve in horror.

He turned to Sterren and said, "Get them out of here."

Then he turned and ran from the room.

The petitioners stared after him in astonishment.

Sterren stepped forward and told them, "The Great Vond is ill. He had hoped that he would be able to hear petitions regardless, but it appears that the gods would have it otherwise." He hesitated, and continued, "And I'm afraid that's why he refused your petition; while his illness persists, his magic is somewhat limited, and to light the sky as you ask would be too great a strain upon his health."

The petitioners looked at him uncertainly as he spoke, and he saw fear appear on the spokesman's face. Sterren thought he understood that; after all, when the king is sick, the kingdom is in danger. That old proverb would hold true all the more for an emperor, and a young emperor of a young and still-unsteady empire at that.

Worst of all, Vond was an emperor without an heir.

"Don't worry," Sterren said soothingly. "It's not that serious."

He hoped the lie would not be obvious.

"What can we do?" the spokesman asked.

"Go home, harvest your peaches as best you can, and don't worry unduly. If you know the names of any gods, you might pray to them on the emperor's behalf, and I'm sure healing charms wouldn't hurt." He took the spokesman's arm and led the party back down the hall to the door.

Once again, a single rap opened the doors, and Sterren escorted the little party out into the hall. There he raised his voice and called, "The Great Vond is ill, and all audiences for today are cancelled!" He repeated it in Semmat. "If you wish to, you may stay in the area and check with the guards daily, and present your petitions when the Great Vond has recovered, or you may put them in writing, and give them to any guard or servant with instructions that they be delivered to Chancellor Sterren, who will see that they are read by the Great Vond as soon as his health permits. If you cannot write, there are scribes for hire in the village."

The little crowd milled about again, muttering uneasily.

"That is all!" Sterren announced firmly. He turned to the four servants at the doors and dismissed them.

That done, he turned and headed for the stairs. He kept his pace slow and dignified until he knew he was out of sight of the petitioners, and then broke into a trot, heading directly for Vond's bedchamber.

As he had expected, he found Vond there, sitting in a chair and staring at the gaping hole, edged with bits of glass and leading, that had once been the window overlooking the courtyard gardens.

"I can't even fix the window," Vond said without pre-amble as Sterren entered.

"I'll have the servants take care of it immediately," Sterren said.

"Sterren," Vond wailed, "I can't even fix the damned window! I can't do *anything*! I can't afford to lose my temper; I was struggling as hard as I could to shut out the magic down there, but you heard my voice, you felt the wind. How can I live without magic?"

"I didn't feel any wind," Sterren said truthfully. "I saw your clothes move, so I knew what happened, but it didn't reach me. You had it *almost* under control. It will take prac-tice, that's all. Most people live their whole lives without magic. You ask how you can live without it; ask how *long* you can live *with* it."

Vond turned and glared at him. "You did this to me," he said bitterly.

"You did it to yourself," Sterren retorted. "And who-ever did it, it's done now, isn't it?"

"Oh, gods!" Vond burst out, throwing himself from the chair to the bed. "And the nightmares have already begun!"

"You've only had one so far," Sterren pointed out, "and that was right after working the mightiest magic any war-lock has ever performed. Perhaps, if you use no more magic, you won't have any more nightmares."

"Oh, get out of here!" Vond shouted.

Sterren retreated to the door. "I'll send the servants to fix the window," he said as he left.

Thirty-Nine

There were no nightmares that night, or the next, and Vond grew more optimistic. He stayed sequestered in his apartments, but spoke of venturing forth again, and taking up his role as emperor, when he had adjusted to using no magic.

Even the rain on the second day did not seriously dampen his spirits. If anything, this sign that he was no longer controlling the weather seemed to cheer the warlock.

On the third night his screams woke the entire palace. Sterren took the stairs three steps at a time on his way to Vond's chamber.

Two guards and Vond's valet were already there, staring in shocked silence as Vond, hanging a foot off the floor, beat on the north wall of the room with his fists.

"Your Majesty," Sterren called, "remember, use your feet!"

Vond looked at him unseeingly, and then seemed to emerge from a daze. He looked down, and then dropped to the floor and fell to his knees.

He knelt there, shaking. Sterren crossed to him and put an arm around his shoulder.

"You," he said, pointing to one guard, "go get brandy. And you, go get an herbalist." They hurried away.

The valet asked, "Is there anything . . . ?"

"Go find the theurgist, Agor," Sterren said.

The valet vanished, leaving Sterren alone with the terrified warlock.

He looked up at the wall, where a small smear of red showed that Vond had scraped his hand on the rough edge of a stone.

"Why were you hitting the wall?" Sterren asked.

"I don't know," Vond replied. "Was I?" He looked up, saw the streak of blood, then looked down at his injured hand, puzzled.

"Was it the nightmares?" Sterren asked.

Vond almost growled. "Of course it was, idiot!" He looked up at the blood again, and asked, "Was I flying?"

"Yes," Sterren said.

"I used magic, then. No matter how careful I am, the nightmares can *make* me use magic. It's not fair!"

"No," Sterren agreed, "it's not fair."

The guard returned with the brandy, and Sterren helped steady the glass as Vond drank.

When the warlock had caught his breath again, he asked, "Did I say anything?"

"No," Sterren told him, "I don't think so."

The guard cleared his throat.

Sterren glanced at him. "Was there something before I got here?" he asked.

"He was crying, my lord," the soldier said, "and saying something about needing to go somewhere. I couldn't make out all of it."

Then the herbalist arrived.

Half an hour later Vond was in bed again, feeling the effects of a sleeping potion the herbalist had brewed, and the little crowd of concerned subjects was breaking up, drifting out of the imperial bedchamber one by one.

Sterren departed and headed back up for his own room.

The incident had shaken his nerves. It had been easy enough to say that Vond had to go, but to watch him slowly being destroyed by the Calling was not easy at all.

Sterren was not sure he could take it.

Perhaps, he thought, it was time to go home to Ethshar. Vond could not follow him. The old Semman nobility was scattered and powerless, save for Kalira and Algarven, and they would have no particular reason to want him back.

But no, he told himself, that was cowardice. Not that he was particularly brave, but it was worse than ordinary cowardice. He had created the whole situation; to run away and leave it for others to clean up the mess was despicable. It went beyond cowardice, and into treachery.

It would be cheating, and he was an honest gambler. He did not cheat. He did not welsh.

He would stay, and watch what he had wrought.

He almost reconsidered two nights later, when another nightmare sent Vond blazing into the sky like a comet. He awoke and fell to earth a mile north of the palace; Sterren and a dozen guards marched out to fetch him back.

Forty

On the twenty-fourth of Leafcolor, 5221, Sterren awoke suddenly and was startled to see sunlight pouring in his bedroom window. It had been two sixnights since he had slept the night through, without being awakened by another of Vond's Calling nightmares.

He sat up, and realized that he was not alone in the room, that he had been awakened. He blinked, and recognized the man who had awakened him as Vond's valet.

"What's happened?" he asked.

"He's gone," the valet said.

Sterren wasted no time with further questions; he rose and followed the servant at a trot through the palace passages, back to the warlock's bedchamber.

The bed was empty, and not particularly disturbed; the coverlet was thrown back on one side, as if Vond had gotten up for a moment, perhaps to use the chamberpot, and had not yet returned.

The often-repaired window to the courtyard was open.

Vond was gone.

It was over; whatever it was that lurked in the hills of Aldagmor had taken another warlock.

Sterren almost wanted to laugh with relief, but instead he found himself weeping.

When he had regained control of himself, he asked the valet, "What time is it?"

"I don't know, my lord; I awoke an hour or so after dawn, I think, and came in and found it like this, and went straight to fetch you."

Sterren nodded. "All right," he said. "You go find whoever takes care of such matters, and see to it that the Imperial Council is in the council chamber an hour from now. I need to speak to them."

The valet hesitated. "What do I do here?" he asked.

"Nothing," Sterren said. "Leave it just the way it is. The Great Vond might come back."

With a shiver, Sterren realized that might even be true. Nobody knew what happened to warlocks who gave in to the Calling. None had ever returned.

But Vond had been more powerful than any other warlock who ever lived, and warlocks had only existed, and therefore only been vanishing, for twenty years. Nobody really knew whether Vond might come back.

But quite frankly, Sterren doubted it.

Back in his room he had someone fetch him a tray of breakfast pastry, which he ate while bathing. When he was washed, fed, and dry, he took his time in dressing in his best tunic and breeches, combing his hair, brushing out his freshly-grown mustache — he was almost, he thought as he looked at the mirror, ready to grow a proper beard.

When he was thoroughly satisfied with his appearance, he headed for the council chamber.

All seven councillors were there waiting for him; Lady Kalira, anticipating his arrival, was at the foot of the table, leaving room for him at the head. He marched in and took his place.

"The Great Vond," he announced, "has moved on to a higher plane of existence."

"You mean he's dead?" Prince Ferral asked.

"No," Sterren said. "Or at least, I don't think so."

"You'll have to explain that," Algarven remarked.

Sterren did, not concerning himself with the truth.

Warlocks, he explained, did not die the way ordinary people did. They vanished, transmogrified into pure magic.

The nightmares and other ills that the Great Vond had been suffering were his mortal body's attempts to prevent this ascension.

"He's gone, though?" Prince Ferral demanded.

"He's gone," Sterren admitted, "but we don't know if it's permanent. It's only twenty years since warlockry was first discovered, and the Great Vond was the most powerful warlock the World has yet seen. We really don't know whether he might return or not."

The councillors watched Sterren carefully, and he looked them over in return, trying to judge how many of them believed him.

He couldn't tell. After all, these were all expert politicians. They could hide their opinions quite effectively.

Then Lady Kalira asked the really important question, the one that Sterren had called this meeting to answer.

"What now?" she said.

"I don't know," Sterren admitted.

"Well, what do you *think*?" Algarven asked.

"I'm not sure," Sterren said. "We could really just go on the way we have been. After all, nobody outside the palace has seen Vond in almost two months now. Nobody has to know that anything has changed."

"I don't know about that," Algarven said. "I don't think we can keep it secret forever. The servants will know, and they'll talk."

The others nodded in agreement.

"We could take Lord Sterren's approach," Lady Kalira suggested, "and say that he's gone, but he'll be back."

"Do we *want* to go on as we have?" asked Lady Arris of Ksinallion. "We could put everything back the way it was, couldn't we?"

"Could we?" Algarven said. "What would we do with this palace?"

Everyone began talking, and Sterren lost track of who was saying what.

"Why should we go back to stupid little border wars?"

"Why break up the strongest nation in the Small Kingdoms?"

"What if the peasants don't want to switch back?"

"What about all the roads he built?"

"We could be beheaded for treason!"

"How would we divide up the imperial treasury?"

It was Lady Kalira who settled the matter by asking, "Do you really want someone like King Phenvel back on the throne?"

That settled it; the Empire of Vond would continue.

"What about a new emperor?" Prince Ferral asked.

"Who?" Algarven asked in reply.

"If we pick one of the deposed kings, we'll have rebellions in the other provinces," Lady Kalira pointed out.

"What about Lord Sterren?" Lady Arris asked.

Sterren thought he sensed a current of approval, and he blocked it quickly. He had thought this all through once before, when Vond had appointed him to handle the details of government.

"No," he said, "I'm not interested. I didn't want to be warlord of Semma, I didn't want to be Vond's chancellor, and I *certainly* don't want to be your emperor!"

Lady Kalira started to speak, and Sterren cut her off.

"You don't need an emperor," he said. "The Hegemony hasn't got an emperor. Sardiron hasn't got an emperor. They get along just fine."

"What *do* they have?" Prince Ferral asked.

"The Hegemony has a triumvirate — three overlords who form a sort of council. And Sardiron has a council of barons. We have a council here; we don't need an emperor."

"You're suggesting, then, that the Imperial Council be the highest authority?" Algarven asked.

Sterren nodded. "Exactly," he said.

"And what," Lady Kalira asked, "of our chancellor? What will you do?"

"Retire, if you'll let me," Sterren said. "I'd like to settle down quietly, find some sort of honest work — though I certainly wouldn't mind if you want to vote me a pension, or maybe even an appointment of some sort."

Lady Kalira rose and glanced at the other councillors. "I think," she said, "that we need to discuss this by ourselves."

Sterren bowed. "As you wish, my lady," he said. "If you need me, I expect to be at Semma Castle."

She bowed in return, and Sterren left the room.

As he strolled down the hill on one of Vond's fine paved roads, he whistled quietly to himself.

It was over. He had discharged his responsibilities. He had cleaned up the mess he had created.

He had won Semma's war, but in the process of winning it he had unleashed Vond and destroyed Semma. Now he had removed Vond, but had kept his good works, his empire, intact. He could not be warlord of Semma, since Semma was gone, and now he was no longer chancellor of Vond.

He was free. He could go home to Ethshar if he wanted, or he could stay where he was.

He was crossing the market before the castle gate when a soldier spotted him and waved.

He waved back.

"Lord Sterren," the man called in Semmat, "what about a game of three-bone?"

Sterren looked over, thinking of the feel of the dice in his fingers. At that thought, somewhere in the back of his mind, he thought he heard a faint silent buzz — or perhaps even a whisper.

He shuddered.

"No, thanks," he called. He turned his gaze away, up toward the castle.

He saw Princess Shirrin standing on the battlements, watching him approach. He waved.

She smiled, and waved back.

Startled, he stumbled and almost fell, then caught himself and walked on.

She must finally have forgiven him for allowing her father to be deposed, he realized. She could not possibly know yet that Vond was gone.

He could explain it all to her now, explain how he had known Vond was doomed, and that to resist him would only lead to disaster. She would welcome this explanation, he was sure. She would welcome *him*.

He thought he just might stay in Semma after all.

Epilogue

Sterren lay on his bed, enjoying the view of warm afternoon sunlight and contemplating his future. Marriage to Princess Shirrin seemed delightfully inevitable. Nobody seemed disposed to evict him from his comfortable tower room in Semma Castle, and nobody objected to his presence at the table at meals, so he had free food and shelter and was in no great hurry to find another home, or any genuine occupation.

Life was good.

A polite knock sounded.

He ignored it for a moment, too comfortable to want to move.

A much less polite knock sounded.

He sighed and sat up as the second knock was followed by someone pounding on his door and calling, "Lord Sterren! We must speak with you!"

"I'm coming!" he shouted in reply.

Reluctantly, he rolled off the bed and onto his feet, crossed the room, and opened the door.

"What is it?" he demanded.

Then he saw who was in the corridor beyond.

The entire Imperial Council was standing there.

For a moment he stared at them silently, and they stared back.

"What is it?" he asked again. "What do you want?"

Lady Kalira spoke, while the others remained grimly silent.

"Lord Sterren," she said, "for the past two sixnights we have tried to do as you suggested, running the Empire ourselves. For the most part, I think we have succeeded. However, some problems have arisen that we find ourselves unable to deal with. We spend our time in pointless bickering over the most trivial issues, and when we try to vote, someone invariably abstains and we find ourselves in a tie, and the arguments start all over again."

Sterren blinked, and said, "So what?"

"So," Lady Kalira said, glaring balefully at him, "your system is not working."

Sterren felt a sudden sinking feeling in his gut.

She paused for a moment, and then continued, "Furthermore, we have some doubts about the nature of our authority. We are all accustomed to living under monarchy, where one person holds the final say. We aren't comfortable having that power divided — particularly when it *stays* divided because our votes end in ties."

"What does this have to do with *me*?" he asked, afraid that he knew.

"Lord Sterren," Lady Kalira said, "you brought the warlock here, and in doing so you destroyed all the established hierarchies. You served as his chancellor, which gave you an authority nobody else in the Empire now possesses. We need an authority, a king or an emperor, who can settle these endless little disputes, and the only authority we can all agree on is yours."

"But I don't want it!" Sterren protested.

"That's exactly why we chose you as emperor," Lady Kalira explained. "How could we trust someone who hungered after power?"

"I won't do it," Sterren said.

"Lord Sterren," Lady Kalira said, "you have little choice. You arranged for your Imperial Council to have absolute power, did you not?"

"Yes, I did," Sterren began, "and I . . ."

"In that case, your Majesty," she interrupted, "if the

Council's power is absolute, you must yield to it — and it is the will of the Council, determined by unanimous vote, that you, Sterren of Semma, be named emperor of Vond."

Sterren stared at her. He realized what he had just done. In admitting that he had arranged for the Council to have absolute power, he had tacitly admitted that he, himself, had the authority to grant such power, and he could hardly deny the Council's right to return it. He fumed for a moment, and then burst out, "I am *not* going to be an emperor!"

"As you wish, your Majesty," she said, bowing. "Tell us then what title you prefer."

"Vond is the emperor," he pointed out. "I can't be emperor."

"Vond is gone," Lady Kalira replied.

He looked over the seven faces before him, all of them determined. "You all want me in charge?" he demanded.

All seven nodded, but he thought one or two might have hesitated.

"Suppose I refuse?"

"If you refuse, your Majesty," Lady Kalira said, "I'm afraid that I will be forced to resign from the Council, and I believe several others will resign as well."

He looked over the faces and saw no hint of yielding.

Lady Kalira said, "Need I point out that if the Council resigns, the Empire will fall apart? I expect that the old kingdoms would revive, and that you would probably be considered a traitor by the nobility of Semma."

That was true enough, and Princess Shirrin was one of those nobles.

Besides, he thought the Empire was a good thing — he saw no point to all the petty little kingdoms it had replaced.

"Oh, hell," he said. "You could appoint me regent, I suppose."

Smiles of varying intensity appeared on four of the seven faces; the other three he couldn't read.

"Lady Kalira will serve as my chancellor and vice-regent, of course," he said.

Her smile had been an intermediate one; it vanished completely, and she opened her mouth to protest.

Then she stopped as she saw the look of satisfaction on his face.

"As your Majesty wishes," she said, reluctantly. She hesitated. "Will you be moving back into the Imperial Palace?"

"Let me think it over," he said. He stepped back into the room, and waved in dismissal. "You may go," he said.

The councillors turned away, when a thought occurred to him. "Lady Kalira!" he called.

She turned and waited as the others continued down the stairs.

"That vote," he asked. "Was it really unanimous?"

She smiled. "On the second ballot," she said.

Then she turned and headed for the stairs.

The Vondish Ambassador

The New Ethshar Novel—Coming in 2009!

Chapter One

A stiff east wind was blowing, bearing the scent of salt and decay from the beaches beyond the city wall. Such a breeze was chilly and uncomfortable, but it could bring ships into port quickly, cutting travel time, and that might mean happy merchants looking for laborers to unload their cargo. Captains and owners pleased by a quick passage tended to pay well, so Emmis of Shiphaven ambled up New Canal Street with an eye on the sea, watching for any inbound vessel, rather than following his usual morning routine of a stroll up Twixt Street to Shiphaven Market. If that unseasonable wind dropped, leaving ships becalmed in the bay, any hope of being overpaid by cheerful merchants would drop with it.

The richest cargoes were usually landed at either the Spice Wharves or the Tea Wharves, across the canal in Spicetown, but the Spicetown dockworkers had their own little bands and brotherhoods, and Emmis was not particularly welcome. In fact, Emmis was not welcome there at all — not since Azradelle's wedding. The Shipping Docks and Long Wharf here in Shiphaven were more informal, though, if only because the work wasn't as steady. Nobody in Shiphaven would mind an extra pair of hands.

Emmis had made his living as an extra pair of hands for some time now. It wasn't a career with impressive prospects, but he got by.

He reached the mouth of the canal and walked out on the seawall, peering out through the tangle of masts and yards at the Spicetown docks, trying to see whether any ships were out beyond the docks, running before that lovely wind. He shaded his eyes and gradually swiveled his head to the left, toward open water.

There! A ship with red and gold sails, hauled over on the port tack, with a long multicolored banner streaming from the mizzen, was swooping across the bay. She looked to be southern-rigged, which meant she was from somewhere beyond the river-mouth at Londa in the Small Kingdoms, and she was clearly heading toward Shiphaven. Her helmsman seemed to be steering for either Pier Two or Pier Three.

Emmis turned west along the seawall to Pier One, where he cut over to the street; he kept a careful eye out to sea, watching the ship's approach.

It was headed for Pier Two, he decided. Even with the strong wind, then, he didn't need to hurry; he would be there before the ship came in. He slowed his pace.

The ship was starting to reduce sail now, slowing for her final approach. Emmis watched with mild interest, observing how well the crew handled their duties — their performance might provide some indication of how he might get the most money from them for the least work.

They did well enough; the mainsail was furled quickly, without any corners flapping free. The jibsails came down smoothly, then the topsails, until only the topgallants were still drawing.

When the vessel finally neared the dock, out past the elbow in Pier Two, Emmis was seated comfortably on a bollard, waiting. Rather to his surprise, no one else had appeared yet on Pier Two; presumably the other Shiphaven laborers had all either already found work elsewhere, or had decided to stay inside out of the wind today.

Emmis stood as the ship came gliding slowly in and raised a hand, indicating his availability. A crewman stood in the bow holding a line; seeing Emmis' signal, he nodded and began swinging the rope, building momentum. When he flung it, Emmis was ready and waiting; he grabbed the painter and threw a loop around the bollard he had been sitting on, securing it with a neat clove hitch.

Then he jogged toward the stern, where another crewman was readying another line.

A few moments later the ship was secured alongside the dock, sails furled and gangplank out. Emmis waited by the plank. He knew better than to board any ship without explicit permission from its master, and as yet he had not spotted this vessel's captain. The man at the wheel wore the same faded white blouse and blue kilt as any other sailor, without so much as a hat to set him apart. Emmis assumed he was merely the helmsman.

There was no sign of a pilot, which might be why the ship

was here rather than across the canal in Spicetown; the New-market sandbars could make getting to the eastern wharves tricky. The more experienced foreign navigators often made the approach themselves, rather than paying a pilot's fee, but no one from this ship looked very experienced. Judging by the visible excitement among the crew of this vessel, Emmis doubted most of them had ever been in Ethshar of the Spices before.

Then a hat appeared amidships, emerging from the deck below and rising above the coaming of the main hatch — a large black hat trimmed with a red satin band and a magnificent plume. It was followed by the head wearing it, and then by the rest of its owner.

Emmis watched with great interest as this person emerged.

He was rather short, with dark hair and a brown com-plexion; his beard appeared to have been trimmed recently, but had clearly not taken to the idea and bristled unevenly. He wore a red velvet coat trimmed with gold braid, black piping, and gold buttons, and below the coat were fine black breeches. The coat and breeches both had the look of new and unfamiliar garb.

His boots, when they finally appeared, were well made and, unlike the rest of his attire, well worn.

Several of the sailors — not all, but probably a majority — bowed to this person as he stepped over the coaming onto the deck. Emmis did not go that far, but he straightened up respectfully.

The man in the red coat waved a brief acknowledgment of the bows, then stamped toward the gangplank.

As the man approached, Emmis continued to eye him with interest. The foreigner was at least forty, perhaps over fifty, though his hair showed only the faintest hints of gray. He had the slightly saggy look of a man who had once been fat but had lost weight, not from healthy exercise but because he wasn't eating well. The fancy clothes fit him well and had obviously been tailored for him recently, but he didn't look entirely com-fortable in them.

He paused at the gangplank and looked along the pier, from the seaward end to the warehouses on East Wharf Street. He took note of the sailors who had secured the lines, of the handful of other workers finally making their way out from shore, and of Emmis, standing there ready.

"Who are you?" he demanded, speaking Ethsharitic with a slight accent.

Emmis did bow now. "Emmis of Shiphaven, at your ser-vice," he said.

The foreigner marched across the gangplank and stepped off onto the pier, then turned to face Emmis.

"Do you mean that, or are you being polite?" He had an odd way of drawing out certain consonants; Emmis did not think he had ever heard this particular accent before.

Emmis blinked. "My services are indeed available," he said. "For a reasonable charge."

The foreigner cocked his head to one side. "We will decide later on what is reasonable, but you're hired."

Emmis smiled. "To do what, my lord?"

The stranger did not smile back. "Don't call me that," he snapped. "I'm not a lord."

Emmis wiped his own smile away. "My apologies, sir. I saw them bow."

The foreigner waved that away. "Apology accepted." He turned and shouted, "Fetch my baggage!"

Two of the sailors hastened to obey.

"Come on," the foreigner said, beckoning for Emmis to follow him toward shore.

Emmis did not move. "Sir?"

The foreigner stopped and turned. "Yes?"

"You have not yet told me what my duties are to be, nor my pay. I can't consider myself employed until I know more."

The foreigner nodded. "A reasonable . . ." He seemed to grope for the right word without finding it. "A reasonable thing," he said at last. "*Od'na ya Semmat?*"

Emmis blinked. That last phrase had been completely unintelligible; he had no idea what language it was, let alone what it meant. "What?"

"You don't speak Semmat?" the foreigner asked.

"I never *heard* of Semmat."

The foreigner nodded, which set the plume on his hat bobbing. "Trader's Tongue? Ksinallionese? Ophkaritic? Thanorian?"

"I've *heard* of Trader's Tongue and maybe know a few words," Emmis said warily. "If you're looking for a translator, I might be able to find you one . . ."

"Ah!" The stranger flung up a hand. "There! You see? You know your duties!"

The little knot of other laborers had reached them; the foreigner waved them past, toward the gangplank, where the sailors welcomed them aboard and began directing them. Brass-bound trunks and leather handbags were starting to appear on the dock, lined up beside the gangplank.

"*No*, sir," Emmis said emphatically. "I *don't* know."

The foreigner sighed. "You live here, yes? In Ethshar of the Spices?"

"Yes. I was born here, over near Olive Street." He gestured in the direction of his parents' home. "Now I live behind Canal Square."

"You know the city well?"

"I suppose so, yes." Emmis was not simply being wary in his phrasing; he knew *parts* of the city very well indeed, but there were plenty of places within the walls where he had never set foot — and never wanted to.

"Then I hire you!" the foreigner exclaimed. "To know the city for me. To tell me what I need to know and take me where I want to go."

"A guide?" Emmis frowned. "You want to hire me as your guide?"

The foreigner smacked himself on the forehead with the heel of one hand. "*Guide!* That's the word. I couldn't think it. In Semmat it's *almit*, in Trader's Tongue it's *elfur*, and I could not remember the Ethsharitic. Guide, of course. Yes."

Emmis hesitated. He did not particularly like the idea of showing this overdressed barbarian around the city's sights; he would probably want to see the Arena and the Wizards' Quarter, halfway across town, and might be upset that he couldn't meet the overlord face to face. He would perhaps want to poke around parts of the Old City that Emmis did not care to visit. And people from the Small Kingdoms were notoriously stingy, unfamiliar with the prices charged in the big city . . .

"I will pay a round of silver a day," the foreigner said, interrupting his thoughts. "To start."

"Ten bits," Emmis said automatically. "To start." Apparently *this* foreigner wasn't stingy, as a daily round of silver was generous to the point of extravagance, but that was no reason not to dicker.

Only after he had responded did Emmis realize that by naming a price he had effectively agreed to take the job and could not back out if his price was met.

"Done!" The foreigner held out a hand . . .

The Vondish Ambassador

On Sale from Cosmos Books in 2009.